I0699822

AQUACAPRI WHISPERER

ACROSS THE AQUACAPRI:

THE ETERNAL SAGA OF AQUA AND CAPRI

VALENTINO TRAVALDI

COPYRIGHT

Title: AquaCapri: Whisperer Across the AquaCapri: The Eternal Saga of Aqua and Capri

Author: Valentino Travaldi

Copyright © 2025 Valentino Travaldi. All rights reserved.

First Edition Publication: October 2025

Self-Published: A Constellary Ordo Press Book
City of Starlight · Year of First Dawn

ISBN (Paperback Adult Edition):9781969666087

Library of Congress Control Number Permalink:
https://lccn.loc.gov/ Pending

Cover and Interior Design: © 2025 by Valentino Travaldi

Language: English, with original elements in Aquarii Tongue

Set in EB Garamond

Printed in the USA

Thank You for Purchasing an Authorized Edition of this Book

This book is a work of fiction. Names, characters, places, events, and incidents are either the product of the author's imagination or used in a mythopoetic context. Any resemblance to actual persons, living or dead, or real events is purely coincidental. No part of this publication may be reproduced, stored in a retrieval system, or transmitted in any form or by any means—electronic, mechanical, photocopying, recording, or otherwise—without the prior written permission of the publisher, except in the case of brief quotations embodied in critical articles or reviews.

The **Aquarii language**, including all terms, phrases, and scripts, is an original creation of Valentino Travaldi and is protected as part of this literary work. Unauthorized replication or use of the Aquarii lexicon, either in full or in part, is strictly prohibited. The AquaCapri:*Whisperer Across the AquaCapri:The Eternal saga of Aqua and Capri* series and all associated realms, characters, and mythologies are trademarks of Valentino Travaldi. All rights reserved under international copyright law. For inquiries, permissions, or licensing requests, visit:
Website: www.aquacaprisaga.com

△ **Derivative Work Declaration**
Title of Original Work:
AquaCapri:Whisperer Across the AquaCapri:The Eternal Saga of Aqua and Capri
Author: Valentino Travaldi

Statement of Derivation:
This work is a wholly original creation and is not based upon, derived from, or adapted from any preexisting copyrighted material, whether literary, cinematic, visual, musical, or otherwise. All characters, settings, names, languages (including the Aquarii Tongue), worldbuilding elements, plots, maps, seals, and mythic structures within this saga are the sole intellectual property of the author. Any resemblance to other works, real persons, or existing mythologies is purely coincidental or used within the bounds of fair use for the purpose of homage, transformation, or education.

Protected Derivative Versions Include:
- Whisperer Across the AquaCapri – Deluxe Edition(Hardcover)
- Whisperer Across the AquaCapri – Adult Edition(Paperback)
- Whisperer Across the AquaCapri – eBook Adult Edition
- Whisperer Across the AquaCapri – Youth Edition(Paperback)
- Whisperer Across the AquaCapri – eBook Youth Edition
- All Aquarii Tongue lexicons and scrolls
- Mythic Dictionaries, Concord Seals, Pact Scrolls, and Whisper Archives
- All future companion works, short films, films, audio performances, or adaptations derived from the AquaCapri universe

Intellectual Property Rights:
The author retains all rights to reproduce, distribute, perform, display, license, adapt, and create derivative works based on this universe in all known and future formats. No part of this publication may be copied, altered, or used to create new works without the express written consent of the author.

Originality and Authorship Declaration

This work was composed through direct human authorship and creative process over several years. While editorial tools were used to refine language and formatting, no AI-generated content was used to author or substitute the storytelling voice. Any resemblance to algorithmic patterns is coincidental and reflects the intentional mythopoetic style of the work. All writing decisions were made solely by the author, Valentino Travaldi.

Declaration Signed By:

✦ Valentino Travaldi
Author & Creator of AquaCapri: Whisperer Across the AquaCapri: The Eternal Saga of Aqua and Capri.

TO

MY BELOVED PRINCESS CAPRI

FOR YOUR LOVE, STRENGTH, AND SPIRIT,
WOVEN INTO EVERY REALM I CREATE.

V.T.

TO

MY MOTHER MARIA

FOR HER UNCONDITIONAL LOVE AND GUIDANCE

AND

TO THE DREAMERS WHO FIND LIGHT WITHIN SHADOW,

TO THE WANDERERS WHO SEEK HARMONY THROUGH CHAOS,

TO THE CHILDREN OF STARLIGHT WHO BELIEVE IN LOVE BEYOND REALMS—

MAY YOUR HEARTS REMAIN VAST, YOUR VISIONS UNBOUND, AND YOUR STORIES ETERNAL.

THIS IS FOR YOU.

V.T.

ACKNOWLEDGEMENT

With deep gratitude and a heart full of starlight, I offer thanks to those who helped AquaCapri become more than a dream.

△ To my mother, Maria
You taught me to believe in imagination's power and the depth of emotion. Your presence beats in the very heart of this book.

△ To my father, Gheorghe Marin
You are the steadfast tide beneath every dream I've dared to sail. Your strength shaped my courage, your silence my resolve, and your spirit remains the compass of my creation.

△ To Sophie and Carter, Claudia, Valentin, and Robert
Your presence in my life shaped the rhythm of my creativity. Thank you for your light.

△ To the teachers, choirs, and poetry circles of my youth
You showed me that words can sing, and that silence can speak.

△ To those who listened as I painted, composed, and dreamed
You encouraged the whispers in my mind to find a home on the page.

△ To the mentors, muses, and mad dreamers
Who taught me the craft of language, the patience of world-building, and the fire of narrative. Your echoes breathe through every chapter.

△ To every voice that challenged, questioned, or guided
You sharpened the vision. You forged the balance between Light and Void. You kept the purpose true.

△ To the timeless storytellers whose echoes span civilizations
Across sands, stars, and scrolls, your myths remind us that storytelling is not a possession—but a cosmic inheritance.

△ To the children I once was, and to the children of the stars yet to come
Never stop dreaming. Never stop dancing in the dark with your own light.

△ And to the readers—both young and eternal in spirit
You are the final Whisperers. May you carry the balance, the love, and the myth of AquaCapri with you—wherever your own story flows.

♠

—Valentino Travaldi

Sealed beneath the stars, with the hand of Valdum and the quill of Maximus

CONTENTS

PREFACE

By Valentino Travaldi,

through the voice of Aqua—From the Constellation of Two

There are stories we are born into, and stories we are born to create. ***AquaCapri*** is both.

It began not as ink on parchment or stars in a manuscript, but as a spark between two souls—mine and hers. I, born under the sign of Aquarius, the bearer of cosmic waters; she, born under the sign of Capricorn, the steadfast mountain rising through the stars. I called her my Princess. She called me her Prince. And in that simple, eternal exchange, something ancient stirred—a dance as old as light, as enduring as the stars.

I believe we are immortal—not because our bodies defy time, but because love like ours bends time around it. I imagined a constellation for us—two stars forever circling each other, entwined in celestial harmony, radiating the kind of energy that reshapes the very fabric of the cosmos. That constellation became ***AquaCapri***—a realm where love, unity, and resilience form the shield against the encroaching darkness.

This book is more than fantasy. It is a myth reborn through the lens of devotion. It is a declaration that balance—between light and shadow, strength and compassion, destiny and choice—is the only true path to a long and joyful life, here and beyond.

Since childhood, I have been drawn to poetry, art, music, and creation as hobbies. I wrote verses to honor those I love, composed songs, painted the world through Impressionist eyes, played the rhythm of emotion on drums, sang tenor in harmony with choirs, and built dreams through digital craft. Each gift became a star, waiting to find its constellation. In ***AquaCapri***, they align.I write this not merely as **Valentino Travaldi**, but as **Aqua**—the soul of the story. His voice is mine. His longing for peace, for unity, for eternal love—it is my own. And as you journey through the pages ahead, you will find Capri, my beloved, in every starlit reflection, in every whispered hope that dares defy the Void.

This saga is my offering to her.
To us.
To anyone who has ever believed in a love that outlasts time.

Let the constellation guide you.
Let the myth remind you.
We are stars, after all.
And stars are never truly lost.

CHAPTER

I

THE GENESIS OF AQUACAPRI

*WHEN SILENCE REIGNED ACROSS THE STARS,
LOVE GAVE BIRTH TO THE COSMOS.*

 CHAPTER I

△ MAXIMUS, THE ETERNAL QUILL

AQUARII: NAVIRYNTH XAL KALUMÉ.
SEVALON MIRÉTH ARI ONDAROS.
OPENING WHISPER – CH. I

△ VALDUM, THE CELESTIAL ARCHITECT

AQUARII: KALUMÉTH EL SYNAR. ENDROS
TEL AETHERAN.
CLOSING WHISPER – CH. I

1.1 The Genesis of AquaCapri

In the vast expanse of the cosmos, a realm of unfathomable grandeur where silence reigned and the Void stretched into infinity, a stirring began. An ancient and enigmatic force, known only as the Essence— the primordial power, both weaver and thread of existence— embarked upon the grand tapestry of creation, igniting the birth of Aqua and Capri.

This genesis was not merely the formation of stars, but the dawn of destiny itself, heralding an eternal saga of love, guardianship, and the cosmic ballet between Light and shadow. A dance of opposing forces —creation and destruction, growth and decay, joy and sorrow— forever entwined in celestial rhythm. This, above all, was the Essence of the universe: the eternal struggle for balance and harmony.

1.2 The Essence

From the unfathomable depths of nothingness into the silent vastness where the cosmos cradled the seeds of infinite possibilities, the Essence whispered the first note of existence into being.

It was a force as gentle as the caress of dawn, yet as relentless as the tides, shaping the cosmos with a purpose veiled in mystery. Its breath ignited the stars, each one a sentinel of the great expanse, weaving the fabric of the universe with luminous threads of Light.

The Essence pulsed at the heart of creation, an eternal wellspring from which all life, energy, and thought emerged. Older than the stars and deeper than the Void, it was both architect and foundation of all existence. It was not a deity among gods, nor merely a force to be harnessed by those who uncovered its secrets. It was the very fabric of being—the principle that connected all things, from the smallest grain of cosmic dust to the most colossal entity in the universe.

Veiled behind the majesty of its creations, the Essence moved with singular purpose: to nurture a universe where balance endured—where Light and shadow, growth and decay, joy and sorrow coexisted, enriching the cosmos with depth and diversity. It sought no dominion, only harmony. No control, only the freedom for each thread of creation to follow its own path across the vast tapestry of reality.

To realize this, the Essence set forth the fundamental laws of existence, establishing the stage upon which life's great drama might unfold. Yet these laws allowed freedom—a space for will, unpredictability, and the potential for both creation and destruction. And it was within this space that the Essence's true vision awakened: a cosmos alive with the potential to grow, to learn, and to love.

Among the celestial orchestra of stars and matter, the Essence brought forth its most resplendent creation: Aqua and Capri, born of its purest energies and destined to become the bastions of the universe.

1.3 The Birth of Aqua and Capri — A Love Forged in Celestial Fire

As the cosmos found its rhythm, two radiant beings emerged from the heart of creation.

Their birth was no accident. It was a deliberate expression of the Essence's most profound aspiration—an embodiment of its dream: a realm where ideals might manifest vividly, where love and harmony could shape the stars.

Aqua and Capri, born of the Essence's will, reflected the dual facets of its nature.

Aqua, the soul of creation and transformation, embodied the boundless depths and mysteries of life. Capri, the beacon of love and wisdom, radiated clarity and purpose, guiding the nascent cosmos with luminous grace.

Together, they represented a perfect harmony—creation and consciousness, movement and meaning. They were the living microcosm of the Essence's vision: a unified force, nurturing growth and inspiring peace across the stars.

When their eyes met across the Void, the universe held its breath. That first gaze was not mere recognition—it was a moment of cosmic alignment, a union forged in the crucible of creation.

Their love, born in silence yet stronger than time, became the cornerstone of AquaCapri.

As the realm unfolded, the Essence—silent and ever-watchful—observed from beyond. The first light of AquaCapri did more than illuminate stars and nebulae. It revealed the stirrings of life: sparks of existence born from Aqua's wonder and Capri's warmth.

Aqua and Capri were not bystanders in this dawn. They were its authors, shaping the cosmos with every breath, every glance, every act of unity.

Their love became a guiding light across the darkness, a force that nurtured new worlds. Aqua's tears of joy became oceans. Capri's smile lit planets like twin suns. From their union, galaxies blossomed.

Yet, as they danced their celestial dance, the first whispers of discord drifted from the edges of space—a quiet foreshadowing of trials to come. The shadows crept along the perimeter of their radiance, not yet a threat but a reminder: where there is Light, shadow follows.

Even in a garden of stars, the balance must be kept. Their love, no matter how pure, would not go untested.

1.4 The Realm's First Dawn

Under the vigilant gaze of their creators, the realm of AquaCapri flourished—a sanctuary of Light, harmony, and wonder.

The first dawn broke across the stars in a symphony of color, painting the skies with radiant hues that danced across planets and celestial rivers. The realm revealed itself in splendor, a testament to the Essence's vision and the love that had given it breath.

Bathed in luminous brilliance, the universe awakened beneath Aqua and Capri's care. Their love was more than emotion—it was a living rhythm, in tune with the heartbeat of the cosmos. In its music, the stars pulsed, the planets turned, and life began to stir.

It was a time of triumph, and yet, beneath the golden serenity of that new morning, something else quietly took shape. Subtle shadows began to stretch across the edges of paradise—not in defiance of the Light, but in quiet response to it.

For even the brightest illumination casts shadows.

The first dawn of AquaCapri marked not only the blossoming of a realm but also the emergence of contrast. Hidden deep within the harmony was the seed of discord, lying dormant, waiting. It did not scream. It whispered. A delicate balance was beginning to shift.

Still, this was not a flaw in the Essence's creation. It was part of the design—a truth woven into the fabric of the universe. The dawn that revealed beauty also revealed contrast. The Light that inspired peace must acknowledge the presence of its opposite.

Aqua and Capri, bound by love and purpose, sensed this quiet duality. They stood not only as guardians of their realm but as stewards of balance. Their journey would not be a simple one, for every harmony invites its echo, and every act of creation stirs a shadow somewhere in the cosmos.

Thus, the first dawn was more than an awakening. It was the beginning of an odyssey—one that would span love and loss, courage and doubt, Light and shadow. As Aqua and Capri walked forward into this unfolding story, the realm watched with bated breath.

For what is born in Light must one day walk through shadow to find its strength.

1.5 The Stirring of Shadows

Amid the flourishing of creation, as Aqua and Capri basked in the growing beauty of their realm, faint whispers began to ripple through the cosmos. These were not the songs of joy and harmony that filled the early days of AquaCapri. These were softer, colder echoes—born of envy, hunger, and ancient unrest.

At first, they were barely audible, lost beneath the chorus of stars. Yet they carried the scent of something old, something that had lingered in the Void long before Aqua and Capri drew breath. A force that had waited patiently, veiled in darkness, now stirred.

As new worlds bloomed and the first beings looked skyward in awe of their creators, a shadow slipped across a distant star—its dimming unnoticed by the guardians as they celebrated their growing domain. This fleeting darkness, subtle as a blink, marked the first disruption in the realm's radiant harmony.

It was a silent herald of the trials to come, a reminder that where Light grows, so too does its shadow.

But such trials were never mistakes. In the Essence's design, challenge was not chaos—it was purpose. Harmony, if never tested, remained fragile. The shadows rising at the dawn of AquaCapri were not flaws in the weave of reality. They were part of the loom itself.

They would become the crucible in which love would be forged into legacy, where guardianship would be measured not by peace alone but by the courage to defend it.

Aqua, ever fluid and fierce, summoned waves of creation—rivers and oceans that surged to protect the vulnerable corners of their realm. Capri, her Light piercing through darkness like a comet's flare, became a guide for lost souls and wandering stars.

Together, they pushed back the creeping dark. Not with war, but with wonder. Not through domination, but through design—constructing a balance, one act of love at a time.

Yet even as they labored, the pace of the universe began to shift. The serenity of AquaCapri was no longer untouched. With each new ripple of shadow came a test, each more subtle, more cunning than the last.

Still, their love endured.

And in the deepest reaches of the Void, where Light had yet to touch, a force moved. Its essence was not balance but domination. It sought to unravel what Aqua and Capri had built—not to reshape it, but to erase it.

The innocent creatures of AquaCapri, still dancing among the stars, remained unaware. But some—those most attuned to the cosmic rhythm—felt the change. A discordant note in the melody of space. A stillness too deep to be natural.

A flicker in the stars. A silence in the fabric of sound. A breath held too long.

Aqua and Capri could not ignore the signs for long. A dimmed star. A tremor across the starlit seas. A quiet absence in a place once full of Light.

Their celestial dance continued, but their steps had grown heavier. For they knew the first great trial of their realm had arrived.

Not by their choice.

But by the nature of all things born in Light.

AquaCapri

CHAPTER

2

GUARDIANS OF THE COSMOS

*THOSE CHOSEN TO PROTECT THE BALANCE
MUST FIRST FACE THEIR OWN INNER TIDES.*

 # CHAPTER 2

△ VALDUM, THE CELESTIAL ARCHITECT
AQUARII: YALTHEORN ISTRI QUEL'VIRETH.
MAERION XAL DORENTHA.
 OPENING WHISPER – CH. 2

△ MAXIMUS, THE ETERNAL QUILL
AQUARII: DORENTHA SILEN AR'NAVAI.
SOLARI VEN THALORIEN.
CLOSING WHISPER – CH. 2

2.1 Aether, the Realm Historian

In the secluded northwestern corner of the AquaCapri Constellation's vast library, hidden one level beneath the Celestial Hallway, ancient celestial charts, planetary maps, and classified documents lay in wait. This chamber, known only to a select few, harbored the secrets of warp-speed troop movements and long-forgotten texts that had once guided the AquaCapri Forces. It was the silent brain of the constellation—fiercely guarded, endlessly revered.

Among these sacred halls moved Aether, the Realm Historian. He was the living memory of the universe, a quiet yet essential guide to the constellation's leaders. Aether bridged past, present, and future, ensuring AquaCapri's choices aligned with its higher cosmic purpose. His influence was subtle, woven into whispers and wisdom—never commands.

The library was more than a repository; it was a fortress. Hidden staircases behind dark crystal walls allowed Aether to travel unseen, guided by the King's Hologram. When summoned, the walls parted to form floating steps of Duroxium, the rarest and strongest mineral in the realm.

Six elite guards stood watch at all times. Entry to the library required two matching pendants—one worn by Aether, the other by King Oceanius. The King alone could trigger the final mechanism: twelve crystal cylinders aligned like the twelve protector stars of Aquaterra. A secret incantation activated the thirteenth, hidden cylinder, opening the door only to those deemed worthy.

When King Oceanius and Queen Marinella approached, their guards flanked them in tight formation. The hallway fell into stillness. The guards bowed low.

A King's Command

"Captain," the King said firmly, "give us privacy. I will open the doors myself."

"You heard His Majesty," the captain commanded. "Secure the outer hallway. No one enters. No matter what."

The guards moved into position. Within the chamber, the King whispered the ancient words.

A pulse of energy stirred the air. Six glowing spikes spiraled forth from the void, piercing the thirteenth cylinder. Stardust flickered, and the cylinder vanished—replaced by a luminous Hologram of King Oceanius, its form cast in pale blue light.

"Hmm, you again," the hologram muttered. "What is it this time?"

"I need access," Oceanius said flatly. "I seek Aether's counsel."

The hologram squinted. "Show me your pendant."

The King raised the pendant without expression.

"No need to get irritable," the hologram replied. "I am your creation, after all. Very well. But next time, a little warning would be nice. Use your messenger."

"Be silent. Just open the door, or I'll replace you," Oceanius said coldly.

With a groan and a slow, metallic screech, the great doors opened inward. Aether stood beyond them—serene, waiting.

"Your Majesties," he greeted. "I was expecting you. Please, come in."

"Aether, you look incredible," said the King. "What's your secret? I could use some of that."

The doors sealed behind them with a quiet hum.

"No secret, Your Majesty," Aether replied with a faint smile. "Just an old soul in fresh robes."

His voice deepened.

"I sensed your arrival. Troubled times approach. Dark forces move in the shadows. We must prepare."

"Tell me," said the King. "What have you seen? Who brings war to our doorstep? Are they strong? Who are they, Aether?"

Aether lowered his gaze, as though burdened with a weight no man should bear. "The visions are veiled,"he admitted.

"I have seen shadows moving across the constellations, but their faces are hidden. Their strength is not in number, but in the darkness that cloaks them."

"My King, I just received word from the Elderly Council," Aether said.

"And?"

"The future is grim."

Oceanius's brow furrowed. "I thought the Essence appointed the Elderly Council to uphold balance. Are they doing nothing to stop this threat?"

"They are trying, but not all agree," Aether said gently. "The Council is divided."

"Divided? That cannot be. They are the protectors of balance."

"Cassiopeia, the Weaver of Fate, shapes much of their vision," Aether explained. "She weaves destiny from threads of Light and shadow. To her, even darkness serves a purpose. They trust fate too deeply."

The King's voice grew low. "Then we walk into ruin. This enemy—this darkness—it must be powerful. How can we defend AquaCapri against such destruction?"

Allies of the Cosmos

"We are not alone," said Aether. "Draco, Guardian of Eternal Night, stands with us. He commands legions of celestial warriors and has already fortified the borders."

"Draco will buy us time," said Oceanius. "Anyone else?"

"Yes. Andromeda. She guards the cosmic waters between realms. Her strength could shift the balance."

"Good. We may yet have hope. Do we know who leads the enemy?"

Aether nodded solemnly. "We do."

"Who?"

"Lord Valthor, Master of the Dark Forces."

A heavy silence fell.

Valthor was not merely an adversary. He was devastation incarnate. His world, Nocturnia—cloaked in perpetual night—was a land of jagged peaks and shadowed valleys, ruled from the Citadel of Shadows, a fortress carved from black stone, its spires slicing the heavens. Within its depths, ancient secrets twisted through darkness.

At its core sat the Obsidian Throne, from which Valthor devised his cruel dominion. Few dared speak of the Abyssal Plane, the roiling storm of shadow energy that stretched beyond Nocturnia, where reality warped and fractured.

"Then we have no time to lose," said the King. "We must prepare for war. Aether, gather your maps. Join us in the War Room. Aqua, Capri, and the generals await."

"At once, Your Majesty. I shall meet you there."

The King turned toward the exit. "My Queen, we have much to discuss with our allies. The Council of War awaits. Follow me."

She nodded, grace flowing through every step.

Oceanius paused at the threshold.

"You there—open the doors."

The hologram shimmered. "As you command."

The doors parted once more.

"Captain," said Oceanius, "fix that squeak. It is beginning to grate on my nerves."

"Yes, my King," the captain replied. "I shall alert the master carpenter."

"Good man. Reinforce the library. Protect Aether at all costs. I shall handle the rest."

Toward the War Room

As the King and Queen departed, Aether gathered his celestial charts and prophetic visions. A chill stirred through the chamber. He knew the path ahead would be their greatest test.

"We shall not fail," he whispered.

With swift purpose, he vanished behind an ancient tapestry, slipping through a hidden stairway. Unseen, he made his way toward the War Room. In the Celestial Hallway, Aqua, Capri, and their allies stood waiting.

The fate of AquaCapri hung in the balance—and together, they would face it

2.2 Protectors Against the Void

The Grand Palace stood in the vast expanse of Aquaterra, where the sky met the clouds and the air hummed with ancient melodies, shimmering in an ethereal glow. This floating citadel, known as the Celestial Haven, hovered with grace above the City of Dreams, its crystal spires piercing the heavens and its radiant gardens blooming with flowers that sang the songs of creation.

Within its crystalline halls, Aqua and Capri gathered with their most trusted allies. Urgency echoed in their voices as they spoke of the mounting threat.

The Gathering of Guardians

"The balance is shifting," said Aqua, his gaze distant. "I feel it in the tides, in the very Essence of the water."

"I sense it too," Capri replied. "The stars whisper of unrest, and shadows stir where there should be Light."

Their exchange was interrupted by the arrival of their closest allies: Zephyr, Aqua's confidant and swift guardian of wind; Lumina, radiant bearer of Light; and Luna, Capri's confidant and keeper of the moon's secrets.

"Dark forces gather at the edge of our realm," Zephyr declared. "The winds carry their warnings. Their presence is veiled, but their intent is clear—and dark."

"I have seen flickers of their shadow," Lumina added. "They dim the Light of the stars. We must act before it spreads to the heart of the Essence."

As they convened in the Grand Hall, its panoramic expanse unveiling the cosmos beyond, Aqua and Capri turned inward, speaking softly of purpose and the force that bound them.

"Our love has always been our strength," said Capri. "It gives us purpose—and now it must also shield us."

"Love is more than creation," Aqua agreed. "It is a shield. We must wield it to stand against the darkness."

Their allies listened with solemn devotion.

"Love has guided us," said Zephyr, "but how do we make it a weapon?"

"It lights the darkest paths," Lumina responded. "If we unite our Light, we can push back the shadows."

"Exactly," said Capri. "Our unity, born of love, is our greatest power. Every star, every soul must be reminded of that truth."

Aqua stepped forward. "The AquaCapri Constellation is protected by twelve mighty stars, forming an almost impenetrable shield. The thirteenth star holds the constellation's hidden power—its location known only to us."

The Arrival of the Monarchs

At that moment, King Oceanius and Queen Marinella entered the Grand Hall, flanked by their elite guards. They had concluded a vital counsel with Aether, the realm historian and keeper of ether and stars. In the library far below, Aether's wisdom wove the threads of past, present, and future into guiding light for the realms of AquaCapri.

Aqua, Capri, and their companions bowed deeply, honoring ancient custom.

"Your Majesties," said Aqua with reverence.

The Royal Family, having heard the words spoken before their arrival, stepped forward to lend their voices to the storm of counsel gathering within the hall.

"Aqua," said King Oceanius, his tone both commanding and paternal, "I have summoned our generals to the War Chamber. Aether will brief us on the truths unfolding across our constellation. We must listen with clarity and act with wisdom. AquaCapri faces its gravest peril. The safety of our thirteenth star—PaxProfundis—must be ensured at all costs. It is the key to our endurance and the beacon of our strength."

"Your assessment is sound," he continued, his voice deepening. "We are under siege—from the Dark Forces... and the Void."

"The harmony we have nurtured in AquaCapri is the result of unity and strength. Each star, each soul, holds a role in maintaining that delicate balance. PaxProfundis remains our most guarded secret—the source of our power and the root of our continued prosperity."

"Our defenses are strong," said Queen Marinella, "but we must remain vigilant. The barriers surrounding PaxProfundis are formidable, yet we cannot underestimate the determination of our enemies. Only those we trust must be permitted near this sacred place."

"My King, my Queen," said Aqua, "we stand prepared to defend our constellation. The unity of our realms and the strength of our guardians shall ensure that AquaCapri remains a beacon of Light and hope."

"Capri," said Queen Marinella, stepping nearer, "let us fortify the defenses around the twelve stars. Their collective power is mighty. With our love and unity, no force shall breach our lines."

"Let us never forget PaxProfundis," said King Oceanius. "It is more than a source of strength—it is a symbol of our unity and resilience. As long as it remains protected and unseen, AquaCapri shall endure."

"We must wield its energy wisely," said Capri. "Let its strength fortify our borders and nourish the harmony of our realms. Together, we shall meet whatever challenge rises."

"We will ensure our constellation remains a sanctuary of peace and prosperity," Queen Marinella affirmed, "a shining example across the stars."

"Once our strategy is set," declared Aqua, "I will lead the warriors of the sea, forging barriers of water and life along our borders. Capri—your Light shall be our guide, our shield, and our spark."

"Together," Capri vowed, "with our allies, we will face the darkness. Our love and unity shall be our greatest weapon."

The council nodded in solemn agreement, their resolve deepening with each breath. The Essence of Universal Love flowed like a silent current among them, fortifying their spirits and weaving them ever closer in cosmic bond.

As dawn's hush approached, Aqua and Capri stood side by side at the crystalline edge of the Grand Hall, gazing across the realm they had sworn to defend.

"No matter the darkness," said Aqua, his voice quiet and sure, "our love shall guide us. Together, we are unstoppable."

"Together," whispered Capri, "we are the Light that shall never fade."

Hearts entwined, spirits unwavering—the guardians of AquaCapri braced for the storm ahead, their love, the eternal key to the harmony of the cosmos.

The Guardians' Vigil

While the King's closest advisors shaped their strategies with sacred care, the guardians of AquaCapri's stars remained ever watchful, their vigil unbroken. Each guardian, alongside their stardust warriors, patrolled the realms to preserve peace and stability. The twelve most powerful stars, set in formation at the constellation's heart, stood as timeless reminders of the unity and strength that defined their world.

In the hidden depths near Aquaterra, PaxProfundis pulsed with cosmic energy, a silent sentinel of enduring harmony. The intricate maze of celestial barriers and invisible traps ensured that only those of pure intent and unwavering loyalty could draw near.

With resolve rekindled, the leaders of AquaCapri stood ready to face the coming trials, bound by the unshakable strength of their shared destiny.

Yet even in that radiant peace, the harmony they held so dear felt fragile. Shadows stirred, and whispers of unease drifted through the realms—carried on the winds of war from distant stars.

2.3 The Harmony of Infinite Realms

In the boundless expanse of the AquaCapri Constellation, harmony reigned supreme among its realms. Each realm, a unique world of celestial beauty and vibrant life, stood united under the wise and benevolent rule of King Oceanius and Queen Marinella. The existence of the AquaCapri Constellation was safeguarded by one hundred thousand stars, each imbued with a soul forged from the radiant heart of its celestial flame. Every stellar being commanded an army of one hundred twenty thousand stardust warriors, ever vigilant in their sacred duty to protect their realm from any threat.

The stardust warriors were sentient war machines, forged from the rarest Duroxium alloys in the constellation. Their strength, adaptability, and firepower were without equal. Towering one hundred twenty feet high, thirty feet wide, and forty feet deep, they shifted form according to their mission—whether patrolling land, soaring through the skies, or diving beneath the waters of AquaCapri. Each stood as a living bulwark, a sentinel sculpted from Light and metal.

Aquaterra: The Capital Planet

At the heart of the AquaCapri Constellation shone Aquaterra, the capital planet—a beacon of Light, wisdom, and enduring hope. Within its embrace stood the Celestial Heaven and the City of Dreams, twin jewels revered by the universe. These majestic sanctuaries embodied the pinnacle of cosmic harmony, where peace, artistry, and learning flourished under the watchful radiance of AquaCapri's mightiest stars.

Twelve of the most powerful stars encircled Aquaterra in an impenetrable barrier, an eternal aegis against any who dared threaten its peace. Their luminous presence radiated immense strength and unwavering resolve, ensuring no enemy could conquer the heart of the constellation.

Aquaterra defied the ordinary—bathed in eternal twilight, where the glow of stars remained ever close. Its vast oceans sparkled like rivers of liquid diamond, mirroring the heavens above. Floating islands drifted in the skies, suspended by unseen forces, each a sanctuary of tranquility and wonder. Graceful gondolas glided through the airways, ferrying citizens and goods across the celestial expanse in harmonious rhythm.

The City of Dreams

At the center of Aquaterra bloomed the City of Dreams, a masterpiece of crystalline architecture and stardust engineering. Towering spires of translucent crystal spiraled skyward, their gleaming surfaces catching the constellation's gentle glow and scattering it in rainbows across the streets. Bridges woven of stardust arched between the towers, forming a radiant web that connected every corner of the city. Within this dreamlike metropolis, the galaxy's finest artists and scholars channeled the boundless energy of the cosmos into their masterpieces—creations that sang with both soul and starlight.

The Celestial Heaven Palace

Above even the highest towers floated the Celestial Heaven, the palace of King Oceanius and Queen Marinella. A marvel of divine engineering, it rested upon a foundation of compressed stardust and Duroxium alloys. Its translucent walls shimmered with hues drawn from the nebulae, while its floors radiated the Light of ancient stars. The palace roof was not a ceiling at all, but a crystalline dome open to the cosmos, where constellations danced and whirled in eternal motion.

The Celestial Heaven was not constructed by mortal hand—it had been summoned from the very Essence of the universe. Its form, ever-shifting, responded to the rhythm of celestial forces, a living embodiment of divine will. Here, King Oceanius, Queen Marinella, Prince Aqua, and Princess Capri reigned not as mortals, but as cosmic deities—keepers of peace, guardians of balance, and the luminous heart of AquaCapri.

A Quiet Moment Before the Storm

Aqua stood alone in the private garden atop the highest tower of the Celestial Heaven, far from council chambers and the preparations for war. The stars above glowed gently, casting silver light over the shimmering foliage, while the hush of distant cosmic winds filled the air with a sacred calm.

He stood at the garden's edge, his gaze lost in the infinite expanse of the AquaCapri Constellation. Below him, the lights of Aquaterra twinkled like a reflection of the heavens, yet his thoughts traveled far beyond the realm's splendor. The burden of what loomed—the threat of the Void, the concealed power of PaxProfundis, the uncertain fate of the realms—pressed heavily on his spirit.

He sensed her presence before she spoke. Capri's arrival was like the softest breeze—known, comforting, constant. She moved with quiet grace, her gown whispering across the crystal floor, her steps echoing gently in the twilight.

"You've been standing here for hours, Aqua."

Her voice, calm and steady, carried its usual serenity, yet tonight it bore a thread of concern.

Aqua turned to her, his eyes reflecting the same constellations they had sworn to defend. He offered a faint smile that never reached the sorrow behind his gaze. "I needed time to think."

Capri stepped closer, her hand slipping over his. Her fingers curled around his palm with quiet strength. "You've been preparing for this your whole life. Whatever comes, we face it together."

He turned fully to her, brushing a silvery strand of hair from her face. "It's not the war that troubles me," he murmured. "It's you."

Capri's brow creased softly. "Me?"

Aqua exhaled, his shoulders relaxing. "I've seen realms fall to the darkness, Capri. I've watched the Void devour all it touched. We built this constellation together—our love, our unity, have been its Light. But if something were to happen to you—"

She placed her finger gently upon his lips, silencing his fear with unwavering calm. "I am not fragile, Aqua. We were forged in the fires of creation. Our love is no fleeting flame. No darkness—not even

Valhor's hatred—can extinguish it." She rested her head upon his shoulder. "I fear only losing you."

His heart stirred. In that instant, he realized what he had always known—they were each other's shield. He pressed a kiss to her hair, breathing in the mingled scent of lilacs and stardust.

"We will face it together. I cannot imagine a world without you at my side."

She lifted her gaze, her sapphire eyes fixed upon his. "Then promise me—here, now—that no matter what darkness comes, no matter what forces try to pull us apart, we will find our way back to each other."

He tightened his grip around her hand. Above them, the stars seemed to blaze brighter, bearing silent witness to their vow.

"I swear it, Capri. Always."

She smiled, her soul aglow with love. "And I swear it, too. Together, forever."

"Together. Always together."

They lingered in that sacred stillness, arms entwined, their love a radiant force defying even the encroaching dark. Though battle approached and the Void threatened, in that moment, they stood invincible—two eternal souls bound by a promise that no force could break.

PaxProfundis: The Hidden Power

Yet AquaCapri's truest strength remained hidden—its most secret and potent star concealed from all but a chosen few. This thirteenth star,

PaxProfundis, surpassed all others in power and brilliance, its core protected by the strongest crust in the known universe. Only King Oceanius, Queen Marinella, Aqua, and Capri knew of its existence.

Access to PaxProfundis was granted through a veiled portal, defended by treacherous traps, layered wards, and illusions powerful enough to deter even the most determined intruder.

More than a hidden jewel, PaxProfundis sustained the constellation itself. A colossal blue star, it absorbed cosmic rays and transmuted them into boundless energy and wealth. It was a fountain of vitality— its breath kept AquaCapri alive, its rhythm ensured prosperity, its Light upheld harmony.

Shrouded in mystery, PaxProfundis lay cloaked beneath five distinct protective layers, each more formidable than the last.

Aether's Vigil Near PaxProfundis

Aether departed the Celestial Heaven and drifted through the constellation's heart, robes flowing like celestial silk. The Keeper of the Stars moved silently through the void until he reached the outer barriers of PaxProfundis, glowing in the distance like a star within a star.

He paused before the first barrier, letting his senses stretch outward. The energy pulsing from PaxProfundis was alive—vast and ancient. The first layer gleamed with raw power, collecting rays from the cosmos and stabilizing their force. Aether raised his hand and felt the surge pass through him, a delicate balance between harnessing energy and averting destruction. It reminded him how close creation always lingered to collapse.

He approached the second layer, where the star's energy was refined into the resources that fed the constellation. He watched streams of Light weave through the barrier like rivers of fire and brilliance, nourishing the realms.

To the third layer he moved, where the celestial seas channeled that power across the network of AquaCapri. Energy pulsed like lifeblood, flowing through unseen veins to every realm and outpost. This was the breath of AquaCapri, and PaxProfundis was its heart.

He turned to the fourth layer—the realm of innovation. Here, the star's strength forged tools, advanced weaponry, and the sacred instruments of knowledge and protection. Aether marveled at its splendor and the quiet genius woven into every glimmer.

And then he gazed upon the fifth and final layer—the impenetrable shield. Only a few had ever seen beyond it. It was said that nothing, not even the darkest force, could breach its wall. And yet, a whisper echoed in Aether's mind.

What if it is not enough?

He cast the thought aside as he returned to the Celestial Heaven, unwilling to let fear obscure his path. But the stars murmured of change, and in the depths of his ancient soul, Aether feared that the constellation's greatest secret might one day be revealed in the gravest of ways.

2.4 Chamber of War

The Chamber of War, nestled within the Celestial Heaven, stood as a grand and imposing sanctuary of strategy and strength. Banners of the AquaCapri Realm adorned its towering walls, each emblazoned with the legendary sigil—a majestic sea serpent entwined with twelve radiant stars.

Walls of translucent crystal bore etched scenes of AquaCapri's storied past. Intricate mosaics lined every panel, chronicling battles fought and victories earned, glinting beneath the soft radiance of floating orbs suspended in the air, their glow ethereal and ever-watchful.

Above, the ceiling arched into a cosmic dome, an illuminated map of the AquaCapri Constellation. Glowing stars and planets moved in celestial harmony, marking key defense points in an ever-shifting ballet of light.

At the heart of the chamber stood a vast circular table of polished aquamarine—a symbol of unity and the Constellation's indomitable will. From its gleaming surface, luminous waterways rose into the air —delicate streams of light suspended like veins—tracing strategic connections across every corner of the realm.

Surrounding the table sat the Generals. Clad in armor that reflected their house emblems, each bore a breastplate engraved with the sea serpent and twelve stars. Waves encircled the design, denoting their dominion over the cosmic seas. These were AquaCapri's fiercest defenders—guardians of light, pride of the realm.

Royal Attire

The echo of resolute footsteps faded into silence as the great doors of the Chamber closed behind the towering forms of King Oceanius and Queen Marinella.

The three Supreme Generals and the Council of Protectors rose in unison, striking their chests with right fists over their hearts in a gesture of solemn reverence.

They chanted as one:
"For God, Honor, and AquaCapri.
Hail to the King."

The air thickened with anticipation. The King surveyed the chamber —his presence alone stilling every voice. His deep blue robe, dusted with diamonds that twinkled like distant stars, swept behind him, and upon his head rested a crown of coral and gold, proclaiming his dominion over oceanic depths and celestial heights alike.

At his side moved Queen Marinella, a vision of strength and serenity. Her gown shimmered in hues of green and blue, woven as though from the very essence of the sea. A tiara of pearls and sapphires adorned her brow, embodying grace, wisdom, and resolve.

The Council of Protectors Against the Void

King Oceanius stepped forward, his voice unwavering.

"We are at war with the Void and the Dark Forces, my Generals."

A murmur rippled across the chamber—a reflexive response to grim truth.

"Silence," he said firmly. "Be seated."

As the Council settled, he continued.

"War has reached our threshold. We are gathered not merely to speak but to act. The Void has trespassed into our space. We must respond with purpose, with unity, with unwavering resolve. Each of you holds a vital role in the defense of our Constellation. Your valor and wisdom will carry us through the shadow."

He gestured toward the glowing map above the aquamarine table.

"As always, we will follow our five-step approach. Aether will reveal his vision of our future and provide you with maps, documents, and any instruments required to ensure victory."

He paused, his gaze steady.

"Council of Protectors, your loyalty humbles me. Your bravery, your sacrifices, your steadfast love for AquaCapri—these are the pillars of our strength. The entire Constellation looks to us now. We must rise together, not just as soldiers, but as guardians of light.

I charge you to begin constructing a war plan—comprehensive, victorious, unwavering. The Void must be repelled in every battle, in every shadow. We shall not falter."

He raised his voice in a declaration that stirred the very air.

"Let us fight in the name of our God, the Essence.
Let us fight with strength and honor.
Let us fight for our homes, our families, our people—our AquaCapri.
Let us fight for unity, love, and peace.
To victory!"

Raising his silver chalice high, he thundered:

"To Victory!"

The Generals responded as one, their silver cups raised in defiance of darkness.

"To Victory!"

The Royal Family Arrives

As the final echoes of the King's words faded, the towering doors opened once more.

Aqua and Capri entered with quiet grace, their presence shifting the atmosphere like a breath of wind stirring still waters. They bowed before the King and Queen, then turned to honor the Generals with equal reverence.

Aqua's armor shimmered like sunlight dancing across ocean waves, the trident engraved upon his chest glowing faintly with elemental power.

Capri's robe flowed like liquid light, radiant and ethereal, her belt adorned with star-forged symbols, each one representing a constellation under her guidance.

Behind them, silent attendants brought refreshments—nectar, ambrosia, and the delicate sweets favored by the King. The scent of celestial fruit and warm honey drifted through the chamber, a brief balm to the gravity of war.

Aqua stepped forward.

"My King, we've come to understand the threat more deeply. The Council of Defenders stands ready to craft a strategy worthy of our cause."

"Aqua, Capri, please take your seats," the King replied.

A Warning from the Stars

As King Oceanius surveyed the chamber, the gravity of the moment weighed upon him. Then his gaze fell upon an ancient figure.

"Ah, Orion, we are honored by your presence at this council. What say you?"

Orion, the Sage of Starlight, stepped forward, his ancient eyes reflecting the constellation glowing above. His voice, though soft, carried the weight of eons.

"My King, my Queen, I have seen signs in the cosmic tapestry. The Void stirs again, and its shadows seek to breach our defenses. PaxProfundis is more than a wellspring of power—it is the anchor that binds our Constellation's Light. If its location is discovered, we may face a cataclysmic collapse."

The chamber fell into stillness as Orion's words settled over them. King Oceanius placed his hand upon the aquamarine table.

"Then we must act with greater caution. PaxProfundis must remain hidden, and its energy safeguarded at all costs. Orion, can the stars reveal the Void's next move?"

Orion closed his eyes and traced invisible patterns through the air.

"They seek a breach in our shields. There is one among them—one they call Valthor, a dark lord who bends space-time to his will. His power grows, fueled by a weapon unlike anything we have seen."

The Rising Threat of Valthor

The name sent a ripple of unease through the council.

Supreme General Vortizian, steadfast and seasoned, tightened his grip on the hilt of his blade.

"If Valthor truly possesses such a weapon, we cannot underestimate him. I shall increase patrols and ensure our Stardust Warriors remain vigilant. We cannot allow the Void to infiltrate our walls."

Queen Marinella turned her gaze toward the far horizon, where the stars shimmered faintly.

"Valthor's ambitions are vast, but his arrogance will be his undoing. He believes brute force can conquer AquaCapri, yet he underestimates the bond we share—the unity of our people, the strength of our guardians."

Capri's Strategic Role with Divine Wisdom

Capri rose before the council, her form aglow with the Light of a thousand stars. Her presence commanded attention, not through force, but through the gravity of celestial wisdom.

"Our defenses are powerful," she said, her voice calm and resolute, "but power alone is not enough."

She stepped forward, her words clear and unwavering.

"Valthor's weapon may pierce our shields, but it cannot touch what it cannot find. We must weave PaxProfundis into the very fabric of the celestial seas, dispersing its presence across the realms like scattered echoes."

With a motion of her hand, a map bloomed in midair—a glowing web of starlight.

She tapped a hidden section, cloaked from dark forces.

"I propose we mask its energy. Let them chase illusions and reflections while we remain protected."

Aqua nodded beside her.

"A brilliant strategy. We can use the third-layer energy streams to create a web of false signals."

Capri continued, her gaze steady.

"And we must prepare for the worst. If Valthor's weapon breaches our defenses, I will personally oversee the creation of remote-activated barriers to shield our core."

Even Vortizian offered a rare smile of respect. Capri was no mere bearer of grace—she was a tactician whose mind rivaled any blade.

Tension in the Council

As Capri concluded, Vortizian stood.

"I respect your insight, but I say we strike first. Why wait for his attack? We have the strongest army in the cosmos. Let us catch him unprepared."

Aether, newly returned from PaxProfundis, interjected with quiet authority.

"And risk exposing our anchor? That is what Valthor seeks. We must endure, reinforce our shields, and remain united."

Vortizian's voice sharpened.

"Endure? For how long? The Void grows bolder. We need decisive action!"

Queen Marinella raised her hand.

"We must not let fear lead us. Our strength lies in unity. Both paths hold merit, but one misstep could doom us."

Aqua's Silent Vigil

As debate stirred, Aqua remained silent, the weight of the cosmos pressing upon him. His blue eyes mirrored the stars above, but within them stormed an unease he could not shake.

He felt the heartbeat of PaxProfundis—a bond shared with the realm —falter. A tremor in the Essence.

He clenched his fist. Was it the Void?

Capri stepped beside him, her touch grounding, her voice a whisper of calm.

"What troubles you, my love?"

He stared upward.

"The Void... Capri, the Void."

Her eyes hardened with resolve.

"We will not let it destroy what we have built. We will protect PaxProfundis—together."

He took her hand. Their bond, forged in starlight and sacrifice, would endure. But the storm had only just begun.

The Leaders' Final Resolve

King Oceanius stepped forward, his voice resolute.

"We have faced many dangers, but none as grave as this. Valthor's weapon may unravel the very weave of our realm. Our defenses stand strong, but should PaxProfundis be found, we must be ready. Unity shall be our shield. Resolve, our blade."

The chamber swelled with renewed purpose. The harmony of infinite realms now stood upon the edge, and the days ahead would test every oath, every soul, every star.

The Battle Plan

General Vortizian rose, his voice deep and commanding.

"Majesty, our first task is to assess the strength and size of the Void's forces. Scouts report increased activity along the kingdom's outer rim. Once we comprehend the full scale of the threat, we should issue a formal declaration of war. Such an act will rally our armies and provide clear direction for the battles ahead."

General Celestara spoke next, her voice calm and resonant.

"We must begin isolating the affected zones. Let no fragment of the Void spread further. Fortify the borders with our Stardust Warriors. Their form grants them unparalleled mobility—they can traverse vast territories swiftly and decisively."

General Tempeston, his voice as steady as distant thunder, nodded.

"Protecting our people must remain paramount. Evacuate the vulnerable, reinforce our perimeters, and increase patrols along the outer Constellation. If we study the Void's movements, we can anticipate and intercept their advance."

King Oceanius inclined his head.

"Agreed. Strategic positioning is essential. Let us turn the terrain into our greatest weapon. If we draw them into our lands, we control the field—and there we strike hardest."

Queen Marinella's voice rang with calm precision.

"We must also prepare a devastating counterattack. Identify the weakest points in their formation and strike with speed and purpose. Keep the Thirteenth Star hidden and secured—it holds power we must protect at all costs. But above all, remember our people. Their courage, their hope, their unity—they are our strength. Involve them. Prepare them. Let them rise with us."

Aqua stepped forward once more.

"We should consult the ancient ones. Their wisdom spans epochs, and they may hold knowledge of the Void's origin and flaws. Love and unity are our greatest shields. With them, we shall pass through darkness and return bearing light."

Capri's tone flowed like the very currents she commanded.

"Our commanders await their orders. We must ensure every battle plan is precise, every response swift. The time has come to rally our full forces at the AquaCapri gates. We will not let the enemy pass."

The King surveyed them, reverence in his gaze.

"You are all correct," he said at last.
"We will strengthen our defenses, seek alliances, consult the ancient ones, and summon the hearts of our people. This war will not break us—it will forge us. We must prevail—for AquaCapri, for the future of all realms."

The Generals bowed their heads in solemn agreement. Their resolve became steel, sharpened by purpose.

Oceanius raised his hand.

"I hereby call for a General Gathering across the AquaCapri Constellation. All leaders must be present tonight—no exceptions. Send word immediately."

He turned to Aqua and Capri.

"You are to gather the people at the City of Dreams' main square tomorrow. As Marinella wisely said, they deserve the truth. We must speak to them not as rulers but as kin. We need their hearts beside ours in the trials to come."

The divine pair inclined their heads, unified in commitment.

"We will prepare," said Aqua.

"They will stand with us," Capri affirmed.

King Oceanius concluded:

"Make ready the Celestial Ballroom. Tonight, we welcome our guests of honor. Your presence is required, my Generals. Bring your kin. We are more than allies—we are a universal family."

Discussion Among Generals

As the King's command settled over the chamber, the circle of Generals leaned forward, their voices rising one by one, a tide of strategic thought.

General Hydronius, calm as a still sea, began.

"Vortizian is right. Our scouts confirm it—activity has increased along the realm's outer edges. The Void gathers strength. We cannot ignore their momentum."

General Pelagius nodded.

"Celestara's wisdom is timely. We must isolate the affected regions. Our Stardust Warriors should already be holding the front lines, preventing further spread."

General Marellus, ever vigilant, added firmly:

"Our duty lies first with our people. Tempeston's call for evacuation is justified. The vulnerable must be protected, and our bastions must rise swiftly."

General Thalassar, eyes as sharp as reef-blades, allowed himself a faint smirk.

"As the King proposed, we'll use our terrain against them. Let the Void stumble into our traps. They expect fragility—we shall show them cunning."

General Aquarion leaned in.

"We must also extend our reach. Communication with neighboring constellations is essential. Their alliance may turn the tide."

General Ceto responded swiftly.

"I will oversee evacuations and fortify the strongholds. No shadow shall pass our gates."

General Nereus, the silent sentinel, spoke with calm certainty.

"Our Stardust Warriors are ready. Their forms shimmer across the skies—they await only the word to strike."

General Tritonis stood with fire in his eyes.

"Why wait? Let us strike first and strike hard. Let the Void learn fear again."

Ondine, poised and unwavering, cut through his fervor.

"That is reckless, Tritonis. We must protect the people. A premature assault may shatter more than it saves."

General Aquilon raised a hand to calm the tide.

"There is truth in both paths. A balanced strategy—aggressive defense supported by coordinated evacuations—may serve us best."

General Delmar, the youngest, spoke with urgency.

"But hesitation is dangerous. The longer we wait, the more the Void gains. We must act—decisively and now."

The chamber quivered with tension until General Maritna rose. Her voice, gentle as moonlight, stilled them.

"Enough. Now is not the time for division. We must act as one. Defend with strength. Evacuate with wisdom. Fortify with resolve. Unity is our greatest weapon. Let that be our strategy."

A moment of silence followed, then nods of assent. The tide had turned. The strategy had become a single, rising wave.

ShadowVeil

In the shadowed recess of the War Room, away from the radiant orbs and open discourse, stood ShadowVeil—the Eclipse Spy. Cloaked in silence and masked by magic, he watched not only the words spoken, but the hearts behind them.

Then—a flicker. A subtle tension in the air.

Among the servants, one valet moved with calculated restraint, checking his surroundings too often. He walked not with grace, but with caution.

As the royal family departed for a brief recess, ShadowVeil followed, slipping through a hidden corridor, veiled in illusion. He trailed the valet through the City of Dreams, winding down into Aquaterra's vibrant underbelly. The cobbled streets glowed with taverns and shops, yet the valet passed all light and laughter, drawn toward a hidden chapel nestled between old stone and new marble.

Behind the chapel's altar lay a concealed door, guarded by two sentries. The valet approached, revealing a pin beneath his robe. A signal. He was of the Shadow Syndicate—an elite spy of King Stonewall of Capricorn.

ShadowVeil's mind sharpened. Stonewall, Capri's father, was no stranger to preemptive tactics—but this crossed a line.

As the guards opened the hidden door, ShadowVeil dissolved his illusion and stepped into the glow.

"Excuse me," he said evenly. "You do not belong here."

He stepped forward, calm and unshaken.

"Hmm. An unexpected guest. How shall I address you? Highness? Lord? Or... traitor?"

The spy froze. The guards reached for weapons—until ShadowVeil drew back his cloak to reveal the trident sigil etched in steel. They hesitated.

The spy bowed low, voice trembling.

"Please, master. I am only a servant. I meant no harm."

"Perhaps," said ShadowVeil, circling him. "But you crossed sacred ground. Speak clearly—if you desire mercy."

"I serve King Stonewall. I was sent to observe preparations... and ensure Princess Capri's safety."

"Loyalty to one's King is noble," ShadowVeil admitted. "But your method is not. Come."

The Interrogation

They returned to the palace. The War Room buzzed with motion and voices. Without pause, ShadowVeil presented the spy before the King.

"Your Majesty, I bring before you an intruder—a spy of the Shadow Syndicate, disguised as a servant."

The King's gaze darkened.

"Speak."

The spy lowered his eyes.

"I am an agent of King Stonewall. My mission was to gather information... to protect Princess Capri. Capricorn stands with you."

Queen Marinella's voice held cold composure.

"Let Capricorn's support be proven. ShadowVeil—hold him. Interrogate him. We take no chances."

ShadowVeil bowed and led the spy away. Yet fate had more to reveal.

An Unexpected Visitor

As they moved through the corridors, a presence emerged from shadow.

ShadowBlade.

One of Capricorn's most feared master spies.

"Release him," ShadowBlade said. "Or face the consequences."

ShadowVeil did not flinch.

"ShadowBlade. No arrival message? No audience with the King? Hardly diplomatic."

He tilted his head.

"Personal... or official?"

ShadowBlade sighed and produced a scroll.

"Official. Our Master Diplomat Zynara arrives tonight. I came first. I regret the intrusion."

"Regret noted," ShadowVeil replied.

"I carry a message from King Stonewall," said ShadowBlade. "Deliver it at the General Gathering. Keep it sealed until then. And yes—your streets are still treacherous. I see you've survived."

"I always do," said ShadowVeil, accepting the scroll.

"Tell your King a storm is coming. We'll aid him if needed. But let him prepare."

"I will. But I want my man released."

"Only if he hears this," said ShadowVeil, turning to the spy.

"AquaCapri stands united. No unannounced spies shall tread our halls. Let this be your first and final warning."

ShadowBlade's gaze narrowed. Then, turning to the spy, he said:

"You heard him. No more secrecy. From now on—use the front door."

The spy bowed low.

"Never again, master. I swear it."

"Then we return," said ShadowBlade.

Spy Report and Secrets Shared

As they walked the shadowed streets, ShadowVeil broke the silence.

"You know something. Speak."

"Only if you trade," said ShadowBlade, smirking.

ShadowVeil obliged.

"They plan to sabotage the Celestial Convergence. Break the alliance before it forms."

ShadowBlade nodded.

"In return—listen well. The Void has forged a new weapon. It is beyond anything we've faced. Be prepared."

Their exchange ended. ShadowBlade disappeared into the chapel's hidden gate. ShadowVeil remained, staring into the darkened door, his thoughts heavy.

Inside, the air was thick with myrrh and flame. Tapestries of forgotten gods lined the walls. Was this chamber a sanctum... or a portal?

Only time would tell.

Return to the War Room

ShadowVeil returned to the Celestial Heaven. The War Room stirred with urgency. Generals leaned over maps. Aether moved between them like starlight incarnate.

Approaching the throne, ShadowVeil bowed low.

"My King, urgent news. The Void possesses a new weapon—unlike any before. They also intend to sabotage the Celestial Convergence. We must move swiftly."

King Oceanius straightened.

"Your insight is a light in shadow. We shall act at once."

Thus, the guardians of AquaCapri steeled themselves for what was to come. Darkness gathered on the horizon, but they would not meet it with fear.

They would rise, as one. United. Unbroken.

And in the shadows, ever watchful, stood ShadowVeil—ready.

2.5 The General Gathering at the Celestial Ballroom

The Celestial Ballroom of the Celestial Heaven Palace stood as a breathtaking expanse, crafted to inspire awe and reverence. Its cathedral ceiling, soaring impossibly high, appeared to brush against the stars themselves. Five rows of towering pillars lined each side of the vast hall, carved from shimmering moonstone and inlaid with constellations that recounted the legends of AquaCapri's creation. The air shimmered with cosmic energy, carrying the distant harmonics of the stars.

This was no mere place of celebration—it served as a living monument to unity. On this night, more than half a million beings from across the AquaCapri Constellation had gathered—royalty, emissaries, warriors, and diplomats—each present to reaffirm their devotion to the Light and forge lasting alliances against the rising darkness.

Above, the ceiling reflected a living map of the realms under King Oceanius' protection. Each star pulsed like a heartbeat—a luminous reminder of what stood to be lost.

At the head of the hall, the King stood regal and commanding. Clad in oceanic robes of dark blue and silver, his presence mirrored the depths of the sea. Beside him rested his trident, its surface aglow beneath the celestial light. Every motion exuded power and clarity; his call to gather had been born from dire news—the Void had breached the constellation's sacred borders.

At his side stood Queen Marinella, her gown a cascade of liquid light. Though her serene expression betrayed little, she clutched a sapphire pendant—an ancient artifact of immense power, worn only in moments of great peril.

Together, they embodied the realm's foundation, their presence alone enough to quell the storm of unease gathering within the hall.

The Circle of Guardians

At the center of the ballroom, the Twelve Guardians of the Cosmos had taken their places around a vast round table.

Aqua and Capri sat at the forefront, radiant in their celestial strength. His eyes mirrored the cosmic deep—calm, resolute, eternal. Her gown shimmered like woven twilight, and her gaze, serene yet piercing, bore readiness for what lay ahead.

Around them sat legends of renown.

Orion, Sage of Starlight, bore a silvered beard and a softly glowing staff—his presence evoking a star born to mortal form.

Chronos, the Timekeeper, sat unmoving in robes of shifting sands, his eyes reflecting the eternal balance of order and chaos.

Luminarion, Sovereign of Radiance, shone with a halo of light, his very presence a beacon against the encroaching Void.

Aether, Keeper of the Stars, studied the holographic map before him, his mind a boundless library of cosmic lore.

Solis, the original Flame of the Sun, emanated ancient wisdom, his aura pulsing with equilibrium and fire.

Zephyr, confidant to Aqua and Champion of AquaCapri, kept one hand close to his star-forged blade—ever vigilant, ever ready.

Nyx, Guardian of Night and Dreams, cloaked in woven shadow, held the mysteries of slumber and foresight.

Gaia, the Lifebringer, wore a living gown of vine and bloom, the scent of growing things trailing in her wake.

The Supreme Generals

Nearby, three Supreme Generals observed in solemn silence.

Vortizian, twilight-armored master of water and time.

Celestara, calm and vigilant, her armor etched with star-born sigils.

Tempestor, born of storm, watched from the shadows, elemental power humming softly through the air around him.

The Gathering Commences

As the gathering commenced, voices mingled with the gentle chime of crystal. Emissaries from distant constellations exchanged measured greetings. Yet beneath the surface, unease coursed like an unseen current.

ShadowVeil, the Eclipse Spy, entered in utter silence, his cloak trailing across the marble like a wisp of the void. He glided toward the royal table, his sharp gaze observing every motion. His arrival, though without fanfare, shifted the atmosphere—a silent herald of what approached.

As guests found their seats, conversation faded. King Oceanius stepped forward, raising his trident high. A profound stillness fell over the hall—as if even the stars above had paused to listen.

"Guardians of the Cosmos. Lords and emissaries of the realms. Honored guests," he began, his voice vast and resonant as the ocean's tide. "We are gathered not merely in celebration, but in preparation for trials that approach swiftly."

"The AquaCapri Constellation has long stood as a beacon of harmony, illuminating the stars with its peace. Yet now, shadows gather. The Void presses against our borders—not only threatening our lands, but the freedom and love all life holds sacred."

His gaze swept across the hall, pausing briefly on emissaries from distant realms.

"But we do not stand alone," he continued, as the ballroom lights shifted to illuminate the honored guests, their garments shimmering beneath the celestial glow. "You, our allies, have come not only in body—but in spirit, in resolve. Your presence fortifies us."

A murmur of assent stirred through the assembly.

"Yet tonight, we celebrate," he said, his expression softening. "We share a feast, a moment of unity—for it is love that gives us strength. The storm looms, but tonight, we remember why we fight."

As the king lowered his trident, the mood eased. But before music could begin, another voice rose—clear and unwavering.

Aqua's Oath

Aqua stepped forward, his gaze reflecting starlight.

"My friends," he began, "our king speaks true. We are bound by more than peace—we are bound by purpose. The Void threatens all we cherish, yet they do not understand the Light we bear within."

His voice echoed like a wave of starlight through the great hall.

"They believe they can extinguish us. Reduce us to ash and silence. But they are mistaken. We are the children of constellations—the flamebearers of hope. The stars we protect shine brighter than their deepest darkness."

The hall pulsed with rising energy as his words took root in every heart.

"To those who journeyed far, know that your allegiance is remembered. The bonds between us cannot be broken."

He paused, his tone gentling. "So tonight, let us remember the beauty of what we protect—our homes, our people, the love that endures. Let this night remind us why we shall not fall."

He raised a chalice.

"To unity," he declared. "To Light. To victory."

The hall erupted with thunderous applause. For a fleeting moment, joy reigned. Yet beneath the celebration, the truth remained—war loomed near.

Arrival from Capricorn

Celestial music swelled once more, and laughter returned in hushed tones. The realms stood firm in their unity, though shadows whispered at the edges.

Then came the voice of a herald:

"Presenting Master Diplomat Zynara of the Capricorn Constellation, emissary of King Stonewall and Queen Terra, accompanied by the Supreme Generals of Capricorn."

All turned to see her enter.

Zynara moved with regal grace, her robes flowing like starlight over velvet. Though famed as a diplomat, few knew she also served as Capricorn's master spy. Behind her marched three Supreme Generals, clad in celestial armor that gleamed with the Essence of stars.

Reaching the royal dais, Zynara bowed deeply.

"Your Majesties," she said, her voice both smooth and unwavering, "I bring apologies for our delay. The path from Capricorn was fraught. Yet we are here now, bearing the full strength and support of King Stonewall and Queen Terra. Capricorn stands with AquaCapri. We will not allow darkness to eclipse the Light."

King Oceanius nodded, his eyes sharp. "Your arrival speaks louder than words, Master Zynara."

Queen Marinella offered a serene smile. "Your loyalty honors us."

Zynara bowed once more and withdrew to a quiet alcove, where a shadow awaited.

Secrets in the Shadows

ShadowVeil emerged from the dark.

"Master Zynara," he murmured, "you arrive at a critical hour."

Her eyes narrowed slightly. "Indeed. Unity is our greatest weapon now."

They exchanged only a few words before Veil's tone shifted, quiet and sharp.

"Your assessment? And... is there more?"

Zynara hesitated, then whispered, "The Void grows stronger. Organized. Capricorn holds, but only just. And yes—there is a message. A scroll meant only for your King's eyes."

Veil nodded. "Then it shall be done."

The Hidden Warning

As the last strains of music faded, ShadowVeil approached the throne once more. He bowed, then presented the sealed scroll.

"Your Majesty. This comes from Zynara. It cannot wait."

King Oceanius took it with care. "A game of riddles, Veil?"

"Not this time. Speak the words 'Love and Unity'—you'll see."

The king spoke the words.

Magic shimmered through the air as ancient symbols formed across the parchment, glowing with a sacred light. Diagrams emerged— maps, notes, and warnings. The hall darkened slightly.

The scroll revealed Nocturnia—Lord Valhor's stronghold—and critical intelligence detailing troop movements, Void weaponry, and, most grave of all... Riftbreaker.

A weapon capable of breaching all five barriers that shielded AquaCapri.

Worse still—it threatened to annihilate entire star systems.

The king's voice dropped, barely more than breath.

"This... changes everything."

"We must act now," said ShadowVeil.

The king turned, his voice rising once more as he faced the assembly.

The Declaration of War

"My friends. What we now know is dire. This is no longer a battle—it is survival. The Void possesses a weapon beyond imagination. Unity is no longer a choice. It is the only path forward."

Silence gripped the hall.

Then—calm, resolute, unwavering—he declared:

"The time has come. The AquaCapri Constellation must declare war upon the Void and its dark legions."

He raised his voice, fierce and clear.

"For the Essence. For our homes. For love and peace. Let us rise!"

The ballroom thundered in reply:

"To victory! To victory! To victory!"

CHAPTER

3

WHISPERS OF DISCORD

*NOT ALL DANGER COMES FROM BEYOND—
SOME THREATS ARE BORN WITHIN.*

 # CHAPTER 3

△ VALDUM, THE CELESTIAL ARCHITECT

AQUARII: VELARITH NOX'AL DRAVON.
ELUNETH XAL VIRE.

OPENING WHISPER – CH. 3

△ MAXIMUS, THE ETERNAL QUILL

AQUARII: VIRE SEVANOR XAL KREION.
NOCTIR VALEA'RIN.

CLOSING WHISPER – CH. 3

3.1 Whispers of Discord

The day following the General Gathering, the harmony within the AquaCapri Constellation—though radiant and resilient—was not immune to the quiet whispers of discord that began to seep through its vast expanse. Despite the strength of King Oceanius and Queen Marinella's rule and the ever-vigilant presence of their one hundred thousand stars and the mighty stardust warriors, a delicate fracture had formed. A crack that, if left unattended, threatened to widen into a chasm of uncertainty.

Beneath the glimmering skies of the Celestial Heaven, where stars sang in ancient symphonies, the heart of Aquaterra—the capital—throbbed with unease. The once-serene streets, lined with crystalline structures that shimmered with blue starlight, now echoed with faint murmurs of doubt. Citizens who had long basked in trust and assurance found themselves questioning the readiness of their defenses. The Void's presence loomed like an invisible veil, stirring quiet unrest among even the most faithful.

Aqua's Silent Reflection with Divine Authority

Upon the grand Starlight Terrace, Aqua paced alone, his gaze fixed upon the horizon of the capital. Radiant with cosmic Light, his eyes glowed with the power of a thousand stars, mirroring the swirling constellations etched into the ceiling above. He was not merely a ruler —he was a god, born of the very Essence that shaped the universe. With each breath, he felt the pulse of AquaCapri's infinite energy.

And that yes pulse—was no longer in perfect rhythm.

The stars, once harmonious in song, now murmured of an encroaching darkness.

His bond with PaxProfundis—the hidden core of their strength—was deeper than any. He could sense the immense force within it, a primordial current that powered their entire realm. Yet something had shifted. A subtle disruption, like a distant tremor across the cosmic expanse, threatened to shake the very foundation of their existence.

He was not alone for long.

Capri approached with quiet grace, her presence glowing with starlight, her steps soundless. She needed no words to sense what troubled him; their connection transcended speech.

"Aqua,"she said softly, her voice a melody woven from the spheres."The Void weighs upon you."

His expression darkened. His voice was low, a reverberation that drifted through the stillness.

"I feel it, Capri. The Void no longer lingers at the edges of the cosmos—it creeps into our realms. PaxProfundis is protected for now, but Valhor is cunning. He watches, waits, probing for weaknesses."

Her eyes ignited with celestial fire as she placed a hand over his.

"We won't let him through. PaxProfundis is beyond comprehension. With it, even the deepest darkness will fail to eclipse us. Together, we protect what is ours."

His brow furrowed.

"Have you heard the murmurings? The people are growing restless—questioning our readiness, doubting our strength."

"I have," she replied, stepping closer. "The winds carry whispers of fear. Our people look to us for certainty, but doubt has taken root."

He turned to her fully, shoulders heavy with responsibility. But her nearness steadied him—she was his center in every storm.

"We cannot let fear fester," he said firmly. "The Void feeds on division. If trust falters, it opens the very door we must keep sealed."

She rested her hand gently on his arm.

"Then we won't let it. Our unity is our power, but we must remind them. Show them we remain steadfast in the face of whispers and shadows."

His resolve returned, carved from her reassurance. Their love—battle-tested and divine—was the cornerstone of all they led.

"Call the generals," he commanded. "Summon our leaders to the Chamber of War. We must speak directly to the people. Make them ready for the battles ahead."

She nodded, sensing another truth beneath the surface.

"There's more," she whispered. "This unrest—it's not just fear. Something stirs these whispers. Shadows are rising, and we must prepare to face them."

He turned again to the stars beyond the capital's edge, jaw tight.

"Then we face them—together."

Bathed in the morning glow, the two stood side by side, their bond unbroken. But while they moved to calm the hearts of their people, an unseen threat loomed—one poised to test the very soul of the realm.

Cracks in the Unity

Across Aquaterra, the whispers festered. Quiet factions emerged, stirred by the spreading unease. Where unity once thrived, quiet rifts began to form. In distant districts and hidden alcoves of the Crystalline Arcades, murmurs turned to hushed conversations—and conversations to subtle dissent.

Among the citizens, those who once stood in unwavering solidarity now found themselves questioning the strength of the bond they had long trusted. Even within the revered Council of Twelve, disagreements began to stir. Views on how to confront the Void and the unease it bred began to diverge.

The Void's touch—unseen and intangible—had begun to coil around the minds of the realm.

To quell the rising tension, Aqua dispatched Zephir—the swiftest of their messengers—with word of a gathering. In the Grand Plaza, under the towering statues of past heroes and vibrant banners of AquaCapri, citizens assembled in growing numbers. Their faces bore the weight of uncertainty, their eyes seeking comfort.

Aqua and Capri ascended a crystalline podium carved from stardust, the crowd swelling below. Capri stood radiant, her gown stitched with glowing constellations. Beside her, Aqua's armor shimmered, marked with the symbols of the stars. He raised his hand. Silence swept over the plaza.

"Citizens of Aquaterra,"he called out, voice resolute."I come to speak of the fears I know many of you feel. Whispers have reached my ears. I understand them. The Void is a ruthless force, relentless in its hunger for chaos. But hear this—our realm is shielded by twelve celestial stars, guardians that remain impenetrable against the darkness."

He surveyed the crowd, his voice flowing like the deep currents of the sea, drawing strength from their shared past.

"We stand on the brink of war. Sacrifices will be made. But our strength lies in unity—the kind the Void cannot comprehend. The stardust warriors, born from the stars, are ready. Above, the vigilant birds of Aquaterra patrol the skies, ever watchful, ever loyal."

As he spoke, many eyes turned skyward. The winged sentinels soared above, feathers gleaming in the light, guardians of the realm.

"I know fear has settled in some hearts,"he continued, his voice softer yet steady."But King Oceanius and Queen Marinella have entrusted me with a promise—Aquaterra remains protected by the stars, our eternal guardians. These are not merely orbs of light; they are forces of protection, unwavering in their vigil."

The crowd stirred—some with hope, others still uncertain. Capri stepped forward, her voice like a balm.

"The stars shall not falter,"she said gently."And neither shall we. We have faced darkness before and risen stronger each time. Our bond is our light. Let us not grant the Void what it desires—a fractured spirit. Trust in one another. Trust in what we are."

Aqua took her hand, their unity on full display. The people looked on, reminded of the strength their rulers shared.

"Remain calm,"Aqua called."Live your lives. Trust in our defenses. The battle may rage beyond our borders, but the heart of AquaCapri remains strong. As long as the stars shine—we remain united."

A calm, rippling through the gathered crowd, settled over the plaza. The doubt had not vanished, but it had been subdued.

"Let the Void hear us,"he concluded."Let it know—we may be threatened, but we will never be broken. We are AquaCapri. Children of the stars. And we shall never bow to shadow."

The crowd erupted into cheers—strong, unified, luminous.

And though the whispers of discord had been hushed, for now, the Void lingered. Watching. Waiting.

3.2 Emergence of Shadows

As Aqua's voice reverberated through the grand plaza of Aquaterra, its tranquil cadence soothed the crowd. Like the calming tide of the sea, his words washed over the worried citizens, assuring them of their safety. For a fleeting moment, the fear in their hearts began to ebb, replaced by the familiar warmth of his presence. However, unbeknownst to them, in the farthest reaches of the AquaCapri constellation, a new menace stirred—a threat that grew not from the Light of their world but from the depths of its shadows.

Far from Aquaterra's shimmering spires, beyond the protective energy fields of the constellation's core, the shadowy star of Umbria lay in eternal darkness. The once-glowing star had long been swallowed by

the Void's influence, now a blackened fortress, serving as the seat of the Shadow Forces—remnants of the Void's legion. In the star's heart, beneath a sky where no Light had pierced in eons, the shadow council gathered. These dark figures, clad in armor forged from the Void itself, were the architects of chaos, plotting AquaCapri's downfall in secrecy.

The chamber they convened in was vast, the walls carved from obsidian stone flickering with eerie violet flames that cast long, twisting shadows. Each step echoed ominously as if the ground trembled in anticipation of the impending chaos.

At the head of this assembly sat Lord Umbra, a devoted ally of the Master of Dark Forces, Lord Valthor. His presence was a living embodiment of darkness itself. His face, masked beneath a hood that swallowed all Light, was unseen, but his voice—deep, commanding, and dripping with malice—filled the room like a chilling wind.

"The time is ripe," he began, his words heavy with purpose.

"AquaCapri's harmony is fragile. The balance they so cherish teeters on the edge. They are blinded by their love, by their misguided belief in unity. We shall exploit this weakness. We will strike at the heart of their strength—sow discord where there is trust and let their alliance crumble from within."

The council murmured in agreement, their voices a collective whisper of dread. Lord Umbra's cold certainty was infectious, and his power over his subordinates was undeniable.

At his side stood Lady Xyn, a figure as calculated as she was cruel. Her armor shimmered with the deep hues of night, accented by jagged blades etched with the ancient runes of the Void. Her eyes, gleaming with cold precision, scanned the gathered council before she spoke.

"Our agents have already infiltrated their realms, slipping through their defenses unnoticed. These fools bask in the Light, blind to the shadows creeping ever closer. We will spread like poison in their midst, whispering falsehoods and feeding their insecurities. Doubt will be our greatest weapon. It will be too late by the time they realize what's happening."

She paused, letting her words sink in, her voice oozing with a venomous promise.

"Let them doubt their leaders. Let them question their gods. Their downfall will come not from the strength of our armies but from the fear in their hearts."

The assembly nodded in unison, their confidence growing as the plan solidified. The council was a mix of generals and spies, masters of deceit and war, each eager to play their part in the coming storm.

From the shadowed corner of the room emerged Kraytor, the silent enforcer of the Void. A hulking figure whose loyalty was matched only by his brutality, Kraytor's presence reminded AquaCapri of the force that would soon rain down upon it.

"I will lead the charge,"Kraytor rumbled, his voice low and gravelly as if scraped from the bowels of the Void.

"Let the skies of Radiantia burn. Let their stardust warriors falter before us. When the battle begins, there will be no mercy, no retreat. We will darken their brightest star and cast its ashes to the winds."

The imagery of Radiantia, the beacon of Light in the AquaCapri constellation, falling under the assault of the shadow warriors sent a shiver through even the most hardened of the council members.

For Radiantia, it was not just a star; it was a symbol of hope and a beacon that inspired the defenders of AquaCapri. If Radiantia fell, so too would the morale of the entire constellation.

The council's strategy was to wage war and undermine AquaCapri from within, turning its strength into weakness. The stars that formed the heart of AquaCapri's defense were interconnected by bonds of trust and unity—bonds that the Shadow Forces sought to sever, strand by strand.

"Their unity," Lord Umbra concluded, rising from his obsidian throne, "is their weakest link. Once doubt spreads like a shadow over their Light, they will break. And when they do, we will be there to claim their world, to drag their shining constellation into the endless night of the Void."

His words echoed through the chamber, a dark promise of what would come. The gathered figures of the Void bowed their heads in respect, each ready to execute their part of the plan with deadly precision.

Outside the fortress walls, the star of Umbria remained cloaked in darkness, an unholy Void where no Light dared shine. But within, the forces of the Void readied themselves.

The shadow warriors, cloaked in black, awaited the signal to launch their assault. They moved with deadly grace, silent and unseen, trained for the sole purpose of infiltrating AquaCapri's defenses and igniting chaos from within.

Meanwhile, in the distance, the defenders of AquaCapri were none the wiser. In their pristine armor, radiant with the Light of their stars, they prepared for battle against an enemy they could see—unaware that the actual threat lay hidden in the shadows, waiting for the perfect moment to strike.

The Shadow Forces, empowered by their patience and bolstered by the doubt they had sown, were ready to set their plan into motion. The seeds of discord had been planted, and soon, they would watch as AquaCapri's unity unraveled before them.

The shadows had emerged, and the real war was about to begin.

Masters of Manipulation and Deceit

In the darkened recesses of the Shadow Fortress, a new council gathered—the Masters of Manipulation and Deceit. Unlike the brute force and direct strategies employed by the front-line Shadow Forces, this group operated in the shadows, their influence subtle, their power derived from the mind rather than the sword. Their mission was clear: fracture the alliances that bound AquaCapri's leaders, causing confusion and mistrust to fester within their ranks.

The chamber where they convened was unlike the war rooms of the Void's generals. Here, silence was the weapon, and deception its blade. The air was thick with an almost tangible malice, a coldness that whispered of lies yet to be told. Flickering black flames cast jagged shadows across the faces of those gathered, their expressions masked in deep concentration.

At the head of this group stood Sectrix and Mirage, the twin architects of deceit. Sectrix, tall and gaunt, wore a permanent smirk that hinted at his delight in twisting truths to suit his needs. His pale, sickly complexion only accentuated the shadowy darkness that clung to him. Mirage, his partner in deceit, was the embodiment of illusion—her form ever-shifting, as though reality itself could not hold onto her. Where Sectrix was the mind behind the lies, Mirage was the face that embodied them, her beauty and fluidity of form allowing her to slip into any role, any shape, to mislead and confuse.

Sectrix spoke first, his voice a soft hiss that snaked through the room,

"The key to unraveling AquaCapri is not through brute force but through a whisper, a suggestion. We will begin by casting doubts upon the leaders. Their strength lies in their unity, but unity is fragile. All it takes is a single thread to unravel it."

Mirage, her form flickering like a mirage in the desert, added,

"The people of AquaCapri worship their leaders as if they are gods. We will show them the truth—that even gods can fall, that their intentions are not as pure as they seem. Let them question, let them wonder. A simple rumor is all we need to set the seeds of mistrust."

The twins planned to infiltrate AquaCapri through subtle, carefully placed rumors. They would spread whispers of betrayal, secret pacts between leaders and enemies, and hidden motives that would force the people to question those they had trusted for so long.

At the opposite end of the table sat Vexalia, draped in shadowy robes that concealed her form. Her eyes glinted with malice as she plotted her next move. Vexalia specialized in inflaming the hidden envies and grudges that lay dormant in even the strongest alliances. She was not content with merely planting the seeds of doubt—she sought to water them, to watch as they grew into hatred.

"Let them turn on each other," she hissed, her voice a cold breeze in the room.

"The alliances of AquaCapri are not as perfect as they seem. There are always rivalries and jealousies. I will find them, and I will stoke them into flames."

Vexalia's expertise lay in exploiting the emotions AquaCapri's leaders worked so hard to suppress. She would manipulate old wounds, reminding allies of past slights, inflaming hidden resentments between leaders and their generals. What once were mere embers of tension would become infernos of conflict, threatening to tear the constellation apart from within.

But the council's final and most dangerous member was Nethermind, a being cloaked entirely in shadow, whose very presence radiated an aura of unease. Nethermind was a master of fear and chaos, feeding on the emotions stirred by Sectrix, Mirage, and Vexalia. Where they sowed seeds of discord, Nethermind ensured they would grow into full-blown chaos.

"Fear,"Nethermind spoke, his voice a hollow echo,"is the greatest weapon of all. Once it takes root, it spreads like a disease. AquaCapri will fall not because of our might but because of their fear. Fear of the Void. Fear of failure. Fear of each other."

His powers allowed him to amplify the anxieties and doubts that the others planted, turning minor suspicions into crippling paranoia. His touch was invisible, his influence spreading like an infection, unseen until it was too late.

Together, the Masters of Manipulation and Deceit crafted their strategy. Sectrix and Mirage would begin their misinformation campaign, infiltrating the very fabric of AquaCapri society. Vexalia would twist and turn allies against each other, inflaming resentments until friendships and alliances shattered. And Nethermind would wait in the shadows, amplifying the chaos until it engulfed the entire constellation. Their plan was set along with their goal to cripple AquaCapri from within, leaving it vulnerable to the impending invasion of the Void.

In the darkness of the Shadow Fortress, their laughter was low, cold, and filled with the promise of destruction. The game had begun, and AquaCapri would never see them coming.

Clandestine Wraith, Zarvok the Shadowweaver

As the Masters of Manipulation and Deceit finalized their plans, a figure appeared silently in the darkened chamber, his arrival marked by a sudden chill that dimmed the already flickering flames. Cloaked in shifting shadow, he moved with a grace that made his presence almost imperceptible—save for the faint whisper of his long robes trailing across the cold stone. This was Clandestine Wraith, Zarvok the Shadowweaver, the unseen master spy of the Void and the Shadow Forces.

Zarvok needed no weapons, no armor. His presence alone instilled unease. He thrived in the forgotten corners of the cosmos, his hooded face hidden in darkness save for two glowing red eyes that seemed to pierce the souls of all who dared to look his way. His skill in subterfuge was unrivaled, and his loyalty to the Master of Dark Forces, Lord Valthor, was absolute.

Without a word, he took his place at the table, his form merging seamlessly with the surrounding gloom. Sectrix, ever the instigator, offered a smirk at the spy's arrival.

"Ah, the master of shadows finally graces us with his presence. I trust you've been weaving your webs, Zarvok?"Sectrix's tone held a hint of sarcasm, though it quickly faded beneath Zarvok's icy gaze.

"Your schemes are merely distractions,"Zarvok replied, his voice like a breeze whispering through a crypt.

"The real power lies in subtle movements, in whispers behind closed doors. I have already sown the seeds of their downfall."

Mirage, shifting her form into that of one of AquaCapri's most trusted diplomats, smiled sweetly.

"Perhaps,"she said, mimicking the diplomat's voice with unsettling perfection,"but we prefer a more... dramatic approach."

Zarvok did not flinch. He simply turned his attention back to the matter at hand.

"While you distract them with illusions and falsehoods, I will undermine their defenses from within. The council will not know who to trust, and when the time is right, I will strike—crippling them before they even realize I was ever there."

Zarvok's Action Unfolds

At the same time, far from the Shadow Fortress, Zarvok's shadowy projections moved silently through the Grand Halls of Celestial Heaven, the seat of AquaCapri's leadership. None noticed the veil of mist that clung to the walls, seeping through the cracks of ancient stonework. No one saw the flickers of darkness that passed by unseen, their movement too quick, too quiet to register.

Deep within the war chambers, Supreme General Vortizian and General Tempestor debated strategies for the imminent assault. Their voices were calm, confident, brimming with conviction. But Zarvok knew better. He lingered just beyond the glow of the crystal torches— an invisible observer cloaked in shadows so complete that not even the most powerful beings could detect him.

"The Void stirs,"said Tempestor, his tone laced with concern.

"But we will be ready. Our defenses are strong."

Zarvok allowed a faint smile to form beneath his hood. Strong, perhaps, but not invulnerable. One lower commander had already heard his whisper—subtle doubt planted like a seed, now taking root.

The ripple would soon begin, spreading distrust like poison in still water.

"Strong defenses mean nothing,"he murmured to himself,"if you cannot trust those who stand beside you."

As the generals exited the chamber, Zarvok moved like vapor, drifting through the corridors. With a flick of his hand, the shadows on the wall twisted then reshaped into the form of General Vortizian—voice, posture, and presence replicated flawlessly. He turned toward a nearby guard, speaking just loud enough for the words to reach him.

"Our allies grow weak. We may need to reconsider who we trust."

The guard, startled, snapped to attention. The familiar voice echoed in his ears, though the source was unclear. Still, the words burrowed into his thoughts. Doubt clouded his certainty. The seed had been planted.

The Gathering of the Masters

Back within the Shadow Fortress, Sectrix and Mirage discussed the rhythm and reach of their misinformation campaign. Meanwhile, Vexalia stood before the great cosmic map, her fingers tracing the star paths of AquaCapri's defenders with meticulous care—like an artist plotting ruin with every elegant sweep.

Suddenly, the darkness in the chamber deepened. Zarvok emerged once more, stepping forth from the very walls as though he had been one with the structure.

"It is done,"he said, voice low and unwavering.

"Their defenders begin to question one another. The seeds of doubt are spreading. Soon, they will turn on themselves—and the real war will begin."

Sectrix chuckled, his gaunt face curling into a satisfied grin.

"Perfect. While they busy themselves with imagined threats, we'll strike where it truly matters."

Mirage, flickering in and out of her phantom forms, offered a smile equally wicked.

"Let them fall into their own darkness. It makes our work so much easier."

But Zarvok's expression remained cold. He had no taste for theatrics. His focus was fixed on the ultimate goal—the destruction of AquaCapri's leadership from within. Every whisper he placed, every fear he stirred, was a thread in his masterwork. Yet even as he worked with his companions, his crimson gaze never fully softened. He remained ever-watchful—for betrayal among allies was as dangerous as resistance from enemies.

The Master of Dark Forces had charged him with more than mere infiltration. Zarvok was also judge and executioner in the shadow ranks. Any treachery, any deviation from the master's will, would be punished swiftly—and silently.

As the chamber filled with the low hum of dark laughter, Zarvok remained unmoving. A shadow among shadows. A wraith beneath the storm.

The Masters of Manipulation and Deceit may have been the hand that cast the stone, but Zarvok would ensure it struck the heart.

The darkness thickened around him as his quiet laughter, barely more than breath, drifted into the air—blending with the cold whispers of the Void.

And across the constellation, the defenders of AquaCapri remained unaware of just how close the darkness had crept.

How close it was to consuming them whole.

3.3 Seeds of Conspiracy

Amidst the rising conflict, the seeds of conspiracy began to take root in the highest echelons of AquaCapri. A shadow crept ever closer to the heart of the kingdom, through the gilded halls of Celestial Heaven, where the royal advisors convened. Among them, two of the realm's most trusted figures—Advisor Talssa and Advisor Aegir— now stood precariously at the edge of betrayal.

Talssa, long renowned for her fierce intellect and strategic prowess, held the coveted role of Master of Arcane Affairs. This appointment granted her unmatched access to the kingdom's ancient archives and mystic knowledge. Her influence over the royal family stemmed from her sway in magical matters, particularly those involving PaxProfundis. Though King Oceanius was a master of war, he often deferred to Talssa's counsel in arcane decisions. No magical act or defense was undertaken without her approval.

Yet now, she saw her role not as a guardian of knowledge, but as a gatekeeper to power long suppressed.

In her private chambers—walls lined with towering shelves of tomes and forgotten scrolls—Talssa summoned Aegir. The firelight flickered against old stone, casting long shadows that danced like conspirators on the wall. Her voice, low and deliberate, held both urgency and veiled ambition.

Talssa: "Aegir, you must see it. PaxProfundis holds more power than they let us perceive. King Oceanius clings to balance, always cautious, always restraining. Why should we sit idle, bound by limitations, when we could reshape AquaCapri—make it eternal?"

Though hesitant, Aegir could not ignore her words. As Advisor of Maritime and Trade Affairs, his power lay in controlling the realm's vast naval fleets and economic lifelines. His insights shaped policies that affected AquaCapri's trade routes and its stability within the constellation's waterways. Aegir could topple entire sectors or bolster them with the flick of a quill. He leaned closer, brow furrowed, his voice tight with conflicted loyalty.

Aegir: "You speak of reshaping the kingdom as though it were a simple matter. PaxProfundis may be powerful, but tampering with it could invite ruin. Whatever their faults, Oceanius and Marinella have kept us safe. This idea of yours—it's dangerous."

Talssa's eyes flashed, her lips curving into a smile as sharp as a blade concealed in velvet.

Talssa: "Dangerous? Yes. But these are dangerous times. The Void forces rise. War nears with every breath. And what does Oceanius do? He hesitates. What if they're not strong enough to lead us through what lies ahead?"

She turned away, stepping to the tall window that framed the vast starry canvas of AquaCapri. Her voice grew distant, contemplative, and hard.

Talssa: "I've read the ancient texts. There are rites—rituals that could unlock PaxProfundis entirely. But they refuse to hear me. The royal family clings to outdated ideals. They grasp at the past while the future slips beyond reach."

Aegir began to pace, his hand drifting to the hilt of his ceremonial blade. He had heard whispers—rumors of these forbidden texts hidden in the dark folds of the kingdom. But treason against the crown? That was a line he had not yet crossed.

Aegir: "You walk a perilous path, Talssa. PaxProfundis is not a plaything. It could destroy as easily as it could save. I won't be part of something that could fracture the kingdom from within."

She turned back toward him, her face unreadable, but her eyes glowed with a darker fire as if another voice whispered within her. Indeed, Zarvok the Shadowweaver had already been whispering to her mind, feeding her doubt, sharpening her hunger. She stepped forward, her voice a whispered storm.

Talssa: "I'm not asking you to destroy the kingdom, Aegir. I'm asking you to help me save it. Together, we can master the full power of PaxProfundis. The royal family—they are rigid and blind. We must act before hesitation becomes our downfall."

Her words lingered in the chamber like a binding spell.

As the days passed, their actions turned bold. Under Talssa's subtle direction, they began maneuvering through the court. She cloaked her research in the service of the king, pretending to devise protective enchantments. In truth, she delved deeper into forbidden knowledge, plotting her own rise.

Aegir, still uncertain, began rerouting naval supplies to hidden coves and securing silent alliances with factions who no longer trusted Oceanius's leadership. Though he didn't fully share Talssa's vision, he feared what would come if the kingdom stood unprepared.

In the dim corridors of the palace, Zarvok watched, cloaked in shadows. The Shadowweaver's cold satisfaction mirrored the stillness of the void.

Talssa, now driven by ambition, followed the path Zarvok had quietly laid. She believed PaxProfundis could grant her dominion—and that the royal family stood in her way.

Zarvok, master of deception, moved unseen. His shadowy power allowed him to whisper directly into the minds of his targets, feeding their deepest doubts.

When Talssa wavered, he spoke of her potential. When Aegir faltered, Zarvok twisted his fear into justification.

Zarvok: "Talssa, you see what they cannot. Why follow a king who leads blindly? PaxProfundis awaits the will to wield it. Oceanius, Marinella—they are relics of yesterday. You are tomorrow."

Talssa didn't question how he always knew just what to say. She had stopped questioning altogether.

Aegir, too, felt the weight of those whispers, though Zarvok now wore the voice of an old friend.

Zarvok (in disguise): "The kingdom falters. You've seen it. Oceanius's restraint will be our ruin. Someone must act, or there will be nothing left to protect."

Aegir: "I want only to protect AquaCapri. But turning on the king and queen... it could break everything we've built."

Zarvok: "Sometimes, the old must fall for the new to rise. You know that truth. It has always lived in you."

Thus, the conspiracy—nurtured by doubt, ambition, and shadows—took root within the celestial halls of AquaCapri. Talssa and Aegir, once loyal defenders of the crown, now stood on the verge of treason. Their thoughts are no longer their own. Their ambitions are shaped by a master of whispers.

Conspirators of Equilibrium

In the shadowy confines of a hidden cave deep within the AquaCapri realm, the Conspirators of Equilibrium gathered under the pale glow of moonlight. Their faces were dimly lit, each bearing expressions of caution and guarded suspicion. The air crackled with tension as the next steps in their delicate dance between Light and darkness hung in the balance. The question of loyalty now hovered over them like a storm about to break.

Stilvren, the Silver Archer, was the first to speak. Ever precise and composed, her voice sliced through the silence like one of her arrows.

Stilvren: "We've delayed the Light forces enough to give the Void room to maneuver, but something feels... wrong. Our efforts falter at the last moment. My aim is true—but the outcomes suggest otherwise."

Her silver eyes flicked toward Aetherwind, the Ethereal Voyager, where suspicion gleamed like steel. She had been watching him closely.

Stilvren: "Perhaps someone among us is not as loyal to the cause as they appear."

The accusation was unspoken, but its weight settled on the group like a suffocating mist.

Zeyra, Mistress of Breezes, frowned. Her fingers moved as if stirring invisible winds. Her voice was light yet laced with hidden strength.

Zeyra: "Stilvren is right. Our winds should have scattered their formations, yet they regroup with uncanny precision. It's as though someone is guiding them... or warning them."

She paused, her gaze locking on Aetherwind.

Zeyra: "Perhaps we should consider how the Light forces seem so prepared for our strikes."

Cyrus, the Skyward Refractor, lingered in the shadows near the archway, arms folded, his presence quiet but charged—like the calm before a storm. His voice, low and edged with windborne clarity, sliced through the room's tension.

"I've sensed it as well. Whenever I shift the upper currents or scatter stormwinds to mask our movements, they seem to adapt before the change even reaches them. It's as if the skies whisper our intentions before we act. That's no coincidence," said Cyrus. He stepped forward, eyes fixed on Aetherwind.

Cyrus: "You're the only one who moves between dimensions, Aetherwind. How do we know you aren't feeding information to the Light?"

The suspicion burned between them.

But Aetherwind, calm as ever, met their eyes. He had expected this moment. Luminarion had warned him. His voice was smooth, each word measured.

Aetherwind: "You accuse without evidence. My ability to traverse dimensions is why I'm valuable. I've brought intelligence no one else could reach."

His gaze lingered on each conspirator, steady and clear.

Aetherwind: "If the Light forces are prepared, it's because they're adaptable. Underestimating them would be a fatal error. I am not your enemy. I stand with you—to preserve balance."

Yet the room remained heavy with doubt.

Stilvren stepped closer, her hand resting near the bow on her back.

Stilvren: "Words won't silence suspicion. You vanish and return with riddles. Your motives remain unclear. If you want our trust, you'll need to earn it through more than vague reassurances."

Before Aetherwind could respond, a voice slithered through the shadows.

From the darkness emerged Zarvok, the Shadowweaver. His very presence chilled the room. His form was wrapped in flowing tendrils of shadow, his steps silent, yet his aura screamed menace. The conspirators exchanged wary glances. Zarvok's ties to the Shadow Forces were no secret—and his sudden arrival raised more questions than anyone dared to speak aloud.

Zarvok: "Ah, trust. Such a fragile thread, isn't it?"

His voice, serpentine and smooth, filled the chamber as he glided forward. His eyes gleamed with predatory intelligence, and the curve of his smile was as thin as a blade.

Zarvok: "I couldn't help overhearing your... concerns. A crisis of faith, it seems. How tragic."

He paused before Aetherwind, his smile deepening.

Zarvok: "You've always been quiet, haven't you? Drifting between worlds, never anchored. It must be easy to hide secrets when you're bound to nothing."

Aetherwind's expression hardened. Yet he stood firm, composure intact.

Aetherwind: "Speak plainly, Zarvok. Are you here to stir doubt, or do you bring purpose?"

Zarvok chuckled, a whisper against the cave walls.

Zarvok: "Oh, I bring many purposes. But today, I come... as a friend."

He turned from Aetherwind, addressing the room like a conductor, to an orchestra of unrest.

Zarvok: "The Shadow Forces have watched the tides of power in AquaCapri with great interest. You, my dear conspirators, have done well in maintaining equilibrium. But tell me—what happens if the balance were shifted just a little... toward darkness?"

The air grew colder.

Cyrus answered first, his voice a landslide of certainty.

Cyrus: "We're not servants of shadows, Zarvok. Our mission is balance, not domination."

Zarvok shrugged, amused.

Zarvok: "Balance, domination—aren't they reflections of the same coin? One must rise to keep the other in check. Right now, the Light grows unchecked."

Zeyra crossed her arms, her voice sharp.

Zeyra: "Why should we trust you? The Shadow Forces care nothing for balance. You crave control."

Zarvok raised a hand, feigning innocence.

Zarvok: "True. Shadows have their interests. But—for now—our goals align. Without shadow, the Light would stagnate. Isn't that why you resist? To stop such decay?"

Aetherwind watched carefully. The moment was delicate. While the others argued, he silently reached through the veil of space—his thoughts extending across dimensions—to contact Luminarion. A warning. A plan. A tether of Light in a place of shadows.

Stilvren cut through the debate with finality.

Stilvren: "Enough. We don't need Zarvok. We are the Conspirators of Equilibrium. Our charge is to preserve balance—at any cost."

Her gaze sharpened as it turned toward Aetherwind.

Stilvren: "But to do that, we must trust one another. Completely. If even a trace of doubt remains, we will not survive."

Aetherwind met her eyes without flinching.

Aetherwind: "You have my loyalty, Stilvren. To balance. Always."

The chamber fell silent. No one spoke. But the tension lingered—quiet, coiled, waiting.

The meeting ended without a resolution. One by one, the conspirators slipped away into the night, leaving only shadows behind.

And Zarvok remained, hidden in the dark, his grin curling like smoke. The seeds of doubt had been planted.

But Aetherwind, ever the silent spy, had begun planting seeds of his own, woven with threads of Light. In the shadows of AquaCapri, the balance continued to tilt.

And only time would tell in which direction it would fall.

Aetherwind's Covert Plan

In the radiant halls of the Citadel of Dawn, Aetherwind
appeared through the shimmering veil of dimensions, arriving to meet with Luminarion. The light cascading through the chamber's crystalline walls reflected a purity and serenity unique to the sovereign's sanctum. Yet beneath the tranquil glow, a quiet urgency stirred.

Luminarion, seated upon a throne bathed in golden radiance, turned his wise gaze toward Aetherwind. His presence filled the chamber with warmth and calm, though his voice carried the weight of vigilance.

Luminarion: "The shadows gather around you, Aetherwind. The balance we have worked to preserve hangs by a thread. Yet I trust your judgment. What news do you bring from the conspirators?"

Aetherwind bowed slightly, the weight of his most recent encounter with Zarvok still heavy on his shoulders.

Aetherwind: "Suspicion runs deep, my lord. They question my loyalty, as we anticipated. But Zarvok's interference complicates matters. He pushes them toward darkness, trying to tip the scales. Stilvren and Cyrus are the most susceptible to his influence."

Luminarion's brow furrowed, though the serenity in his expression did not waver. Rising from his throne, he crossed the chamber and placed a steady hand on Aetherwind's shoulder. The touch pulsed with radiant reassurance.

Luminarion: "Zarvok is a cunning adversary, but this too was foreseen. His intrusion will reveal more than it hides. You must remain steadfast. The Light depends on your vigilance now more than ever."

He turned toward the towering window that overlooked the vast sprawl of AquaCapri, where the stars shimmered like eternal sentinels. His voice shifted, taking on a more contemplative tone as he revealed the deeper purpose of his strategy.

Luminarion's Grand Strategy

Luminarion: "We cannot allow the balance to break entirely. But we must let the conspirators believe they're succeeding. You must guide them subtly, allow them to act as though of their own volition, yet keep the Light beyond true danger."

He turned back, his radiant gaze meeting Aetherwind's with unwavering intensity.

Luminarion: "Stilvren, Cyrus, Zeyra... they are pieces in a larger game, though they do not see it. The balance they seek is but an illusion—an illusion we must uphold until the Light reclaims its rightful place."

Aetherwind nodded, grasping the full weight of his role. Luminarion's plan was clear: allow the illusion of balance to exist, even as the Light slowly reclaimed dominion.

Aetherwind: "Zarvok's influence grows daily. He's spreading discord. Stilvren has come to trust no one. Cyrus's resolve is faltering."

Luminarion offered a faint, knowing smile tinged with sadness.

Luminarion: "Let Zarvok weave his webs. The darkness always consumes itself. So long as you remain within, watching, guiding—we shall be ready."

The Conspirators' Growing Discord

Back in the conspirators' secret hideout, the group gathered once again. This time, the tension was even higher as Stilvren stood at the center, her silver eyes scanning the room for any signs of betrayal.

"Zarvok's words linger, and I can't ignore them. The Light is growing stronger by the day, and if we don't act decisively, the balance will be shattered,"said Stilvren.

Cyrus, pacing at the back of the room, spoke up, his tone gruff and conflicted.
"We've done everything we can to maintain the balance. But maybe

Zarvok is right. Maybe we must let the shadows rise for a time—to remind the Light that it cannot remain unchallenged,"said Cyrus.

Zeyra stepped forward, her presence like a calming breeze, though her voice carried an edge.

"You're talking about risking everything. If the shadows grow too strong, we might be unable to regain the balance. And then what? AquaCapri falls into darkness?"said Zeyra.

Stilvren narrowed her eyes, frustration mounting.

"And what if we do nothing? What if we sit idly by and let the Light consume us all? Do you want that?"said Stilvren.

The argument escalated, voices rising and overlapping. Once solid in their pursuit of balance, the group's unity now showed cracks.

Aetherwind, sensing the moment was ripe, stepped forward with measured calm.

"Enough,"said Aetherwind.

His voice cut through the noise, and the room fell silent. He stepped into the center, his presence commanding attention.

"We cannot let doubt tear us apart. Balance is our mission, and we must remain focused. Zarvok may have his own agenda, but we have ours. We need to stay the course,"he said.

He paused, allowing his words to settle.

"Stilvren, your concerns are valid. The Light is growing, and we must ensure it does not tip the scales. But allowing the shadows to rise unchecked is too dangerous. Cyrus, you must see that,"said Aetherwind.

Cyrus looked away, his jaw clenched, but he did not argue.

"We need to act with precision. Subtlety should define our methods in the field. The balance we seek is delicate and can only be maintained if we work together. No more rash decisions. No more doubting each other,"said Aetherwind.

The others nodded, though the tension had not entirely dissipated.

Stilvren, still wary, spoke once more.

"Fine. But if I find out that anyone here is playing both sides... they will not live to see the Light's next dawn,"said Stilvren.

Her gaze lingered on Aetherwind a moment longer than necessary.

The Shadow Forces' Growing Influence

Meanwhile, in the darkened corridors of the Void's stronghold, Zarvok met with his master—the unseen Lord of the Void, Valthor.

His voice, dripping with satisfaction, echoed in the darkness. "The seeds of discord have been planted, my lord. The Conspirators of Equilibrium are divided. It won't be long before they tear themselves apart,"said Zarvok.

A voice replied from the shadows, deep and menacing.

"Good. Continue to stoke the flames. Let their doubt consume them. And when the time is right... we will strike,"said Lord Valthor.

Zarvok bowed, a smile playing at the corners of his lips.

"As you command,"he said.

The game was set, and the pieces moved into place. Aetherwind played both sides, and Zarvok manipulated the conspirators from the shadows. The balance between Light and Dark teetered on the edge.

Fractures Among the Conspirators

The Conspirators of Equilibrium gathered once again, this time in a secluded forest clearing beneath the veil of night. The air was thick with tension, charged by the simmering distrust that had grown since Zarvok's arrival. The darkness whispered through the trees, and within the clearing, unity stood on the edge of collapse.

Stilvren, ever sharp and unrelenting, spoke first. Her words were as precise as the arrows she wielded.

Stilvren: "I grow tired of waiting. We've delayed the Light long enough, yet the shadows remain weak. If we are to preserve balance, we must allow darkness to rise—or everything we've worked for will be undone."

Her gaze landed on Aetherwind, suspicion burning behind her silver eyes.

Stilvren: "You, Aetherwind. Always vanishing. Always gathering 'intelligence' that leads us nowhere. Perhaps it's time you explain your true role in all of this."

Aetherwind stood unshaken, his expression unreadable as he addressed the challenge.

Aetherwind: "My role is the same as yours, Stilvren—to preserve balance. Just because the results aren't immediate doesn't mean we've failed. If we push too far, the Light will retaliate. We could lose everything."

Zeyra stepped forward, her motions fluid as wind through leaves. Her voice was diplomatic, but a thread of frustration wove beneath it.

Zeyra: "You speak of patience, Aetherwind—but how long should we wait? The winds of change are moving fast. The Light grows stronger each day. You talk of balance, but you act like a stone in the path."

She paused, narrowing her eyes.

Zeyra: "It almost feels as if you're stalling us."

Cyrus, arms crossed, finally spoke. His deep, gravelly voice rumbled like tectonic plates shifting beneath their feet.

Cyrus: "Enough patience. We've made sacrifices. Fought battles. And still, the Light gains ground. I begin to wonder if someone here has a different agenda."

His gaze settled on Aetherwind, heavy and direct. The implication was clear.

Aetherwind knew the moment had come—he had to deflect suspicion or risk losing control of the group.

Aetherwind: "You're letting Zarvok twist your thoughts."

He stepped forward, voice steady and resonant.

Aetherwind: "He's the one pushing for chaos. He wants to drag AquaCapri into the Void. Will you really let a creature of shadows lead you?"

Silence fell.

He pressed on, seizing the moment.

Aetherwind: "Yes, I gather intelligence. But it's for our mission. For balance. Zarvok wants dominance, not harmony. He would destroy us if it served the Void. Do any of you truly believe he fights for us?"

As the last word left his lips, a whisper passed through the wind.

From the darkness stepped Zarvok, his presence thick and chilling, as though the shadows had manifested him from the very night. His voice, a soft, venomous hiss, cut through the stillness.

Zarvok: "How quickly trust decays when fear takes root."

He smiled—a thin, cold expression—and moved with the ease of a specter through the circle.

Zarvok: "You speak of balance. But balance is meaningless without strength. The Void has waited long enough. The Light grows bold. It is time for darkness to reclaim its place."

Stilvren, eyes sharp, stepped toward him.

Stilvren: "We're not your pawns, Zarvok. We do not serve the Void."

Zarvok chuckled, voice layered with mockery.

Zarvok: "And yet, with each action, you already serve it. Every step you take, every ounce of doubt—you walk the edge willingly. Whether you admit it or not, the darkness is already in your bones."

He turned his attention to Aetherwind, the mockery fading.

Zarvok: "And you... always playing both sides. They may not see it, but I do. You hide behind the word 'balance,' but you've guided them toward the Light since the beginning."

The air stilled.

Aetherwind held firm, stepping into the space between Zarvok and the others.

Aetherwind: "I guide them toward truth. Toward balance. The Light and Void exist in tandem. One without the other is ruin. I am the bridge. Not your enemy."

His voice turned resolute.

Aetherwind: "If we follow you further, the balance collapses. AquaCapri falls into eternal shadow. Is that what you want?"

No one answered.

Then, slowly, Cyrus spoke, his tone quieter now.

Cyrus: "I don't trust Zarvok. He serves only the Void. We cannot let him lead us."

Zeyra nodded, her gaze returning to Aetherwind.

Zeyra: "Aetherwind is right. If we tip too far, we lose what we've sworn to protect. Balance must be maintained."

Stilvren, still tense, lowered her hand from her bow.

Stilvren: "Perhaps. But the Light cannot go unchecked either. We tread a thin path—and we must tread it carefully."

Zarvok's gaze narrowed, the grin gone.

Zarvok: "You think this moment a victory. But darkness is patient. When the Light dims—and it will—the shadows will return."

With that, he vanished, melting into the trees as though he had never been there.

The forest fell silent once more.

The Conspirators' Fragile Unity

The conspirators stood together, fractured yet not broken. For now, the balance held.

Aetherwind turned away from the clearing, stepping into the shadows between dimensions. A portal shimmered into existence before him— a quiet rift leading back to the Citadel of Dawn.

There, beneath the crystalline spires of Light, he sent word to Luminarion.

Aetherwind: "The shadows stir, but the Light still holds. The final move nears."

Aetherwind's Return to the Citadel of Dawn

After the tense confrontation in the clearing, Aetherwind slipped through dimensions, his heart burdened but his resolve unbroken. The weight of his double life—guardian of Light among those who wavered in shadow—pressed heavily upon him. When he reappeared in the radiant halls of the Citadel of Dawn, he stepped into serenity itself.

The sanctum glowed with luminous calm. Here, light flowed through crystalline walls, bathing every stone in warmth. It was a place where time moved with grace, far removed from the scheming whispers of the Conspirators.

Luminarion awaited him, seated upon a throne of golden fire. The Sovereign of Radiance radiated tranquility, but his eyes remained vigilant, filled with wisdom older than the stars.

Luminarion: "You have done well, Aetherwind. The Conspirators still stand together, though Zarvok's influence runs deeper than even I anticipated."

Aetherwind bowed respectfully, his tone measured.

Aetherwind: "Zarvok has sown the seeds of doubt, but I've begun to push them back toward balance. Still, Stilvren and Cyrus remain wary. They hover at the brink. Zarvok is relentless. He won't stop until he drags them into the darkness."

Luminarion rose, his robes cascading like a waterfall of morning light. He moved with deliberate grace, the air around him humming with sacred power. With a reassuring hand, he touched Aetherwind's shoulder.

Luminarion: "Zarvok thrives on division and fear. But he is also short-sighted. His shadow reveals what he means to conceal. The Conspirators are not our greatest threat—yet. The Void gathers, and we must prepare."

He walked to the vast star-crystal window that looked over AquaCapri's celestial canopy. Countless stars shimmered across the sky like silent witnesses. Then his voice changed—lower now, more solemn—unveiling his deeper plan.

Luminarion: "The balance cannot be broken outright—but it must appear fragile. Let the Conspirators believe they tip the scales. You will guide them gently, unseen. Let them think their path is their own. Keep the Light just beyond risk and the Void from overwhelming."

He turned again, eyes alight with ancient clarity.

Luminarion: "Stilvren, Cyrus, Zeyra... they are noble, but they do not understand. Their balance is an illusion. And yet, that illusion buys us time. Time enough for Light to rise once more."

Aetherwind nodded, feeling the weight of the plan settle within him. It was delicate—this orchestrated illusion—but necessary.

Aetherwind: "Zarvok's hold tightens. Stilvren now trusts no one. Cyrus's resolve is crumbling. He's begun to question everything."

Luminarion gave a faint, thoughtful smile.

Luminarion: "Let Zarvok press harder. His pride will undo him. The darkness always forgets the resilience of Light. And as long as you remain our eyes among them, we will not be surprised."

Aetherwind bowed again, though the strain of his mission flickered across his face.

Aetherwind: "And what of Zarvok? I fear he plots something we have yet to see. His power grows, and the Shadow Forces are poised to strike."

Luminarion's gaze turned knowing, his voice calm but certain.

Luminarion: "Zarvok is clever, but he underestimates the truth. Let him gather his forces. Let him believe he holds the upper hand. When the hour comes, we will meet him with Light."

He stepped close once more, his presence a beacon against the darkness closing in.

Luminarion: "Remember this, Aetherwind—the darkness always thinks it has the advantage. But it is the Light that endures. You are our key. Hold your course. Even when the shadows deepen, I will walk beside you."

Zarvok's Plot Deepens: The Shadow Forces Gather

Deep within the swirling mists of the Void, Zarvok stood before the hidden throne of the Master of the Void. The air around them pulsed with malignant energy, thick with the weight of ancient, malevolent power.

Zarvok's eyes gleamed with anticipation.

Zarvok: "The Conspirators are fracturing, just as you foresaw. Aetherwind believes he holds their loyalty, but doubt festers. Soon, Stilvren and Cyrus will be ours."

From within the darkness, the Master of the Void finally stirred. His form remained obscured as a silhouette of ancient entropy.

Master of the Void: "Aetherwind is the key. Turn him, and Light will collapse from within. Feed his conflict. Make him question his loyalty. Even the brightest star can be extinguished."

Zarvok bowed low, his grin dark and triumphant.

Zarvok: "As you command, my lord. Aetherwind will fall. And when he does, so will the Citadel of Dawn."

The Plot Thickens

Back in AquaCapri, the Conspirators of Equilibrium gathered in secret—Stilvren, Cyrus, and Zeyra—this time without Aetherwind.

Trust in him had waned. Whispers had become convictions. And now, judgment loomed.

Stilvren: "He speaks of balance, but I see hesitation. Secrets. He hides something. We can no longer trust him."

Cyrus, conflicted yet stern, nodded slowly.

Cyrus: "If we cast him aside, we lose our link to the dimensions beyond. But... I agree. He isn't telling us everything."

Zeyra, arms folded, her tone a cautious breeze.

Zeyra: "We need proof. We can't act without it. But we must be wary of Zarvok's influence. We cannot let fear drive our hand."

Stilvren stepped closer; her voice steeled with quiet resolve.

Stilvren: "Then we watch him. We gather the truth ourselves. If he serves the Light, we will find out. And if he does..."

She let the sentence hang unfinished but understood.

Their once unified cause now splintered. Suspicion had taken root. And far away, Aetherwind, unaware of their gathering doubt, stood closer than ever to the edge of betrayal.

Light and Shadow Converge

The stage was set. The balance hung by threads woven of lies, half-truths, and fragile hopes.

Aetherwind, torn between loyalty and deception, now walked the narrowest of paths. With each step, he straddled the edge between friend and foe, between salvation and betrayal.

Zarvok, convinced his manipulations had taken root, moved confidently in the shadows, tightening the noose around the Conspirators' trust. His whispers had become convictions, his doubts —dividing lines.

Meanwhile, high within the Citadel of Dawn, Luminarion prepared—not for a clash of swords, but for a confrontation of destinies. Light and shadow would soon collide, not only on the battlefield but within the very hearts of those who once claimed to uphold balance.

The Conspirators of Equilibrium, once united in purpose, now teetered on the edge of schism. Their mission to maintain harmony had become clouded by fear, doubt, and hidden allegiance.

And Aetherwind—who held both their trust and their suspicion— would soon be forced to choose not only between light and darkness but between illusion and truth.

The storm approached.

And in its eye, the fate of AquaCapri awaited.

3.4 Chamber of Ligh

The Chamber of Light was where Aqua and Capri gathered with their most trusted generals inside the luminous Hall of Stars.

Adorned with radiant constellations and crystalline pillars, the chamber pulsed with celestial elegance—its very architecture meant to inspire resolve. But today, that beauty bore tension. A heavy silence wrapped the chamber as the Void's growing threat cast its dark tendrils over AquaCapri.

Aqua stood at the head of the room, regal yet calm. Capri stood beside him, graceful and poised, though her eyes shimmered with the burden of war to come. Around the luminous table sat Generals Vortizian, Celestara, and Tempestor, each bearing expressions of readiness laced with concern.

Aqua's voice echoed confidently:
Aqua:"The Void forces gather. They come for Aquaterra—our cities, our people. We must act quickly to preserve all we hold sacred. Our realm must be fortified without delay—and that includes safeguarding PaxProfundis."

At the mention of PaxProfundis, unease flickered among the generals. The ancient power it held was both a blessing and a burden.

Capri stepped forward, her voice firm but composed:
Capri:"PaxProfundis is our heartstone. If it falls, the entire constellation will falter. And worse—there are whispers of betrayal within our own walls. We cannot let treachery fracture our defenses."

General Vortizian, steward of AquaCapri's waterways, spoke with the depth of the ocean in his voice:
Vortizian:"Our fleets are prepared, my king and queen. But this war is

twofold—there are enemies without and enemies within. We must find and remove the traitors in our midst."

Celestara's voice followed, threaded with starlight:
Celestara:"The Void's strike will be swift. Our barrier fields need to be reinforced with celestial force. But without better intelligence on this internal threat, we risk blindspots we can't afford."

Capri met the generals' gaze, unwavering:
Capri:"ShadowVeil has been activated. He is tracking whispers, decoding lies, moving through the unseen. If we are to defend PaxProfundis and Aquaterra, we must identify the traitors before they strike."

The conversation turned tactical—lines of defense, interrealm communication, and magical shielding—but beneath every strategy lay the same question: Who among them might already be compromised?

The Scroll's Revelation

Far from Aquaterra, within the radiant halls of Luminarion's palace, ShadowVeil emerged from the darkness. In his gloved hands rested a sealed scroll—its wax bearing the Capricorn sigil.

The golden palace, aglow with solar magic, stood in sharp contrast to the shadows carried in that parchment.

Luminarion stood ready, his expression calm yet charged.
Luminarion:"What news do you bring, ShadowVeil? This scroll carries more than words."

ShadowVeil, face hidden beneath his obsidian hood, laid the scroll upon a crystalline altar. With a steady hand, he whispered the unlocking spell:

"Lux Veritas."

Light flared. The scroll opened on its own, its contents lifting as shimmering glyphs suspended in the air. Luminarion's eyes narrowed as the message unraveled—a warning from King Stonewall of Capricorn, passed through ShadowBlade himself.

The Scroll's Message:

"To ShadowVeil, Master of the Order of Equinox, and Luminarion, Sovereign of Radiance:

The Void's corruption runs deeper than your borders. Among your highest ranks are those who serve the Shadow. We have identified several: Talssa, Aegir, and more yet unnamed.

They whisper rebellion. They conspire in darkness. And they are not alone.

Void-aligned spies walk your cities without hindrance, gathering secrets and undermining hope.

Strike now, before their treachery becomes fatal. Time is not your ally.

Capricorn stands beside you—but you must act first.

—King Stonewall"

The final line burned brighter, compelling immediate action.

Luminarion:"Talssa and Aegir... So our suspicions were true. But now, we have proof."

ShadowVeil:"They must be neutralized before they breach our sanctum. If they gain access to PaxProfundis..."

Luminarion:"Summon your agents. Unmask the spies. Eliminate the traitors. The time for shadows is over."

ShadowVeil:"It will be done. Their betrayal ends today."

This battle would not be fought with legions—but with silence, secrecy, and precision.

The Order of Equinox

Luminarion approached ShadowVeil once more, as he was already deep in thought.

Luminarion:"There's more. Aetherwind, our informant among the Conspirators of Equilibrium, has revealed a deeper thread. Some among the Defenders themselves—Stilvren, Zeyra, Cyrus—have fallen. They seek to disrupt our shield grid from within."

ShadowVeil's voice grew cold:
ShadowVeil:"Aetherwind walks a dangerous line, but his instincts are rarely wrong. If what he says is true, we cannot wait."

Luminarion:"Coordinate with him. Stop this internal rot before it spreads. The Void's next assault is imminent—and if our defenses fail, PaxProfundis will be theirs."

ShadowVeil nodded, disappearing again into the folds of shadow.

In a hidden interdimensional chamber, Aetherwind stood at a glowing portal, waiting. ShadowVeil entered without a word. Their eyes met—understanding passed between them instantly.

Aetherwind:"They'll strike tonight. They've infiltrated three key nodes of our shield system. If they succeed, the capital will be exposed."

ShadowVeil:"Names?"

Aetherwind:"Stilvren. Zeyra. Cyrus. They once sought equilibrium, but they've crossed into something darker. If not stopped, they'll open the gates for the Void."

ShadowVeil:"Then we strike preemptively. I'll deploy my agents to intercept."

Aetherwind:"We've tracked their movements. They're overconfident —tonight, they'll act. Let's end this before it begins."

The Operation

As night fell over Aquaterra, ShadowVeil's agents moved like wraiths through alleys, rooftops, and arcane portals. Their task was clear: stop the sabotage before the shields fell.

At the first defense node, three cloaked figures worked under starlight —Stilvren, Zeyra, and Cyrus. They moved with haste, each one corrupted by a false sense of balance that now served the Void.

But their movements had not gone unseen.

From above, the silent strike began. Veil's agents emerged, weapons drawn, magic charged with precision.

ShadowVeil descended like night itself—cutting through illusions, parrying Cyrus's attacks. Zeyra attempted to vanish into wind, but was caught in an arc of lunar chain. Stilvren raised a barrier, but Veil's ShadowBlade pierced through its core.

Cyrus fought with elemental fury, his connection to earth churning stone beneath his feet. But his strength was no match for Veil's focus. With one clean strike, he fell—blade through heart, silence following.

ShadowVeil:"Your betrayal ends here. AquaCapri will not fall to your delusions."

His agents secured the scene. Across the city, other nodes were likewise reclaimed. The treason was silenced before the Void could exploit it.

By dawn, the defense grid shimmered once again with full power. The sabotage had failed.

Reporting to Luminarion

The sun had barely risen when ShadowVeil and Aetherwind stood before Luminarion in the Citadel of Dawn. The chamber was calm, its golden glow reflecting a moment of reprieve.

ShadowVeil:"The traitors were neutralized. The defense systems hold. We are secure—for now."

Luminarion's radiant eyes met theirs with steady strength.

Luminarion:"You've done well. The Light endures because of you. But this was only the first strike. The Void is watching. It will come again."

Aetherwind:"Then we stay ready. Let them come. We'll meet them with truth and fire."

Luminarion:"Indeed. And as long as the Light is guarded by those like you, AquaCapri shall not fall."

ShadowVeil bowed silently, disappearing into the shadows once more. Aetherwind followed, the scent of starlight still clinging to his cloak.

The war for AquaCapri had begun—but in the battle of whispers and shadows, tonight belonged to the Light.

3.5 The First Rift

Beyond the known borders of AquaCapri, across the infinite stretch of the Cosmic Seas, subtle ripples began to disturb the fabric of space. These disturbances, though faint, were deliberate—a malignant pulse seeking to breach the realm's defenses.

The stars above Aquaterra glittered with their usual harmonious glow to the casual observer, casting an illusion of eternal peace. But deep within the Void between them, something dark and ancient stirred, testing the boundaries that had long safeguarded AquaCapri from invading forces.

Commander Tethyrian, one of the most revered Stardust Guardians, drifted above the Celestial Seas, attuned to the delicate balance of cosmic energies. His silver-blue armor shimmered with reflected starlight, and his sharp eyes scanned the space beyond. For days, he had sensed it—an anomaly growing, subtle yet undeniable, like the first tremor of an impending storm.

The First Warning

Tethyrian froze mid-flight, his connection to the cosmic currents amplifying the disturbance. This was no natural phenomenon. Something—or someone—pressed against the very fabric of their realm. Pressing a gauntleted hand into the stardust flow, he felt the slight, unnatural dissonance in its rhythm. His jaw tightened as a memory clawed its way back—of a distant star lost to the Void because he had hesitated too long.

Tethyrian:"Not again..."

With a thought, he sent a warning rippling through the stardust network, its urgency spreading to the farthest corners of the constellation. The alert reached Supreme General Vortizian, stationed at the heart of Celestial Heaven.

Tethyrian:"I've detected an anomaly—a breach in the cosmic fabric. The Void is testing our defenses."

A Gathering Storm

On the terrace of the Celestial Citadel, Supreme General Vortizian, master of water and time, stood silent, storm-gray eyes narrowing as he received the message. His presence commanded attention, his armor a swirling blend of blues and silver, humming with latent power. Thought turned swiftly to action.

Vortizian:"The Void stirs once more..."

His voice rumbled like distant thunder. Turning to his aides, his tone sharpened, each word cutting with urgency.

Vortizian:"Prepare the forces. We must be ready."

Across AquaCapri, its greatest defenders began to mobilize. Yet beneath that surface response, in the quietest corners of the palace, shadows moved faster than preparations for war.

The Rise of Betrayal

In the shadows of AquaCapri's inner sanctum, Advisor Talssa stood silently, her gaze sharp, measuring every motion, every change in the cosmic winds. PaxProfundis—the concealed star pulsing with unimaginable energy—had become her fixation. She no longer viewed it as a sacred force to be preserved but as the key to reshaping the constellation itself, a tool through which she could bend reality to her vision.

Beside her, Aegir, a fellow advisor and longtime confidant, shared her ambition, though cloaked in a more measured caution.

Talssa:"The disturbance... it's a sign. An opportunity. The Council doesn't grasp the true potential of PaxProfundis."

Her voice was hushed, tinged with impatience and belief.

Aegir:"If we push too far, Talssa, we risk everything. The Void is not to be underestimated."

But her expression only grew harder, eyes glittering with the fever of purpose.

Talssa:"The Void is a distraction. PaxProfundis is the key to control, not chaos."

Unbeknownst to them, their thoughts had already been subtly twisted.

In a recess cloaked in darkness, Zarvok the Shadowweaver, master spy of the Void, observed in silence. Hidden behind veils of illusion, his presence went undetected. His whispers had been few, precise, and devastating. Doubt had taken root. Ambition had been fed. And now, the first fractures in AquaCapri's leadership began to spread.

The Rift Opens

Across the cosmic expanse, the ripple transformed into a fracture—a gaping tear in AquaCapri's long-impervious defenses. The Void had found its passage.

Above Aquaterra, the skies darkened as if the stars themselves were being devoured. From the widening rift, formless shadows poured into the realm, their coming not announced by sound but by an overwhelming, unnatural silence.

The Shadow Forces, led by the formidable Lord Umbra, descended upon the City of Dreams. Their very presence bent the laws of reality, warping the air and fraying the light. These were no mere soldiers— they were hunger incarnate, shadows forged by ancient malice and intent.

At the palace gates, Aqua stood still, gaze locked on the darkening heavens. His royal blue robes danced with the rising wind, his aura bright but tinged with uncertainty.

Aqua:"Capri... Can we truly stop this? Can I?"

Beside him, clad in silver and gold armor, Capri radiated with brilliance. The light of PaxProfundis surged through her veins, alive, vibrant, unwavering.

Capri:"We will. Together. The light within us is stronger than the darkness that seeks to consume."

Even as they prepared to defend their realm, the seeds of conspiracy deepened their roots. Within the palace walls, trust frayed, and the silence of betrayal grew heavier.

The Battle for Aquaterra

The sky cracked open as the Shadow Forces surged forth in full assault.

The Stardust Warriors—beings sculpted from the essence of stars—descended in unison. Their towering forms, forged within the collapse of suns, glowed with celestial intensity. Like intricate machines crafted from constellations, they moved as one, gliding through the skies with impossible precision.

The clash was immediate. Blades of brilliant light met twisted shadow, and the battlefield erupted into a storm of violence and luminescence. Each warrior fought with flawless rhythm—every strike calculated to the breath of a star. Their metallic forms hummed in resonance with the very pulse of the realm, their armor shimmering in tones that sang of order and unity.

At the forefront, Aqua and Capri led with breathtaking harmony. His hands called forth tidal waves of stardust that crashed upon the enemy like celestial tsunamis while she hurled radiant beams that carved through the invading darkness, illuminating the night. Their energies danced together—fluid, fierce, and fused by love and purpose.

General Vortizian stormed the battlefield, wielding his dominion over water and time. With every gesture, whirlpools erupted beneath the enemy, swallowing soldiers whole and freezing seconds mid-air to redirect the chaos. Yet, for every foe vanquished, two more emerged from the Rift's depths.

Below, fear spilled into the streets of Aquaterra. The city's people, long protected by peace and harmony, now faced a nightmare birthed from the stars' forgotten corners. The invasion was no distant tale—it had come to their gates.

Astor, a young soldier stationed at the city's edge, watched as a monstrous shadow closed in. His sword trembled, knees barely holding.

Astor:"For AquaCapri!"

His voice was brave, but his eyes betrayed the fear that swelled within.

At the final breath before defeat, a Stardust Warrior intervened—its blade striking the shadow down in a flash of blazing energy. Astor lived. Many others were not so fortunate.

The colossal defenders, standing at 120 feet tall and crafted from nearly indestructible Duroxium alloys, moved with both elegance and deadly force. They were more than machines. They were protectors—intelligent, responsive, and alive with purpose. Their forms shifted mid-battle—some sprouting luminous wings, others reshaping limbs into weapons of staggering power.

Their systems pulsed audibly, echoing like the heartbeats of stars. Every motion was exact. Every maneuver the product of celestial design.

From the Celestial Citadel, Vortizian re-established control. In his command chamber, bathed in glowing sigils and stardust-infused consoles, he directed the flow of battle with calm authority.

Vortizian:"Section Three—Aerial units to the northern quadrant. Seal the breach. Section Nine—Engage the left flank. Shields at eighty percent. Do not let the breach widen."

The response was instantaneous. Shields shimmered into formation, absorbing waves of dark energy and returning them as redirected bursts that blasted into the Void. The sound of their coordination was like the rhythm of a divine mechanism—clicks, pulses, vibrations. AquaCapri's defenses, forged over eons, moved with infallible grace.

Still, the Shadow Forces pressed forward, multiplying through the darkness that flowed from the rift. Yet the defenders stood resolute. And in the skies above, the elemental forces of Aqua and Capri raged with radiant fury.

Even as the stars dimmed and the earth trembled beneath the battle's weight, AquaCapri did not yield. But victory carried with it a chilling undercurrent—an uneasy sense that this clash had only opened the first wound.

Aqua and Capri's Determination

Back on Aquaterra, momentum began to shift. The battlefield, once shrouded in shadow, now pulsed with growing light. The Shadow Forces, disorganized and recoiling, found themselves no match for the radiant onslaught led by the Stardust Warriors and their celestial commanders.

Aqua lifted his hands, summoning the celestial seas to rise. In response, a gleaming barrier of stardust encircled the capital, casting a radiant dome over its heart. Capri, focused and fierce, added her own power—light from PaxProfundis flowing from her palms, weaving through Aqua's shield and reinforcing it with a brilliance drawn from the core of creation.

Capri:"Aqua, we must strike now. The rift is weakening, but if we don't seal it completely, the Void will continue to claw at our defenses."

He met her gaze, his blue eyes reflecting both the cosmos and the burden of leadership. The expectations of countless stars bore down on him, but beside her, doubt turned into resolve.

Aqua:"We fight for all of AquaCapri. For every star in this constellation. The Void will not claim us."

Their hands moved in unison. A torrent of cosmic energy surged forth, rippling through the battlefield. Beams of piercing light cascaded into the rift, overwhelming the shadows and collapsing the breach upon itself. With a final pulse, the tear sealed shut, and the silence that followed was not one of peace—but of wary reprieve.

Yet safety remained elusive. What had been torn open in the sky now echoed as fractures within.

The Rift Within

As the heavens stitched themselves back together, so too did the illusions of unity begin to unravel. A different kind of rift—one invisible to the eye—grew wider in the hearts of those who watched from within the palace walls.

King Oceanius, standing atop the citadel's highest tower, raised his voice, a clarion call meant to rally.

Oceanius:"This rift is but the beginning. We must stand together, or we will fall."

But his words, though strong, struggled to drown out the quiet murmur of unrest. The seeds had been sown. Doubt had taken root.

The battle for AquaCapri had only just begun. The greatest threat now came not from without—but from within. Trust, once ironclad, began to falter.

And unseen amidst the wounded corridors and quiet halls, Zarvok spun his web. He moved like vapor, listening, sowing, recording. Each whisper of dissent he gathered, each betrayal he fed, was passed to his master—Lord Valthor. The Void's aim was not merely to conquer. It was to corrode.

Lord Valthor's Vision

Far beyond the reaches of light, within the deepest chamber of the Void, Lord Valthor stood atop a jagged precipice inside his citadel of shadows. Ethereal projections of the battle shimmered before him, hovering like dark mirrors carved from smoke.

Tall, cloaked in shifting darkness, his presence absorbed the very light around it. Valthor was less man than manifestation—a living wound in reality, eyes gleaming with an inner fire that neither time nor fate could extinguish.

His vision was not born of chaos but of control.

Valthor:"The universe has long been ruled by imbalance..."

His voice echoed through the obsidian halls, carried on tendrils of shadow that whispered secrets only he could understand.

"Light, with its arrogance, claims dominion over all. But without darkness, their precious glow would be meaningless."

He did not crave the annihilation of light—but its subjugation. In his philosophy, only balance—under his rule—could bring cosmic truth.

AquaCapri was not his enemy. It was his fulcrum.

Valthor:"Let them resist. Let them fight."

He addressed the dark that swirled and listened.

"Every battle sharpens my blade. The light may have claimed this day, but the Void is eternal. In time, they will understand the universe's true nature."

"They think light will save them. But they fail to see... their light is nothing without the dark."

His final whisper came not with rage but with prophecy.

Valthor:"AquaCapri will be the first to fall. And when it does, the stars will follow. The Void will bring balance. And I... will be its guide."

As the last of the invaders fled and the Stardust Warriors resumed their vigilant watch, their forms towering and aglow with readiness, silence returned to the realm—but it bore new meaning. The rift had been sealed, but deeper wounds had formed.

Within the palace, ambition festered. Doubt crept. And in places where once only unity had lived, something colder now stirred.

The Seeds of Betrayal

As the forces of AquaCapri repelled the Shadow Forces, hidden within the palace, Talssa and Aegir exchanged a glance. The battle may have been won, but the war within the kingdom had just begun.

The subtle manipulations of Zarvok had planted seeds of doubt in their minds, and with each passing day, those seeds grew stronger. Talssa:"The Void is not our enemy, Aegir. They are simply another force, another aspect of the universe. And PaxProfundis... its true power remains untapped."

Aegir hesitated, still uncertain of Talssa's growing obsession with the hidden star."If we push too far, we risk losing everything."

But Talssa's ambition had taken root. The Void's shadow had reached her heart, and Zarvok's whispers guided her now."No, Aegir. This is only the beginning. PaxProfundis is the key to controlling not just AquaCapri but the entire cosmos."As the last of the Shadow Forces retreated, the Stardust Warriors returned to their vigil, their towering forms reshaping and realigning into their original defensive postures.

The rift had been sealed, but the battle had left more than physical scars. Within the palace, the cracks of doubt and ambition had widened.

CHAPTER

4

THE COUNCIL OF TWELVE

UNITY DEMANDS SACRIFICE, AND LEADERSHIP DEMANDS VISION.

 # CHAPTER 4

△ MAXIMUS, THE ETERNAL QUILL

AQUARII: SALENDIR VIRATHA'KAEL. LUMAE XAL AQUARITH.

OPENING WHISPER – CH. 4

△ VALDUM, THE CELESTIAL ARCHITECT

AQUARII: THALORION KEL'DUNARI. KAELIS VINTRA SOMNAR.

CLOSING WHISPER – CH. 4

4.1 Aqua's Kin: Guardians of Elements

After the Battle for Aquaterra, the Crystal Table shimmered in the heart of the Temple of Elements, mirroring the glow of the constellations above. Each star pulsed with memory, each flicker a tribute to battles won and those yet to come.

The vast, ancient Temple now welcomed a gathering unlike any other —the Council of Twelve. This was no mere assembly of warriors but a convergence of beings whose power could shift the tide of the cosmos. Strength and wisdom radiated from each presence in the chamber.

At the table's head stood Aqua, his gaze sweeping across the council, meeting expressions etched with exhaustion, resolve, and sharpened readiness. Though the battle for Aquaterra had been grueling, the war against the Void had only begun. They had come not to celebrate but to chart the path forward—how to protect the realm and strike before the enemy regrouped.

Encircling the luminous table were the Elemental Vanguard, the Elemental Artisans, and the Champions of the AquaCapri Constellation—each an anchor to the realm's survival.

Thalassa, the new Protector of the Water Realms, sat in serene silence, her stillness evoking the hidden depths of the sea. Successor to Aqualith, she wielded water with both grace and fury, capable of healing—and obliteration.

Beside her, Ignatius, the Flame Warden, rested his crossed arms atop the table, faint embers smoldering along his bronze skin. He had risen in Pyronix's stead, his tempered fire ready to blaze should the council choose aggression.

Next sat Boreal, the Frost Guardian, his quiet contemplation reflecting the steady chill of glaciers. Though untested in direct combat against the Void, his command of terrain and strategy made him essential to the council's next move.

One seat remained hauntingly vacant—the place once held by Cyrus, now fallen to treachery. Aqua's eyes paused there, heavy with remembrance, before shifting to the other side of the chamber.

There, the Elemental Artisans held their place. Verdantia, the Green Whisperer, gazed out a stained-glass window, lost in thought. Her forests had begun to heal Aquaterra, though she knew the fragile calm would not last.

Next to her, Voltar, the Stormcaller, drummed fingers against the table, soft electric pulses rippling through the air—impatient and potent.

Beside him, Tempesta, the Tempest Wielder, exuded quiet control. Though her exterior was calm, storms brewed within her veins.

At the far end, Lunarix, the Moonshadow, observed in silence. Sentinel of shadows, she pierced veils and pathways no other could see.

Completing the sacred circle were the Champions of the AquaCapri Constellation.

Solarion, the Radiant Vanguard, glowed softly with the warmth of the sun, his presence a beacon of hope and courage.

Celestine, the Star Weaver, sat beside him, her serenity a quiet strength, her starlit gaze revealing the fire of unwavering purpose.

Auroria, the Harmony Keeper, folded her hands in calm focus, a living symbol of balance and inner peace.

Lastly, Valorus, the Shield of Valor, sat like a stone sentinel—solid, silent, and ever vigilant, his essence forged in the crucible of both creation and destruction.

Aqua raised his hand. The crystalline hum of the Temple quieted as the meeting began.

"We have won the battle for Aquaterra,"he said, his voice deep and even."But the Void will return. We cannot wait for their next move. We must strike before they recover."A murmur of agreement flowed around the table.

Ignatius was the first to respond, his voice crackling like dry leaves catching flame."We mustn't let the Void believe they can attack us and retreat untouched. We gather our strength and burn through them before they rise again."

Boreal's cool tone followed, slicing through the heat."Charging blindly will cost us dearly. The Void feeds on chaos. If we move without a plan, we become their prey."

Thalassa nodded."The ocean does not thrash without reason. It watches, waits—and then crashes with purpose. We must do the same. Anticipate, then strike."

Verdantia leaned forward, her green eyes alert."Nature stirs. The ground quakes, the winds shift. The Void is gathering; that much is clear. But we delay too long, and they'll rise stronger."

Voltar's fingers drummed again, lightning threading the table's edge."Storms build along the realm's borders. We can harness that power—strike with it, surprise them."

Tempesta, composed and measured, added,"We command the skies, but they'll expect that now. The Void isn't blind. If we use the environment, they will be ready with counterforce."

Lunarix finally spoke, her voice like a secret wind."Darkness shrouds their movements, but I've traced hidden paths within their territory— routes they use to shift their forces. We strike there, sever their lifelines, bleed them slowly."

Solarion's radiant voice followed."We are Light. We don't wait for the dark to envelop us—we illuminate the field. Our response must be swift, unmistakable."

Celestine nodded gently."And in that Light, we must inspire our people. Their hope empowers us. Without it, even victory would be hollow."

Auroria added,"Balance is our ally. Too much haste invites collapse. But hesitation is just as deadly. We must act with purpose."

Then Valorus spoke, voice deep as the earth's bones."When the moment comes, I will lead. But our forces must be prepared. The Void will not yield easily."

Aqua took in every word, his mind weaving the threads of strategy."We will not wait for the Void to strike again,"he said firmly."But we will strike with precision, not recklessness.

Lunarix, you will lead a reconnaissance mission through the shadow paths you've uncovered.

Voltar, Tempesta—prepare the skies. When the time comes, we'll ride the storm.

Thalassa, Ignatius, Boreal—your forces will lead the charge. But not before the Void reveals its weakness."

Nods circled the table, a silent pact of unity. The plan had begun.

After the Gathering – A Dark Presence Approaches

As the council members filed out, voices hushed but burning with intent, Aqua remained behind, joined by his closest allies.

Pyronix and Aqualith, though no longer active Guardians, had returned as trusted advisors. Their insight was too valuable to leave behind. Zyrion, the Gale Knight, stood silent and alert, his sharp gaze scanning the chamber's shadows.

Aqua stood at the Crystal Table, one hand pressed against its flawless surface. The weight of what was to come bore down on him. At his left, Aqualith leaned against a silver-veined pillar, his quiet watchfulness a calming presence. To his right, Zyrion's fingers tapped the hilt of his blade, the rhythm a signal of gathering tension.

Across the room, Pyronix paced with blazing impatience, fire flickering from his fingertips with every stride.

"We cannot sit idly while the Void gathers strength,"Pyronix growled."Every moment we waste is another step toward our end."

Aqua's reply came like the deep calm of ocean depths."If we rush blindly into their trap, we risk everything. This realm cannot withstand a careless assault."

Zyrion's voice cut through."Waiting won't save us either. We've seen the omens—the sky trembles, the stars whisper. They're coming. If we hesitate, we hand them the field."

Aqualith's voice rolled gently through the space."We must not divide before the battle begins. Balance is the only way forward. Strike and shield must move as one."

Pyronix's fury surged."Balance? They'll devour us if we hold back. We must scorch them—leave nothing behind."

Aqua's gaze held steady."And if we destroy ourselves in that blaze? The Void waits for us to falter. We cannot let pride be our undoing."

The air pulsed with unspoken defiance. Zyrion stepped forward."If you won't lead us to battle, I will. The winds won't wait on patience."

Aqualith raised his hand between them, steadying the storm."There is wisdom in both. Patience is not passivity. But urgency, without wisdom, is suicide. We need both."

Pyronix halted, flames dimming but present."How long do we wait?"

Aqua's reply was unwavering."Not long. But when we move, we move with thunder. We strike when least expected—and strike true."

A sudden ripple stirred the air—subtle, yet undeniable. Every presence in the Temple felt it.

Zyrion narrowed his eyes."Something's here."

The great doors trembled. A gust burst inward, carrying with it the unmistakable scent of the Void—decay and despair. Shadows slithered across the walls, merging and twisting into grotesque forms. The Void had sent its messengers.

Pyronix responded first, fire erupting from his fists as he lunged forward."Finally,"he growled, flames igniting around him in a blazing aura.

"Wait!"Aqua's voice rang clear, but Pyronix was already in motion.

The creatures lunged, their forms shifting like liquid darkness. Pyronix struck with fury, fire clashing against shadow. For a moment, he held the upper hand, his light searing through the gloom—until the shadows slipped past his flames, tendrils wrapping around him.

"Aqualith!"Aqua called.

With swift grace, Aqualith stepped forward. Water surged from the crystal pools lining the chamber, rising in flowing ribbons. A single motion from his hand sent the water wrapping around Pyronix, suppressing the fire just enough to loosen the Void's grip.

"You're reckless,"Aqualith said softly as the water fell away.

Pyronix growled, eyes burning but silent.

Zyrion lifted his hand. The winds obeyed. A massive gust swept through the Temple, scattering the remaining shadows like dust before a storm.

Stillness returned, but the message had been sent.

The Void was watching. Preparing.

Aqua's voice dropped, cold and sure."This was a probe. A test. They're measuring our readiness. They'll return."

Zyrion sheathed his blade, his face unreadable."Unity is fragile, Aqua. Make sure it doesn't break when the storm arrives."

As the winds settled and the waters calmed, Aqua stood alone at the center of the Temple. The Crystal Table shimmered with distant starlight, yet shadows had touched its edge.

The Void had made its move.

Now, it was their turn.

The Guardians would rise—not just with might, but with unity.

They had to.

4.2 Capri's Circle: Mystics of Time

The Observatory of Infinity, perched high among the celestial towers of Aquaterra, was a sanctuary where time itself seemed to yield. Its walls, crafted of shimmering glass, gave the illusion that the stars and constellations beyond were close enough to touch. Above, the observatory's great dome remained ever open, revealing a sky in constant motion—visions of possible futures unfolding across the cosmos like drifting veils. The air here was dense with the murmurs of time, and the current of existence slowed as though granting the Mystics more space to ponder, feel, and gaze beyond the veil of the present.

The purpose of the gathering was clear. The Void was stirring once more, its tendrils reaching toward Aquaterra. The Mystics of Time, under Capri's guidance, had convened to seek insight and prepare. Though powerful, these seers and visionaries approached the future with care—for even the lightest misstep could ripple through eternity.

Capri stood at the heart of the assembly, regal yet serene. Her gown, a cascade of midnight blue, shimmered with stardust under the constellation's glow. A crescent moon adorned her crown, its pale light echoing her bond with the stars and the rhythm of time. Her foresight, while not as potent as the other Mystics', was woven with a deeper understanding—balance and cosmic harmony were her compass.

Beside her stood Luna, her most trusted confidant, cloaked in silver and shadow-blue robes that mirrored the moonlight. Her eyes, deep as the Void yet glittering with starlight, reflected the very heavens above.

Capri turned from the stars to face Chronia, the Seer of Time. Pale-haired and tranquil, Chronia stood by the crystal table, her silvery robes flowing like morning mist. Her gaze, faintly glowing, focused not on the now but on the infinite strands of time stretching before her. Her power was vast, yet even she hesitated to peer too far, wary of unraveling too much.

"Can you not see where this path leads, Chronia?"Capri's voice was soft, yet urgency clung to each word."Can you not tell us how to prevent this war?"

Chronia's eyes did not stray from the stars. Silence lingered like mist before she spoke.

"The future is not a single thread, Capri. Every choice we make weaves new patterns. Some paths lead to victory—but others..."Her voice faltered, and sorrow flickered behind her eyes."Others end in ruin. The Void grows stronger. The further I look, the more the future fractures."

Capri's expression darkened as she paced across the translucent floor, the stars beneath her feet shimmering with each step. She felt the storm building.

"If there is a way to change our fate," she said, "we must find it. We cannot let Aquaterra fall."

Allies from the Stars

Lumina, the Bearer of Light, stepped forward, her golden robes aglow with a soft radiance that seemed to rise from within her. Her essence was tied to the stars and the cosmic light that sustained all life. She sensed the subtle shifts in celestial energy—and lately, that light had grown dim beneath an encroaching shadow.

"The Void creeps closer," she said, her voice gentle yet charged with intensity. "I feel its fingers in the Light. Each star flickers under its influence. The cosmic balance is tipping. We must act now."

Capri turned toward her, unease deepening. "How long do we have?"

Lumina's gaze rose to the sky, her golden irises reflecting the swirling constellations. "Not long. The disturbance grows stronger with each passing moment. If we wait, the Light itself may falter."

Before Capri could answer, the great doors of the observatory opened, and the Defenders of Capricorn entered—warriors from the neighboring constellation, summoned in this time of need. Clad in dark armor traced with silver, they bore the might of their realm, where earth met stars in solemn unity.

At their head strode a towering figure whose presence silenced the chamber. His armor gleamed beneath the celestial dome, and his voice carried the weight of galaxies.

Origon: "Princess Capri, I am Supreme General Origon of Capricorn, at your service."

Origon was a master of elemental forces, able to channel cosmic energy into destructive torrents or shields of impregnable force. His prowess on the battlefield made him a guardian few dared challenge. Under his command stood the Starfire Elite—warriors trained to wield cosmic energy with unmatched precision. They were Capricorn's first line of defense.

His loyalty to King Stonewall and Queen Terra ran as deep as the roots of his realm. To him, honor was infinite, and duty to Capricorn sacred.

Behind him stood three of his most trusted generals:

General Firn, the Ice Vanguard, commanded blizzards and sculpted barriers from frozen air. His Frost Guard excelled in arctic warfare, their resilience unmatched. As unyielding as ice, Firn revered Stonewall's strategic brilliance and would die for his king.

General Caelix, the Sky Sentinel, ruled the upper winds, wielding lightning and storm. His Aerial Fleet flew faster than sound, piloting creatures and crafts alike. As boundless as the skies he patrolled, Caelix was a fierce protector of his constellation.

General Tervigon, the Earthshaker, wielded seismic power, tearing the ground with thought alone. His Groundbreakers tunneled beneath enemy lines, striking from below with surgical precision. Solid and immovable, Tervigon viewed King Stonewall as the foundation of all stability.

Origon: "Princess Capri, we have come to lend our strength. The Void threatens us all, and Capricorn stands ready to fight by your side."

Capri inclined her head in solemn gratitude though her mind remained with the Mystics.

"Your arrival is timely, Supreme General Origon. The Void's reach widens—and we may need more than magic to protect Aquaterra."

Threads of Time

Luna, who had been silent until now, finally spoke. Her voice, calm and resolute, carried a thread of deep concern.

"Magic will not be enough. The Void is twisting time itself. Even our visions are growing unclear. We must strengthen not only the defenses of the stars but the timelines themselves. Only then can we hope to hold them back."

Chronia sighed, her pale eyes dimming as though shadowed by a thousand futures."It is true. The threads of time are unraveling. The more I search, the more I see the Void's influence expanding—stretching across eras, weakening us before the first blade is drawn."

Capri's heartbeat quickened. She had always known the Void was dangerous, but to unravel time? That was a threat beyond comprehension.

"Then we must act swiftly,"she declared, her voice firm with conviction."We will fortify the stars and the fabric of time. But we must act together. Our strength lies in unity."

Lumina stepped forward again, her radiant presence intensifying.

"I will channel the energy of the stars,"she vowed."I will bolster the cosmic Light, let it shine so brightly that it burns away any shadow seeking to take root in Aquaterra."

Chronia nodded, though her gaze remained heavy."I will mend what I can in the tapestry of time. But it will not be easy. The Void's corruption is insidious—it clings to moments we thought safe."

Supreme General Origon, ever the stalwart, rested his hand on the hilt of his sword."The Defenders of Capricorn will see to it that no dark force reaches your borders. We will guard the realms and defend your Mystics while they work."

Capri turned to Luna, her voice softer yet just as steadfast."And we will stand ready, my friend. We will preserve the balance. Together, we will protect Aquaterra."

Luna's gaze shimmered with starlight as she nodded."We will not let the Void consume our Light, Capri. Our bond is unbroken—and it shall remain so."

As the meeting drew to a close, both Mystics and Defenders knew the path ahead was perilous. The Void had already begun to distort the very weave of reality, and time was slipping from their grasp. But with their combined powers—and the unwavering strength of their unity —they would not face the darkness alone.

Above them, the stars shifted once more, and in their radiant dance, the fate of Aquaterra—and perhaps all of AquaCapri—trembled in silence.

4.3 The Pact of Protection

The Hall of Elements pulsed with cosmic energy as the ceremony of the Pact of Protection neared. Its shimmering walls mirrored the assembly—Guardians of Elements and Mystics of Time—gathered beneath one solemn vow. Overhead, stars drifted through the crystal dome, shifting slowly as if bearing silent witness to the moment. Each constellation shimmered with an ancient awareness, watching history unfold once more.

The Guardians and Mystics approached the Pillar of Eternity, laying their hands upon its surface—feeling its warmth, sensing the depth of the promise soon to be sealed. Yet beneath the sacred calm, tension laced the air. The future hovered in uncertainty, the silence between heartbeats filled with unspoken questions.

At the center stood Aqua and Capri, their bond as sovereigns of AquaCapri anchoring the gathered hosts. But before the Pact could be sealed, the arrival of the Defenders of Capricorn cast a deeper gravity over the gathering. Their leader, Supreme General Origon, flanked by his generals—Firn, Caelix, and Tervigon—had remained silent through most of the assembly. Now, their silence broke.

Origon stepped forward, imposing and resolute, his celestial armor shimmering like the night sky itself. When he spoke, his voice bore the weight of countless battles—fought not only in defense of Capricorn but for the enduring honor of his realm.

"Capri. Aqua. Guardians. Mystics. You gather here to unite your strength against the Void. But know this—the Void is not easily vanquished. It is relentless, cunning, and it thrives on every fracture, every seed of doubt."

All eyes turned as Origon addressed the Guardians."Capricorn has battled the Void for eons. We have seen its shadows seep through the stars and consume entire constellations. My generals and I have stood upon the front lines. Though we've driven it back, it never dies. It waits—for unity to crumble, for strength to wane."

General Firn, the Ice Vanguard, stepped forward. His glacial gaze swept the hall, armor forged from the frost of distant worlds gleaming in the subdued light.

"Aquaterra stands as a beacon, yes. But the Void creeps beneath surface strength. It will not only strike from without—it will corrode from within. It will turn friends into foes, poison thoughts, and unravel purpose. We must meet it not only with might but with unshakable resolve. Ice can fracture—but when held firm, it endures."

General Caelix, the Sky Sentinel, stepped forth. His eyes, sharp as the winds he commanded, glinted with purpose. Storm-carved symbols adorned his armor.

"The Void seeks to cloud your mind—like the sky before a storm. But we know the sky's wrath. We'll harness its winds, its fury, and let lightning answer darkness. Yet, we cannot do this alone. We need you —Guardians, Mystics—to stand beside us. The air will grow thick with doubt, but the storm we summon will roar with fury, not fear."

General Tervigon, the Earthshaker, moved with thunderous weight, each step sending subtle tremors across the floor. His voice rumbled, deep and powerful, like tectonic unrest before a quake.

"Aquaterra rests on strong foundations, yes—but even bedrock can fracture beneath relentless strain. The Void will burrow below, seeking to unmoor what you've built. But with us—the Groundbreakers—no darkness shall seep through. We will shake the earth itself to repel the Void and be the bedrock of your defense."

Origon turned to the Pillar of Eternity, then back to the assembled hosts.

"The Defenders of Capricorn stand ready to bind our strength to yours. But let it be known—once this Pact is made, there is no turning back. The Void will come for us all, and it will not rest until all is devoured. We must be vigilant—prepared to meet it at every breach."

Silence swept the Hall. Origon's words lingered, heavy and immutable.

Capri, eyes steady, turned from the generals to Aqua.

"They speak truth. This is no mere war—it is a war for existence itself. The Void will stop at nothing. We must stand together—more united than ever."

Aqua stepped forth, voice resolute.

"Then let it be so. Guardians. Mystics. Capricorn. Together, we fight. And the Void will learn—we are not to be trifled with."

Capri turned to Luna.

"Are you ready?"

Luna's starlit gaze met hers. Her silver robes glowed like moonlight.

"Always. We'll hold the line—whatever comes."

Together, they moved toward the Pillar of Eternity. The energy in the Hall intensified—rising with each step. One by one, Guardians, Mystics, and Defenders placed their hands upon the sacred stone. A gentle glow ignited at every touch. The air itself began to hum—a resonance of power far beyond any single will.

Origon placed his hand last. Light surged from the Pillar, energy swirling throughout the Hall.

"By the strength of Capricorn, by the stars above—we swear to stand united against the Void. We will not falter. We will not fail."

The hall echoed with unified voices:

"We swear to protect the Light, to guard against the Void, and to uphold the balance of the realms."

As the last vow resounded, the Pillar of Eternity blazed with radiant fire, sending a wave of energy through the Hall. Overhead, the stars shimmered—as if the cosmos itself had bowed to the power of their oath.

Hope filled the air. Yet beneath it all, the Void lingered—watching, waiting.

The Pact had been made. But their unity, their strength... would soon face its truest test.

CHAPTER

5

THE DANCE OF DESTINIES

EVEN IN PEACE, DESTINY STIRS BENEATH THE SURFACE.

 # CHAPTER 5

△ MAXIMUS, THE ETERNAL QUILL
AQUARII: CELESTRION VAL'DARETH.
SYMPHARA XAL INTRAE.

 OPENING WHISPER – CH. 5

△ VALDUM, THE CELESTIAL ARCHITECT
AQUARII: FURION ASTRAE XAL THANIEL.
TORITH VEL SYMPAR.

CLOSING WHISPER – CH. 5

5.1 The Celestial Ball

The Grand Hall of Aquaterra shimmered with Light, a living mosaic of color cascading from the towering crystal chandeliers suspended high above the vaulted ceiling. Banners representing each allied realm lined the luminous walls, their emblems glowing faintly in the golden ambiance of the evening. Above, stars embedded in the ceiling glowed with ethereal brilliance—mirroring the vast cosmos outside and reminding all gathered of the unity hard won through countless battles.

On this night, the Celestial Ball was more than festivity—it was defiance in its most radiant form. A declaration of resilience, it blazed as a beacon of hope against the encroaching darkness. The event had been summoned by Aqua and Capri to commemorate their first triumph over the Void at the Battle for Aquaterra. Dignitaries from across the constellations had arrived in solidarity, and the atmosphere was thick with the hum of shared resolve.

Near the entrance stood King Stonewall and Queen Terra of the Capricorn Constellation, surrounded by their most loyal generals and spies. Among them, Supreme General Origon watched the hall with a steady gaze, his captains at his flank. Their presence was a silent affirmation—the Pact of Protection would be honored.

At the summit of the grand staircase, Capri observed the throng below, her poise both serene and commanding. Draped in a gown that rippled like moonlit water, she embodied elegance shaped by purpose. Beside her stood Aqua, regal in deep-blue ceremonial armor—a living emblem of unity. Their eyes met across a moment of silence, and a quiet, knowing smile passed between them. This night belonged to them both—a shared moment carved from triumph and purpose.

As they descended, the room fell still. He extended his hand, and she received it with grace. Each step they took together was a rhythm of harmony and power. They reached the center, and music unfurled into the air—a melody that seemed born from stardust and woven with memory. Their movements flowed like twin comets dancing through the heavens, a tapestry of love, leadership, and luminous destiny.

Around the perimeter, murmurs of quiet intrigue began to rise as dignitaries exchanged whispers beneath the shimmering glow. Zynara, master spy of the Capricorn realm, offered a subtle glance toward ShadowVeil, AquaCapri's elusive sentinel of secrets. Their silent exchange carried the weight of hidden truths, and with Aetherwind— the dimensional infiltrator of Equinox—at their side, they moved with purpose toward the royal pair. The timing was precise. The dance had ended. The moment had come.

Tension simmered beneath elegance. Every word in this hall mattered. Every breath had consequences.

ShadowVeil leaned toward Zynara, his voice barely a whisper."The spy ring is no more. Aquaterra's streets are cleansed. Many were seized, and interrogations have begun under the Order of Equinox. Zeyra and Stilvren..."He paused."Their betrayal runs deep. We did not foresee it."

Zynara's face, carved in calm, revealed nothing. But a flicker passed through her eyes—acknowledgment, perhaps regret."And Aegir?"

His response was a shadow cast across the moment."Dead. A dagger to his heart. Likely silenced before revealing more. But Talssa..."He hesitated again, his tone edged with frustration."She vanished. Zarvok warned her. She fled—into the arms of Lord Umbra."

Aetherwind, who had until then remained an observer, finally spoke. His voice was soft, but each word landed with weight."The scroll from King Stonewall did not lie. The ring ran deeper than any had guessed. We were ready, but Aegir's loss... complicates the road ahead. His mind held keys we may never recover."

Zynara gave a single nod, her gaze drifting across the hall to where Capri now conversed with Queen Terra. Her voice, though distant, rang with elegance undercut by urgency:"Lord Umbra will not wait long."

ShadowVeil's expression darkened."He was wounded during the last clash, but he gathers strength. Talssa sees him now as a guardian. If we fail to act, she will strike—and not alone."

Zynara's eyes narrowed."Then we will strike first. I will dispatch agents. ShadowBlade will lead them."

From behind the pillars, ShadowBlade emerged, his presence as quiet as it was ominous. His dark eyes glinted with quiet menace."Talssa is ruled by fear. That makes her dangerous—but traceable. I'll find her."

Their discussion halted as the great doors creaked open, the sound slicing through music and murmur alike. A hush fell. All eyes turned.

From the shadows stepped a figure cloaked in living darkness, gliding with unearthly grace. The air grew heavier with each of his movements, and a cold whisper ran through the hall. The envoy of the Void had arrived.

Aqua stepped forward. His voice echoed across the marble floor, unwavering."What message do you bring from the Void?"

The envoy's voice was quiet, but its resonance blanketed the room like fog."The Void extends its hand again. Accept our terms, and peace may still be yours. Refuse, and the next tide will leave no stars standing."

Stillness. Then Aqua's tone sharpened his stance firm."We have no need for your peace. This constellation stands as one. We will meet your shadows head-on."

A faint smile touched the envoy's lips, a crescent of disdain."So be it. But remember—stars, too, eventually fade."

Without further word, he turned and vanished into the dark as easily as he had come. His presence lingered, a phantom draped over every soul in the room.

The atmosphere, once alive with celebration, now pulsed with quiet unease. The ball had turned. No longer merely a celebration of victory —it was now a gathering beneath the storm's approach.

Aqua returned to Capri. Without words, their hands found each other. Their touch said enough. United they stood, beneath joy, beneath warning.

And then Krytor stepped forward.

The Silent Enforcer—barely more than a shadow—paused at the threshold. His voice, though barely above a breath, carried a depth that froze time itself.

"Before I go,"he said, with a cold edge honed by ancient wars,"remember Radiantia. A realm once radiant, a beacon among the stars. Its defenders were mighty—your famed Stardust Warriors. Relentless. Proud. Yet, in the end, even they could not hold."

Gasps spread across the hall like ripples through water, and the memory of Radiantia swept over the gathering like a cold tide. The Stardust Warriors—towering titans forged from Duroxium alloys, guardians of light and realm—had once stood unshaken. They might have shaped legends. Their fall had shattered illusions.

Krytor's voice remained calm, merciless."Wave upon wave of Shadow Warriors descended. Black tides smothering light. With every assault, Radiantia dimmed. Its defenses held... until they didn't. Until only ruin remained. Ash where brilliance once burned."

A hush engulfed the chamber. Even the air seemed still. The memory of that fallen world—of heroes outmatched and obliterated—struck at the hearts of every leader present. The tale was not a threat—it was history. A lesson. A wound.

Krytor stepped farther into the shadowed silence, his form blurring at its edges."Your warriors were machine-like. Noble. Fierce. But relentless is not invincible. And light, when isolated, becomes a beacon for destruction."

A tremor ran through the room as if the very stars above mourned.

"Radiantia,"Krytor whispered,"was merely the beginning. More will fall. If you continue to resist the inevitable, your constellation shall suffer the same fate."

His gaze—cold and pitiless—swept the hall, catching Aqua, Capri, and every figure of power in its reach."No unity can shield you from what has no form. The Void finds the cracks. And when it does, your fall will echo even louder than Radiantia's."

With those final words, Krytor turned. His form dispersed into darkness, leaving only silence behind.

The music never resumed.

Aqua's voice broke through at last, low but steady. "Radiantia will not be our fate. Where the Void brings silence, we bring songs. Where it spreads shadow, we kindle stars."

Capri gave a solemn nod. "Let them come. We are not what we were—we are more."

But as the starlit hall remained still, the truth settled among them like dew: the celebration had ended, and the war had already begun.

5.2 A Symphony of Stars

The Celestial Ball had dazzled with grandeur and unity, a shining testament to the strength of AquaCapri's alliance. Yet Krytor's chilling words—his reminder of Radiantia's fall—lingered like a specter above the festivities. As guests filed into the Symphony Hall, that darkness still clung to them. The space itself was wondrous—vast and ethereal, its starlit walls gleaming with ancient radiance, and its ceiling mirroring the night sky, where each star pulsed faintly, as if alive. Despite the shadow looming in their hearts, the chamber retained its sanctity, a quiet ode to harmony.

One by one, dignitaries and warriors took their seats for the evening's grand performance—A Symphony of Stars, a convergence of music and magic from across the realms. More than entertainment, the performance stood as a symbol—an artistic fusion of diverse cultures, each melody a strand woven into the great tapestry of unity. Yet Krytor's warning clung like a silent wind, whispering doubts, stirring unrest just beneath the surface.

As the first celestial notes floated through the hall, Capri sat beside Aqua, her thoughts drifting like leaves in a storm. Though she held a composed posture, her spirit stirred uneasily. The unspoken weight in the air pressed down on them all—fear, uncertainty, a faint tremor in the soul of the realm. Beside her, Aqua felt it, too. His hand found hers beneath the table, a quiet offer of comfort. She welcomed it, but even his touch could not entirely quiet the sense of unraveling.

Not far from the couple, King Stonewall and Queen Terra of Capricorn listened in composed silence, their faces a careful balance of appreciation and tension. As the music climbed in intensity, Terra leaned subtly toward Capri, her voice a whisper laced with steel.

"That creature Krytor... his words were more than a warning. They were a test. They want to know if we'll fracture under pressure."

Capri's gaze remained fixed on the performers, but her mind turned inward."They'll find no weakness in us,"she murmured."But their aim is clear—corrode us from within, seed doubt until unity shatters."

Stonewall's deep voice echoed quietly from Aqua's other side."Umbria is their core. Take it, and the tide may turn in our favor."

Aqua didn't shift his gaze from the stage, but his voice was sure."Umbria alone won't be enough. We must strike with finality. No hesitation. If we want to send a message, it must thunder through the stars."

Terra nodded, eyes narrowing with purpose."Then Umbria must fall. Our Celestial Warriors will be unleashed. Their cosmic rays will turn the shadows to nothing. We'll show the Void their dominion ends now."

In a nearby section of the hall, the Supreme Generals of Capricorn conferred with AquaCapri's military elite. Seated in deliberate formation, their voices were hushed, yet their presence exuded urgency.

Supreme General Origon leaned in, flanked by his seasoned captains."The last battle revealed our miscalculations,"he said, voice low but unwavering."The Stardust Warriors fought with honor, but the number of shadows summoned surpassed expectations. This time, we strike fast. We give them no breath, no ground."

AquaCapri's Supreme General, Celestara, nodded, eyes sharp."Our Cosmic Ray weapons are our edge. But precision is paramount. A mistimed strike, and we lose not just the advantage—but lives."

From the far side of the table, Tempestor joined in, arms crossed and tone resolute."No mercy. When we descend on Umbria, we leave nothing standing. The Void will have no sanctuary, no walls behind which to scheme."

As the symphony soared, so too did the gravity of their conversation. What had begun as a celebration of art was now a council of war cloaked in music. Each chord that echoed through the chamber accompanied the silent crafting of destruction. A great assault was being orchestrated, one that sought not just victory—but total obliteration of the enemy's stronghold.

In the darker recesses of the hall, beneath muted starlight and veils of shadow, four figures gathered—Zynara, ShadowVeil, Aetherwind, and ShadowBlade. Their voices scarcely rose above the music, yet each word carried the weight of fate.

"Talssa hides within Umbria,"murmured ShadowVeil, gaze fixed not on his companions but on the room's many exits."We must reach her before she compromises more. The knowledge she carries could undo everything we've built."

Zynara's expression remained unreadable, but her voice was laced with conviction."We move with precision. Silent, surgical. No trace. She cannot strike again."

ShadowBlade gave a subtle nod."Our agents already follow her trail. Once she's in custody, the Order of Equinox will handle the rest. We'll know all she knows."

Aetherwind, calm yet firm, added,"We can't delay. She grows bolder by the hour. Zarvok won't let her linger—his reach extends deep. We've seen his shadows slither into every crack."

The four exchanged glances, their unspoken oath renewed. Justice would be swift. Talssa's betrayal would not go unanswered.

Yet even as decisions turned to sharpened strategies, something unseen stirred in the ether. The music shifted, flowing into a delicate, haunting melody—like starlight whispering across a dying world. It reached deep, touching chords within Capri's spirit. She closed her eyes, allowing the sound to guide her inward. And then, the vision came.

The stage blurred. In its place rose flames—roaring, all-consuming. The great cities of AquaCapri lay in ruins, their spires crumbling, their crystal domes cracked and fading. Above them, the stars had dimmed. Where constellations once sang, there was silence. Shadows moved like sentient fog, slithering across ravaged lands. The Void had won.

Her breath caught as her eyes flew open. Panic flickered across her face as she turned toward Aqua, fingers gripping his with sudden force. Her voice quivered, barely audible above the music.

"I saw it... the fall of AquaCapri. Everything... devoured by the Void. We couldn't stop it."

Though his face remained composed, Aqua's heart raced."A vision,"he said softly, locking eyes with hers."One of many paths. But not the only one."

Capri shook her head."It felt so real. Too real. We can't afford false hope. The Void waits for comfort to soften us. It waits for us to believe we've already won."

His grip tightened."Then we stay vigilant. We give it no opening, no breath. We fight with everything we have."

The final note of the symphony rang out—long, crystalline, echoing through the chamber like a prayer lost in the stars. A silence followed, deeper than before. The hall was still but not at peace.

Krytor's shadow lingered. Capri's vision loomed. And the war ahead pressed ever closer.

What had begun as a celebration was no longer a symbol of unity but a solemn overture to a coming storm. As guests quietly departed, their faces bore the weight of what they had seen, heard, and now feared. The real battle had not yet begun—but they all felt its breath on their necks.

5.3 Echoes of Fate

The days following the Celestial Ball were steeped in an uneasy stillness. Though celebrations lingered in the air, an undercurrent of tension threaded through the heart of Aquaterra. Subtle, strange disturbances began to stir—unmistakable signs that the Void's shadow was drawing nearer.

Within the War Chamber of the Celestial Heaven Palace, King Oceanius stood before a vast constellation map, its shimmering lines connecting the stars of AquaCapri and its surrounding realms. Across from him, King Stonewall of Capricorn sat with a stern gaze, his jaw clenched under the weight of their discourse.

"We can't keep pretending we have the upper hand,"said Stonewall, his voice low but edged with frustration."The Void is growing stronger—bolder. Radiantia's fall was only the beginning. If we hesitate now, the next battle could be our last."

Oceanius didn't lift his eyes from the stars."I understand the threat. But to strike without caution could leave us vulnerable. Strategy must guide us."

Stonewall's fist tightened against the armrest."Strategic or not, we're losing ground. We must strike Umbria while we can—cripple their ability to regroup. The Void thrives on momentum. We must shatter it."

Oceanius's brow creased beneath the crown of command."Even if Umbria falls, the Void is without end. New threats will rise. How do we defeat a force that knows no limits?"

Stonewall leaned forward, eyes burning."By refusing to fear it. If we falter, if we let doubt take root, we've already lost. We have the

Celestial Warriors, the Guardians, and the combined might of AquaCapri and Capricorn. We must wield it."

Oceanius finally turned to him."And yet, the greatest danger may not be their numbers—but the erosion of our will. Unity must be our strongest weapon."

Meanwhile, in the suspended gardens of the Celestial Palace, Queen Marinella and Queen Terra stood amidst their attendants. The gardens floated like verdant islands in the sky, brimming with otherworldly flora that shimmered beneath the light of the stars. Though tranquil in appearance, the air between them was charged with determination.

"We cannot leave our fate to the whims of destiny,"Terra said firmly."Our people look to us for strength. If we waver, they will, too."

Marinella nodded, her gaze luminous beneath the starlight."We've come too far to let fear dictate our path. The Void is powerful, yes— but we possess the will to shape our own fate."

"Then we must act,"Terra urged."We've relied on our warriors and our defenses, but that isn't enough. We must show the Void we are not reacting—we are creating our own future."

A soft, resolute smile played on Marinella's lips."And we will. We are the heartbeat of these constellations. Our strength lies in unity—our unwavering resolve to protect what we've built. The Void will not claim that from us."

Their words rang true across the celestial winds, a reflection of the resolve radiating through the halls of the palace. Yet even as courage grew within its walls, signs of encroaching darkness surfaced across the realm. Whispers of moving shadows haunted Aquaterra's streets, stars flickered inexplicably, and a strange chill began to spread—subtle yet undeniable echoes of the Void's encroachment.

It wasn't long before Aqua stood beside Celestine in one of the palace's elevated observatories, their eyes cast upon the constellations that shaped their destiny. The chamber was silent, save for the distant hum of starlight. Yet Celestine, ever the pillar of calm and insight, appeared burdened by what she had seen.

"I've read the signs,"she murmured, her voice a fragile echo."The Void's power is escalating. I fear we may not hold it back much longer."

Aqua turned, concern etched across his face."We've faced shadows before. We will again."

Celestine shook her head slowly, her gaze seeming to pierce the veil of time."This is unlike any shadow we've faced. It spreads faster than we can prepare. Even our Guardians—the strongest among us—cannot contain it indefinitely. The Void is patient... and it is wearing us down."

Aqua's jaw clenched."Then we fight harder. We find a way."

But even as he spoke, a flicker of doubt threatened his resolve. Her words hung heavily in the space between them. The Void was no longer a distant force. It was everywhere—unseen but ever-present, unraveling the Light they had struggled to preserve.

Before another word could be said, the palace trembled beneath a sudden, violent jolt. Above, the stars pulsed erratically, and a dense pressure filled the air.

A guardian burst through the chamber doors."Sire! The outer realm of Aetherion is under siege. Shadows swarm the skies!"

Aqua's heart pounded, but he stood firm."Summon the Guardians. We will not let this go unanswered."

Celestine's eyes brimmed with fear, but she nodded."The time we feared has come. The war begins now."

As the alarm resonated through Aquaterra's spires, the Guardians assembled in unity. The first true battle had arrived, one that would test not just the strength of their weapons but the endurance of their spirit. The forces of Light were prepared to rise—but the question lingered like an echo in the cosmos:

Could they withstand the endless hunger of the Void?

CHAPTER

6

SHADOWS CREEP CLOSER

BEFORE THE BATTLE BREAKS, THE SOUL IS TESTED.

 # CHAPTER 6

△ VALDUM, THE CELESTIAL ARCHITECT

AQUARII: SHALANOR TEVIR XAL MAEL. ORUN'THEL DRAYEN SOM.

OPENING WHISPER – CH. 6

△ MAXIMUS, THE ETERNAL QUILL

AQUARII: MAEL'DROS VIRAN.

CLOSING WHISPER – CH. 6

6.1 The Gathering Storm

The air inside the Celestial Heaven Palace was thick with unease. Polished marble floors gleamed beneath the soft glow of floating lanterns—each one representing a constellation pledged to AquaCapri. The ceiling stretched high into the heavens, painted with celestial maps that shimmered with stardust. Yet this was no night for wonder. A storm brewed—not of wind or rain, but within the very fabric of the realms.

In the shadows of the Grand Hall, Zyrion, Champion of Winds, stood silently, his gaze fixed on the darkening horizon beyond the palace's protective shields. His thoughts were clouded, heart heavy with whispers of war. The memory of Radiantia's fall still burned in his mind.

A soft, slithering voice broke his silence.

From the shadows emerged Noxar, his dark robes curling like smoke, his presence dimming the surrounding light. Darkness clung to him as if he were its source. Malice glinted in his black eyes, a twisted smile playing across his face. He moved like a wraith—his steps silent, never quite touching the ground—as he approached.

Noxar: "You seem troubled, Zyrion. Is the weight of your crown becoming too heavy?"

Zyrion's hand drifted to his sword hilt, his stance rigid as he turned. Noxar's voice slithered, smooth yet venomous—like a serpent cloaked in words.

Zyrion: "You have no place here. Leave before I scatter your ashes to the winds."

Noxar chuckled—an eerie, hollow sound that echoed along the marble halls.

Noxar: "Ashes, is it? Such conviction. But deep within, you know the truth, don't you? This Light you cling to... honor, duty, loyalty—it binds you. Chokes you."

He drew closer, his shadow stretching behind him like smoke, winding around the pillars.

"The Void offers something else. Freedom. Power. True power—not the paltry crumbs AquaCapri grants its champions."

Zyrion's eyes sharpened, yet Noxar's voice pressed on, velvet and poisonous.

Noxar: "Picture it. The skies of Planet Umbria are yours to command. No chains of service. No thrones to answer to. With us, you could rule —not kneel. The Void is boundless. Infinite. What is AquaCapri in comparison?"

Zyrion tightened his grip, knuckles white.

Zyrion: "The Void deals in ruin. I will not betray my people. I am the wind—and the wind does not bow to shadows."

Noxar's smile faded for a breath, then returned—deeper, darker.

Noxar: "You resist now. But the Void waits. It watches. Soon, you'll see the Light for what it is—a prison. When that moment comes, remember this: darkness always finds a way in."

A faint rustling stirred the silence beyond the archways. Caspian, a spy of Capricorn hidden in the alcoves, held his breath. Cloaked in the colors of night, he had tracked Noxar into the palace on orders from Zynara, tasked with uncovering traitors within AquaCapri. What he heard confirmed the worst—treachery whispered at the heart of the realm.

Zyrion's gaze flicked toward the shadows, instinct sensing movement. Before he could speak, Noxar's eyes narrowed.

Noxar: "And what do we have here? A rat in the dark?"

Caspian stepped into view without hesitation, dagger in hand, its edge catching the light.

Caspian: "Your schemes end here, Noxar."

His voice cut through the hall—sharp, unwavering. He had walked through the depths of darkness before and would not be cowed.

Noxar's sneer deepened. With a casual flick, a blade of shadow formed in his hand. In a blur of motion, he lunged. Steel met shadow.

Too fast.

Caspian stumbled back, a searing pain slicing across his arm. He gasped—darkness bled into the wound, deeper than the blade should have cut.

Zyrion moved like a tempest. In a sweep of silver light, his sword flashed from its sheath, wind curling around him in a protective vortex. He struck at Noxar—but the emissary dissolved into black mist before the blade could find flesh. His voice lingered, disembodied and mocking.

Noxar: "This is only the beginning, Zyrion. Soon… you will see. The Void claims all in the end."

Silence followed. The shadows stilled. Noxar was gone.

Zyrion dropped beside Caspian, inspecting the wound. The spy clutched his bleeding arm, his face pale but determined.

Caspian: "We… we need to warn the others. The Void runs deeper than we thought."

Zyrion nodded, his expression grim.

Zyrion: "We will. But first, healers. That wound bears dark magic—it must be cleansed."

Caspian gritted his teeth and rose with Zyrion's help.

As they left the Grand Hall, footsteps echoing through the corridor, the air behind them hung heavy with unease. Noxar's offer had been refused—but his poison remained.

Within the palace, rumors began to churn. Whispers flickered like embers—of betrayal, of corrupted loyalties, of shadows lurking beneath gilded loyalty. Friend-eyed friend with doubt. The Guardians' bond, once a fortress, was beginning to fray.

Zyrion led Caspian through the crystal corridors of the Celestial Heaven Palace, each step echoing like a drumbeat of approaching war. Though the halls shimmered with Light, shadows clung to the edges of his thoughts.

Who else had been approached? Who had already yielded?

He had resisted Noxar's temptation—but the voice of the Void had struck chords too close to truth. In silence, his mind turned to the others. Guardians. Generals. Mystics. Would they all stand firm... or falter?

Outside the palace, winds stirred unnaturally, brushing against the energy shields with a low hum. The cosmos beyond, once serene, seemed unsettled—stars flickering with unease. Even the heavens held their breath.

In the palace's heart, the whispers deepened. Paranoia crept like ivy through the ranks. Allies grew wary. Suspicion cracked once-solid foundations. Unity, once absolute, began to tremble beneath the strain of unseen threats.

The name Noxar passed from lips in hushed tones. Eyes watched the corridors, not for enemies from without—but traitors from within.

Zyrion's thoughts churned. Had others heard the same offer? Had they, too, been promised skies to command freedom from chains?

The Void's power was not brute strength—it was seduction. Corruption cloaked in promises. The real war was not of sword or spell but of belief.

He looked to Caspian, who leaned against him with fading strength, pain etched deep in his brow.

Zyrion: "Hold on. We're almost there."

The spy nodded faintly.

Caspian: "Whatever happens... don't let them turn us against each other."

Zyrion did not answer, but his silence was a vow.

As they reached the healing sanctum, priests of light rushed to Caspian's aid. Zyrion turned away, the fire in his chest cooled only by dread. He needed to speak to Aqua. To Capri. The Guardians must convene. There was no more time to wait.

Far beyond the domes of the palace, past Aquaterra's orbit, the Void Forces gathered.

A great churning sea of blackness swirled silently in the vacuum, flecked with shadows and ships of impossible geometry—a void craft that shimmered like broken reflections. From within, entities stirred— ancient, hungry, watching.

The storm was not coming.

It had already begun.

6.2 Whispers in the Dark

The once-tranquil kingdom of AquaCapri now quivered beneath a veil of unease. It began subtly—mysterious whispers drifting through the streets of Aquaterra, weaving themselves into the hearts and minds of its people. At first, faint and elusive, these murmurs soon grew in strength and number. They carried grim tidings—of shadows hidden within Light, of betrayal festering among the Guardians, and of the Void creeping steadily toward the heart of the realm.

Fear ignited like wildfire, sparking anxiety in every corner of the kingdom. The once-unified citizens began gathering in hushed circles, casting cautious glances at familiar faces. Could anyone be trusted? Could they even trust their leaders?

The Celestial Heaven Palace, the radiant seat of Light and power, echoed with the same tension. Capri, ever the calming force, had sensed the shift—not just in the kingdom, but in Aqua himself. For days, he had grown distant, his once-unshakable resolve now clouded by doubt. The sacred bond they shared—once unbreakable—felt strained, as though the whispers of the city had seeped into the palace walls and now drove a wedge between them.

Capri had tried to reach him. Each attempt had been met with silence or evasion. But tonight, she would not yield. Tonight, she would find him and face whatever truth awaited.

She found him in the Chamber of Stars, standing alone beneath the vast cosmic map etched into the vaulted ceiling. The stars above pulsed faintly—the light of those they had sworn to protect. Even their glow seemed diminished, mirroring the uncertainty blanketing their realm.

Capri stepped forward, her voice calm but resolute.

Capri:"Aqua."

Her voice carried through the chamber, but he did not turn. His gaze remained fixed above, the weight of their universe etched into every line of his posture.

Capri:"We need to talk."

A silence passed before Aqua answered, his voice low, distant.

Aqua:"Is this really the time, Capri? The Void presses in from all sides, our enemies multiply beyond reason—and you wish to talk?"

His tone cut deep. Capri wasn't merely seeking conversation—she sought understanding, healing, and unity. She stepped closer, undeterred.

Capri:"Yes. Because something is wrong. You've been pulling away. The people feel it, and I feel it. Fear is spreading, and whispers are growing louder. Now more than ever, we must stand as one. But you... you're slipping away from me."

Aqua's fists clenched at his sides. At last, he turned toward her. The light in his eyes—once blazing with certainty—was dimmed, replaced by something Capri had never seen in him before. Doubt. Fear.

Aqua:"Do you think I don't feel the weight of all this? That I'm blind to the shift in our realm? I was entrusted to guard this kingdom, to defend the Light. And yet..."

His voice faltered. Capri's heart tightened. She stepped forward, her hand reaching for his.

Capri:"And yet what?"

Aqua lowered his gaze, ashamed.

Aqua:"And yet I am failing. We are failing. The Void grows stronger no matter what we do. It seeps into our world, into our people... into us."

His voice dropped to a whisper, heavy with despair.

Aqua:"I can't protect them. I can't even protect you."

Capri's breath caught. She had always seen Aqua as a force of nature —unyielding, immovable. But now, standing before her, he seemed fragile, as though the heavens themselves were pressing down on his soul.

Capri:"You don't have to carry this burden alone. We are in this together. You have me, the Guardians, the entire constellation standing beside you."

A flicker of hope sparked in his eyes, but it was quickly smothered by the storm of doubt within him.

Aqua:"But what if together... isn't enough?"

Capri stepped closer, placing her hand on his arm. Her touch was warm, steady—filled with the love and courage she had always given him.

Capri:"We are enough. You are enough. The Void thrives on fear and division. But love... unity... that is our true power."

Suddenly, the air shifted. The lights flickered. A chill crept through the chamber. Capri's fingers brushed the hilt of her sword.

A whisper echoed—faint yet chilling.

Voice:"Love and unity... are weakness."

From the shadows, a figure emerged, peeling itself from the darkness. Its body rippled like living smoke, eyes gleaming with cruel light.

Lord Umbra—the shadow assassin of Planet Umbria—stood before them. A blade of pure Void was clutched in his hand, so dark it devoured the light around it.

He advanced soundlessly toward Capri, his intent unmistakable.

In an instant, Aqua moved, summoning a radiant barrier between them. Celestial light flared from his palms, forming a shield.

But Umbra's form twisted around the barrier, his blade arcing toward its mark.

Capri spun, drawing her sword in one seamless motion. Metal clashed with Void. A shockwave rippled through the chamber, Light battling Shadow.

Aqua:"You dare attack her in our home?"

His voice thundered with fury, his hands blazing with the light of a thousand stars.

Umbra smiled, a cruel curl of darkness. He twisted through their attacks, his form slipping between shadows.

Umbra:"The Void is already here, Aqua. You cannot stop us. Your Light is a flicker, soon to be snuffed."

He struck again, his movement a blur—shadow and malice entwined. Capri met him blow for blow, her sword radiating with celestial might. Yet Umbra's agility was unparalleled. Aqua launched a wave of radiant energy, crashing toward the assassin—but Umbra dissolved into smoke and reappeared behind Capri, blade raised.

She spun just in time, slashing upward, yet again striking only mist.

Aqua:"Enough!"

He unleashed a brilliant burst of power. The chamber was flooded with Light so pure it forced Umbra back. The assassin's form flickered, his control wavering. But he reformed quickly, eyes burning with triumph.

Umbra:"The Void is patient. We will wear you down, piece by piece, until nothing remains. This is just the beginning."

With one final, twisted grin, Umbra melted into shadow. He vanished into the darkness that had birthed him, his voice lingering in the cold air.

Umbra:"The royal family is not untouchable. Soon, the Light will fall."

Capri lowered her blade, her breath unsteady. The chamber still hummed with the echo of battle. Beside her, Aqua's hands pulsed with fading Light. Their eyes met—no words were needed. The danger was real, immediate.

Capri:"They've already infiltrated the palace."

Aqua's expression hardened, his jaw set with renewed purpose.

Aqua:"If they reached us here, at the heart of AquaCapri, then nowhere is safe. We must strengthen our defenses. Someone from within is helping them."

Capri nodded, though her spirit felt heavy. The whispers, the fear, the doubt—they weren't incidental. They were weapons. The Void had declared war not with armies alone but with poison in the soul of the realm.

Now, it was clear—the royal family was no longer just a symbol of hope. They were the primary target.

They stood in silence beneath the celestial map, its stars dimmed, its constellations shrouded. The truth loomed larger than any constellation above them: the Void had arrived.

This was no longer just a war for their kingdom. It was a battle for their lives.

Capri:"We must be ready. The Void will stop at nothing. It will consume everything we love."

Aqua reached for her hand, his grip steady. The distance between them, once widened by fear, was now bridged by resolve.

Aqua:"We will stand together. No matter what comes—we will not let them take our home. Or each other."

But even as they vowed to protect each other and their realm, the whispers endured—spreading through the streets of Aquaterra, casting long, ominous shadows upon the Light.

6.3 Allies of the Night

The great Council Chamber shimmered with celestial flames, its grandeur unrivaled in all of AquaCapri. Vaulted ceilings mirrored the constellation maps above, and gleaming walls bore the sigils of the Guardians. Yet tonight, the flickering light cast deep shadows over the assembled council—a reflection of the division and dread growing among them. The coming storm loomed near.

At the chamber's center, Aqua and Capri presided with solemn expressions. Around them sat the Guardians, their faces bathed in the gentle glow of floating orbs. A crackle of anticipation filled the air, for two unexpected figures had arrived—defectors from the Dark Forces.

Suspicion thickened as the strangers entered. Cinderspark, tall and fierce, eyes glowing like embers, walked beside Dreadmare, a towering mass of twisted metal and fractured starlight. Once a Star Warrior, Dreadmare had turned his back on the Void and sought refuge within the very walls he had once opposed.

Every gaze locked on the pair. In these uncertain times, trust had become a rare treasure. To many, the notion of former enemies joining their ranks was unthinkable.

Cinderspark's voice rang out first—measured, unwavering, laced with the weight of war-worn truths.

Cinderspark: "We come with an offer, but not without demands. We hold knowledge—critical knowledge—of the Void's designs. But in exchange, we ask for positions of leadership among your Guardians."

A hush fell. Discontent stirred like a wind among the council.

Zyrion, Champion of Winds, broke the silence, eyes narrowing on the newcomers.

Zyrion: "Leadership? After fighting against us, now you seek to stand among us? How can you expect our trust?"

Dreadmare stepped forward, voice like thunder rumbling deep within.

Dreadmare: "Because you must. If survival matters, you will listen. The Void is unlike any threat you've faced. It is ruthless and knows your every flaw. We've seen their playbook, walked their warpaths."

He paused, gaze sweeping the council.

"Without us, AquaCapri will fall."

Tension gripped the chamber.

Aqualith, Aqua's advisor, leaned forward. His voice, though soft, bore the firmness of deep waters.

Aqualith: "We have faced the Void before. What makes this time different?"

Cinderspark's eyes flared. Her words struck like fire.

Cinderspark: "Because now, they seek the Essence of Light itself. The Void won't stop at realms or warriors—they aim to consume existence. And those they find worthy, they will corrupt."

Dreadmare shifted his gaze to Zyrion, his tone suddenly razor-sharp.

Dreadmare: "I heard them speak your name, Zyrion. Noxar and Lord Umbra. You were marked. They believe you can be turned, just as others were. Perhaps... it has already begun."

The chamber froze. Accusation thickened the air like smoke.

Zyrion rose, jaw clenched, his eyes ablaze.

Zyrion: "You question my loyalty?"

Dreadmare's voice dropped into a dark growl.

Dreadmare: "Your loyalty is in question, whether you see it or not. The Void seeps into even the strongest. I've witnessed it. Lived it. If you wish to prove yourself—do so in battle."

Zyrion's hand flew to the hilt of his blade.

Zyrion: "Then let the Light judge us."

The challenge had been cast. There was no turning back.

The council chamber emptied swiftly, its occupants drawn toward the Arena of Stars, where honor was tested in combat. The Guardians, once unified, now walked with divided hearts. This was more than a duel—it was a crucible for loyalty, a forge for trust, a battlefield that might seal the fate of AquaCapri.

Under the celestial dome of the arena, Zyrion stood ready, sword gleaming in the starlight. Across from him, Dreadmare towered like a mountain of war, his frame etched in metal and fire.

Silence blanketed the gathering crowd. The duel was no longer about two warriors—it was about the fractures running beneath their feet, the echoes of unity unraveling.

With a gust of movement, Zyrion struck. He was wind incarnate—fluid, swift, graceful. His sword whistled through the air, striking true, but Dreadmare raised his shield, the clash of metal on metal reverberating like thunder.

Dreadmare: "You're fast, Zyrion. But speed cannot protect against the Void's corruption."

Zyrion said nothing, eyes locked on his foe. He moved again, blades slicing through the air like dancing currents. Dreadmare held fast, absorbing the fury with grim resolve. His fists swung like hammers, each blow a trial of strength.

Light and metal met in a symphony of violence. Zyrion weaved like a storm; Dreadmare endured like the mountain. Precision versus power. Spirit versus steel.

The Guardians watched, breathless. Hope and doubt warred within them. Whispers passed—was Dreadmare truthful? Was Zyrion vulnerable?

But neither faltered. The battle had no victor. Only questions.

Time blurred. The duel raged like a storm with no end. Zyrion and Dreadmare stood locked in the arena's center, weapons lowered but grips still tight. Sweat beaded their brows, breaths heavy with exhaustion, yet neither stepped back—neither conceded.

From the edge of the arena, Cinderspark raised her voice, clear and resolute.

Cinderspark: "Enough. This battle proves nothing. The Void wins when we fight each other. Continue this, and you do their work for them."

A long silence followed. Zyrion and Dreadmare exchanged a look—wariness, defiance, understanding. They stepped back, ending the clash in a draw.

But the damage had been done.

The Guardians dispersed slowly, the arena's silence now filled with uneasy murmurs. The division once hidden now lay bare. Doubts once whispered now echoed freely. The duel had not restored unity—it had splintered it further.

In the growing quiet, Zyrion sheathed his sword. As he turned from the arena, his heart bore a weight he had not known before. Dreadmare's words clung to him like a shadow.

The Void had spoken his name.

Had it already begun?

Beneath the starlit dome, the battle for AquaCapri took on a new form. No longer was it a war of weapons alone—but of conviction, of will, of soul.

Brother now stood wary of brother. Warriors, once united, eyed each other with guarded hearts. The Void, cunning and cold, had cracked the surface of their trust, and now, darkness seeped through.

And in that moment, one truth shimmered in Zyrion's mind with terrible clarity:

This was no longer just a fight for survival.

This was a battle for the soul of AquaCapri.

AquaCapri

CHAPTER

7

THE SIEGE OF SERENITY

THE TRUTH, ONCE BURIED, NOW IGNITES THE SKIES.

 CHAPTER 7

△ VALDUM, THE CELESTIAL ARCHITECT

AQUARII: TORAN VIRANTH XAL VEKIR. SHAL'DRYN ESTEL'NAR.

 OPENING WHISPER – CH. 7

△ MAXIMUS, THE ETERNAL QUILL

AQUARII: SERENYTH KALAN'MIR.

CLOSING WHISPER – CH. 7

7.1 The Clash of Powers

The long-feared battle had arrived.

The Void forces, ruthless and unrelenting, launched an unprecedented assault on Aetherion—a once-pristine planet that exuded serenity within the constellation of AquaCapri. Aetherion, known for its celestial waterfalls cascading from floating cliffs and its forested tranquility, now stood as a battlefield. The champions of AquaCapri rallied to defend the planet and preserve cosmic balance, knowing that failure here would mean the collapse not just of a world but of the entire constellation's defenses.

At the helm of the AquaCapri forces stood Aqua and Capri, leading with grace and boundless might, their bond to nature and cosmic energy guiding every movement. Alongside them marched the elite:

Celestine, guardian of cosmic energy, twisted the fabric of space to summon storms of starlight.

Lumina, bearer of light, unleashed rays so pure and fierce they blinded the encroaching darkness.

Zephyr, master of wind, turned each gust into a slicing tempest, commanding the skies as his domain.

Draco, dragon-blooded commander of the Celestial warriors, towered like a living storm—his mere presence struck terror into the Void's legions.

Then came the Pact of Protection Guardians—elemental beings bound by oath and soul to Aqua and Capri, unflinching in their cause.

Yet, the true backbone of their defense was the army of Stardust Warriors—120,000 titanic, mechanized protectors forged from unbreakable Duroxium alloys. Blessed with shape-shifting prowess and newly crafted cosmic ray weaponry, they stood as the last, towering line between peace and annihilation.

At their helm, Aetherion's Star Warrior, an ancient sentinel of incalculable strength, guided their every move with stellar precision.

Before the assault, Aetherion was paradise—a sacred harmony untouched by war. Twin suns cast soft light on crystal-clear waterfalls; the forests whispered with vibrant life. But when the Void breached space's veil, the atmosphere shifted. Skies dimmed. Waters churned. The planet's song was drowned beneath the growls of war machines and the screech of unleashed cosmic energy.

The Stardust Warriors advanced. Each step of their colossal frames sent tremors racing through the ground—rivers surged, trees toppled, mountains fractured. The skies, once filled with radiant peace, now split with fire and shadows as the war unfolded in heaven and on earth.

At the forefront of the enemy storm loomed Umbra, Lord of Shadows, bearing the Riftbreaker—a devastating relic forged to pierce AquaCapri's strongest defenses. His forces poured forth: countless and merciless. But against the Stardust Warriors' cosmic rays, even the Void's might faltered. The beams disintegrated shadow beasts in blinding flashes of celestial power.

The serenity of Aetherion shattered as the first wave struck. The air turned heavy with despair. Aqua's eyes narrowed, his gaze fixed on the dark rift unraveling the sky, from which shadow soldiers spilled like an endless tide. The Void moved as a living stormfront, swallowing light, drowning hope. Waterfalls that once shimmered like liquid crystals now ran crimson.

With radiant precision, the Stardust Warriors unleashed destruction. Each blast of cosmic rays turned nightmares to dust. But with every victory, more Void forces emerged from the abyss, as if darkness itself were endless.

Aqua stood at the battle's edge, his presence a calm eye in the storm. Every movement was deliberate, guided by a strategist's mind and a warrior's instinct. With a mere gesture, the rivers and falls surged—roaring torrents summoned by his will swept across the battlefield, drowning entire battalions of Void soldiers. He was not merely commanding the water—he was its fury incarnate, Aetherion's wrath given form.

Yet, Aqua knew brute force alone would not turn the tide. Amidst the chaos, another war unfolded—one within his heart. He felt the growing pressure of Umbra's presence, the cold press of shadow brushing against his soul. The Void was more than an invading force; it was a reflection of doubt, fear, and unraveling order. It sought not only to conquer but to corrupt.

At the planet's heart, Capri raised her arms to the heavens, her fingers weaving a dome of protective light above the AquaCapri forces. Her brow glistened with effort, her eyes shut in focus as she channeled Aetherion's life force. Stardust and radiant energy spiraled around her, forming a vortex that deflected the Void's relentless curses. Her magic pulsed in time with the planet's own rhythm.

But within her raged a different battle. As the power of creation coursed through her, so too did the burden of destruction. The Void's energy scraped at her shield, each wave of darkness like poison seeping into the edge of her spell. Holding the barrier required everything—body, mind, and soul. Yet she refused to falter.

Her thoughts flickered to Aqua, standing amid the storm with unyielding strength. Their bond gave her strength—not just as rulers, but as kindred souls. Love, unshaken by chaos, became the foundation of their resistance. It was a love that refused to be undone, even by the Void's consuming hunger.

High above, Umbra watched from within the swirling clouds. His form shifted like vapors, only his piercing eyes visible through the storm. He studied Aqua with interest—there was power there, yes, but also something fragile. Umbra's lips curled into a faint, knowing smile.

To him, darkness was not destruction—it was transformation. Light and shadow, he believed, were never meant to destroy one another but to coexist in eternal tension. The Void was not malevolent. It was:

Change. Evolution. Balance.

He descended.

With him came silence, a void so thick it silenced even the screams of war. The moment his obsidian blade clashed with Aqua's water-forged sword, the ground trembled, and the heavens recoiled. The force of their duel was apocalyptic—each blow, the echo of galaxies colliding. Aqua's strikes were sharp and resolute, while Umbra's movements flowed like the darkness itself—ungraspable, inevitable.

But in the midst of combat, something shifted.

Aqua began to hear Umbra's voice not just in the air but within himself. His words, spoken not in malice but with ancient clarity, pierced the fog of war:

"You fight against me, but do you not see? The darkness is within you, Aqua. It is within us all. Without the Void, there can be no light. You are bound to me, as I am bound to you."

For a fleeting moment, Aqua faltered—not in strength, but in certainty.

The teachings of the Elderly Council returned to him. Their scrolls spoke not of victory but of harmony. Light and dark—two sides of one coin. Each incomplete without the other.

And so the battle took on new meaning.

Aqua's Revelation

As Aqua battled Umbra, a deeper clarity awakened within him. He no longer fought to destroy the darkness but to restore equilibrium. The Void was not a foreign plague—it was a cosmic truth that had grown distorted, unrestrained in its hunger. Aqua realized that defeating Umbra meant tempering the Void, not erasing it.

His strikes shifted. Each move now carried purpose—measured, thoughtful, resonating with an inner wisdom. He struck not to end Umbra but to hold him back, to realign the scales.

Umbra's form flickered with uncertainty. In Aqua's eyes, he saw no hatred—only understanding. The light did not seek to erase him; it sought peace. For the first time in eons, the Lord of Shadows faltered.

"I see it now, Umbra,"Aqua spoke, voice steady as the tides."You're right—light cannot exist without darkness. But that doesn't mean we have to drown in it. The balance has shifted because the Void seeks to consume, not coexist."

Umbra's expression twisted."You think yourself wiser, Aqua? The light consumes, too. It spreads, suffocates, and erases shadow without thought. You pretend it heals, but even healing can destroy."

Aqua's voice remained calm."The light gives life, not because it must, but because it chooses to. The Void takes. It must be reminded—power is not purpose. We are defined not by what we wield, but how we wield it."

Umbra hesitated. The wind stilled. Even the battlefield paused as if listening.

But then came a roar—not from Umbra, but from the dark horizon.

Voidbringers.

Shadow-infused monstrosities, created to nullify the Stardust Warriors' light-based weaponry, burst through the sky like falling stars of darkness. Their presence twisted the air, unraveling the harmony Capri had so carefully woven into her protective dome.

The Stardust Warriors faltered. Their cosmic rays dimmed, their systems distorted. The Voidbringers drained not just energy but hope.

Capri felt the rupture in her spell. Her hands trembled as the dome began to crack, darkness threading through its luminous weave. She turned her gaze toward PaxProfundis, the core of AquaCapri's defense, now vulnerable beneath the fraying shield.

And yet, in that desperate moment, a strange calm overtook her.

She closed her eyes and reached deeper—into the ley lines of Aetherion, into the breath of the stars. There, she found not opposition but unity. Light and dark. Heat and cold. Chaos and peace. They pulsed together, not as foes, but as partners in the dance of existence.

With renewed focus, Capri altered the spell.

The dome shifted—no longer pure light but a radiant fusion of light and shadow. It shimmered like a nebula, its energy pulsating in rhythm with Aetherion's core. The Voidbringers reeled. Their own darkness, once an advantage, now found itself mirrored and neutralized.

At the height of battle, Aqua and Umbra met in one final clash. Their blades collided in a burst of brilliance and void, sending shockwaves across Aetherion. Yet this was no longer a duel of destruction.

Aqua had changed. His strikes flowed like water through rock—persistent, patient, unstoppable. Umbra, though fierce, began to bend beneath the tide.

And then a convergence.

Capri's shield and Aqua's sword—light and shadow, love and power—united. A radiant beam surged skyward from Aqua's blade, laced with cosmic waters. Capri's dome became a conduit, channeling this energy across the battlefield. The Void forces wavered. The Voidbringers cried out as the fusion of forces unraveled them from within.

PaxProfundis was saved.

The battlefield fell into silence. The smoke parted. Aetherion's skies began to clear.

But it was no victory in the traditional sense. Aqua and Capri knew that the war was far from over. It was a reprieve—a moment to breathe, to reflect, to prepare.

They stood amidst the shattered terrain, not as triumphant heroes but as stewards of the balance. Around them, the remnants of war flickered with both sorrow and hope.

Aqua turned to Capri, his voice quiet but resolute.

"The darkness will always be there, Capri. We can't destroy it. But we can keep it from consuming everything. Together, we can hold the line."

She nodded, eyes shimmering with stardust and weariness.

"It's not about light or darkness," she said. "It's about harmony."

7.2 The Battle for AquaCapri continues

The battlefield surrounding the Crystal Citadel stretched out like a dark scar upon the once-serene landscape. The sky churned with ominous clouds, weighed down by the suffocating presence of the Void. In the distance, the towering Citadel, a symbol of hope and Light, stood resilient but flickering under the growing strain. The glow of its shields flickered against the encroaching darkness.

The ground beneath the defenders trembled as the Void's forces launched relentless waves of attacks. Massive, monstrous war machines, with their twisted, blackened forms, spewed destructive energy that drained the very life force from anything it touched. These war machines, each unique in its design and capabilities, were a terrifying sight to behold. At the front lines, Aqua stood tall, his hand gripping the hilt of his stardust-forged sword, his eyes locked on the enemy. His voice, calm yet commanding, cut through the chaos around him.

Aqua (to his soldiers):

"Hold the line! We cannot let them breach the Citadel. Our home, our future—it all depends on this!"

The soldiers around him, their armor marred with the marks of battle and their faces weary from endless fighting, straightened at his words. Their unity, a testament to their shared purpose, was a sight to behold. With renewed determination, they raised their weapons and charged forward, meeting the Void's forces head-on. Above, the battle raged in the sky. Sleek, silver warships piloted by the Star Warriors engaged with the Void's dark crafts, their energy blasts lighting up the sky in bursts of brilliance. The battlefield below reflected the clash between Light and Darkness, the struggle of two forces vying for dominance.

Inside the Crystal Citadel, Capri stood at the helm of the command center, her fingers tracing the edges of the shimmering battlefield map before her. Her mind tracked the battle with precision, but her heart was tethered to Aqua, who fought bravely below. Their bond, forged through love and battles, made every distant sound of clashing swords and blasts feel personal as if each strike reverberated through her own soul. The thought of losing him was a weight she could not bear.

Capri (to Luminarion, Sovereign of Radiance):

"We need more power in the shields. If they fall, the Citadel will be overrun, and we'll lose everything."

Luminarion's golden aura, usually serene and powerful, flickered under the strain. His voice, though calm, carried the weight of the ongoing battle.

"I am channeling every drop of radiance I have, Capri. But the Void's power is immense and growing. Reinforcements are essential on the western front."

The communication channel buzzed with static as Valorus, general of the Star Warriors, spoke.

"We're spread thin, but I'll send whatever forces I can muster. We must hold until reinforcements arrive."

Capri's heart constricted. She could sense Aqua's strength waning, the battle slowly taking its toll on him. She longed to be beside him, fighting as they had always done, united on the battlefield. But now, her duty was to defend the Citadel and ensure their forces remained organized and focused.

Capri (to herself):

"Aqua... how much longer can you hold out?"

Aqua moved through the ranks of the Void's twisted soldiers, his stardust blade cutting through them with precision. Each strike felt heavier, and each movement was slower as exhaustion crept in. He was a force to be reckoned with, but even Aqua could feel the weight of the enemy pressing in, wave after relentless wave. The ground quaked beneath his feet with the Void's war machines, and the roar of battle filled the air above him.

For a moment, Aqua faltered, knocked back by an explosion that sent him sprawling. His vision blurred, and for a heartbeat, his thoughts drifted to Capri.

"Capri..."he whispered under his breath, his grip tightening on his sword.

Valorus, fighting nearby, saw the momentary falter and shouted, cutting through the noise.

"Aqua! Focus! We need you here! Capri is strong. She's leading the defense. Right now, we need to push them back!"

Aqua nodded, pushing the concern from his mind, though the worry still lingered in his heart.

"I know, Valorus. But I feel her... something is wrong. I should be with her."

With a surge of determination that seemed to defy the odds, Aqua charged forward again, cutting through the enemy lines with renewed ferocity. His resolve was unshakable, a beacon of hope in the midst of chaos.

"We fight together, or not at all."

Inside the Citadel

Capri's eyes never left the map, but her mind was on Aqua. She could feel his exhaustion as if it were her own, the shared connection between them growing stronger with each passing moment. The shield around the Citadel flickered once more, and the pit in her stomach deepened. If the defenses fell, if the Void breached the walls, they would be lost.

Capri (whispering to herself):

"Aqua... stay with me. We're so close."

Luminarion's voice cut through her thoughts, the strain evident even in his usually composed tone.

"Capri, the western defenses are failing. We need immediate reinforcements, or the Void will overwhelm us."

The Breach

Suddenly, a tremor ran through the Citadel. The shields faltered, and in that moment of weakness, the Void's forces surged forward. Dark, twisted soldiers flooded through the breach, their forms spreading terror and corruption in their wake. The battlefield descended into chaos as the Voidbringers wielded their energy-draining weapons, tearing through the defenders.

A powerful blast threw Aqua to the ground. His head spun, and for a brief moment, everything went dark. The sounds of battle grew distant, muffled. All he could think of was Capri, her presence a distant Light in his mind.

Aqua (to himself, gasping for breath):

"Capri... I don't know if I can keep going."

But he had no choice. With great effort, he pushed himself to his feet, bloodied but unbroken. His sword gleamed with stardust, and with a roar, Aqua unleashed a torrent of energy, driving the Void's forces back.

"For Capri. For AquaCapri."

The Final Push

Inside the Citadel, Capri felt Aqua's strength surge through their bond, a jolt of energy that steadied her resolve. She straightened, her voice clear as she issued the final command.

"Prepare for the last assault. We hold this Citadel, no matter the cost!"

Luminarion, his radiance now blazing like the heart of a newborn star, nodded.

"The Light will not fail us today."

Raising his arms, he channeled the power of the Radiant Heart into the Citadel's core. A flood of golden Light erupted from within, bathing the battlefield in brilliance.

As the radiant Light combined with Aqua's water magic, a swirling tempest of energy formed. The storm of Light and water swept across the battlefield, blinding the Void's forces and sending them retreating into the shadows from whence they came. The defenders, renewed by the combined strength of Aqua and Capri, pushed forward with a final surge, forcing the Voidbringers back.

Aftermath: A Victory Won

When the battle was finally over, the ground was littered with the remnants of the Void's forces. The air was heavy with the scent of smoke and ash, but the Citadel stood strong, its Light flickering but alive. Aqua, battered but unbroken, made his way back to the Citadel. His first thought, his only thought, was of Capri.

When their eyes met, the weight of the battle lifted. They ran to each other, collapsing into a fierce embrace.

Aqua (barely audible, his voice heavy with relief):

"Capri... we did it."

Capri (tears welling in her eyes, her voice trembling):

"I thought I lost you."

Aqua (holding her tighter):

"Never. From now on, we face the darkness together. Always."

In the Great Hall

Later, the leadership of AquaCapri gathered in the Citadel's Great Hall. The air was thick with exhaustion but also with the pride of hard-won victory. King Oceanius and Queen Marinella stood at the head of the room, their presence regal and commanding.

King Oceanius (addressing the leaders):

"Today, you have proven the power of unity. Through your bravery, AquaCapri stands strong."

Queen Marinella (smiling warmly):

"The Void may come again, but we will be ready as long as we stand together. This victory is yours, and it will echo through the stars."

Valorus, ever the stalwart general, nodded, his voice measured but resolute.

"We fought well today, but we cannot rest. The Void will not give us peace."

Luminarion (his voice thoughtful, the golden Light still faintly emanating from him):

"The Void's power grows, but there is something it will never understand—our unity, our Light. That is our greatest strength."

His gaze fell upon Aqua and Capri, their bond palpable to all.

"You two, more than anyone, remind us that balance is our key. Light and darkness must coexist, but together, we will always endure."

Aqua (his voice steady and clear):

"Together, we are stronger than the Void. We will protect this realm, no matter the cost."

Capri, standing at his side, nodded in agreement, her voice firm and resolute.

"The battle may be over, but the war is far from won. We'll be ready."

With the Light of the Citadel shining brightly once more, the leaders dispersed, their hearts heavy but hopeful. AquaCapri had weathered the storm, but the real war was only beginning.

7.3 Sacrifices and Salvation

The battlefield stretched beneath a bruised sky, a solemn graveyard of shattered hopes and lingering despair. The once-glorious Crystal Citadel, a radiant beacon at the heart of Aquaterra, now bore the deep scars of battle. Its shimmering walls, once symbols of invincibility, were cracked and marred by the relentless siege. The Citadel's protective shields flickered faintly, like a dying star clinging to life. Smoke rose from the scorched earth, carrying with it the scent of ash and blood. Heroes and enemies lay side by side, their bodies forever etched into the soil, their struggle imprinted on the realm itself.

Survivors, their steps slow and weighted with exhaustion and sorrow, moved among the fallen. Their eyes, hollow from the strain of battle, swept over the faces of the dead, searching for comrades who had not survived the siege. Yet amidst the devastation, a glimmer of relief remained—the Citadel, though battered, still stood. In their shared grief, they found a bond that not only strengthened their resolve but also united them in a way only shared suffering can. This unity, born from the ashes of war, stood as a testament to their resilience and shared purpose.

Aqua, his once-glimmering armor now charred and dulled, stood at the entrance of the Citadel. His eyes, filled with determination, also carried the heavy burden of grief as they surveyed the scene—the fallen bodies of his people, the broken weapons, and the shattered defenses. His body ached with exhaustion, and his mind was clouded with the memories of the battle.

Stardust Warriors, once radiant beings born from the stars, now lay motionless, their eternal Light extinguished. His heart ached, but he could not show it—not now, not while so much still rested on his shoulders.

Beside him stood Capri, her ethereal beauty undiminished despite the grime and blood that stained her white gown. Her presence commanded respect, even in the aftermath of such devastation. Aqua longed to reach for her, to hold her and share in their mutual grief, but the mantle of leadership held them both apart. They were rulers now, bound by duty, even as their hearts silently reached out to each other. The weight of their leadership was a heavy burden, one that threatened to crush them under its weight.

Aqua (thinking): We've won the battle, but at what cost? How many more lives will we sacrifice before this war is over?

The Gathering of Leaders

Within the cracked, weathered walls of the Citadel, Aqua and Capri gathered their most trusted leaders. The room was heavy with the weight of loss yet laced with an unspoken determination.

Luminarion, the Sovereign of Radiance, stood tall, his golden aura now dimmed. However, his staff still emitted a faint, steady glow. His usually serene expression was clouded with sorrow, his radiant eyes scanning the faces of his comrades as though searching for answers to questions even he could not fathom.

Valorus, the Commander of the Stardust Legions, stood beside Luminarion. His posture was rigid, but the fire in his eyes had not dimmed. Blood trickled from a wound on his brow, but he seemed unaware; his fierce gaze locked on Aqua and Capri. The tension in the room was palpable, each leader struggling to reconcile their relief at victory with the terrible cost they had paid. His eyes, usually ablaze with determination, now held a glint of sorrow, a testament to the emotional toll of the battle.

Luminarion (softly): "We have won this battle... but was the price too high? So many of our brightest stars have fallen."

Valorus, still seething from the heat of battle, his voice sharp as a blade, responded:

"Every life lost was a blow to the Void. They will remember this day, and they will tremble in fear."

His words rang out, fierce and defiant, but even in his strength, the burden of the fallen weighed on him. His hands clenched at his sides as though, by sheer force of will, he could undo the devastation they had endured.

Capri, her voice steady yet thick with sorrow, spoke next:

"The sacrifices made today will never be forgotten. We fought for the safety of Aquaterra and for our future. But we must remember the price of every life lost. We cannot become hardened to it."

Her words, though gentle, were firm. They hung in the air like a quiet storm, rippling through the room. Even General Vortizian, his long blue cloak torn from battle, remained silent, his gaze cast down in respect. Celestara and Tempestor, equally battle-worn, exchanged a solemn glance before bowing their heads. In their shared silence, a bond of unity and shared responsibility was palpable. Their respect for the fallen was a silent vow to honor their sacrifice in the battles to come.

Aqua, his voice filled with quiet grief yet underpinned by resolve, said:

"We must honor the fallen by fighting on. Their sacrifice cannot be in vain. The battle is over, but the war is far from won. We must be ready."

His words, a testament to their resilience, echoed across the battlefield, a rallying cry for the battles that lay ahead.

The Aftermath – The Battlefield

After the council, Aqua and Capri walked together across the ruined battlefield, the weight of leadership pressing heavily on their hearts. Luminarion followed behind them, his soft glow casting a gentle Light over the wreckage and the dead. The ground was littered with the remnants of war—twisted weapons forged from the fires of AquaCapri, now mixed with the dark, malevolent artifacts of the Void. A stark contrast between Light and darkness, locked in eternal conflict.

Aqua knelt beside the body of a fallen Stardust Warrior, a young soldier whose Light had been snuffed out far too soon. He placed his hand over the warrior's chest, whispering a quiet prayer for their soul to find peace among the stars from which they had been born.

Aqua (thinking): You fought bravely, and now your Light joins the heavens once more.

Nearby, Capri moved silently through the rows of the fallen, her steps slow and deliberate, her heart heavy with grief. Her hand lingered on the cold skin of a fallen Mystic, one who had served her loyally for centuries. She fought the rising tide of tears, knowing she had to remain strong for her people. She remembered the times they had shared, the battles they had fought together, and the laughter they had shared in times of peace.

As they passed among the dead, Valorus approached, his usual fierce demeanor tempered by the quiet grief in his eyes.

Capri (gently): "Valorus, do you regret what we've done here today? Do you think the price was too high?"

Valorus, his voice low and rough, replied:

"I mourn for every soul lost today. But regret? No. If we hadn't fought as we did, the Void would have torn us apart. Sacrifices must be made for the greater good."

Capri, her voice soft but resolute, responded:

"Yes, but we must ensure we don't lose ourselves in the process."

Valorus' fierce gaze softened, and for a moment, his hardened exterior cracked.

"That is for you and Aqua to decide, my lady. But know this: we will follow you, no matter the cost."

The Solemn Ceremony

As the survivors gathered in the central courtyard of the Citadel, a reverent hush fell over the crowd. The courtyard, once a place of celebration and unity, had been transformed into a memorial. At its center stood a large, circular altar, upon which were placed starstones —one for each fallen soul. Their glow was soft yet unwavering, a reminder of the warriors who had given their all for the realm.

Luminarion stepped forward, raising his staff high into the sky. The Light from his staff mingled with the fading sunlight, casting a warm glow over the assembled. As the names of the fallen were read aloud, each stone was placed into the ground, creating a new constellation within the Citadel itself—a permanent reminder of their sacrifice.

Aether, Keeper of the Stars, stood at the head of the altar, his voice carrying across the courtyard with ethereal grace.

"For each star that has fallen, a new Light will rise. We honor them not with words but with a promise—their Light will guide us, even in the darkest of times."

Aqua's heart felt impossibly heavy as he approached the altar to place the final starstone into the ground. His hand lingered on the cold stone, his fingers trembling as the weight of the day pressed down on him. He felt Capri's presence beside him, her quiet strength bolstering him.

Capri (softly): "These stars are not just our past, Aqua. They are our future. We fight for them. For us."

Her voice trembled slightly, revealing the vulnerability beneath her regal facade. Aqua turned to her, and in that moment, the weight of their leadership seemed to lift, if only for a heartbeat. They were no longer rulers but two souls bound by love and shared sacrifice.

Aqua (quietly): "We will honor them, Capri. And we will finish this war in the Light together."

Tools of War

As the ceremony concluded, Luminarion and Chronia, the Seer of Time, gathered the remnants of the Void's weapons. Twisted and dark, the artifacts were imbued with a malevolent energy that seeped into the very air around them. The Mystics carefully collected each weapon, preparing them for study, hoping to uncover a way to counter the Void's dark magic.

Luminarion, his radiant eyes troubled, spoke quietly to Aqua and Capri.

"We must understand these weapons. The Void's magic is more insidious than we realized. It reaches deeper than we thought, into the very fabric of our realm."

Capri, her voice resolute, replied:

"Study them, Luminarion. We cannot afford to be unprepared for whatever comes next."

As night fell, the new constellation of starstones in the courtyard began to glow brighter, a beacon of hope amidst the encroaching darkness. Aqua and Capri stood together at the edge of the courtyard, hand in hand, their gazes fixed on the stars above. The battle had taken much from them, but as long as they had each other—and the Light of the fallen to guide them—they would continue to fight.Aqua (softly): "We will honor their memory, Capri. And we will make sure this war ends in Light."Capri (whispering):

"Together, Aqua. Always together."

CHAPTER

8

HEART'S ECLIPSE

THE REFLECTION OF FEAR LIES THE PATH TO STRENGTH.

 CHAPTER 8

△ MAXIMUS, THE ETERNAL QUILL

AQUARII: THALUN XAL AURELIETH.
SEVARAN DOXAL MIRAV.

 OPENING WHISPER – CH. 8

△ VALDUM, THE CELESTIAL ARCHITECT

AQUARII: AURELIETH VAL'TORUN.

 CLOSING WHISPER – CH. 8

8.1 The Darkness Within

The Shadow Caverns stretched endlessly, a labyrinth of twisting obsidian formations that seemed to drink in all Light. The air hung heavy with despair, thick with a suffocating chill that pierced the bones. In this forsaken place, even the faintest sound was consumed by the oppressive silence, and the cold winds, howling through the tunnels, carried the echoes of lost souls. Their wails magnified the growing sense of doom that seemed to seep from the very stones. The landscape mirrored the unease swelling within Aqua and Capri as the toll of war cast its shadow over their hearts.

At the edge of a subterranean lake, Aqua stood, his reflection swallowed by the water's ink-black surface. His hands clenched tightly at his sides, and the once-vibrant glow that enveloped him had dimmed to a pale, muted hue. Thoughts of failure gnawed at him, each one a jagged edge, digging deeper into his resolve.

"Aquaterra..."Aqua's voice broke the silence, barely a whisper, heavy with regret."I've led it to the brink of ruin. The Void grows stronger with each passing day, and I stand powerless as our people suffer."

The shadows seemed to creep closer, thickening as Capri approached, her radiance dulled by the darkness that filled the cavern. She reached out, placing a hand on Aqua's shoulder. Yet the warmth that once flowed freely between them felt distant, strained."Aqua, we are not alone in this,"she said softly."We have the Council, the armies, and—"

Aqua spun toward her, frustration flashing in his eyes."Is it enough, Capri? Every battle we fight costs lives. Every day, the Void tightens its grip. I feel their darkness... growing inside me."

Capri took a step back, her own insecurities rising to the surface."Do you think I don't feel it, too? Do you think I don't question my strength every day? We're supposed to be united, Aqua. But sometimes... I feel us slipping apart as if the war is pulling us in different directions."

Their words hung in the air, heavy with emotion. This wasn't just a war against an external enemy—it was a battle within themselves, within their love. The Void they feared, a manifestation of their deepest fears and insecurities, wasn't just encroaching on their realm; it was creeping into their hearts, sowing doubt and fear.

A soft shuffle echoed through the cavern as Aether, the ancient historian of AquaCapri, stepped forward. His eyes, always calm and knowing, now held a flicker of unease."The stars have whispered to me,"he began, his voice a low murmur, heavy with the weight of countless centuries."Another storm is coming—one that will consume not only realms but hearts. You must stand strong, not just in battle, but within. The greatest threat to AquaCapri may not come from the Void... but from the darkness within your souls."

Aether's words lingered in the oppressive air, a truth neither Aqua nor Capri wanted to face. The silence between them deepened, a chasm widening as they realized the gravity of their internal struggle. Their love, their bond, was their greatest strength—and their most vulnerable weakness.

Chamber of Light

In the Chamber of Light, Luminarion and ShadowVeil convened. The chamber was a masterpiece of ethereal design, its walls bathed in a soft golden glow that pulsed in harmony with the stars. The ceiling above resembled a vast, starlit sky, a constant reminder of the eternal dance between Light and shadow.

ShadowVeil moved silently through the chamber, his dark cloak merging seamlessly with the shadows, his presence more of a whisper than a man."The Void grows nearer than you know, Luminarion,"he said, his voice barely audible yet sharp as a blade."AquaCapri's defenses are weakening. Even among our own, whispers of betrayal have begun to spread."

Luminarion, his radiant form aglow with celestial Light, nodded solemnly."I have sensed it, too. The Light dims in the hearts of many, and even the Elder Council feels the strain. They suggest drastic measures."

"Drastic measures?"ShadowVeil's tone was laced with curiosity.

"They propose invoking the ancient magic of our ancestors, "Luminarion replied, his brow furrowing with concern."A fusion of their wisdom and power to form an unbreakable shield around AquaCapri. But such magic hasn't been summoned since the Great Eclipse."

ShadowVeil's eyes gleamed with intrigue from beneath his hood."Desperate times indeed, Master of Light. Be cautious in guiding the Council. Such power comes at a cost."

Without another word, ShadowVeil melted back into the shadows, leaving Luminarion standing alone, deep in thought, the weight of the looming decision heavy upon his shoulders.

8.2 A Love Tested

Back in Aquaterra, Aqua presided over a war council with his most trusted generals. The tension in the room was palpable, a shared weight pressing down on every soul present. The air grew heavy as strategies were debated and plans laid for the battles to come. Yet, none could prepare for the interruption that followed.

A messenger arrived, his breath ragged, fear dancing in his eyes. Aetherwind, ever vigilant, was the first to intercept him, his hand steady on the hilt of his sword.

"My lord,"the messenger gasped, barely able to find his voice."It's the Princess. She's been taken—ambushed on her way back to the Celestial Heavens Palace."

A sudden, chilling silence fell over the council. Aqua's heart seemed to stop, his mind racing through every dark possibility, each worse than the last. His eyes burned with fierce, unrelenting fury as he rose abruptly.

"Who?"His voice, sharp as a blade, echoed through the chamber.

"Noxar... and Zarvok,"the messenger stammered, his body trembling under Aqua's intense gaze."They've taken her to Umbria."

Aetherwind stepped forward, his voice cold and resolute."There's no time to waste, Aqua. The Void will not wait."

Aqua's decision came swiftly."Prepare the forces. We march now. I will lead the rescue myself."

The council burst into motion, but Aqua's thoughts were consumed with Capri. He could feel her absence like a wound in his soul.

Capri's Capture

Capri had been returning to the Celestial Heavens Palace, her thoughts still lingering on the recent council of the Mystics. Her escort was small but capable, moving swiftly across the neutral territories between Aquaterra and the outer realms. They had just passed into a shadowed valley when the attack struck with sudden, lethal precision.

Zarvok, ever the master of deception, had infiltrated her guard, disguised as one of her most trusted warriors. Alongside Noxar, they had waited for the perfect moment, the tension building like the gathering of a storm.

The ambush was brutal. The Void forces, hidden in the surrounding shadows, descended upon them with calculated ferocity. Capri's guards fought valiantly, but the attack was too sudden, too overwhelming. Zarvok, using his shadow-shifting powers, isolated Capri, binding her in dark, ethereal chains before she could summon her celestial powers. The dark magic of the Void clung to her, draining her strength. Though her heart raged with defiance, her body weakened.

Noxar watched from the sidelines, a cruel smirk twisting his lips. "It is done," he murmured, his voice as cold as the winds of Umbria.

As they dragged her toward Umbria, Capri's spirit remained unbroken, her eyes blazing with fury. She would not submit—not to the shadows, not to the Void. Yet, as the jagged spires of the dark fortress loomed on the horizon, she felt the weight of her captivity pressing down on her like a crushing tide.

Mission to Planet Umbria

The mission to Umbria began under a veil of secrecy. Aetherwind, Caspian, Dreadmare, Cinderspark, and a select group from the Order of Equinox moved like shadows through the dark labyrinths of the Void's stronghold. Their objective was clear: rescue the princess, arrest the traitor Talssa—who had aligned herself with the Dark Forces—and extract her to face justice before King Oceanius, Queen Marinella, and the Guardians. But for Caspian, the mission held a deeper, more personal vendetta. He sought to end Noxar, the shadow agent whose treachery had caused Caspian untold suffering.

"We're close, but Talssa knows this fortress better than anyone,"Aetherwind muttered, his voice low and filled with urgency."Stay sharp; we have to be prepared for ambushes."

The air grew thicker, the darkness pressing in on them like a living thing. The walls, black as obsidian, seemed to swallow the light from their torches, turning each step into a trial of will. There was a foul, almost tangible energy in the air—a heavy malice that clung like mist. Every corner they turned felt like the jaws of the Void closing in on them.

Dreadmare gripped his weapon tighter, his voice gravelly."If Talssa really betrayed us, she's not going to make this easy. We need to keep moving before—"

Suddenly, the ground trembled as distant explosions rocked the fortress. The assault had begun outside. Supreme General Celesta and her warriors were launching their attack. The plan was in motion.

"Move fast, and stay quiet,"Aetherwind commanded, his keen senses guiding them forward.

Capri's Defiance

Far deeper in the fortress, Princess Capri sat in cold defiance, her wrists bound by dark chains that glowed with Void energy. The room was dim, the jagged walls like teeth, and every breath felt heavy with the weight of shadow magic. The silence in the cell was broken only by the occasional crack of distant lightning, each flash illuminating her bruised form. Yet, even in captivity, Capri's spirit remained unbroken. She glared defiantly as Noxar approached, his form a silhouette of darkness. Behind him loomed Zarvok, his eyes glinting with cruel amusement.

"You truly think Aqua will come for you?"Noxar sneered, pacing in front of her like a predator toying with prey."Do you believe your love can withstand the darkness that grows inside him? He won't save you. Not this time."

Capri lifted her head, her voice unwavering despite the pain."I know he will come. And I know our love is stronger than any Void you can summon."

Noxar laughed darkly, his face inches from hers."Love? It is a weakness. It has already cost you everything. Look at where you are, Princess. A prisoner in the heart of Umbria, the last place light will ever touch. Your kingdom burns, and your people fall into despair— all because you believed in him."

Capri's heart wavered for a moment, the words cutting deep. She remembered the day they parted, the uncertainty in Aqua's eyes. But she pushed the doubt away, her gaze hardening.

"You're wrong, Noxar. Aqua will come. And when he does, you'll regret every word you just said."

Zarvok, watching from the shadows, chuckled darkly."Let her keep her delusions. It will make breaking her all the sweeter."

Even as they mocked her, the distant sounds of clashing steel echoed through the fortress halls.

Battle Outside the Fortress

Meanwhile, outside, the forces of AquaCapri had descended upon Umbria with unrelenting force. Supreme General Celesta led the charge, her shining armor reflecting the blinding light of the Celestial Warriors who flanked her.

Overhead, Zephyr, Guardian of Winds, whipped the sky into a furious storm, using his powers to turn the very atmosphere against the Void forces. The dark army struggled to maintain its defenses, their ranks thinning since the failed assault on Aquaterra. Now, the relentless onslaught from Celesta's forces threatened to overwhelm them. The cries of battle rang across the desolate landscape while bolts of energy crackled through the air like stars falling from the sky.

Celesta raised her sword high, her voice ringing out."For AquaCapri! We press on! Break their lines!"The warriors surged forward with renewed energy, their weapons gleaming in the dim light of the darkened world. The ground trembled beneath their feet as the clash between light and shadow intensified. Zephyr rode the wind, his speed unmatched, leaving destruction in his wake. Yet, even as the AquaCapri forces pressed forward, they knew the true battle lay within the fortress walls.

Aqua's Rescue Mission

Inside the fortress, Aqua and his elite team moved with purpose. His heart thundered in his chest, every fiber of his being focused on one thing: finding Capri. He could feel her, the faint connection between them pulling him deeper into the fortress.

"Aqua, we have to be careful. This place reeks of traps,"one of his warriors cautioned, glancing nervously around at the oppressive darkness.

Aqua's voice was firm, his determination unyielding."We don't stop until we find her. Keep moving."They pressed forward, but the darkness fought back. The shadows themselves seemed alive, twisting and shifting around them. Suddenly, figures emerged from the dark, their forms barely distinguishable but their intent clear. Zarvok had set his trap.

"Ambush!"Aqua shouted, drawing his sword just in time to block a lethal blow. The battle erupted in the narrow hallway—steel clashing with shadow. Aqua's team fought with everything they had. Aqua himself moved like a force of nature, his sword a blur of light as he cut through the enemy. For every shadow he struck down, two more appeared. Still, Aqua pressed on, his heart filled with fear and urgency. He couldn't be too late. He wouldn't be too late.

Caspian's Duel with Noxar

As Aqua fought through the labyrinth, Caspian finally found his quarry. Noxar stood in a darkened chamber, his blade drawn, a cruel smile on his face.

"I've been waiting for this,"Noxar taunted, twirling his sword as if the duel were a mere game to him."Did you really think you could defeat me? You've already lost, Caspian."

Caspian's eyes narrowed."The only one losing here is you, Noxar. I'm going to end this."

The clash was immediate and violent. Noxar fought with deceptive speed, his strikes a flurry of shadow-infused blows meant to confuse and overwhelm. But Caspian had trained for this. Every swing of his blade was fueled by righteous anger, and with each clash, the rage inside him burned hotter.

"You cost me everything!"Caspian growled, pushing Noxar back with a powerful strike."Your lies, your treachery—they end here."

Noxar grinned, but his confidence began to falter as Caspian drove him toward the edge of the chamber. Finally, with a roar of fury, Caspian struck down his enemy, his sword piercing Noxar's chest. As Noxar's body crumpled to the ground, Caspian felt the weight of revenge lift from his heart.

The Battle with Lord Umbra

They neared the center of the fortress, where they were met by a dark presence—Lord Umbra. Aqua's eyes narrowed as the towering figure of the Void leader emerged from the shadows, his form almost merging with the darkness itself. Lord Umbra's voice rumbled through the halls like distant thunder.

"You've come for her, haven't you? Foolish prince. Do you think your love can conquer the Void? I am the darkness, the very force that will swallow your precious light."

Aqua, his sword already drawn, stepped forward, his eyes blazing."You will not keep her from me."

The battle that followed was brutal and unrelenting. Lord Umbra, wielding the power of the Void, summoned shadows that lashed out like living tendrils, each one aiming to snuff out Aqua's light. But Aqua fought back with a fury that surprised even Lord Umbra. His love for Capri fueled his strength, and every swing of his sword sent waves of radiant energy cleaving through the shadows.

At one point, Lord Umbra managed to knock Aqua to the ground, his dark tendrils wrapping around the prince like serpents. For a brief, agonizing moment, Aqua struggled, the weight of the Void pressing down on him.

"You will never win," Umbra hissed. "She will be mine, and the light will die with her."

But Aqua, fueled by unyielding determination, summoned a surge of energy from within. With a roar, he shattered the shadow chains and leaped to his feet. His sword, now blazing with the light of a thousand stars, struck Lord Umbra with a force so powerful it sent the dark lord staggering back.

At that moment, Supreme General Celesta and her warriors arrived, launching a coordinated attack that overwhelmed Lord Umbra's defenses. Trapped and weakened by the assault, Lord Umbra attempted to retreat into the shadows, but Celesta's warriors, using their celestial magic, sealed him within a barrier of light. Bound and powerless, Lord Umbra was finally captured.

Aqua Finds Capri

At last, Aqua burst into the cell where Capri was held. The sight of her, battered but alive, brought a surge of relief that nearly buckled his knees. He rushed to her side, cutting through the dark chains that bound her wrists.

"Capri," Aqua breathed, pulling her into his arms. "I thought I'd lost you."

Capri, her voice soft but unwavering, leaned into him."You'll never lose me, Aqua. Not as long as we stand together."

Their moment of reunion was brief. The fortress still echoed with the sounds of battle, and the war was far from over.

Talssa's Arrest

As the battle inside the fortress raged, Aetherwind had been pursuing a different target—Talssa, the traitor. Using his ethereal abilities, Aetherwind slipped through the fortress, following the faint traces of Talssa's magic. He found her deep within the fortress, hiding among the shadows, her face twisted in fear.

"Aetherwind..."Talssa whispered, her voice trembling."You don't understand. I did what I had to—for AquaCapri."

"You betrayed us,"Aetherwind replied coldly, his eyes filled with disappointment."You aligned yourself with the Void. There's no justification for that."

Talssa made a desperate attempt to escape, but Aetherwind was too fast. With a swift motion, he bound her in a magical net, her powers rendered useless.

"Your fate will be decided by the Royal Court,"Aetherwind said, his voice hard as stone."You'll answer for your treachery."

Victory and Return to Aquaterra

With Lord Umbra captured and Talssa in custody, the forces of AquaCapri had won a decisive victory. As the dark fortress crumbled around them, Aqua, with Capri by his side, led the victorious warriors out of the shadows and into the light. On the battlefield outside, Celesta and Zephyr rallied the remaining forces, driving the Void army into retreat. The enemy, demoralized and leaderless with Lord Umbra's defeat, scattered, leaving the AquaCapri forces to claim the field.

As they prepared to return to Aquaterra, Aqua and Capri stood together, their hands intertwined. The battle had been won, but the war was far from over. Their love, tested by the darkest of trials, had endured, but the shadows still loomed.

"We've won today," Aqua said softly, his eyes on the horizon. "But the Void is not finished."

Capri nodded, her expression solemn. "No, but as long as we stand together, we will face whatever comes."

With the captives in tow, the AquaCapri forces returned to Aquaterra, their victory a beacon of hope. Talssa and Lord Umbra would face justice, and the realm would prepare for the next battle. But for now, the light had triumphed over the darkness, if only for a moment.

In the Ruins of Umbria

Lord Valhor met with his two most trusted lieutenants, Lord Malagorath and Lord Moroseth. The fortress, once a symbol of power, now lay in ruins, its walls crumbling and the air thick with the stench of sulfur and ash. Despite the recent defeat at the hands of AquaCapri's forces, the Void soldiers stood their ground on the ruins of Umbria, but at the cost of devastating destruction for the planet and their leader, Lord Umbra.

Valhor remained composed, his gleaming black armor untouched by the battle's devastation.

Lord Malagorath paced angrily, his voice a low growl."We were annihilated, Valhor. Our legions are in shambles. How do you propose we rebuild before AquaCapri strikes again?"

Valhor's eyes gleamed with dark amusement."From the ashes, we will rise. This war is far from over. AquaCapri may have won a battle, but the Void is eternal. Their forces weaken with every skirmish, while we are born of darkness, unyielding. I have already begun recruiting new soldiers from the depths of Umbria."

Lord Moroseth eyed Valhor warily."And what of your ambitions, Valhor? We all suffered losses, yet you remain unscathed. Do you not think we've noticed?"

A faint smile tugged at Valhor's lips."I am the Void incarnate, Moroseth. Where others fall, I ascend. My strength lies in more than just numbers. Let AquaCapri bask in their fleeting victory. When the time comes, the Void will consume them, and I shall lead that final wave."

As the Void lords continued to plot, suspicion lingered between them, their unity as fragile as the ruins around them. Valhor's ambitions remained shrouded in darkness, his true intentions known only to himself.

8.3 The Fading Light

The Solarium, once the radiant heart of Aquaterra's warmth, now stands as a mere shadow of its former self. The vast crystal ceiling, crafted to magnify the sun's brilliance, had once filled this sacred chamber with a golden glow. Now, that light is dimmed, barely more than a flicker, as the Void's encroaching darkness seeps into its very foundation. The once-shimmering walls, which mirrored the stars, now absorb the little light that remains, casting long, foreboding shadows that stretch like claws across the chamber floor.

In the heart of this dimly lit space, Aqua and Capri stand together, their figures bathed in the muted glow, their faces etched with both weariness and relief from the recent rescue. The war outside may still rage, but here, within the Solarium, they allow themselves a fleeting moment of respite. Their bond remains a beacon of hope in the encroaching darkness.

Capri steps closer, her voice barely a whisper, thick with emotion.

"I thought I lost you... back there, in the Shadow Caverns."

Aqua lowers his head, his voice laced with fatigue.

"I thought the same. It's as if the Void isn't just outside, but inside too —creeping into our hearts, our minds."

Capri's hand gently rests against Aqua's chest, her fingertips tracing the etched lines of his armor as if reminding herself that he is still here.

"But we're still here, Aqua. Together. That's what matters. The darkness can't win if we don't let it."

Aqua looks up, meeting her gaze. Her warmth and presence, even amidst the fading light, are a beacon of strength.

"You're right. But with each battle, I feel the weight... like I'm not enough to protect Aquaterra. Or you."

Capri's soft smile, tinged with sorrow, radiates a quiet strength.

"We've never fought alone, Aqua. Not truly. It's our bond, our love, that's always been our strength. That's how we'll endure."

The two stand in silence for a moment, hands entwined, finding solace in each other's presence. The faint light of the Solarium flickers with a renewed glow—a subtle reminder of the hope that lingers even in the darkest moments. But beneath that fragile hope, tension coils, a reminder of the battles yet to come. They've survived this night, a testament to their resilience, but the war looms ever closer.

The silence is broken by the arrival of Chronia, Seer of Time, whose robes flow like liquid starlight. Her distant eyes reflect the countless futures she has glimpsed. She steps into the chamber, her presence unsettling, as though she carries the weight of a thousand unsaid truths.

"Aqua. Capri,"Chronia's voice carries the calmness of the cosmos, yet her tone bears an ominous edge.

"There is something you must know."

Capri turns, concern clouding her expression.

"What is it, Chronia? What have you seen?"

Chronia's gaze, though softened, weighs heavily.

"The future is not set, but in every path I've seen, there is a price to be paid. A great cost. To save Aquaterra... one of you may have to sacrifice everything."The words hang in the air like a curse. Aqua's heart tightens as his grip on Capri's hand grows stronger. Silence fills the chamber, heavy with the foreboding of what this vision means.

The words hang in the air, thick and suffocating. Aqua's heart tightens as his grip on Capri's hand grows stronger. The silence in the room deepens, suffused with the weight of Chronia's words, which settle upon them like a shroud. Each breath becomes a struggle, burdened by the looming shadow of doom.

Capri's voice trembles, though she remains resolute.

"There must be another way. There always is."

Chronia's head shakes gently, the starlight of her robes dimming.

"Perhaps. But the Void's darkness grows stronger with each passing moment. Your love, as powerful as it is, may not be enough to vanquish it. You must prepare for the possibility that victory will demand the ultimate price."

Aqua steps forward, his voice steady and determined.

"We've faced the impossible before, and we will again. If it comes to that... if one of us must fall, then we will face it together."

Capri squeezes his hand, her resolve unyielding. A silent vow passes between them. No matter the cost, they will stand together—even if it leads them to the edge of their own destruction.
Chronia's expression remains unreadable as she watches the two.

"The choice is yours to make. The path is not set, but the moment will come. I only hope you are ready when it does."

As Chronia turns to leave, the dim light of the Solarium flickers once more, casting twisting shadows across the floor as if echoing the darkness that inches ever closer. Aqua and Capri stand in silence, their love a fragile flame amidst the coming storm, knowing that their greatest challenge may be the choice between life and loss.

Before Chronia exits, she pauses. Her voice, soft yet haunting, echoes across the chamber.

"I have glimpsed a vision of AquaCapri teetering on the edge of oblivion. The Void's forces, led by powers unimaginable, will overwhelm the realms unless one among you makes the ultimate sacrifice.

The Starlight Pendant holds the key, but it exacts a heavy toll."

She continues, her tone distant as though she sees the future unfold before her.

"Only in the deepest shadow can Light truly be seen. When the moment arrives, the Pendant will show you the path, but the sacrifice... will be inevitable."

With that, Chronia fades into the darkness, leaving Aqua and Capri to grapple with the weight of the future she has laid before them.

CHAPTER

9

THE QUEST FOR THE STARLIGHT PENDANT

TO SAVE THEIR REALM, THEY MUST RETRIEVE THE LIGHT HIDDEN BEYOND TIME.

 # CHAPTER 9

△ VALDUM, THE CELESTIAL ARCHITECT
AQUARII: NARETH DORAL SA'VYN.

 OPENING WHISPER – CH. 9

△ MAXIMUS, THE ETERNAL QUILL
AQUARII: VELNAR XAL KIRETH.

 CLOSING WHISPER – CH. 9

9.1 The Summit Before the Storm

The Grand Council Hall shimmered beneath the constellations that circled like watchful sentinels above. Suspended in the heart of Aquaterra, this sacred chamber had witnessed the rise and fall of stars, the forging of alliances, and the pronouncements of destiny itself. Tonight, it would echo with a new oath—one that would shape the fate of AquaCapri.

Aqua and Capri stood at the center of the circular dais, their presence radiant, their resolve unwavering. Light danced across Aqua's ocean-hued robes, rippling like a tide stirred by the breath of eternity. Capri, adorned in a gown woven from refracted starlight, exuded both grace and command. Together, they faced the gathered Mystics, Generals, Guardians, and Sovereigns—the ancient defenders of the constellation.

The air was still, not with silence, but with reverence.

Aqua raised his hand, his voice steady, carrying the gravity of a ruler and the intimacy of a brother to all who served.

"We have called you here not to seek counsel but to share our path. The darkness spreads faster than prophecy foretold. We cannot wait for fate to act—we must move before the Void reaches the soul of our realm."

Capri's voice followed, clear and resolute.

"Our course leads us to the Starlight Pendant, a relic of immense Light hidden beyond the edge of memory. We will also seek the Elemental Alliances, long dormant but vital if we are to restore balance to the cosmos."

A low murmur rippled through the chamber, echoing off the crystalline walls like distant thunder.

Aqua continued, addressing the room with the weight of a sovereign who entrusts his kingdom to those he most honors.

"While we embark on this sacred journey, AquaCapri must not falter. We entrust its defense to the might and wisdom of those who remain."

He turned to General Valorus, whose armor shimmered with embedded constellations.

"You shall lead the Star Warriors across all constellations. Ensure that every realm stands vigilant and ready. The battle is no longer coming —it is here."

Valorus bowed his head, his voice a low rumble of steel.

"The stars shall not sleep, my lords. Not while I draw breath."

Aqua then faced Supreme General Vortizian, stationed beside the royal banners.

"You are to lead the defense of AquaCapri itself. The constellational barrier, PaxProfundis, and all celestial arteries are under your guardianship."

Vortizian nodded, his expression immovable as the tide.

"I shall defend our home until the sea ceases to flow."

Capri lifted her gaze to the far edge of the chamber, where two luminous figures stepped into the Light—Supreme General Celestara and Supreme General Tempestor.

"Celestara," Capri addressed, "you will fortify the Luminary Citadel and wield your celestial shields to protect the elemental nexus points."

Celestara bowed, her silver-and-gold aura gleaming like dawn.

"The stars themselves shall guard AquaCapri, my queen."

"Tempestor," Aqua continued, "cloak our kingdom in your storms. Shroud us from the Void's gaze."

Tempestor's voice rolled like distant thunder.

"My fury shall be the veil through which no shadow may pass."

King Oceanius, robed in flowing blue that shimmered like sunlight upon waves, stood with quiet strength.

"You leave us for a noble cause, but know this—you do not leave us unarmed. All of Aquaterra stands with you."

At his side, Queen Marinella placed a hand over her heart, her eyes reflecting both pride and sorrow.

"And the sea sings your courage. We shall carry your Light in your absence."

Aqua stepped forward, raising a radiant artifact—a Celestial Anchor, pulsating with threads of golden energy.

"This will bind us to you across stars and storms. If the Void strikes, call, and we will come."

Zephyr, Luna, and Galeonix stood behind Aqua and Capri, quiet but resolute. Each bore the sigils of the Elements, prepared to face the unknown. They would join their sovereigns on the perilous journey—united, unyielding.

To their sides, Aqualith and Pyronix stood ready, each commanding a force of elite warriors—guardians of the mission.

Luminarion, Sovereign of Radiance, stepped forward.

"And if the stars grow silent?"he asked.

Capri met his gaze.

"Then let us become the Light ourselves."

A solemn stillness fell.

From the shadows, ShadowVeil exchanged a knowing look with Aetherwind, the hidden gears of protection already in motion. Zynara and the spies of Capricorn stood like still statues, waiting to intercept betrayal should it slither forth.

Aqua's voice rose once more.

"Guardians of the Constellation—should AquaCapri fall under siege, fight not with fear but with purpose. Let no realm falter. Let no traitor rise. Let no Void take root."

Capri stepped beside him.

"And should we fall, then may our sacrifice buy you victory. If we succeed—when we succeed—we will return with the Pendant and with the power to end this war."

One by one, the assembled protectors crossed their fists to their chests, their hearts beating as one. Light spread from soul to soul, a silent vow that echoed through the chamber.

The dawn of departure neared.

And so, with shields lifted, plans laid, and fates entwined, the summit ended.

The storm would come.

And they would face it—apart, but never alone.

The constellations bore witness as the summit dispersed,

each soul carrying the weight of what was spoken,

each heart beating toward an uncertain dawn.

Far beyond the veil of starlight, the ancient powers stirred—

and the path to the Starlight Pendant began to awaken.

9.2 Journey Through the Nebulae

The Nebulae Pathways loomed ahead like a living, shifting entity, their swirling clouds of blues, purples, and pinks twisting in a mesmerizing dance of light and shadow. The vast celestial labyrinth stretched endlessly, hiding danger at every turn. Stars shimmered within the mist, bending and refracting in the dense fog, creating illusions that disoriented even the most experienced travelers.

At the head of the group was Aetherion, the legendary Star Warrior. His glowing armor reflected the soft, ethereal light of the nebulae as he moved with purpose, his gaze sharp, scanning for threats. He had faced the annihilation of his star and home planet, saved by his brilliance and strategy. Still, even he could feel the weight of uncertainty pressing down upon them.

Aetherion's thoughts: I've seen planets fall. I've calculated the course of a thousand battles. But the Nebulae... this place is where even the stars lose their way.

Beside him, Aqua gripped his glowing staff, its light cutting through the shifting mist. He and Capri walked side by side, their bond unspoken yet palpable in the silence. The weight of their responsibility lay heavy on both of them. They had faced dark forces before, but something about the Nebulae felt different—more personal, more dangerous. Zephyr, the nimble and swift guardian of the winds; Luna, the serene guide of moonlight; and Galionix, the Guardian of the Winds, flanked them. A small force of warriors led by Pironix and Aqualith
followed, their armor shimmering under the nebula's ever-shifting hues. They were prepared for battle, their training and experience a shield against the unknown, but unaware of the tests that awaited them.

Glowing orbs known as Nebula Wisps floated lazily through the Pathways, pulsing with a soft, alluring energy. They appeared as gentle guides, but Aetherion's calculating mind saw through their deception. He raised a hand, halting the group.

Aetherion: (calm but firm)"These wisps... they aren't what they seem. Follow them too closely, and we'll be led into a trap—gravitational wells, energy storms. They're as treacherous as the Void itself."

Aqua nodded, his sharp gaze sweeping the environment. His connection to water, so often a source of guidance, felt distant and tenuous in this strange space.

Aqua: (grim)"We trust our instincts, not the lights."

Beside him, Capri felt the weight of the Nebulae pressing upon them as though the very stars were conspiring against them. Shadows flickered at the edges of her vision, dissolving into mist and reappearing just as quickly. The Pathways were alive, and they were watching.

Capri: (quiet, her voice threaded with concern)"These paths... they're like nothing I've ever seen. It's as if the stars themselves are trying to lead us astray."

Aqua's gaze softened as he looked at her, though the determination in his eyes did not falter.

Aqua: (resolute)"The Nebulae respond to our thoughts, our emotions. We have to stay focused, Capri. If we waver, we'll lose our way."

Nebulon Appears: The Guardian's Warning

Without warning, the mist parted, revealing a figure emerging from the swirling clouds—Nebulon, Guardian of the Nebulae. His form shimmered and shifted, composed of stardust and light, his body a constantly reforming silhouette. His voice resonated like distant thunder, vibrating through the vast expanse.

Nebulon: (ominous, yet inviting)"The Nebulae are not easily traversed. Only those with pure hearts and clear minds will find the way. But beware—each step you take echoes through the cosmos, and the Pathways will challenge you at every turn."

He floated beside them, neither friend nor foe, his presence both a guide and a test. Nebulon was here not to help but to measure their worth.

Aetherion eyed the guardian warily, his mind already formulating strategies. Every step in the Nebulae could be their last, and he knew that.

Aetherion: (quietly to Aqua and Capri)"We can't trust anything here. Nebulon may test us, but the Pathways are designed to exploit our weaknesses. Stick to the plan—no deviations."

The First Trial: The Unraveling of Courage

As the group pressed deeper into the Pathways, the atmosphere grew heavier, the colors darkening, taking on more ominous hues. The mist seemed to thicken, and the very ground beneath their feet shifted between solidity and nothingness. The Nebulae were warping reality itself.

Suddenly, Capri halted, her breath catching in her throat as the mist before her swirled and transformed. She saw herself standing alone in an endless void, the stars dimming and fading until there was nothing but cold, empty space.
Aqua, Aetherion, Zephyr, and Luna—all of them vanished, leaving her adrift in the dark.

Capri: (whispering, her voice trembling)"I can't... I can't lose them."

The overwhelming fear of abandonment clawed at her. Her steps faltered, and the emptiness threatened to consume her. Every fiber of her being screamed that it was real—that she had already lost the ones she loved.

Aqua rushed to her side, his voice calm but firm, cutting through the darkness.

Aqua: (steadying her)"Capri, it's not real. This place is playing tricks on us. We're here—right beside you."

Capri's vision flickered, the void retreating as Aqua's words broke through the illusion. She closed her eyes, focusing on his voice, her heartbeat slowing as the fear began to ebb.

Capri: (softly)"I know... but it felt so real."

Aetherion's Strength Tested

While Capri fought her fear, Aetherion found his mind under siege. The Nebulae conjured visions of his carefully laid plans crumbling, entire battles lost because of one mistake. His mind, so used to controlling every detail, now showed him chaos—his home star and planet obliterated because of his failure.

Aetherion: (gritting his teeth)"No... I've planned for every outcome. I can't fail."

But the Nebulae fed on his fear of imperfection, of letting down those who relied on him. He saw his warriors falling, his strategies unraveling like threads.

Aqua interrupted the spiral of doubt

Aqua: (firm)"Aetherion! You've never failed us before. Don't let these illusions make you doubt yourself."

Aetherion's vision flickered, Aqua's voice slicing through the fog of fear. Slowly, the vision dissolved and Aetherionsteadied himself.

Aetherion: (with renewed determination)"Right. This place thrives on doubt. We won't give it that."

Zephyr and Luna's Trial: Unity in Motion

Further behind, Zephyr and Luna faced their own trial. Zephyr, usually so swift and untouchable, felt his winds slipping out of control. The air, once his ally, became chaotic, swirling against him. Beside him, Luna felt her light dimming, the serenity of the moon replaced by overwhelming darkness.

Zephyr: (gritting his teeth)"I can't control it! The winds... they're betraying me."

Luna: (calm but strained)"The Nebulae feed on imbalance. We have to move as one, Zephyr. Feel the harmony between us."

Her voice was like a tether, grounding him. Together, they synchronized their powers. Luna's calming light blended with Zephyr's winds, creating a balanced force that cut through the chaos. The storm quieted, and they moved forward in unison, proving that only through unity could they overcome the trials.

Galeonix's Trial: Overcoming the Fear of Weakness

At the back of the group, Galeonix, the fierce warrior and Guardian of the Winds, faced her own test. Her winds, once under her perfect control, now swirled chaotically around her. She had always been the embodiment of strength, but here, her greatest fear—the fear of weakness—manifested before her.

In her vision, she stood in the midst of a battlefield, but her strength had left her. She watched as her allies fell, unable to wield her power to save them.

Galeonix: (whispering, despair creeping in)"No... I can't be weak. Not now."

But the Nebulae thrived on her fear, amplifying her feelings of helplessness. The winds slipped further from her grasp. But then, something shifted within her. She wasn't alone. The winds, though chaotic, responded to her renewed sense of purpose.

Galeonix: (steadying herself)"I am not my fear. I am stronger than this."

With renewed determination, she forced back the illusion, and the winds once again obeyed her command. She had passed the test, but the trial left her shaken. Galeonix knew then that when the time came, she would sacrifice herself if it meant protecting Aqua, Capri, and their constellation.

The Final Confrontation: Facing Their Collective Fears

The group reformed, stronger but not yet victorious. The Nebulae had one final challenge—manifesting their deepest fears into monstrous forms that towered over them.

Aqua faced raging waters spiraling beyond his control, Capri confronted the Void, Aetherion saw the crumbling remnants of his failed plans, Galeonix confronted waves of despair, and Zephyr and Luna were surrounded by chaos.

But this time, they stood together.

Aqua: (calm and resolute)"We face this together. No fear can break us."

Their combined strength surged, each of them drawing from the other.

Aqua commanded the water to form a protective barrier, Capri's light dispelled the Void, Aetherion's brilliant mind found the weaknesses in the illusions and Zephyr and Luna harmonized their powers to cut through the chaos as Galeonix regained her posture and judgment.

The monstrous forms crumbled into stardust, and the Pathways stilled.

Reaching the Starlight Pendant

At last, they stood before the Starlight Pendant, its soft glow filling the now-calm Nebulae. Aqua and Capri reached out together, their hands clasping the pendant, and with it, they dispelled the last remnants of the Nebulae's trial.

Nebulon reappeared, his voice filled with approval.

Nebulon: (echoing)"You have passed the trials of the Nebulae. Your bond is strong, and your minds are clear. The Starlight Pendant is yours."

With the pendant in their possession, the group left the Nebulae, their bond renewed. But as they moved forward, Galeonix lingered. She had passed her test, but the weight of her realization hung heavy on her heart. When the time came, she knew she would sacrifice herself if it meant saving them all.

9.3 The Guardians' Trial

The Celestial Citadel loomed ahead, its towering spires glowing faintly in the heart of the nebula. Pyronix, Aqualith, and their warriors rejoined Aqua, Capri, and their companions—Zephyr, Luna, Aetherion, and Galeonix—as they stood at its base, gazing up at the majestic structure that had stood for eons, a sentinel of cosmic power. The nebula swirled around them, casting a soft, ethereal glow over the ancient stone and shimmering stardust that composed the Citadel's towering walls. The group had the Starlight Pendant, but its immense power was sealed. The key to unlocking it awaited them within the heart of the Citadel.

Standing between them and the key were the Guardians of the Citadel, ancient beings woven from the very fabric of Light and shadow. Towering figures of indescribable beauty and terror, their forms shifted like the very stars in the night sky. Their faces, indistinct and ever-changing, watched in silence as the group approached. A weight of expectation hung in the air, thick with anticipation.

The Starlight Pendant glowed faintly against Aqua's chest, almost as if responding to the energy within the Citadel. But the group knew that the Pendant, despite its beauty, was nothing more than a dormant artifact without the key. Their trials were not yet over.

The largest of the Guardians stepped forward, its form rippling with Light and shadow, expanding and contracting as though the very essence of the cosmos lived within it. When it spoke, its voice was deep and resonant, like the low rumble of distant thunder.

Guardian (with the weight of eons in its voice):

"Though the Pendant is in your possession, its power remains bound. Only through the key can you unlock its true potential. Yet, to claim the key, you must prove yourselves worthy once more."

The Guardian gestured toward the cosmic altar behind it, where an intricate, glowing artifact hovered above a shimmering pedestal. The key, bathed in the Light of the stars, pulsed gently in rhythm with the universe itself. It seemed so close, yet the air between the group and the key was thick with the promise of challenge.

Aqua: (stepping forward, his expression resolute)

"We've faced your trials before and succeeded. Whatever the test, we will face it together."

There was a tension in his voice, one that only Capri, standing beside him, could sense. His confidence was unwavering, but the weight of the responsibility they carried had been building with each step closer to the Citadel. Aqua knew this test would be unlike any they had faced before.

Capri: (placing a steady hand on Aqua's arm, her voice soft but unyielding)

"We stand as one. We have always faced our challenges together, and this will be no different."

Her words, though gentle, held the power of conviction, and Aqua nodded. The Guardians remained motionless, their gaze piercing as if weighing the truth of their words.

Guardian: (its voice a low, rumbling hum)

"The key will be yours if you can prove your unity. This trial is not one of individual strength but of trust. You must work as one or fail as many."

The Cosmic Labyrint

At the Guardian's words, the floor beneath them began to shift. The ground rippled, and the cosmic energy that had been pulsing gently now surged to life. Starlit patterns danced across the floor, swirling into a massive cosmic labyrinth, its walls stretching endlessly into the sky. The labyrinth was alive with the energy of the stars, its pathways shifting and twisting, never remaining the same for more than a moment.

A single glowing thread of Light appeared at their feet, binding them together in a radiant, ethereal bond. The thread connected each group member, its Light pulsing in rhythm with their heartbeats. Should the thread break, the trial would end in failure. This was the ultimate test of their unity and trust.

Aqua's Role

Aqua stepped forward first as the natural leader, his eyes scanning the ever-shifting maze before them. He could feel the weight of the thread tethering them, a reminder that every movement he made would affect the others. He needed to trust them as much as they trusted him.

Aqua: (his voice steady but thoughtful)

"I'll guide us through, but we must move as one. We've always worked together. This will be no different."

The group nodded, determination shining in their eyes. Aqua took the first step, the thread glowing brighter as they all moved forward in unison.

Capri's Insight

Ever attuned to the subtle shifts in energy, Capri felt the labyrinth's movements before they became visible. The very air around them vibrated with the pulse of cosmic power, and Capri could sense where the labyrinth would twist and turn next.

Capri: (her voice a calm, guiding force)

"The path ahead is changing... Shift left. We need to move quickly before it closes."

The group adjusted their steps, following her guidance. The thread of Light connecting them pulsed in response, growing stronger with each synchronized movement.

Zephyr's Role

Suddenly, a powerful gust of wind surged through the labyrinth, threatening to knock the group off balance. The cosmic winds howled, swirling around them with a force that could easily tear them apart.

Zephyr: (gritting his teeth, focusing his energy)

"I've got the winds! Just stay together—I'll keep them in check!"

With a wave of his hand, Zephyr called upon his control of the winds, calming the tempestuous forces that threatened to disrupt their progress. The windstorm subsided, allowing the group to continue forward.

Luna and Aetherion's Contributions

Luna's connection to the stars allowed her to map out hidden paths within the labyrinth. Her eyes, glowing faintly with starlight, scanned the maze ahead, searching for the safest route forward.

Luna: (her voice bright with discovery)

"There's a path just ahead—follow the Light I'm casting. It's faint, but it's there."

She projected beams of starlight onto the shifting walls, revealing a hidden passage. The group followed her lead, moving quickly before the labyrinth could change again.

Aetherion, ever the strategist, observed the flow of time and space around them. He could sense the labyrinth's movements, almost as if it operated on a cosmic clock that only he could read.

Aetherion: (calmly, his mind calculating the next shift)

"The labyrinth follows the stars. It's about to shift again. We need to move now—before the path closes."

His strategic insight allowed them to anticipate the movements of the labyrinth and avoid paths that would lead them into danger.

Galeonix's Strength

As the group pressed forward, the labyrinth walls began to close around them. The cosmic energy surged, threatening to trap them within the twisting corridors. Galeonix, her muscles straining, stepped forward and braced herself against the closing walls.

Galeonix: (her voice a growl of effort)

"Go! I'll hold the walls back—just keep moving!"

Her unmatched strength in battle kept the walls at bay long enough for the group to pass. She dug her heels into the shifting ground, her determination unwavering as she forced the cosmic forces to yield.

The Group Passes the Trial

Step by step, the group navigated the labyrinth, their movements perfectly synchronized. The glowing thread of Light that bound them together pulsed brighter with each successful maneuver. The labyrinth, though treacherous, could not overcome their unity.

After what felt like an eternity, the labyrinth began to fade. The shifting walls dissolved into stardust, and the path ahead cleared. The cosmic altar stood before them once more, and above it hovered the key, glowing with celestial Light.

The Guardians, silent until now, stepped forward once more. Their forms still shifted between Light and shadow, but there was a new reverence in their presence.

Guardian: (its voice deep and reverberating)

"You have proven yourselves worthy. The bond between you is unbreakable. The key is yours."

The key descended slowly, its glow illuminating the faces of Aqua, Capri, and their companions. Aqua reached out, his hand trembling slightly as he grasped the key, feeling its ancient power flow through him.

Aqua: (his voice filled with awe)

"We did it... together."

Capri: (her voice soft, yet filled with pride)

"The Pendant will unlock its power now. But what we've unlocked within ourselves is far greater."

9.4 The Light of Hope

The Heart of the Citadel shimmered with an ethereal glow as its crystalline walls refracted beams of Light, seeming alive, pulsating with energy. With the Starlight Pendant and the key in their possession, Aqua, Capri, and their companions stood on the precipice of unlocking its full potential. As they prepared to face the growing darkness of the Void, they realized that the true strength they carried was not just in the Pendant but in the bond they had forged through trust and unity.

The Starlight Pendant, a symbol of hope and the last defense against the encroaching Void seemed as if the Citadel itself was waiting for the moment when the Pendant's dormant power would be unlocked. Its radiant Light bathed the chamber, yet it held back its true brilliance—its full potential locked away, awaiting the right moment, the right key. Surrounding them was the weight of expectation, the burden of knowing they were standing on the precipice of something far greater than themselves.

Despite their proximity to the Pendant, one final obstacle remained. To awaken its true power, they needed not only the key but also mastery of an ancient spell—one that had been protected for centuries, known only to those deemed worthy.

The group exchanged uneasy glances, their unity a powerful force in the face of what lay ahead. Each trial they had faced before had pushed them to their limits, and now, so close to victory, the air felt thick with tension. Their journey, filled with dangers and triumphs, had prepared them for this moment, but doubts lingered in the back of their minds.

Then, the final Guardian appeared once more before them, its presence commanding and ancient. It was a figure of pure cosmic energy, shifting like a living constellation as if it embodied the very stars themselves. Its form was a swirling mass of light and shadow, its features constantly shifting and changing. The Guardian's Light fluctuated between brilliance and shadow, and its voice, when it spoke, echoed with the hum of the universe.

Final Guardian:

(its voice deep and resonant, vibrating through the room)

"You carry the Starlight Pendant, but its power remains sealed. The key is within your grasp, yet to open the keyhole, you must prove yourselves worthy. The ancient spell lies within your hearts, but it must be unlocked through the strength of your unity and the purity of your purpose."

The Guardian's gaze seemed to pierce through them, looking not at their faces but into their very souls.

Final Guardian:

"Will you accept this challenge and face the final trial? Only then will the keyhole be revealed and the Pendant's power unleashed."

A stillness fell over the room as the group, united in their purpose, stood in quiet contemplation. Aqua and Capri stepped forward, their hands clasped together. They could feel the weight of the other's eyes on them, but they also knew they were not alone in this trial.

Capri:

(her voice calm, though a flicker of uncertainty crossed her features)

"We accept. Whatever challenge lies ahead, we are ready to face it together. We will prove ourselves worthy of the Pendant's power."

Aqua:

(nodding, his eyes unwavering)

"The Void grows stronger with every moment. This Pendant may be our only hope to restore balance. We won't turn back now."

Aqua's voice was unwavering, filled with determination, inspiring his companions and readers alike. The final Guardian's Light flared brightly, illuminating every corner of the chamber as though the stars themselves were watching their next move. The air crackled with energy, and the hum of the Pendant grew louder, resonating with the Guardian's Light. Suddenly, the atmosphere shifted.

The Trial

Without warning, the walls of the Citadel began to shimmer and change. The crystalline walls bent and refracted, transforming into endless mirrors that reflected the group's every movement. The reflections were not true—they were distorted, twisted images, exaggerated versions of their fears, doubts, and failures. The mirrors pulsed with an eerie light, and the reflections began to shift and move on their own.

Final Guardian:

(its voice booming, now sounding more distant as it faded into the shimmering Light)

"This is a trial not of strength but of belief. To unlock the keyhole, you must confront the deepest fears within your heart. Only those who hold onto hope will be able to master the spell."

The room became a maze of mirrors, each one reflecting a different fear. Aqua's gaze was immediately drawn to a reflection of himself—his body cloaked in shadows, his eyes hollow and filled with despair. He watched as his reflection fell into darkness, failing to protect his loved ones, his kingdom crumbling beneath the weight of his failures.

Aqua:

(whispering to himself, his voice filled with shock)

"Is this... what will happen? Is this the future that awaits me?"

Beside him, Capri stared into a mirror that showed her standing in a desolate world, her powers drained, unable to prevent the fall of Aquaterra. In the reflection, she was alone—isolated in a universe where the stars had all gone dark.

Capri:

(her voice trembling, the weight of the vision pressing down on her)

"No... it can't end like this. I... I won't fail..."

Her hands shook as she reached toward the mirror, the fear growing inside her.

Aqua:

(stepping closer to her, his voice firm and steady)

"Capri, look at me. These are illusions—meant to weaken us. This isn't the future. The Pendant's power is built on hope and unity. We've faced worse and come through together. Don't let this break you."

Capri closed her eyes, letting his words ground her. Taking a deep breath, she raised her hand, calling on her Light. A radiant wave burst from her fingertips, crashing into the mirror. The false vision shattered into a thousand fragments, each piece dissolving into stardust.

As the mirror broke, a faint, glowing symbol appeared in its place—the first fragment of the ancient spell they needed to unlock the keyhole.

Facing Their Fears

Each of their companions faced their own mirrors, reflections filled with despair, regret, and overwhelming loss. But one by one, they broke through their fears. Aqua, standing before his own reflection of failure, clenched his fists and stepped forward, a symbol of resilience and determination.

Aqua:

(his voice filled with determination)

"No. This is not my destiny."

With a powerful sweep of his hand, he unleashed a surge of energy, shattering his mirror into pieces. As the glass broke, another fragment of the spell materialized, glowing brightly and joining the first.

The others followed suit. Each of them, guided by Aqua and Capri's unwavering belief, broke through their illusions, destroying the reflections that sought to undermine their resolve. With every shattered mirror, more fragments of the spell appeared, floating in the air like stardust, waiting to be spoken.

Learning the Spell

Finally, the last mirror fell. The ancient symbols of the spell now hovered before them, forming a complete incantation and glowing faintly with celestial energy. The Guardian, now reduced to a faint outline of starlight, reappeared in the center of the room, its light softer and more reverent.

Final Guardian:

(its voice echoing, filled with awe)

"You have faced the darkness within, and hope still burns in your hearts. Now, speak the spell, and the keyhole will be revealed."

Aqua and Capri stood at the center, the group gathering around them in a circle. As one, they began to recite the spell, the words flowing from their mouths like a song carried by the stars themselves. The ancient language felt familiar as if it had always been inside them, waiting for this moment.

"Orravelle luminara, stellae cordis spirara—

Kaelion veritas, e'ravun estelanar—

Virellum thalorien, pax infinita—"

As they spoke, the Pendant began to shift. The glow intensified, and a small keyhole appeared in its center, radiating a faint Light that beckoned for the key.

Unlocking the Keyhole

The key, now shimmering in Aqua's hand, vibrated with a soft hum, responding to the Pendant's call. Together, Aqua and Capri stepped forward, their hearts racing with the knowledge that they were about to unlock the power that could save their realm. With steady hands, they guided the key into the keyhole.

The moment the key touched the Pendant, a blinding Light exploded from its core, filling the entire chamber with radiant energy. The Light pulsed, growing stronger with each beat, until it felt as though the very stars were being born anew in that chamber.

The power of the Pendant coursed through them, filling each group member with warmth, hope, and the realization that they had passed the final trial. The Pendant's power was theirs, but it was not a weapon—it was a force of balance, a Light that would push back the darkness of the Void.

As the Light settled, Aqua and Capri stood at the center, the Pendant glowing brightly between them. They felt its immense power, but more importantly, they understood the responsibility it carried. This power wasn't just for them—it was for all who believed in hope, for all who stood against the growing darkness.

Capri:(her voice quiet, yet filled with renewed determination)

"We've passed this trial... but the final battle is still ahead."

Aqua:

(placing a hand on her shoulder, his voice calm and resolute)

"Together, we'll face whatever comes. And with the Light of the Pendant, we will prevail."

The group stood united, the Light of the Starlight Pendant glowing brightly in their hands. Their journey had been long, and their trials many, but now they were ready. The final battle against the Void was near, and they had the power to fight back.

CHAPTER

10

ALLIANCES OF THE ANCIENTS

VICTORY IS BORN NOT FROM MIGHT, BUT FROM UNITY OF HEART.

 # CHAPTER 10

 △ **MAXIMUS, THE ETERNAL QUILL**
AQUARII: XARNOR XAL VINTHAE.
OPENING WHISPER – CH. 10

 △ **VALDUM, THE CELESTIAL ARCHITECT**
AQUARII: VINTHAE XAL EIRANOR.
CLOSING WHISPER – CH. 10

10.1 The Elemental Pact

After awakening the full brilliance of the Starlight Pendant within the Heart of the Celestial Citadel, Aqua, Capri, and their closest companions stood at the edge of the Nebulae, where light itself bowed before ancient paths unseen by mortal eyes. Around them, cosmic winds stirred with unspoken purpose. The Pendant pulsed softly at Capri's chest, resonating with energies now unlocked — a beacon and a burden.

"We're no longer just protecting AquaCapri,"Capri whispered."We're protecting all that lives and breathes beneath the stars."

Aqua nodded, his voice steady."But we cannot stand alone. We need the First Forces."

Their gazes turned skyward as a great vortex shimmered into existence — a spiral of starlight and elemental essence swirling in silence. This was the threshold to the Elemental Realms, where the Primordial Lords kept their vigil.

As the group stepped forward, time bent and space folded. They crossed not into a place but into a balance — the ancient architecture of the cosmos.

The Realm of Earth – Trial of Endurance

They emerged in darkness, heavy and deep. All sound faded into silence. The Realm of Earth had no sun — it breathed through pressure, heat, and ancient stillness. Towering mountains loomed under a copper sky. The ground vibrated subtly beneath their feet as if listening.

A low rumble cracked the stillness. Without warning, the mountains began to shift — the valley they stood in trembled violently. Great stone pillars erupted from the ground, closing them in. A circle of stone. A test.

Zephyr drew his blade instinctively."We're being watched."

"No,"said Aqua."We're being weighed."

The ground convulsed, splitting beneath their feet. Massive slabs tilted, creating a shifting maze of sheer stone walls. Dust and gravel cascaded around them as the land reshaped with deliberate power.

Capri held onto a rock face, her voice calm but firm."This is no attack. It's a message."

Then, the quake paused. From within the stone rose a colossal figure — vast, unmoving at first — as if the mountain itself had grown limbs. Terranox, Lord of Earth, formed from bedrock and iron-veined soil towering over them. His molten eyes burned slowly, like embers trapped in stone.

Terranox:"The Void crumbles what was built with patience. Yet you come seeking to build anew. Can you withstand the weight of the ages?"

Aqua stepped forward, breathing through the dust, eyes locked with the ancient gaze."We do not seek shortcuts. Only to anchor what is slipping."

Terranox lifted his stone arm, and from the cracked earth beneath Aqua's feet, the path collapsed into a pit. Aqua plummeted downward — no scream, no resistance — only focus. He braced and slammed against the walls, controlling his descent.

At the base of the chasm, he stood alone.

Terranox:"Strength is not in the strike. It is in the stand. Rise through what buries you."

Above, Capri watched as the earth walls began to shift again, sealing Aqua below.

She called down."You are not alone in this. You never have been."

Her voice echoed through the stone.

Then the ground shook again — a controlled tremor. From within, Aqua began to ascend, not by force, but by harmony — following the rhythm of the Earth itself. Stone ledge by stone ledge, the path reshaped, responding to his resolve.

When he reached the surface, Terranox extended a massive hand. Upon it lay the Earthshaper Hammer — veins of silver threading through its deep black surface.

Terranox:"Endurance earns power. But remember: for every wall you build, something must crumble."

Aqua accepted the artifact, its weight monumental — yet balanced. His gaze found Capri's, and through it, he knew that Earth had accepted them.

Capri whispered,"One realm. One bond strengthened."

The Realm of Water – Trial of Surrender

The vortex closed behind them as the ground dissolved beneath their feet. They emerged on the edge of a vast ocean, where the sea stretched endlessly in all directions, dotted with floating islands of crystal, coral, and mist. The water glowed from beneath, shifting between deep blue, silver, and violet.

The air was soft here. Quiet. Yet beneath the peaceful surface, something vast stirred — old and watching.

Zephyr inhaled deeply, brushing his hand across a ribbon of sea mist."This place listens. But it doesn't trust."

Capri stepped forward, her voice barely above the sound of lapping waves."It knows the truth of all things. Water remembers."

A sudden wave surged toward them — not violent, but deliberate. It formed a wide circle around their small island, trapping them within. Then, rising from the ocean like a column of liquid moonlight, emerged Aqualora, Lady of Water. Her body flowed with grace, her face ever-changing — both young and ancient, calm and storm.

Aqualora:"You carry the Starlight, and yet you fear the deep. Why have you come, hearts full of fire, into my silence?"

Capri stepped into the shallow tide that brushed the coral shore."Because we must learn to surrender. Not to give up — but to let go."

Aqualora's eyes darkened. The sea surged again, forming three mirrored figures out of salt and shadow — copies of Aqua, Capri, and Zephyr. The reflections stared back at them, emotionless and cold.

Aqualora:"What do you see when you confront yourselves?"

The copies raised their hands in unison. Torrents of water surged toward them.

Rather than fight, Capri lowered her weapon. She breathed with the tides. Her reflection melted away. Aqua and Zephyr followed — surrendering not to defeat but to understanding.

The tide calmed.

From the ocean rose a pedestal of shell and light. Upon it rested the Tidecaller Trident, humming with the pulse of moon-pulled tides.

Capri stepped forward and took it. The trident trembled slightly in her hands, then settled.

Aqualora:"Tides, once raised, may drown even those you love."

Capri held the weapon close."We'll hold to each other — and rise together."

The ocean parted, revealing a path of glowing water leading onward.

The Realm of Fire – Trial of Control

They rose into a sky heavy with red light, stepping into a land of molten rivers and smoldering stones. The air shimmered with heat. Fire ruled here — wild, alive, barely contained.

From the heart of a volcano, a figure formed — Pyronis, Lord of Fire, all flame and iron and fierce intent.

Pyronis:"You seek fire's blessing? Fire is earned, not given. Control it — or be consumed."

The ground split. Flames surged around Aqua, Capri, and Zephyr, separating them. Each faced a burning mirror of themselves — furious, impatient, chaotic.

Aqua did not strike. He stood still, anchoring his will. Capri closed her eyes, embracing the fire without letting it rule her heart.

The flames recognized their control — not conquest. They faded.

Pyronis approached, drawing from the heart of the volcano the Solarflame Blade, pulsing with the fury of stars.

Pyronis:"Fire creates as it destroys. Will you wield it for vengeance — or for renewal?"

Aqua grasped the blade."For renewal."

The volcano's rumbling dimmed, and the horizon brightened.

The Realm of Air – Trial of Clarity

They ascended into the open sky — a realm of floating islands, mist bridges, and endless blue. The winds whispered secrets from every direction.

Zephyr laughed into the gusts."Now, this is a dance worth joining."

From a swirling gale appeared Zephra, Lady of Air, her form translucent, her eyes sharp.

Zephra:"Wind reveals the truth. What will you see when the world turns upside down?"

The islands broke apart. Winds ripped through the sky, isolating them.

Capri stood still on her drifting isle, letting the storm scream around her. She listened deeper — past fear, past noise — into stillness.

The Windstrider Bow appeared before her, woven of stardust and song.

She accepted it with calm hands.

Zephra's voice was the last whisper before the winds stilled:

Zephra:"Freedom, tempered by wisdom, saves worlds."

The skies opened, and a path of light led home.

Return to Aquaterra

Bearing hammer, trident, blade, and bow, the heroes stepped into the currents of the cosmos once more. But they were not the same. Each realm had changed them — tempered them — made them more than warriors.

As Aquaterra's twin suns rose on the horizon, their homecoming was not just a return.

It was a rising tide of hope.

The Power of Unity would awaken soon.

10.2 The Power of Unity

The Crystal Garden rose like a celestial marvel atop the highest peak of Aquaterra, where sky and earth embraced in a union that felt eternal. Its crystalline pillars reached toward the heavens, refracting starlight into a living kaleidoscope of color. Each structure hummed with ancient resonance, alive with the memories of countless generations. Beneath it, the ground pulsed as though the very Essence of the cosmos flowed below—binding the realms to the infinite beyond.

Above, the stars shimmered, not as distant observers but as sentinels, aware of the ceremony poised to unfold.

The Pact of Protection, once sworn in the mortal halls of Aquaterra, had led to this moment. Yet this was no mere repetition. It was a sacred ascension. Beneath the gaze of the stars, the promise of unity would be fulfilled—not in word, nor war, but in Light.

At the heart of the garden stood an altar, carved from a single slab of glowing, ethereal stone. It emitted a soft radiance, its edges blurred, as if formed not of stone, but woven from the threads of starlight. Around this sacred center, the leaders of the allied realms gathered in solemn unity. Their faces reflected a blend of pride and humility, each soul quieted by the weight of what was to be invoked. They came not merely as rulers, but as guardians—bound by the shared burden of survival. Their unity, forged in battle and anchored in hope, was about to be sealed in the eternal struggle against the encroaching darkness of the Void.

Among the gathered figures stood the finest guardians, sages, and warriors the realms had ever known. At the head stood Solarion, radiant in his armor, his presence exuding the quiet authority of AquaCapri's champion. Beside him, Celestine the Star Weaver wore a robe of spinning constellations, her fingers trailing cosmic thread even in stillness. Auroria, the Harmony Keeper, smiled with serene grace— her voice ready to soothe should even joy grow too vast to bear.

The mighty Valorus, the Shield of Valor and Supreme Protector of the constellations stood like a living monument, his steady gaze scanning the horizon out of habit rather than need. Zyrion, the Gale Knight, with his wind-swept hair and eyes like stormlit skies, exchanged light banter with Solis, Elder of AquaCapri and the Original Sun's Flame, whose laugh warmed the very air around them.

Nyx, Guardian of the Night and Dreams, stood cloaked in midnight hues beside Chronia, the Mystic of Time, whose timeless eyes watched moments pass with reverence. Gaian, Earth Warden, leaned on his staff carved from the roots of the first tree, listening quietly as the conversation ebbed and flowed around him.

Luna, Guardian of the Moon and Secrets, stood beside her daughter, Lunara, the Moon Priestess, both cloaked in gentle silver light. Zephyr, the Wielder of Winds and Change, laughed with Auroran, Knight of Dawn, whose aura always seemed to herald morning even in the deepest night. Aether, the Realm Historian, recited brief verses of ancient epics with Astralis, the Seer of Stars, and Thalor, Architect of the Stars, who quietly etched symbols of celebration into the garden stones.

Near the reflective pool of harmony, Aetherion, reborn Guardian of the Celestial Conflux, stood wreathed in radiant energy, his form flickering like a living constellation. He had once been broken, lost to the Void, yet stood now as a symbol of rebirth. At his side was Sylphara, whose laughter rose like wind-chimes in sunlight, and Liora, Healer of the Dawn, who embraced each returning hero with a touch that shimmered with quiet Light.

Thalassa, Guardian of the Oceans, offered chalices of celestial nectar as guests raised their cups in joy. Celestia, Elder of the Constellations and Mystic of Stars stood beside Luminarion, Master of Light, their presence anchoring the evening in wisdom and radiance. Pyronix, the ever-fiery Master of Flames, shared exaggerated tales of narrow escapes, sparking laughter as Aqualith, the stoic Guardian of Water, patiently corrected him with a smile and a sigh.

Orion, Sage of Starlight, simply listened, his silence carrying the weight of aeons.

And at the heart of them all—Aqua and Capri. Clad not in royal regalia but in humble traveler's robes, they radiated peace, unity, and quiet triumph. When they entered the Crystal Garden, conversation paused, and the entire assembly stood as one.

No speech was required. The clasp of their hands, the serenity in their gazes, and the warm embrace they exchanged with each friend told stories more powerful than words.

It was Solarion who broke the silence first.

Solarion: (smiling)"You return not just with hope, but with Light itself. I see it in your eyes. Welcome home."

Capri: (grateful)"We carried all of you with us. Every breath, every trial... was made easier by your belief in us."

Aqua:"And we return with stories—some terrible, some miraculous—but all shaped by love. Tonight, we rest. Tonight, we rejoice."

Laughter followed. Pyronix was the first to demand the retelling of the sky serpent's downfall in the Nebulae.

Pyronix:"You can't just return and not tell me how you tamed a storm beast the size of a mountain! Was it a spell? A trick? Or did you feed it Aetherion's cooking again?"

Aetherion: (mock indignation)"Careful, flame-breather. My dishes are interstellar delicacies. Even the beast bowed to their power."

Liora: (giggling)"That's not what it looked like. It fled. From both the battle... and the stew."

The garden burst into laughter.

Moments passed like falling stardust—glimmering, brief, precious. Tales were shared, arms were raised in victory, and melodies were played from instruments strung with starlight. Capri danced once with Luna and once with Thalassa. Aqua sparred playfully with Zephyr and bowed deeply to Solis. Nyx gifted dreams in the form of luminous petals, while Chronia marked the evening's time in her cosmic journal, calling it"a moment untouched by fear."

As the night deepened, Luminarion approached Aqua.

Luminarion:"The pendant... is it what we hoped?"

Aqua: (softly)"It is. But it is also more than power. It is memory, unity... love distilled into Light."

Celestia: (nodding)"And love, when shared freely, becomes eternal."

The music slowed, the laughter softened, and the leaders found themselves gazing up at the stars. A new constellation shimmered above them—not born of ritual or command but seemingly formed by the stars themselves to mark this rare reunion.

The night was still. No alarms, no shadows, no threats. Just unity, peace, and Light.

The Next Morning: In the Heart of Aquaterra

Morning light cascaded through the crystal arches of Aquaterra's Radiant Forum, bathing the city in golden calm. The central plaza overflowed with citizens—elders wrapped in memory, children wide-eyed with wonder, and warriors standing in quiet formation. The news of Aqua and Capri's return had traveled like a heartbeat through the realms. And now, their people gathered—not in fear, but in hope.

High above the crowd, a wide balcony of woven starstone extended over the city square. Upon it stood the leaders of AquaCapri, their silhouettes gleaming against the rising sun. At the center stood Aqua and Capri, their hands entwined. Though their garments were simple, their presence illuminated the space more than any crown or robe.

Aqua stepped forward first, his voice calm and expansive.

Aqua:"People of Aquaterra... you have waited. You have endured. And now we return—not with promises, but with proof. Beyond the Nebulae, in the sacred convergence of the Elemental Realms, we were tested—body, spirit, and soul. The journey stripped us of illusion, but it gave us something greater: understanding and the unshakable truth that we are not alone."

He raised the Starlight Pendant, and a surge of Light swept across the plaza. It shimmered like a drop of infinity itself, humming with a power both ancient and alive.

Capri stepped beside him, her voice crystalline and radiant.

Capri:"The Pendant was only the beginning. In each Elemental Realm, we were challenged—not merely with trials of strength, but with reflections of ourselves. The Elemental Lords gave us more than weapons. They gave us wisdom, earned in trust. Let us show you what their faith in us looks like."

With a quiet gesture, four ethereal platforms rose behind them, each bearing an artifact wrapped in elemental Light. As they emerged, Aqua, Capri, and their companions stepped forward—each chosen to speak, each voice carrying memories.

Zephyr:"In the Sky Realm of Zephra, Lady of Air, the winds were not ours to command. We had to listen—truly listen—to the breath of the world. Only then did she offer us this: the Windstrider Bow, carved from the highest gust, strung with silence. It finds only that which resists harmony... and passes by all else."

Aqualith:"Aqualora, Lady of Water, tested not our power—but our stillness. Her realm, both gentle and crushing, taught us that strength flows from patience. From her hands came the Tidecaller Trident—not to command the seas, but to call upon their memory, to heal, to defend, to endure."

Pyronix:"In the searing core of Pyronis's domain, we faced fire not as destruction but as purification. It burned our doubts and forged our resolve. From those embers rose the Solarflame Blade, a sword that remembers the Light of the first sun. It burns only for the truth."

Gaian:"And in the earthen silence of Terranox, Lord of Earth, we were brought low—not to humble us, but to teach us how to rise. The mountain does not speak... but it watches. And when it judged us worthy, it gave us the Earthshaper Hammer—a tool to build, to shield, to awaken the foundations of worlds."

Aetherion:"I once fell to the Void. I remember the silence that devours. But in the heart of the Elemental Realms, I was remade—not in power, but in purpose. These relics are not symbols of dominance. They are promises—promises that we are not forsaken."

Liora:"These are not legends. They are your legacy. The Realms gave us these gifts because they believe in what AquaCapri still stands for—compassion, balance, unity."

Solarion:"You have stood against storms without answers. Now, stand with us in calm and courage. We have the strength. We have the tools. And now, we have the Light."

Capri:"You've given so much... your faith, your resilience, your dreams. Now we give you this: our vow. That we will protect that which binds us all—not just with swords or shields, but with love that no shadow can unmake."

Aqua:"The journey was long, but we did not return empty. We returned as one. And we will rise... as one."

The plaza erupted—not in wild noise, but in something greater: a harmony of voices, a thousand heartbeats thudding in sync. Crystalline chimes rang overhead. The wind stirred. Petals shaped like stars fell from Luna and Lunara's hands. The sun broke fully through the clouds.

Above, new constellations formed, whispering of a future rekindled. And far below, in every corner of the radiant city, hope unfurled its wings once more.

10.3 The Path Ahead

"After the unity forged beneath the stars and the constellation born above the Temple of Stars, Aqua and Capri stepped once more into the quiet sanctum of the Celestial Courtyard."

Nightfall descended over Aquaterra like a velvet shroud woven with ancient stardust. The celestial dome above burned brighter than usual as if the stars themselves watched in reverent silence. Though the echoes of celebration still shimmered in the air—the triumph, the reunion, the feast of unity—beneath it all lay an unspoken truth: the Light had returned... but the Darkness had not retreated.

Within the Celestial Courtyard, where silver vines coiled around marble pillars and crystalline fountains sang songs older than time, Aqua and Capri stood at the heart of a quiet circle. Around them gathered the champions who had risen in defiance of the Void—Zephyr, Pyronix, Aqualith, Orion, and others whose hearts now beat with renewed purpose.

The Starlight Pendant, nestled against Aqua's armor, pulsed with a quiet, conscious rhythm—as though it, too, felt the weight of what was to come. Its Light, no longer dormant but alive with the power of the Elemental Realms, cast a pale glow across the stone floor, mirroring the unity of those who had reclaimed it.

Capri's eyes scanned the horizon, where the sea met the sky in an eternal embrace."We've rekindled hope,"she murmured, her voice as gentle as moonlight upon water."The people believe again. But belief must be guarded, nourished. What we face now is deeper than shadow—it is doubt, corrosion of will, a darkness that seeps rather than strikes."

Zephyr's brow furrowed as he stepped forward."The Void learns. It adapts. Each time we rise, it shifts its form, its strategy. We cannot face it as we did before. This is no longer a battle of strength—it is a war of truth, perception, and trust."

Pyronix, ever ablaze with passion, spoke next. The fire along his shoulders flared subtly, echoing his inner flame."We cannot wait for the Void to decide the time and place of our undoing. It coils in silence, hidden within whispers and doubt. If we hesitate, even for a breath, its darkness will thread itself through the hearts of those we swore to protect."

He looked at the pendant, its Light reflected in his flame-lined eyes."Let our resolve burn hotter than their silence. Let the fire of purpose shape our path—not in vengeance, but in vigilance. We must ignite every realm with the clarity of our mission. Not every battle is fought with weapons. Some must be won with vision."

Aqualith, whose presence stilled even the most turbulent soul, placed a hand upon the fountain beside him, sending gentle ripples outward. His voice was steady as the tides."And yet fire alone cannot hold the night. Harmony must guide our hand. Even the strongest flood may drown what it seeks to protect. Power must be tempered with wisdom... with restraint."

A hush settled over the circle until Orion broke it. His cloak spun from constellations and shimmered as he stepped from the shadows of a marble archway."Beyond the outer constellations, there is a silence where once there was a song. The stars we once navigated by no longer respond. Something has silenced them—not conquered them, but emptied them."

All eyes turned toward him.

"This is no longer merely an invasion—it is a hollowing. The Void consumes essence, not just space. It seeks to unravel identity, to make us forget who we are, why we shine."

Aqua looked around the courtyard. He saw warriors of flame, water, air, and stars—each bearing wounds not visible yet deeper than flesh."The Elemental Realms gave us more than relics,"he said quietly, lifting the Earthshaper Hammer in his hand."They gave us remembrance. The Tidecaller Trident, the Solarflame Blade, and the Windstrider Bow—each is a testament to what endures when the Light is nearly extinguished."

He lowered the hammer and stepped closer to Capri."But these artifacts are not enough. What will save us is what cannot be forged—our unity, our conviction, our willingness to stand even when afraid."

Capri's voice followed his, sure and serene."The Void's deadliest weapon is not destruction—it is isolation. Division. Doubt. It turns light inward until it forgets how to shine. That is why we must speak as one voice and move as one breath. Every star, every soul must feel that they are not alone."

General Valorus, commander of the Stardust Warriors, entered with slow, deliberate steps, his armor echoing with cosmic resonance."Then we must fortify not only our walls but our hearts,"he declared."The veils must be reinforced. The beacons rekindled. The Guardians awakened. The defenses of AquaCapri will be more than shields—they will be symbols."

From the spires above, the bells of the Luminary Citadel began to toll—low, resonant, prophetic. A signal that the next phase had begun.

Chronia, the Seer of Time, arrived in a shimmering haze, her presence folding seamlessly into the moment."Yet even now,"she said,"a final thread remains unwoven. I've peered beyond the edge of what is seen. The greatest threat does not come from the dark... but from within the Light. A fracture—hidden, growing."

Aqua met her gaze."Then we must look inward as we look forward."

"And prepare,"added Capri, placing her hand over the Starlight Pendant."Not just for war, but for the truths it will reveal. Let this Light guide us—through darkness, through deception. May it reveal not only the path but the purpose."

The warriors, mystics, and guardians around them bowed their heads. No command had been given—only clarity.

Then, from the stars, a wind descended. Gentle, eternal. Not of weather, but of fate.

"The path ahead is veiled in shadow,

But fear shall not define you.

Walk it not as warriors alone,

But as bearers of the dawn."

As morning's silver crest edged the eastern sky, the circle dissolved in solemn purpose. Each would go forth—some to ready armies, others to commune with constellations, some to seek out the fractures within.

But they walked away changed, no longer separated by realms or titles.

They were, at last, one force. One Light.

One voice rising to meet the looming dark.

CHAPTER

II

THE LOOMING DARKNESS

THE STORM IS NOT THE END—IT IS THE BEGINNING OF RENEWAL.

CHAPTER II

△ VALDUM, THE CELESTIAL ARCHITECT
AQUARII: KAERINTH XAL MAELORIN.

 OPENING WHISPER – CH. II

△ MAXIMUS, THE ETERNAL QUILL
AQUARII: SERYON VE'MARION.

CLOSING WHISPER – CH. II

11.1 The Return of the Void

The Outlands. Even the name pulsed with ancient dread, echoing with the solemn toll of forgotten ruin. Once a realm of vibrant wilderness on the farthest edge of Aquaterra, it now stood desecrated —its soul torn open by the creeping tendrils of the Void. Twisted, hollowed, and stripped of life, it served as a silent harbinger of the doom threatening to consume all.

Even Aqua and Capri, accompanied by their elite scouts—warriors of legendary renown—appeared dwarfed by the sheer magnitude of desolation that stretched before them.

The ground cracked beneath their feet like brittle bone, long drained of vitality. Each step crumbled remnants of a world that once pulsed with starlight. The Outlands, once basking under Aquaterra's radiant constellations, now lay cloaked in shadow, a wasteland drained of Essence—the very force that breathed life into creation.

The air stank of rot and cosmic decay. It clung to every breeze as if the breath of the world itself was poisoned. Overhead, the skies convulsed —a tempest of black and violet clouds roiling endlessly, pierced by jagged arcs of green lightning. These unnatural flashes briefly lit the silhouettes of dead trees—skeletal, contorted, their limbs raised in eternal agony as if pleading for salvation that would never arrive.

Aqua pressed forward, his eyes once bright with hope now shadowed by grim purpose. His hand rested on the hilt of his stardust blade, its light faint yet unwavering—a pulse of hope from a thousand stars. But here, on the fringes where even the stars were fading, that hope felt paper-thin.

His voice cut through the oppressive silence, low and somber.

Aqua:"This land... it's already surrendered to the Void. If we don't stop this, it won't just be the edge that falls—Aquaterra will follow."

Beside him, Capri moved with measured grace though the land's despair seeped deep into her being. Her staff, normally thrumming with the vibrant pulse of time's current, now whispered only faint echoes as though even time recoiled from this place.

She gazed skyward, where each flicker of lightning revealed the crumbling bones of a world unraveling.

Capri:"It's feeding—on the Essence itself. The Void isn't just killing the land... it's consuming its soul. Just as Orion warned. The stars at the edge—drained. If we wait, Aquaterra could face the same fate."

Their eyes met. No words needed to pass between them. The weight of that truth was enough.

Behind them, even the battle-hardened scouts hesitated. Something unseen pressed down on the group—a darkness not of shadow but of despair. The Void wasn't merely a force. It was a presence, ancient and insidious, eroding resolve and unraveling the threads of existence itself.

Then, ahead—movement.

The ground shimmered with a sickly, pulsing glow. Thick, black ichor bubbled from beneath the soil like a living wound, seeping upward in slow, deliberate spirals. Dark energy bled into the air, heavy as tar. Every breath became an effort, every heartbeat, a fight.

The warriors raised their weapons, senses honed, but spirits dulled.

From the veil of gloom, they came—phantoms woven from nightmare.

The Shadow Wraiths emerged without sound, gliding from the swirling fog like whispers made flesh. Ethereal forms, formless yet menacing, barely discernible save for the eerie violet glow pulsing within their hollow eyes. They moved with unsettling grace, neither bound by gravity nor flesh, as though they were echoes of something lost—something cursed.

Where they passed, the land decayed further still. Cracked soil crumbled to dust, and the dead trees splintered into ash. Their presence drained what little vitality remained, their touch accelerating the unraveling of this place.

A young scout staggered backward, his breath catching as his gaze locked onto the approaching wraiths.

Scout (whispering, trembling):"What... what are those things?"

Before an answer could come, a voice—if it could be called that—slithered through the air, hollow and cold. It seeped into bone, bypassing flesh and thought.

Shadow Wraiths (in unison, disembodied):"The darkness will consume all... There is no escape from the Void..."

A chill swept through the party. Even the most seasoned warriors felt their resolve falter. These were no ordinary foes. They were the harbingers of unraveling.

Aqua stepped forward, jaw clenched, his hand tightening around the hilt of his blade.

Aqua:"They're not like anything we've fought before. One mistake—and they'll overrun us."

Capri raised her staff with calm precision, though her grip was firm, her expression hardened by resolve.

The wraiths surged forward.

The Battle Begins

The first glided with terrifying speed, a blur of shadow and cold. But Aqua moved faster. In a burst of radiant motion, his stardust blade swept through the air. It carved a glowing arc through the gloom, and when it struck, the wraith recoiled with an inhuman shriek, its form unraveling into ribbons of darkness before vanishing into the air.

Light had wounded it. But the victory was fleeting.

Dozens more emerged from the dark—faster, hungrier, relentless.

Each creature danced through the air like smoke laced with venom. Their movements were precise, fluid, and terrifying in their grace. They were not warriors. They were hunger made manifest.

Capri channeled the Essence of time, her staff radiating with ancient force. With a single motion, the world around the wraiths bent. Time itself slowed, distorting their rhythm. Their relentless advance wavered as though caught in a storm of molasses.

Capri:"Now, Aqua!"

He leaped into the distorted current, his blade a streak of stellar fire. Each strike tore through the Wraiths' insubstantial forms, shattering them into violet mist. Again and again, he struck—precision born of desperation. Light against darkness. Essence against Void.

But with every foe they felled, more rose in their place.

And the Void pressed closer.

The battle raged. The sky above seethed with storms of shadow, and below, the Outlands trembled with each clash of Light against Void. Yet the tide would not turn.

The Wraiths poured forth from the ruptured earth—endless, insatiable. For everyone destroyed, another emerged, drawn by the Light they sought to devour. Their violet eyes burned brighter, their voices now a chorus of torment:

Shadow Wraiths:"Surrender... The stars are fading... All will be silenced..."

The very air conspired against them. Each breath was a struggle, each movement a labor. Even Capri, with the Essence of time woven through her veins, felt herself faltering. Her staff, once light in her grip, now seemed burdened with the weight of a thousand years.

Time itself strained beneath the pressure of the Void.

Aqua's blade, though still radiant, no longer danced—it fought. His swings had slowed, his breath now ragged. The once-rhythmic hum of his attacks had become a discordant hymn of defiance. And yet, he held the line.

Capri (gasping):"They're too strong... We can't hold them off forever... We must fall back!"

Her voice trembled, not with fear, but with urgency. She could feel it —their power waning, the land itself siphoning their strength. Every second they remained, the Void fed more greedily.

Aqua turned to her, his eyes blazing with stubborn resolve. He shook his head, the flicker of his defiance unquenched.

Aqua:"Not yet. We push them back. Even if only for a breath."

But now, the Wraiths were closing in—encircling them, stealing the warmth from the air, their ghostly limbs reaching for life to extinguish.

One scout collapsed, overcome by the chill, his Essence nearly drained. Another fell to his knees, weapon slipping from numb fingers. They were breaking—unraveling in the face of the Void's might.

A Final Stand

Capri raised her staff once more, summoning all she had left. The temporal field exploded outward in a final pulse, freezing the Wraiths mid-glide. Their forms shuddered, caught in time's web—but even this would not hold long.

She turned to Aqua, desperation flickering in her eyes.

But he was already moving.

With a cry that echoed through the desolate sky, Aqua lifted his blade high. It pulsed—once, twice—then ignited with blinding radiance. The starlight within surged to life, fueled by raw will and desperation.

He brought it down with a force that fractured the air itself.

The resulting wave of Light engulfed the Wraiths in a searing explosion of brilliance. They screamed—not with pain, but with the sound of their unraveling. One by one, they scattered, vanishing into the abyss from which they came.

The Void, momentarily, was repelled.

But the price was steep.

The brilliance faded.

Ash drifted through the air like snow made of sorrow, settling upon the scorched ground. The battlefield, once pulsing with fury, now stood still—silent save for the labored breaths of the survivors.

Aqua staggered the glow of his blade dimming as it returned to rest. His knees buckled beneath him, and for a moment, he seemed ready to fall—but Capri was there. She caught him, pulling him close, her strength holding against the weight of exhaustion.

Together, they retreated to higher ground, scaling a jagged outcrop where the poisoned wind blew a fraction less cruelly. There, they collapsed side by side. Their chests rose and fell in uneven rhythm, sweat mingling with ash as their senses reeled from the ordeal.

Capri leaned against the cold stone, her voice quiet but edged with alarm.

Capri:"If this is only the beginning..."

She left the sentence unfinished. Words could not contain the dread rising in her heart.

Aqua turned to her, his voice low but steady—hardened like stone shaped by flame.

Aqua:"Then we're in more danger than we ever imagined."

Below them, the Outlands stretched on like a graveyard of the stars. The land was wounded beyond healing, and the Essence leached away. In the farthest reaches, Orion's warning now echoed louder in their minds—the stars at the edge, devoured of their light, their spirit consumed. This was no longer a theory. It was a fact.

Above, the sky churned on, the clouds circling as though the Void itself watched—and waited.

This was not simply a return.

The Void had grown. It had learned. It had fed.

And now, it had come to reclaim all that once defied it.

As Aqua and Capri sat in silence, they knew the truth was no longer avoidable. If they were to stand against the coming tide, it would require more than courage. It would demand unity across all realms, from every Guardian, every Elemental, every warrior who still held Light in their soul.

The hour of war had arrived.

And the greatest battle the universe had ever known now loomed just beyond the veil.

11.2 Shadows Against the Light

Not far from the devastation, across a threshold of ancient ley-lines and weathered starmarks, lay a sacred stretch of Aquaterra—the Plains of Serenity. Once untouched by chaos, it now stood as the final sanctuary before the storm's edge.

And here, the line had been drawn.

The Last Haven

The Plains of Serenity had once been a haven of calm, where winds whispered legends of peace and the sun-kissed rolling hills wrapped in wildflowers. But that memory had faded. Now, the air hung heavy, dense with the weight of war. The sky, once a brilliant twilight blue, had darkened unnaturally as though the land itself recoiled from the coming storm. Shadows crawled across the terrain, cast by clouds that gathered like a mourning shroud, devouring beauty with every passing moment.

At the heart of the defensive line stood Aqua, resolute. His armor—forged from pure stardust—shimmered with the fading Light, each prism refracting beams of hope as though defying the darkness inching ever closer. His gaze swept the horizon, sharp and unyielding. The moment had come.

"This battle,"he began, voice a resonant current of conviction,"will not be like those we've known. The Void does not merely destroy—it devours. It seeks to erase Light, memory, essence. But here, we stand firm. We hold the line. If we falter, if we break, all we love will be lost."

The warriors—knights, archers, mages, and mystics—shifted in their ranks. Their faces bore the scars of fear and resolve. Above them shimmered golden shields drawn from the Starlight Pendant that hung around Capri's neck. Its celestial energy, infused with the blessings of the constellations, cast a protective dome across the plains. For now, it held—but all knew its strength had limits.

Besides Aqua, Capri radiated quiet power. Temporal magic shimmered from her staff, encircling her in ethereal grace. Her presence, serene yet fierce, offered strength to all who looked upon her.

"Unity is our greatest weapon,"she declared, voice clear as crystal, resonating like the stars themselves."Together, we are unbreakable. We are the Light of Aquaterra. And as long as we stand as one, the Void shall find no victory here."

Her words kindled courage. Shoulders lifted, weapons steadied. In that moment, hope swelled brighter than fear.

Then came the first omen

A wind, sharp and unnatural, swept across the plains. It carried the sound of war drums—low, rhythmic, relentless. The earth trembled beneath their feet, a grim herald of what marched toward them. On the distant ridge, shapes emerged—twisted, wrong, their limbs moving with a sickening fluidity. Shadows clung to them like a second skin.

From within that host emerged a figure who seemed to swallow Light itself. His armor was jagged, forged in hate, and his presence exuded malice. His sword—serrated and black—drank the last golden rays of the sun, casting a voided aura that choked the field in dread.

Duskblade. General of the Void.

He lifted his blade, pointing it directly at the defenders. His voice, venomous and cold, sliced through the distance.

"Your Light flickers like a dying star," he hissed. "The Void is eternal. It will consume your realm, your hopes, and your memories. Resistance is futile. All will be devoured."

A ripple of dread passed through the ranks. Fear found its way into even the bravest hearts.

But from the center of the line, Light burst forth—defiant, radiant.

Auroran, Knight of the Dawn, strode forward. His silver armor blazed against the shadows, and his blade, Dawnbreaker, ignited with celestial fire.

"The Light of dawn always breaks the night!" Auroran's voice rang out, a beacon of defiance. "We will not yield to your corruption, Duskblade. As long as even a single ray of Light endures, darkness shall never prevail!"

A roar of approval surged through the ranks.

Aqua tightened his grip on the stardust blade, his expression carved in resolve. From the distant ridge, Duskblade's army began its descent—each step like a war drum pounding against the earth. The very soil quaked beneath their march, a slow, thunderous heartbeat of doom.

The First Clash

The silence shattered with the first cry of war.

The dark creatures surged forth—beings twisted by the Void's foul sorcery. Their forms shifted grotesquely, limbs reshaping with each movement. Their eyes burned with corrupted Light, and as they charged, the world itself seemed to retreat before them.

"For Aquaterra!" Aqua's voice thundered, and with a burst of Light, he leaped into the fray. His blade sliced the air like a comet streaking through the night. Three of the beasts fell in one stroke, disintegrating into ash before their lifeless forms struck the ground.

The defenders charged behind him, their unified force a wave of radiance crashing into the darkness.

At the center, Auroran met Duskblade in a clash of legends. Dawnbreaker struck against the void-forged blade, releasing bursts of brilliance and shadow. Each blow sent tremors across the plains, a battle of opposites: Light seeking to heal, Darkness striving to devour.

"You are nothing but sparks waiting to be snuffed out," sneered Duskblade, each word laced with venom. "The Void is inevitable. Your flame—an illusion."

Auroran parried, his strikes fluid and unwavering. "Even one spark can ignite a thousand stars. And I am far from alone."

Elsewhere, Capri danced through the battlefield. Time bent to her will as she cast weaving spells of protection and slow. The Voidspawn stumbled, their movements distorted in a temporal haze. Arrows pierced the air with precision. Swords flared with enchanted fire. Spells crackled like lightning across the battlefield.

And among the frontline defenders stood four champions, each wielding an elemental relic bestowed upon them by the ancient Lords.

Gaian, steady and unshakable, swung the Earthshaper Hammer, sending shockwaves through the enemy ranks, cracking the very ground beneath their feet. Pyronix, blazing like a living flame, unleashed torrents of fire with the Solarflame Blade, incinerating shadows mid-charge. Aqualith, guardian of tides, wielded the Tidecaller Trident, conjuring waves of crashing water that swept enemies aside. And Zephyr, swift as a storm wind, danced with the Windstrider Bow, losing arrows that split the air with sonic force, each shot guided by the breath of the skies.

Together, they carved through the Void's ranks, their relics pulsing with the raw power of the elements, standing firm beside Aqua and Capri—pillars of hope in a world on the brink.

Aqua remained at the vanguard, his stardust blade a radiant blur, cutting swaths through the horde. But even with his strength, the strain grew heavier with each moment. The magical shields overhead wavered—the Light within Capri's pendant faltering under the ceaseless onslaught.

Amidst the storm, she shouted above the din, her voice urgent and clear."Aqua! The shields are failing—we must reinforce them or fall back!"

He glanced at the flickering dome that had once pulsed with unwavering brilliance. A beat of hesitation. But then, his eyes narrowed.

"We cannot retreat,"he replied, calm and resolute."If the shields fall, Aquaterra falls with them. We hold the line—no matter the cost."

The battle roared louder, unforgiving. The dark magic of the Void bled strength from the defenders, draining Light and resolve alike. One by one, soldiers collapsed—their essence siphoned, their bodies left empty by the creeping shadow.

And yet... they endured.

Auroran raised his voice once more, a cry that pierced the gloom."For the dawn! For the Light! Stand strong, warriors of Aquaterra!"

His words rekindled the fire in their spirits. With renewed fury, the defenders surged forward—magic flaring, blades flashing, shields reforged through will alone. The elemental relics blazed in unison, their power answering the call of unity.

At the center of the storm, Aqua and Capri fought in perfect harmony. His blade struck like the birth of stars; her magic flowed like woven light across the battlefield. She shielded him in moments of peril. He struck down the darkness that dared approach her. Their rhythm was the music of resistance—undaunted and eternal.

Above them, the Starlight Pendant flared, its inner light awakened by their bond, its power responding to their unbreakable union. Beams of pure celestial brilliance lanced out from the heart of the pendant, strengthening the faltering shields and pushing back the tide. The elemental relics resonated in kind—earth, flame, water, and wind igniting together, their symphony stalling the Void's advance.

Still, the darkness lingered.

For every twisted creature that fell, another took its place. The Void was not merely a force—it was endless hunger.

At last, the first wave broke, and the enemy's advance momentarily stalled. A silence, thin and trembling, fell across the battlefield.

But it was not peace.

The horizon remained dark. The storm had not passed—it had only paused. The defenders stood bloodied but unbowed, breathing heavily beneath the tattered sky.

Though the Light held... it flickered.

The true war had only just begun.

11.3 The Threat Beyond

Aqua and Capri stood on the desolate threshold of the Void's Fortress, its presence an overwhelming blot upon the fabric of reality. Behind them stretched the path carved from stars and sacrifice, and before they loomed the final shadow—vast, ancient, malevolent. The fortress rose like a jagged scar etched into the horizon, its spires twisted and cruel, reaching like claws toward a storm-choked sky. Bolts of lightning split the heavens, momentarily illuminating the obsidian walls, each pulse revealing veins of dark energy that throbbed like a living wound.

The ground beneath their feet—cracked, ashen, and lifeless—radiated a cold that sank deeper than the skin. Even the air itself recoiled from the structure as though reality strained to avoid its presence. Light did not merely fade here; it fled, consumed by the hunger of the Void. This was the edge of known existence, the boundary where hope and dread entwined.

Behind them stood their most trusted companions: Celestine, the Star Mystic, whose aura shimmered like constellations in motion, and the four Elemental Lords—Gaian, Pyronix, Aqualith, and Zephyr—each holding the sacred relics bestowed by their realms.
Gaian's Earthshaper Hammer gleamed with the strength of mountains; Pyronix wielded the Solarflame Blade, its fire eternal; Aqualith held the Tidecaller Trident, pulsing with the rhythm of oceans; and Zephyr's Windstrider Bow vibrated with invisible tension, ready to lose the winds of battle. Around Capri's neck hung

the Starlight Pendant, glowing softly as though whispering courage with each beat.

The swirling mist that blanketed the ground writhed with unnatural purpose, moving like a living thing, whispering warnings no ear could fully understand. With every step toward the fortress, the air grew heavier, pressing against them like unseen hands of fear.

Capri broke the silence, her voice steady though her heart pounded with the weight of what was to come."This is it,"she said."The final battle. Everything we've fought for—every one we've lost—it all comes down to this moment."

Aqua nodded, his grip tightening around the hilt of the Sword of Stardust. The blade, forged from the celestial core of fallen stars, glowed with defiance, casting small arcs of Light that pushed faintly against the ever-hungry gloom."We can't afford to fail,"he said."No matter what happens in there... I'm with you. Always."

The mist churned violently, and the ground beneath them trembled. From the swirling dark emerged a towering figure—massive, armored, and seething with malice. The Void Warden. His presence eclipsed all others, a living embodiment of the Abyss. Encased in blackened armor adorned with runes that pulsed like dying suns, his eyes burned with a venomous glow. The air seemed to retreat from him, the Void bending to his will.

"You dare challenge the Void?"His voice thundered, cracking like mountains splitting."You will find only despair beyond these gates. Turn back, or be devoured."

The cold deepened, stealing breath and hope. For a moment, doubt flickered among them. But then Celestine stepped forward, starlight dancing across her skin like a cloak of galaxies.

"The stars have shown me the path,"she said, voice unwavering."It is perilous, but it is true. Even in the heart of the Void, Light can endure."

The Warden sneered."The Light will die here, Star Mystic. Your stars are blind."

Aqua stepped forward, his blade igniting with radiant power."Then let them see us blaze."

Capri lifted her Staff of Time, the ancient wood humming with temporal force. The air around her shimmered, bending ever so slightly as the flow of time itself slowed in obedience.

From the darkness, the Warden unleashed his blade—a towering weapon of shadow forged in the very heart of the Void. He swung in a great arc, tendrils of dark energy slashing through the air. The ground cracked under the impact, sending tremors outward.

Aqua surged forward, intercepting the blow with a clash of star-forged Light. The strike echoed like the cry of the cosmos in pain. Around them, the battlefield came alive.

Celestine raised shimmering shields of starlight, catching blasts of Void energy and dispersing them into bursts of harmless brilliance. The Elemental Lords leaped into action.

Zephyr summoned a gale that tore through the fog, revealing lurking horrors skulking in the mist. His Windstrider Bowsang, each arrow a whisper of vengeance.

Pyronix roared, unleashing the fury of suns with his Solarflame Blade, casting walls of fire that seared through the creeping dark.

Aqualith lifted the Tidecaller Trident, conjuring waves of luminous water that crashed into the enemy lines, each tide washing away corruption.

Gaian, unmoving as a mountain, struck the earth with the Earthshaper Hammer. The ground answered, erupting in jagged stone to block and repel the darkness.

"You are but sparks in a dying cosmos!"the Warden bellowed."The Void consumes all!"

"We are the stars reborn,"Aqua countered, deflecting another devastating strike. His every blow with the Sword of Stardust lit the gloom with hope.

Capri danced through the chaos, her staff slowing the Warden's movements with each precise gesture. She bent seconds into shields and turned moments into weapons."Together!"she called."Stay together!"

Seeing their unity, the Warden unleashed a torrent of darkness—an explosion of tendrils that surged outward, seeking to crush and consume. The Elemental shields cracked. The air itself seemed to shatter.

Then, the Starlight Pendant blazed.

A radiant pulse spread from Capri's heart, pushing the tendrils back. Light poured from the Pendant, flowing into the relics and igniting them with ancestral energy. The Elemental Lords stood taller, stronger —their relics now brimming with awakened power.

With a final cry, Aqua summoned the full fury of the stars. His sword flared brighter than ever, drawing from the Pendant's Light."For AquaCapri!"he roared, launching into the heart of the storm.

Capri, sensing the critical instant, raised her staff high. Time halted. The world froze in a suspended breath. Aqua's strike came swift and true, plunging into the core of the Warden's blackened armor.

The Warden screamed, not in rage—but in fear.

"You may pass... but what lies beyond is far worse than I,"he hissed as his form unraveled, fading into the dust of uncreation.

As silence fell, the mist withdrew. The gates of the Void's Fortress groaned and creaked, opening wide. The sound was not welcome—it was a warning.

Aqua and Capri stood before the opening, their hearts braced, their purpose unshaken.

Capri turned to him."Together, Aqua. We face whatever comes together."

His voice was firm."Always."

And side by side, they stepped into the final darkness—into the unknown heart of the Void—where only their Light could lead the way.

AquaCapri

CHAPTER

12

THE REVIVAL OF HARMONY

*THE STORM IS NOT THE END—IT IS THE
BEGINNING OF RENEWAL.*

 CHAPTER 12

△ **VALDUM, THE CELESTIAL ARCHITECT**
AQUARII: THANDOR XAL ARAVYN.

 OPENING WHISPER – CH. 12

△ **MAXIMUS, THE ETERNAL QUILL**
AQUARII: XEL'VIRE NAX TORUIN.

 CLOSING WHISPER – CH. 12

12.1 The Cleansing Storm

They had stood at the edge of annihilation. At the desolated threshold of the Void's Fortress, Aqua and Capri—joined by Gaian, Pyronix, Zephyr, Aqualith, and the Elemental Lords—witnessed the truth Orion had warned them of: stars dimmed and consumed, their essence stolen by a hunger older than time. The fortress pulsed with malevolence, its spires twisted by the Void's will. It was there, amid the darkness, that Orion's vision became prophecy.

In the stillness after their confrontation, Aetherion, Guardian of the Conflux, appeared—drawn by the ripple of cosmic imbalance. With him came Sylphara, spirit of air and keeper of the unseen winds. They brought a warning—and a path.

"The corruption cannot be undone by force,"Aetherion had said."It must be cleansed from the convergence where Light and shadow meet. You must journey to the Celestial Conflux—the heart of equilibrium. There, the storm awaits."

And so, guided by the pull of the Starlight Pendant and the relics entrusted by the Elemental Lords, the heroes departed the blackened gates of the Void and traveled through celestial currents to reach the place where fate would be reborn.

The Celestial Conflux stretched before them now, a breathtaking and chaotic intersection of realms. Rivers of stardust coiled through the sky, glowing like living veins of the cosmos. The heavens shifted endlessly between day and night, stars burning in full daylight as if the universe itself wavered in allegiance. Above, floating crystal islands scattered rainbow prisms across the land. But overhead, a storm churned—no ordinary tempest, but a gathering of corrupted forces straining to break free.

At the heart of the Conflux stood Aqua and Capri, burdened but unbowed. They had led armies, shielded stars, and defied annihilation, but this moment felt heavier. Their every breath was laced with destiny.

Beside them hovered Aetherion, his form forged of stardust and time, silent and radiant. Sylphara stood near, her shape ever-shifting like wind itself, calm in the face of chaos. Around the circle, the four bearers of the elemental relics took their place:

Gaian, bearer of the Earthshaper Hammer, grounded and resolute

Zephyr, holding the Windstrider Bow, focused as the winds around him danced

Pyronix, wielding the Solarflame Blade, silent and aflame with inner fire

Aqualith, guardian of the Tidecaller Trident, calm as deep waters yet brimming with silent fury

Capri stood at the center, the Starlight Pendant glowing against her chest, pulsing in sync with the storm above—an anchor of hope and harmony.

The ground beneath them thrummed with the heartbeat of creation itself. The air crackled with the scent of ozone, heavy with anticipation. This was the moment foretold. The Conflux would either be their salvation—or their undoing.

The Ritual Begins

The circle formed, and the ritual commenced.

"The Conflux holds power beyond reckoning," Aetherion declared, his voice resonant and unshaken. "But power alone is not salvation. You must move not in dominance—but in harmony."

Sylphara lifted her arms, the wind forming a halo around her. "The air listens only to those who breathe with it. Guide, do not command."

Capri knelt, her fingers pressing into the luminous ground. She reached for the earth's essence, calling forth the rhythm beneath. The Earthshaper Hammer vibrated in Gaian's grasp, resonating with her.

Aqua inhaled slowly. With each breath, he summoned the cosmic waters, channeling them through his soul. The Tidecaller Trident shimmered in Aqualith's hands, its power flowing into the circle. Earth and water—steady, enduring, foundational.

Aetherion's voice rose like a current swirling through the Conflux. "Now, call fire and air. Let the balance be complete."

Sylphara stepped forward, her form dancing like a gale. With a single motion, the winds swirled into the circle, chaotic then calm, responding to her will. The Windstrider Bow sang in Zephyr's grasp, arrows of air notched with invisible precision.

Then came Pyronix. His presence ignited the space. He raised the Solarflame Blade, which roared to life, flames spiraling skyward—but not wild. Guided. Purposeful.

Above, the storm surged in response. The heavens roared.

The Void Strikes Back

As the elements unified, the storm twisted violently. Shadows slithered into the ritual's edge—dark tendrils born of the Void. The air froze. The Conflux pulsed with resistance.

A black lightning bolt struck near Capri, throwing her off balance."We're losing control!"she called out, her voice nearly lost to the howling winds."It's breaking through!"

Aetherion stood firm."You cannot resist a storm and survive it. You must become it. Let the Conflux flow through you. Be wind. Be water. Be flame. Be stone."

Doubt crept into Aqua's mind. The storm bore down, heavy and relentless. The Void pressed its will into the ritual. Were they strong enough?

Then he turned to Capri. Amid the fury, she stood resolute, the Starlight Pendant blazing with Light. Her bond to the earth was unshaken.

"We can do this,"he said, finding strength in her gaze."Together."

Their connection sparked like the first Light at creation's dawn. The others felt it, too. The relics pulsed in rhythm with the Conflux. They did not push the storm—they flowed with it.

The winds no longer screamed; they sang. The flames no longer devoured; they warmed. The water surged not with chaos but clarity. The earth held—not as resistance, but embrace.

A brilliant Light erupted—a wave of cleansing radiance that shattered the encroaching shadows. The Void's essence dissolved in silence.

Where there had been chaos, now there was calm.

The Aftermath

As Light faded into stillness, the Celestial Conflux glowed with restored grace. The rivers of stardust shimmered freely again, unburdened by shadow. The skies, at last, were clear.

Sylphara's voice carried on the breeze."You have done it. The Conflux is yours. The land is cleansed."

Aqua wiped the sweat from his brow, breath ragged. He steadied himself with his own royal Trident, its polished shaft warm from the storm's passing."It's over... for now."

Capri stood beside him, the Starlight Pendant calm at her heart."But the war has not ended. We've won balance, not victory. The Void waits."

Around them stood the silent guardians—Gaian, Pyronix, Zephyr, and Aqualith—each holding their elemental relic: the Earthshaper Hammer, the Solarflame Blade, the Windstrider Bow, and the Tidecaller Trident. None spoke, but their presence radiated unity and resolve.

In the hush that followed, Aqua reached for Capri's hand. Their fingers interlaced—no words needed. A vow lived between them, sealed in silence.

Harmony had returned. Not granted, but earned—through unity, through will, through love.

The storm had not been vanquished.

It had been transformed.

12.2 Rebirth of the Realm

Aquaterra, once a realm cloaked in desolation and despair, now rose as a kingdom reborn. The emerald canopies of its forests stretched toward the horizon, their vibrant leaves swaying gently in the breeze as if dancing with newfound freedom. Rivers that had once carried the poison of the Void's corruption now shimmered like molten silver beneath the midday sun, their currents clear, pure, and full of life. The air, once acrid with the scent of war, was now fragrant with blooming wildflowers, sweet with renewal. At the heart of the AquaCapri Constellation, Aquaterra pulsed anew—its heartbeat synced with the restoration of its people's spirit.

Aqua and Capri stood at the grand gates of the capital, their eyes sweeping across the transformed land. Behind them, the city had been not just rebuilt but reimagined—restored in glory, elevated by celestial grace. Towers laced with cosmic crystals soared skyward, catching starlight and casting it back into the heavens in radiant flares. The architecture blended seamlessly with nature—bridges adorned with flowering vines arched over the winding rivers that flowed through the city's heart, while lush gardens blossomed in every corner, vibrant with color and peace. It was as if the city itself exhaled a breath of joyous rebirth.

Within the capital square, celebration bloomed as fervently as the gardens. Musicians played gentle, lilting tunes, their melodies weaving through the laughter and chatter of the crowd. Dancers spun in graceful arcs, their robes swirling like stardust. Long tables brimmed with fruits, breads, and delicacies, inviting all to partake in abundance. Tapestries adorned the streets, each thread woven with symbols of the cosmos—a reminder of the stars' eternal watch. Citizens moved freely, clad in garments that shimmered like constellations, their steps light, their voices joyful.

And yet, beneath the revelry, Aqua sensed a quiet current of unease. Eyes filled with joy still flickered with uncertainty. Though the great battle had been won, scars endured—etched into the land, etched into hearts. Capri stood beside him, silent but attuned to the same undercurrent. Though the darkness had been vanquished, its echo still lingered.

"They celebrate," Aqua murmured, his tone low and thoughtful. "But I can feel it—the fear. It lingers, even now."

Capri's gaze swept the crowd, her expression solemn. "They've endured too much to forget so quickly. The darkness may have passed, but belief in lasting peace... that takes time."

Just then, the crowd parted like morning mist, revealing two familiar figures—Liora and Thalor.

Liora, healer of soul and flesh, moved with the quiet grace of wind through willow leaves. Her soft robes whispered with each step, the fabric rippling like water touched by Light. She had not only mended wounds but rekindled the spirit of a weary people. At her side was Thalor, the visionary architect whose designs had breathed form into the capital's resurrection. His eyes, reflecting the starlit towers, gleamed with silent pride.

"Liora, Thalor," Aqua greeted, voice warm with gratitude. "What you've done cannot be measured in words. You have restored not just the land—but its soul."

Thalor's gaze swept the skyline, admiration rich in his voice. "It is not merely rebuilt—it is reborn. Every stone, every archway, reflects the constellations above. A testament to our endurance."

Liora offered a gentle smile."The land has healed. The hearts of our people will follow. What they've endured has made them stronger—united."

Aqua looked once more toward the square. Laughter rang through the air, yet he saw it—that flicker of worry in the glances skyward, the subtle edge in their steps, as if expecting shadows to return. He understood what must be done.

He stepped forward and raised a hand. The music softened, and the dancers stilled. Silence fell like a gentle snowfall, all eyes turning to their sovereign.

"My people,"his voice resonated, calm and clear,"we stood at the edge of oblivion. The Void sought to unravel us—to taint our land, our lives, our very spirits. But look around you... Aquaterra lives. It breathes once more. It thrives."

A chorus of cheers rose in response, yet Aqua saw the fear still linger in their eyes. He lifted his hand again, calling for stillness.

"I know,"he continued, voice softer now,"that fear remains. That somewhere within you, there's a whisper that this peace may be fleeting—that the darkness may return."He paused."But let this truth be known: the Light has prevailed. And as long as we stand united, holding fast to that hope, no darkness will ever take it from us."

Beside him, Capri stepped forward. Her presence radiated serene power, her words clear and strong.

"The Void tried to divide us—tried to break us with fear and doubt. It failed. Our unity is our strength. It is this bond that made us victorious. Let fear not claim this moment. Today, we do not merely survive—we rise."

A murmur of understanding passed through the crowd as though Capri's words had loosened something within them—a long-held breath released at last. She turned toward Aqua, and with a quiet nod between them, the message was sealed.

From the front of the gathering, an elderly woman stepped forward, her hands trembling slightly, eyes brimming with emotion. Her voice wavered, but it carried the weight of every heart in the square.

"My king, my queen... we are grateful. Truly. But... what if the Void returns? How will we protect our homes, our children, our lives?"

Aqua stepped down from the platform. The golden Light bathing the square seemed to follow him, and when he reached the woman, he took her hands with the tenderness of kin.

"We will be ready,"he said softly, yet each word carried unwavering strength."The Void is patient—but so are we. We've rebuilt stronger than before. We've learned from our wounds. And you are not alone. Together, we will protect what has been reclaimed."

Tears welled in her eyes, and she bowed deeply. The crowd, moved by the quiet exchange, erupted in renewed cheers that rose like a swell, filling the square with sound and certainty.

Then Liora's voice rose above the clamor, firm and luminous."Time will mend our wounds. But the spirit of Aquaterra—it is already restored. We are not who we were before. We are more."

Thalor stepped forward, his hand outstretched toward the horizon."This city, this realm, is proof of that strength. Every tower, every beam of Light, is forged from resilience. From you."

The music surged anew, and this time, the joy that followed was no longer tempered by fear. Laughter rang out, the dancers returned to the square, and the celebration resumed in full—renewed and unburdened. It was as though the realm itself exhaled, casting off the remnants of sorrow and embracing the dawn of its rebirth.

Beneath the heavens, Aqua and Capri stood together, watching as constellations shimmered in quiet harmony with the joy below. Stars blinked like watchful eyes, blessings from above.

"We've given them their home again," Capri whispered, voice steady.

Aqua's gaze remained fixed on the stars touching the farthest edge of their realm. "And now, we'll make sure it remains theirs."

At that moment, as joy soared around them and the realm pulsed with new Light, they knew—they would face whatever came together. The realm had been reborn. And so had they.

12.3 A New Dawn

The first Light of the new day unfurled across the horizon like a golden veil, casting warm hues over the revitalized lands of Aquaterra. From the soaring height of the Horizon Spire, Aqua and Capri stood hand in hand—silent witnesses to their realm's rebirth. The Spire, a magnificent tower forged of shimmering crystal and starstone, spiraled heavenward in elegant defiance of gravity. Its surface, etched with constellations carved by celestial artisans, glowed faintly in the gentle dawn, each reflection an echo of the cosmic forces that had shaped their destiny.

Here, at the apex of the world beneath a sky not yet fully awakened, the air felt charged with possibility. A breeze stirred the stillness, whispering of renewal as it carried the scent of dew-kissed soil and the faint perfume of blooming wildflowers. Far below, the world exhaled —stirring from a long and shadowed slumber.

The forests, once suffocated by the Void's cruel grasp, now shimmered in the sun's first embrace, their leaves quivering like grateful prayers. The rivers, tainted by battle and burdened with sorrow, flowed again with crystalline clarity, sunlight dancing across their surfaces like celestial blessings. Even the mountains—those solemn guardians that had long stood veiled in mist—gleamed anew, their jagged crowns catching the Light and casting it like beacons across the land.

Capri's gaze swept across the renewed expanse. Her sapphire eyes mirrored the vibrant pinks and golds streaking the sky, though they held the silent weight of memory. Her voice, when it came, was soft, reverent—wrapped in the fragility of truth hard-won.

"We've come so far,"she whispered, her fingers tightening in his."There were moments I feared this dawn would never break... when the darkness felt too deep."

He turned to her, eyes steady and warm beneath the Light. The sun's ascent cast a halo across his features, revealing the quiet strength that had always anchored them. His voice, calm as the still sea after a storm, carried with it the steadfast certainty that had never faltered.

"We stood at the edge of the abyss,"he said, brushing a windblown strand from her face."But we didn't fall. We held on—because we had each other. That's what kept the Light alive. That's what gives me hope even now. As long as we stand together, nothing can break us."

They remained silent, not with fear or grief, but with the serenity born of survival. In that moment, they were more than rulers. They were soulbound—reforged by the fire of trials, shaped by sacrifice, and tempered in the crucible of love. The dawn rising before them was not just Aquaterra's—it was theirs.

As the Light ascended higher, casting golden fingers across the land, Aquaterra seemed to breathe anew. The kingdom—scarred yet unbroken—unfolded like a celestial tapestry. Forests rustled with life, rivers shimmered like molten gold, and the mountains stood tall, their summits ablaze with radiant fire. Every corner of the land whispered of survival and rebirth.

Capri's lips curved into a smile, soft and reverent. She didn't speak at first—she simply gazed out at the horizon, where daybreak painted the sky with promise. Her fingers remained woven with Aqua's, a lifeline not only of affection but of all they had fought to preserve.

"The Light has returned to our world,"she said at last, her voice laced with awe."But it wasn't just the stars or the relics. It was our love that truly guided us. Even when hope dimmed, and the sky fell silent... it was always there. A flame that refused to die."

He looked at her, and in his eyes shone the same golden warmth that touched the land. His voice carried the weight of their journey, each word etched with the certainty forged in trials overcome.

"It will continue to guide us,"he said."No matter what shadows may rise, we will face them as one. This is more than a new day. It's the beginning of our legacy."

Their vow, unspoken yet understood, lingered in the wind that danced about the Horizon Spire. It was a promise born of devotion and tested in fire—one that belonged not just to them but to the realm they had vowed to protect. Below, the realm stirred with quiet joy. Trees swayed as though sighing in relief. Rivers twinkled with the sun's approval. Mountains, now fully revealed, watched in stoic pride.

Yet they knew peace was not permanence. The Void had been driven back but not destroyed. Somewhere beyond the edges of Light, shadows stirred. Challenges still awaited, and time would test their strength again.

Capri turned her face to the sun, eyes closed as warmth washed over her like a benediction. "I've learned something through everything," she murmured. "Love... it's not just a feeling. It's a force. It shapes destinies. It's what kept us walking forward—when everything else was crumbling."

Aqua nodded slowly, his gaze never leaving her. "It is. And it always will be. There will be more battles, more darkness. But as long as love guides us, we'll never lose our way." He turned then toward the glowing horizon, where the sun now hovered just above the land, casting golden fire across all it touched. "This dawn... it's not just Aquaterra's. It belongs to us. To everything we've fought for. And to everything we will build."

The Horizon Spire, eternal and luminous, stood not merely as an architectural marvel but as a symbol of vision, strength, and unyielding hope. Its spiraled form mirrored the vastness of the cosmos —a reminder that their story was part of something far greater. Beneath their feet, the mosaic floor shimmered with fragments of crystal and starstone, shaped into constellations that told the tale of their trials. Every star, every celestial line etched into the floor, marked a battle fought, a darkness overcome, a harmony restored.

The day stretched before them—unwritten, full of promise. Though the sunlight painted the world in radiant hues, a quiet truth lived in their hearts: the memory of what was lost would always linger like a faint echo at the edge of the Light. Victory had been hard-won. Peace is even harder. And still, they knew, it was not everlasting. Darkness did not disappear—it only receded. Somewhere, in the vastness, it would stir again.

Yet, in this moment, they allowed themselves to simply be. To breathe. To feel the warmth on their skin. To stand as two souls bound by love, surrounded by the world they had saved. The Light continued its graceful sweep across Aquaterra—over the forests, across the rivers, into the heart of every restored village. With each ray, it carried the essence of their unity, their sacrifices, their truth. Their love.

As they stood hand in hand, the golden brilliance of the sun embraced them fully. This new dawn was not an ending but a beginning. They had reclaimed the realm, but now came the greater task: to lead it into an age of peace, to heal what could still be healed, to nurture the fragile beauty they had restored.

The final rays of sunlight gleamed in their eyes as they looked across the horizon, their silhouettes cast in gold. The new day had come— quiet, unwavering, eternal. With it, a sense of renewed purpose anchored in something far deeper than strategy or strength. Hope. Love. Harmony.

Together, they would walk into the unknown.

And so, with hands entwined and hearts full of promise, Aqua and Capri turned to face the future—together.

CHAPTER

13

SECRETS OF THE CONSTELLATIONS

TO UNDERSTAND DESTINY, ONE MUST KNOW THEIR ORIGIN.

 # CHAPTER 13

△ **MAXIMUS, THE ETERNAL QUILL**
AQUARII: NURALITH SEL'VIAN.

 OPENING WHISPER – CH. 13

△ **VALDUM, THE CELESTIAL ARCHITECT**
AQUARII: SEL'VIAN XAL TARUUN.

CLOSING WHISPER – CH. 13

13.1 The Hidden Realms

In the sacred heart of the Celestial Citadel, beneath a dome of glimmering crystal etched with constellations older than memory, a secret gathering unfolded in silence. No bells tolled. No heralds announced. Only starlight bore witness as four of the cosmos' wisest gathered with Aqua and Capri in a chamber hidden from the eyes of even the most watchful spirits.

Luminarion, Sovereign of Radiance, stood at the center, his aura pulsing with a serene, steady brilliance. To his right, Chronia, Seer of Time, eyes swirling with endless futures, spoke softly yet with undeniable gravity. Orion, the Star Navigator, traced glowing paths across a stellar map hovering midair, while Aether, the cosmic bridge between dimensions, folded reality's veil like parchment between his fingers.

"You are being summoned to a place forgotten by most, protected by myth, and feared by the Void,"Luminarion said, his voice like sunlight breaking through storm clouds."The Starforge holds secrets forged in the first breaths of the universe. Its knowledge could save all we hold dear—or unmake it."

Chronia stepped forward."We cannot predict what you will find. Time itself veils that place. But it is not fate—it is choice—that must guide you."

Aether added,"You must go as seekers, not conquerors. The Starforger is no mere guardian of relics. It is a being forged of will, born of Light, and older than the Void's first whisper."

Orion's hand hovered over a shimmering thread on the star map."Here,"he said, pointing to a nebula coiled like a serpent of Light."This is where the path begins."

At the edges of the chamber stood a small circle of trusted companions—Zephyr, Luna, Aetherion, and Sylphara—all warriors, friends, and keepers of countless battles past. Each stepped forward as Luminarion drew a radiant sigil in the air, its shape ancient and binding.

"You who bear witness,"he intoned,"are now sworn by starlight and silence. The knowledge of this journey must not pass your lips until the stars themselves grant release. Do you swear?"

One by one, hands touched hearts."We swear,"they said in unison, the vow sealed by a shimmering pulse that passed through them like a wave of Light.

And so, beneath the vault of stars and the seal of sacred trust, Aqua and Capri were sent forth—not as rulers or warriors, but as guardians of possibility.

The nebula surrounding the Starforge shimmered with hues that seemed drawn from the cradle of creation—pinks as tender as a lover's blush, indigos as profound as the endless Void and a golden Light pulsing like the very heartbeat of the cosmos. As Aqua and Capri descended through the thick, star-dusted air toward the celestial marvel below, they felt raw energy crackle around them, each spark resonating in harmony with their very souls.

Aqua's gaze held steady as they approached, yet the slight quickening of his breath betrayed the weight of the moment. His steps were deliberate and cautious as if he could feel the ancient force slumbering within this sacred place. Beside him, Capri's eyes widened—her typically composed demeanor faltering beneath the overwhelming grandeur and scale of the Starforge.

It rose from the swirling mists like a relic of myth—crafted from starstone and rare cosmic alloys that shimmered with an ethereal radiance. Towering walls curved upward, glinting with a Light that pulsed in rhythm with the stars. This was no mere place of creation; it breathed with the rhythm of the universe, alive in its own right.

Capri exhaled, her voice barely more than a breath."It's as if the universe itself is watching us... like every star knows we're here."

Aqua glanced her way, his voice low and measured."Perhaps it is. There's power here unlike anything we've encountered. We must tread carefully. The knowledge hidden in this forge could change everything —both for us and for our people."

She nodded, but awe still sparkled in her gaze. As ever, her curiosity burned brighter than fear.

Deeper into the forge, they stepped until a figure emerged at the chamber's heart—radiant with a Light so pure it outshone the stars. The Starforger stood before them, an ageless being whose form shifted endlessly. A swirling mass of stardust and cosmic energy, it seemed as though the stars' Essence had taken sentient shape. Its presence was overwhelming—timeless, unknowable.

Its voice echoed through the forge, deep and resonant as if the cosmos itself were speaking."You seek knowledge, but know this: what you learn here will shape your destiny in ways even the stars cannot foresee."

Capri took a hesitant step forward, awe still woven through her voice."We seek not power for ourselves, but knowledge—to protect those we love. The Void grows stronger each day. We need something —anything—that might help us stand against it."

The Starforger's gaze, though it had no true eyes—only clusters of radiant Light—seemed to focus sharply on her."The Void is relentless,"it said, each word heavy as a falling star."But power alone will not save your realm. The knowledge you seek carries a price. To wield it is to bend the current of time itself, to ignite events that even you may not command."

Aqua, ever the more grounded of the two, placed a steadying hand on her shoulder. His touch was firm yet gentle—an anchor in the rising tide of revelation."We understand the risk,"he said, voice resolute."But fear must not steer us. Show us what we must see. We will use what we learn with wisdom."

For a breathless moment, the chamber stood still. Then, with a motion as fluid as the shifting constellations, the Starforger lifted its arms. The air thickened, the Light dimmed, and reality itself bent beneath its will.

Before them bloomed a vision: an intricate web of Light stretching across the cosmos, each thread connecting to unseen realms. These were the Hidden Realms—places of untainted beauty, untouched by the Void. One floated above a silver sea of stars, its verdant lands gleaming with life. Another lay nestled in the nebula's heart, crystalline spires pulsing with pure cosmic energy.

Capri gasped, her hand finding Aqua's."It's... beautiful,"she breathed, wonder softening her words.

He, too, was spellbound. But his thoughts raced, weighed by consequence."Could these realms serve as sanctuaries? A refuge beyond the Void's reach?"

The Starforger's voice broke through the vision like thunder through still air."The Hidden Realms are powerful but fragile. If darkness discovers them, their purity will be undone. The balance of all things will falter."

Capri's brow furrowed."If we reveal them, we might save them... or lead the darkness straight to their gates. How can we know what's right?"

Aqua's eyes remained locked on the vision, his thoughts heavy."Perhaps it is wiser to keep this secret—for now. Until we understand the true consequences. We must consult the Mystics and the Elemental Lords. This choice is greater than us alone."

The Starforger's Light dimmed slightly as if in acknowledgement.
"The knowledge I have granted is a double-edged sword. It may shield or sever. Choose wisely, Guardians of AquaCapri—for the fate of many hangs in your hands."

A hush fell across the chamber. The Starforger's words lingered like echoes etched into time, and the immense gravity of the moment pressed down upon them.

At last, Capri spoke, her voice soft yet resolute."We cannot decide this alone. We must return to Aquaterra and seek the wisdom of others. Until then, the Hidden Realms must remain veiled."

Aqua turned to her, admiration glowing beneath the tension in his expression. She had always been bold, but now she was wise."You're right. This isn't just about what we've seen—it's about what it could become. The cosmos itself may change by our hand."

The Starforger inclined its head, its body flickering like a dying star, yet not dimmed in reverence."Then go, and may the stars guide your steps. But remember—secrets crave the Light. Be certain you are ready when they emerge."

With a single, sweeping gesture, the vision faded. The Hidden Realms dissolved into the swirling nebula, leaving only silence—and the weight of knowledge too vast to voice.

They turned to leave, the celestial map clutched tightly in Aqua's grasp. The silence between them was not of discord but of shared burden. What they had found was more than wisdom—it was a responsibility that might decide the fate not only of AquaCapri but of the universe itself.

Together, they stepped once more into the stars—side by side, yet changed. The path ahead shimmered with uncertainty, but the truth was clear:

The Hidden Realms held the key. And their choices would either unlock salvation—or summon ruin.

13.2: The Legacy of Stars

As the final echoes of celestial energy faded from the Nebula surrounding the Starforge, Aqua and Capri stood in quiet reverence alongside Zephyr, Luna, Aetherion, and Sylphara. The revelations within the forge had illuminated more than power—they had awakened a deeper understanding of the universe's fragile balance. But clarity often bred more questions, and the answers they sought now lay beyond strength—hidden in memory and starlight.

It was as they prepared to depart the Nebula that the Veil of Time parted, revealing a new presence.

Chronia, Seer of Time, emerged without sound; her arrival felt before it was seen. The threads of her robe shimmered like woven constellations, her gaze distant and knowing.

"The forge has revealed the nature of your strength,"she said,"but to wield it wisely, you must first understand the truth of the cosmos. The origin of the Void. The cycles that bind all realms. For that, you must journey where few dare tread—into the Library of Eternity."

Guided by Chronia's temporal foresight and Sylphara's celestial intuition, the group embarked aboard the Celestial Ark, traveling through a corridor of collapsing stars and timeless streams of radiant matter. Their destination: the Hollow of Infinity, where memory itself had been given form.

There, within the spiraling core of a drifting asteroid beyond the tether of any sun, the Library of Eternity awaited them.

The Library of Eternity stood beyond the reach of time, nestled within the heart of a colossal asteroid adrift in the silent Void of an ancient star cluster. Vast and ageless, the asteroid cradled a treasure trove of cosmic knowledge deep within its stone core. The library's endless halls radiated a soft, almost sentient energy as though the very stone had absorbed the wisdom of the cosmos. Towering bookshelves, carved directly from the asteroid, spiraled toward an infinite abyss above, each shelf brimming with tomes, scrolls, and artifacts that pulsed faintly—echoing the distant rhythm of the stars.

Aqua, Capri, and Chronia stepped cautiously into the labyrinth of knowledge, followed closely by their companions. The air was thick, not with dust but with the lingering Essence of forgotten centuries. Soft Light from far-off stars filtered through crystalline windows, casting an ethereal glow upon the texts. The scripts seemed illuminated from within, whispering silent tales of worlds long vanished, each syllable aching to be remembered.

Chronia glided ahead, robes flowing like the passage of ages, brushing soundlessly against the stone floor. Her gaze, ancient and wise, shimmered with caution—unspoken but deeply felt. As they delved deeper into the library's depths, Aqua felt a stillness settle over them as though the very air held its breath in reverence of so much history.

"This place,"she began, her voice soft yet resonant,"is more than a repository. The Library of Eternity exists outside the current of time. Here, the truths of the cosmos are preserved—the cycles of life and death, creation and destruction, Light and darkness. But beware... some truths, once uncovered, cannot be forgotten. Knowledge carries its own burden."

Aqua exchanged a glance with Capri. The starlight reflected in her eyes, but beneath her composed expression, he could sense the weight pressing upon her heart. They had come too far, endured too much, for hesitation now. The mission they bore demanded truths long buried.

"We need to know,"she said, voice unwavering."If we're to save our realm, we must understand the past—the origin of the Void and the cycle that binds all things. We can't fight what we don't comprehend."

Chronia paused before a towering archway, its surface etched with glowing cosmic sigils that shimmered at her approach as if recognizing her presence. She traced a single finger along the runes, then turned back toward them.

"There is no return from the knowledge you seek here,"she warned, voice tinged with reverence and restraint."What you learn may change the course of everything."

With a silent nod, she stepped through the archway, and they followed.

The chamber beyond defied description—an expanse so vast it seemed to contain entire galaxies. Constellations shimmered and shifted across its walls, alive with motion, as if the stars themselves had gathered to listen. The ceiling above was not stone but a swirling canopy of stars and nebulae, a reflection of the cosmos in motion. At the chamber's center stood a pedestal of stardust, upon which rested a single tome: The Legacy of Stars.

Its cover was etched with symbols so ancient they defied comprehension. Yet something about them resonated with Aqua, a pull that pressed against his chest like gravity drawn from memory. He stepped closer, feeling Capri's presence steadying him, her silence lending strength.

With a trembling hand, he reached out. The moment his fingers brushed the surface, the tome awakened. Its pages fluttered open, drawn by unseen winds, responding to the call of destiny. The words, written in starlight, danced before his eyes. Though the script was unfamiliar, the meaning bloomed within his mind, undeniable and clear.

He read aloud, voice hushed with awe.

"'The Void... is not merely a force of destruction. It is balance. Born from the same primordial Essence as the stars, it is the necessary counterbalance to Light. The two are intertwined—one birthing the other in an endless cycle.'"

Capri stepped closer, her brow furrowed."The Void is part of the universe itself,"she whispered."It's not just something to defeat—it's something we've always been bound to."

Chronia, solemn, joined them at the pedestal.

"The Void rises and falls with the birth and death of stars,"she said, her voice heavy with countless ages."It ensures creation does not spiral unchecked. But..."She hesitated, eyes drifting toward the ever-moving stars above."There is a prophecy—a final cycle. A chance to break this eternal dance between Light and dark. But to do so... will demand a great sacrifice. One that could alter the fabric of existence itself."

A chill passed through Aqua."A sacrifice,"he echoed, barely audible."What kind of sacrifice?"

Chronia's gaze moved to the shifting constellations, her voice distant.

"To break the cycle requires something beyond it. A force powerful enough to transcend the natural order. But such a force risks unraveling everything—time, fate, even the stars."

Capri's hands clenched."If the Void is part of a cycle... then every battle, every loss—has it all been for nothing? Are we trapped in an endless struggle with no escape?"

Aqua turned to her, pain flashing in his eyes. He took her hand gently.

"Even if the Void is necessary, we can't allow it to consume everything. There must be a way to protect what we love... without destroying the balance. But if sacrifice is required... we must be ready."

Chronia's expression softened.

"There is always a way,"she said gently."But the choices ahead will shape not just your realm—but the destiny of the cosmos. Once you begin, there is no turning back."

For a long moment, silence filled the chamber. The burden of truth pressed heavier than any armor, the knowledge both illuminating and crushing. Aqua and Capri stood on the edge of revelation, the shape of their path altered by what they had uncovered. The truths whispered by the stars were a gift—but one with a cost yet to be paid.

"We have to keep going,"Capri said at last, her voice firm though her eyes shimmered with unspoken emotion."If we can break this cycle... if we can stop the Void from rising again, we have to try. Even if it means..."

Her voice faltered, the weight of her thought suspended in the hush between them.

Aqua's grip on her hand tightened, his tone quiet but steady.

"We'll face it together. Whatever it takes, we face it together."

Chronia stepped forward, her face unreadable.

"There is more you need to know,"she said softly."The Legacy of Stars is only part of the story. Follow me."

They trailed behind her through the winding labyrinth, past endless shelves that stretched like spires into the heavens. Time seemed to bend in these halls, the air holding its breath as they passed into deeper chambers untouched by light or age.

Eventually, they reached a smaller room—dimly lit, intimate, and unbearably still. The space trembled with anticipation as though the universe itself leaned in to listen. Ancient scrolls lined the shelves, their brittle pages curled with age, each one a fragment of forgotten destiny.

At the chamber's center, a single scroll hovered above a pedestal, suspended in Light that pulsed from within.

"This,"Chronia said, gesturing to the relic,"contains the prophecy of the final battle—the one that will decide the fate of the universe. But know this: once it is read, the path ahead will be set. There will be no turning back."

Aqua and Capri exchanged a glance. No words passed between them —only understanding. The war with the Void had already begun. And now, the final threads of destiny beckoned them forward.

With slow reverence, Aqua reached out. The scroll unfurled at his touch, the glowing script revealing itself line by line. The prophecy emerged in full, and with it came the chilling certainty that the end had not yet begun—but was swiftly approaching.

The final cycle loomed, vast and inevitable.

And the greatest sacrifices still lay ahead.

As they stood at the edge of this new awareness, Aqua and Capri understood that their journey through the Library of Eternity had changed them. The knowledge they sought had been found—but it demanded more than understanding.

It demanded everything.

13.3 The Map of Destiny

The Chamber of Destiny lay deep within the heart of the Library of Eternity, hidden from all but the most trusted guardians of AquaCapri. The air was thick with ancient energy, pulsing in harmony with the rhythm of the stars. As they crossed the threshold, guided by Chronia, the Mystic of Time, Aqua and Capri felt the moment's immense weight settle upon them. The chamber had awaited this very juncture—and now, they stood before the heart of the universe's unfolding fate.

It was a circle of power, its walls smooth and radiant, carved from starstone that shimmered beneath a soft, ambient glow. Ancient runes, etched in the forgotten tongues of stars, illuminated the chamber with a quiet hum. Overhead, the ceiling revealed a living dome of the night sky, its constellations constantly shifting, realigning to echo the great turning of the cosmos.

At the center hovered the Map of Destiny, suspended above a translucent crystal table. It did not rest—it floated and breathed, a living mosaic of Light, shadow, and chromatic energy. Threads of brilliance and darkness wove through it in an intricate dance, displaying myriad futures yet to be shaped. It pulsed in rhythm with the universe itself, mirroring their thoughts, reflecting the infinite paths that lay ahead.

Aqua and Capri exchanged a glance—wordless, solemn. This was not a choice of convenience but one of consequence. What lay before them would define not just their own lives but the fate of countless worlds scattered across the stars.

The air within the chamber grew heavy with expectation, as though even the walls held their breath. Shadows lengthened across the starstone, cast by the shifting Light of the map—echoes of the inner turmoil each carried. In this sacred space, destiny could be glimpsed but never promised. The future could be rewritten—but never without a cost.

Chronia stepped forward, her movements fluid and deliberate. She reached toward the map, placing her fingers gently upon its surface. At her touch, the swirling tapestry of Light stirred, revealing fresh possibilities—paths not yet trodden but aching to be known. Her voice, though quiet, carried the gravity of the ages.

"The Map of Destiny is not fixed," she began, her gaze unwavering. "It changes with every thought, every breath, every decision. What you see here are potential futures—paths unwalked, but ones you have the power to shape."

Aqua stepped forward, shoulders squared with resolve, though his eyes reflected a flicker of unease. He studied the living map, watching as the woven threads of Light and shadow responded to his presence —shifting, spiraling, changing course. Futures stretched before him— some radiant with promise, others choked in darkness. He caught glimpses of battles not yet fought, of shattered worlds and faces he cherished—Capri, their allies, even their enemies—interwoven within the endless fabric of fate.

"We must be careful," he said, voice steady but tinged with wary gravity. "Each choice we make here ripples outward, touching not just us but every world. The map shows the way... but it also reveals the cost."

Capri stood beside him, eyes fixed on the shimmering dance of threads. Awe shimmered within her gaze, but beneath it lay unease—a quiet storm of doubt, of responsibility. Every step they took from here could restore the cosmos... or unmake it. One misstep and even the stars might fall.

"This is where it all begins—or ends,"she whispered, her voice barely above breath."But how do we know the right path? These futures... they promise peace, but they also carry ruin."

Chronia moved closer, her hand still resting upon the map. The threads responded, flowing into new patterns—fresh visions unfurling like constellations reborn. Her eyes, luminous with the wisdom of endless timelines, softened.

"The future is a tapestry,"she said calmly."An endless weave of possibility, each thread formed by the hands of those who choose to act. The map is a guide, not a promise. The outcome belongs to you."

The map shifted again, revealing radiant trails—paths of direct confrontation where Light and darkness would meet in decisive battles. These futures gleamed with clarity, filled with action, with purpose. Yet even in their brilliance, the certainty of victory was absent. Each path was laced with danger, shadowed by loss. Other threads, dimmer and twisting, suggested different destinies—futures that shimmered with fragile hope but came with peril. On these, a single misstep could unravel everything.

Capri's breath caught. One of the darker strands unfurled, casting a bleak vision: the stars dimmed, their Essence devoured by the Void. AquaCapri—fallen. She saw herself and Aqua at the precipice of ruin, enemies closing in, Light flickering in their eyes like dying embers.

"This path..."she murmured, voice thick with fear."It could bring peace—but if we fail, all will be lost."

Aqua reached for her hand, his touch firm, grounding. Their eyes met. Within his gaze lived quiet strength—undaunted, unwavering.

"We've walked into the unknown before," he said gently. "And we'll do so again. But we can't let fear lead us. We must trust in each other. That's how we'll endure."

The map pulsed in response, and for an instant, a new image appeared —a fragile vision where Light and shadow coexisted in balance. Fleeting though it was, it seeded hope within them both.

Capri turned to Chronia, who had stepped back. Her expression was unreadable yet touched by quiet understanding. The Mystic of Time folded her hands, her gaze gentle and sure.

"The map shows what may be," she said softly. "Not what must be. You hold the power to shape it. But know this—such power bears a cost. Trust in your bond, your love, and the universe will answer."

A heavy silence settled over the chamber. The walls seemed to press inward, echoing the stillness of fate suspended. Aqua and Capri stood unmoving, eyes locked on the living map. Between them stretched the weight of choice, of futures held in balance. Yet within that silence, they found something solid—each other. Aqua's hand remained in Capri's, the warmth of it anchoring them. "No matter what comes," Capri said, her voice steady and clear, "we face it together."

Aqua nodded. "Together. Always."

They reached out. As their hands brushed the glowing surface, the crystal beneath their fingers grew warm. The map shifted once more —threads aligning, a single path solidifying from possibility into reality. The future remained uncertain, but one truth endured: they would meet it united, trusting in the Light and love that had always guided them.

As they turned to leave, the runes along the starstone walls flared briefly, acknowledging their choice. The path was set—not foretold but chosen. The road ahead remained unwritten, but they walked it with the power of their bond and the will to shape the cosmos itself. Outside, the stars turned slowly, aligning with the choices made within.

CHAPTER

14

THE ECHOES OF TIME

*SOME LOVE EXISTS OUTSIDE OF TIME,
SHAPING ALL THAT FOLLOWS.*

 CHAPTER 14

△ VALDUM, THE CELESTIAL ARCHITECT
AQUARII: VRAXOR TENEBRAL.

 OPENING WHISPER – CH. 14

△ MAXIMUS, THE ETERNAL QUILL
AQUARII: XAL'RETH DONAVIR.

CLOSING WHISPER – CH. 14

14.1 The Timeless Bond

As the Map of Destiny faded into the starlit floor, its final echo resonating through the chamber, a hidden pathway revealed itself—etched in light, winding downward like a stream of time itself. Aqua and Capri, hearts brimming with questions and purpose, followed its pull along with their steadfast companions. Chronia, who had remained behind to safeguard the sacred scrolls, rejoined them moments later, having consulted the ancient glyphs for guidance. Her presence confirmed what the map had already whispered—their journey was not yet complete. Beyond the threshold awaited the Chamber of Echoes, a sanctum veiled within the folds of time, where forgotten truths stirred and destiny awaited its next revelation.

The Hall of Ages stood as an eternal witness to the passage of time. In the heart of the Temporal Realm, where time danced in unpredictable patterns, this ancient structure had seen the birth of stars, the rise and fall of civilizations, and the very Essence of cosmic balance. Its obsidian walls pulsed with the energy of forgotten moments, casting echoes of the past and whispers of the future into the ever-shifting present.

Aqua and Capri stepped through the towering archway, their movements slow and deliberate, as though the weight of millennia pressed upon their shoulders. Each step carried a resonance beyond the now, rippling through unseen threads of time. The air was heavy with reverence, the silence broken only by the soft hum of temporal energy—a rhythm that coursed through the very bones of existence.

The chamber was vast and circular, its obsidian walls adorned with spiraling carvings—symbols of creation and destruction—that depicted the history of the cosmos. Empires had risen and crumbled here, their legacies etched into the stone and lit by the faint starlight that shimmered from above. Overhead, a dome of flawless crystal shifted like the surface of a tranquil lake, reflecting the kaleidoscopic swirl of time's endless flow. It shimmered with visions—moments past and future, flickering like memories suspended in eternity.

Beneath their feet, the polished floor mirrored the cosmos, giving the illusion they walked among stars. The hum of time resonated through their bodies, each heartbeat syncing with the cosmic pulse of the Hall. The sensation was overwhelming—a visceral reminder of the infinite strands connecting them to every heartbeat of the universe.

"Everything feels... heavier here," Capri murmured, her voice barely more than breath.

Aqua, eyes lifted to the lights above, nodded. "Time is watching. It always has."

At the heart of the Hall, a solitary figure awaited—Chronia, the ageless Mystic of Time. She stood as if rooted to the very core of eternity, her presence bending the air around her. Her robes shimmered with a twilight glow, shifting between deep blue and silver as though spun from dusk and starlight. Her gaze met theirs—eyes luminous with the Light of a thousand dawns, carrying a wisdom forged through the slow, patient turning of ages.

"Welcome," Chronia said, her voice soft yet resonant with the gravity of uncounted moments. "You now stand at the crossroads of eternity, where time flows not as a river but as a tapestry—woven from the threads of all that has been and all that may come."

Aqua and Capri exchanged a glance, hearts burdened by the weight of the war they waged. They had come seeking clarity, but with each step forward, the enormity of their task seemed only to deepen.

Chronia extended an arm toward the obsidian walls. Her motion was fluid, measured, as though she moved in harmony with the rhythm of time itself. The carvings began to shift, transforming into vivid, living images—fragments of AquaCapri's past brought to life. Battles long passed reawakened before their eyes, triumphs and tragedies woven into one vast, radiant mosaic.

The scenes changed again, now turning inward—moments from Aqua and Capri's journey. Their first alliance, the forging of their bond, the moments when love had been their weapon and their salvation. These echoes shimmered across the chamber walls like memories reborn, suspended in a sea of light.

"Your bond,"Chronia said, voice steeped in reverence,"is a thread that stretches across time itself. It binds the past to the present and the present to futures yet to unfold. Even I cannot foresee all its power. It is your greatest strength... but also your greatest responsibility."

Capri's eyes settled on an image of Aquaterra, aglow with light and peace. She saw herself and Aqua standing before their people, symbols of unity in a turbulent universe. But then, shadows crept in, and the Light dimmed. The vision twisted—Aquaterra, fractured and broken, consumed by the merciless tide of time.

"What if... we can't stop it?"she whispered."What if this cycle—war, peace, war again—is inevitable? What if we're only delaying the darkness?"

Aqua reached for her hand, anchoring her with his touch."We can't let fear guide our choices. These are visions—possibilities, not promises. Our bond is the one constant, the one force that has always carried us. Together, we can shift what comes."

Chronia stepped closer, her voice now a quiet warning."Your connection is timeless but no less fragile. Like all things, it must be tended to. Every word, every act—no matter how small—echoes across the fabric of existence. Choose wisely."

Aqua's jaw tightened, his gaze distant, thoughts swirling like a storm. For so long, he had borne the mantle of leadership, forging ahead even when the way was shrouded in uncertainty. But now, the doubts pressed harder—was darkness inevitable? Was their fate already sealed?

"How do we know we're making the right choices?"Capri asked, her voice fragile, eyes searching Chronia's for answers."How do we stop this cycle?"

Chronia looked at the crystal dome above. Its surface flickered, shifting through a cascade of potential futures. In one, AquaCapri flourished—its Light extending across the galaxies. In another, it crumbled into ruin, devoured by shadow.

"You cannot predict every outcome,"she said, her tone laced with solemnity."But your bond remains the thread running through all futures. It is the axis upon which your destiny turns. Trust it, and it will lead you true."

Aqua tightened his hold on Capri's hand. His voice was calm, unwavering."Then we trust. In what we are. In what we've built."

Capri looked up at him, her heart heavy yet steady."We've seen what the darkness can do. We've lived through it. But it's never torn us apart. Not truly. As long as we stand together..."

Chronia regarded them with quiet intensity."Time challenges all bonds,"she said gently."But you are not alone in this fight. Others will stand with you. When the time is right, call upon them."

Above, the dome shimmered once more. A fleeting vision emerged—a brighter world where AquaCapri's Light burned radiant and unchallenged. It vanished as swiftly as it came, but in its wake, a spark of hope remained.

"This,"Chronia whispered, her voice now barely louder than the hum of the chamber,"is but one possibility. A glimpse of what may come—if you choose to fight for it."

Capri's breath escaped slowly as her fingers interlaced with Aqua's. Together, they turned toward the archway. The mists of the Temporal Realm stirred beyond, a veil between moments.

They had come seeking answers. What they found instead was a truth more enduring than certainty—hope.

As they stepped into the swirling veil, Aqua spoke with quiet resolve."We'll break the cycle."

Capri smiled, her voice the echo of his."Together."

Behind them, the Hall of Ages grew still. Its walls shifted once more, subtle and slow—as though time itself had acknowledged their vow.

The future awaited—uncertain, infinite, and alive with possibility.

14.2 The Cycle of Ages

After their solemn passage through the Hall of Ages, where echoes of their past and glimpses of cosmic truths stirred something ancient within, Aqua and Capri were summoned by Chronia to a place known only to the Mystics of Time—the Eternal Spiral. It was not a summons of words but of purpose, spoken through the quiet rhythm of time itself. Guided by Chronia's presence and the pull of a deeper calling, they ascended into the Spiral to confront a question that no weapon could answer: Was the fate of all things bound to repeat, or could it be rewritten? With the balance of the cosmos teetering at the edge of renewal or ruin, Chronia revealed that only those who dared face the full weight of time could hope to change it. Their journey into the Spiral was not a battle—but a reckoning.

The Eternal Spiral stretched before them—a vast staircase of translucent crystal that wound endlessly into the stars. Its steps shimmered with the resonance of ancient eras, each tread glowing with faint glimmers of Light drawn from the very Essence of time. Cosmic radiance from distant galaxies danced across the walls, casting a shifting symphony of color over Aqua and Capri, who stood solemnly at its base. The sheer grandeur of the place was overwhelming—each step a monument to the passage of ages, to the rise and fall of forgotten worlds.

Chronia, Mystic of Time, moved with the grace of a being woven into the fabric of the universe. Her robes shimmered like they had been spun from living stardust, and though her voice was soft, it echoed like a whisper from the heart of eternity itself.

"The Eternal Spiral is the universe in motion,"she said, her words carrying a gravity that both comforted and unsettled."Each step is a turn of the cycle—creation, destruction, and rebirth. The rhythm repeats across ages. As you ascend, you will feel the weight of time— the echoes of what was, what is, and what may yet be."

Aqua tightened his grip on Capri's hand, a silent anchor in the vast unknown. His eyes lifted toward the spiral that vanished into the stars above."We've faced darkness before, fought across realms. But this..."His voice dropped to a murmur,"This feels beyond anything we've ever known."

Fingers intertwined, Capri's usual confidence dimmed."What if we're just part of it?"she asked, barely audible."What if everything we've done—everything we've sacrificed—is just another thread in this endless weave?"

Chronia, ascending slowly ahead of them, paused and turned. Her eyes, ancient and vast, held the weight of countless epochs. When she spoke again, her voice was steady with timeless truth.

"The universe is a spiral,"she said."Ever turning, ever echoing. With each revolution come new trials, new hopes... and familiar patterns. To break free, one must find the courage to change—and the strength to sacrifice."

Capri's gaze rose again, following the spiral's endless arc. The path stretched before them like an eternal question. As her heartbeat quickened, visions began to unfold upon the walls around them— spectacles of empire banners flying proudly, only to fall into dust; galaxies spinning like celestial wheels, ablaze before fading into the Void. Every image, every rise and fall, felt like a mirror of their own journey. The weight of recurrence pressed on her soul like a silent tide.

With each step upward, the burden grew heavier. The hum of the universe grew louder—a heartbeat that pulsed not through air but through their very beings. Time no longer felt abstract. It became a force—alive, pressing against their every breath. They were no longer witnesses. They had become part of the Spiral.

Flashes of their past battles danced before them—memories of victory, sorrow, love and loss—reflected in the collapse and resurgence of civilizations etched in light along the walls. The rhythm of existence— conflict, destruction, rebirth—persisted. No matter how hard they had fought, the pattern endured.

Capri's breath trembled. A weight pressed against her chest as despair crept in."We've done this before, haven't we?"she said, her voice strained."We fight, we win... and then it begins again. What if we're destined to lose everything—over and over?"

Aqua turned, steady in the storm of her doubt. His expression bore the strength of battles past, softened by their shared journey."We're not bound by what came before,"he said, his voice unwavering."We carry the past, yes—but we're not chained to it."

Chronia ascended without turning, her gaze distant, her voice carrying the resonance of eons."To change what has always been, you must walk into the unknown. The cycle can be broken—but it requires a sacrifice. Of certainty. Of comfort. Of all that you think you know."

Around them, the spiral shimmered and shifted. The past gave way to visions of the future, weaving themselves into the present. Glimpses emerged—victories over the Void, realms rescued from collapse—but also darker possibilities. Failures. Shadows consuming stars. The gravity of choice bore down on them like collapsing suns.

Capri faltered, her fear surfacing."But how do we know?"she asked, her voice fragile."How do we know that our choice won't just lead us back here? That we're not making the same mistakes again?"

Aqua's eyes flared with quiet resolve."We don't,"he replied."That's what makes the choice matter. We don't know the future... but we know why we fight. We fight for unity, for love. That's our compass."

Chronia stopped once more, her gaze turning back to them. Her eyes shone like time's own flame, bearing the weight of endless tomorrows."The future is not fixed. It is shaped by what you choose—

here, now. You are the Echoes of Time. Bound to its spiral, yes, but not its prisoner. Do not forget this."

The walls of the Eternal Spiral shimmered again, revealing branching timelines—some radiant with harmony, others dark with devastation. The climb was no longer merely physical. It had become an ascent of spirit and soul. Each step tested their resolve, echoing their greatest fears and most sacred hopes. The rise and fall of stars reflected not just history but the struggle within their hearts.

They began to understand—the bond they shared was more than love. It was a force interwoven with the destiny of all things. That connection, so powerful and pure, was now fused with the fate of the cosmos itself. If they faltered, if they gave in to despair, the universe might descend into shadow once more.

The air thinned. Cold crept in with every breath. The hum of the cosmos had become a full symphony, vibrating in their bones. Doubt and hope swirled like twin storms.

Capri's steps slowed. Her voice trembled."What if we're just another turn of the spiral?"she whispered."What if it always ends the same way?"

Aqua halted beside her. His breath came heavy, but his gaze remained fixed upward—then downward, to the path behind them. He turned, meeting her eyes, his voice low but resolute.

"We can't let the past define the future,"he said."We have the power to change the pattern—to become something new. Together."

Chronia remained silent. Her ancient eyes observed, unblinking, unreadable—yet behind them, a flicker of understanding stirred as if even she could not see what might come next.

At last, they reached the summit.

The final step led them into a vast, silent expanse—the edge of time itself. The visions vanished. All that remained was the stillness of the stars, the hush of possibility.

Before them stretched infinity.

Capri's heart raced as she stared into the Void."What now?"she asked, her voice barely a breath.

Aqua stood beside her, eyes on the horizon."Now... we choose."

The universe waited—watching.

Together, at the pinnacle of the Spiral, Aqua and Capri held the power to shape more than their fate. In that suspended moment, eternity listened.

And they knew—however uncertain the future—the story was still theirs to write.

14.3 Future's Promise

The Star Nexus shimmered before them, an ethereal beacon suspended against the dark canvas of the cosmos. Set at the pinnacle of the Eternal Spiral, this sacred place was where time and destiny intertwined. Side by side, Aqua and Capri ascended the final steps—hearts heavy with the weight of their journey, yet uplifted by the awe that surrounded them. Each breath carried the pulse of the universe itself, the very air alive and shimmering with the radiance of a thousand stars.

The walls of the Nexus were no ordinary boundaries—they flowed like rivers of living stardust, shifting and swirling with celestial grace.

Constellations formed and faded in endless cycles, mirroring the breath of existence. It felt as though they had stepped into the very heart of creation, where past, present, and future coalesced into a single, breathtaking tapestry.

At the threshold stood Chronia, Seer of Time. Her presence was serene yet immeasurably powerful. Robes rippled like the sands of an eternal hourglass, and her eyes held the glow of ages—Light untouched by mortal comprehension. She welcomed them without words, offering a silent nod that spoke volumes. Chronia was not merely ancient; she was ageless—a living embodiment of time's eternal rhythm.

"Welcome,"she said, her voice gentle yet resounding like the echo of a forgotten star."To the Star Nexus, where all futures converge, and the paths of time lay bare before you."

A glance passed between the two—fingers intertwining in silent resolve. Here, at the apex of their odyssey, they would witness the future they had fought for, suffered for, and vowed to protect. But were they truly ready to behold it?

As they stepped forward, the floor glowed with quiet brilliance, pulsing with the warmth of suns long extinguished yet still remembered. Each footfall sent waves of Light rippling through the chamber, illuminating the stardust walls with celestial fire. Above, the ceiling expanded into a boundless sky where stars hummed a haunting melody—a cosmic lullaby that echoed within their souls, a reminder of every sacrifice, every trial that had shaped their path.

In the center of the chamber, the air began to shimmer, and the threads of time wove together in radiant strands. A vision was forming.

A vision of the future.

Capri's breath caught as the image unfolded—a universe in perfect balance. Worlds once ravaged by conflict now flourished in peace. The harmony between Light and darkness was no longer a fragile hope but a living, thriving force. Civilizations moved in unison, realms attuned to one another, their energies aligned, their destinies intertwined. The sight was so exquisitely beautiful it brought tears to her eyes.

"This..."she whispered, awe softening every syllable."This is the future we dreamed of. A universe in balance—where Light and darkness exist together, without conflict, without fear."

He remained silent, gaze fixed on the unfolding vision. Hope surged in his chest, yet with it came the familiar weight of responsibility. He felt the pulse of the Nexus beneath his feet and heard the whisper of stars singing their ancient song. This future was real. It was possible. But it would not come without sacrifice.

As the vision shifted, so too did the warmth in Capri's expression. Fleeting peace gave way to moments of loss. Familiar faces—beloved friends, trusted allies, even family—faded into stardust. The cost of this dream became starkly visible. Her heart clenched with sorrow, the grip of uncertainty closing in.

"The cost..."Her voice broke, her hand tightening around his."Can we truly pay it? Is this future worth all we must lose?"

His eyes met hers, unwavering. His voice, though soft, carried the full measure of his resolve."We always knew this path wouldn't be easy. But seeing it—so vivid, so real—it hurts. And yet, if this is the future, we can give those who come after us... then yes. It's worth it. We have to believe it is."

Chronia stepped forward, her presence a stillness that demanded attention. Her gaze was deep as time itself, her voice a gentle echo of cosmic truth.

"The future is a promise,"she said."But also a challenge. The road ahead is marked by trials. Sacrifices will be made—great ones. Yet the reward is beyond imagining. A universe free of the old cycles. A peace that can truly take root."

Capri turned to Aqua, her eyes brimming not only with love and pain but with fierce determination. They had endured betrayals, battles, and the relentless burden of their roles. And still, their bond endured. Deeper than ever. Stronger than doubt.

Together, they would choose. Together, they would rise.

"Then we'll face it together,"she said at last, her voice steady, her resolve like steel wrapped in starlight."No matter the cost. No matter the challenges. We stand side by side. We'll build this future—together."

He looked at her, pride swelling in his chest, love radiating from his soul. In her eyes, he saw not only the strength they shared but the unwavering faith that had carried them through the worst of times. His grip on her hand tightened as he nodded.

"Together,"he whispered."Always."

The vision still shimmered in the Nexus. A glimpse of what might be. Peace. Harmony. Worlds united under a single dream. But so, too, did the shadows of its price. The memory of battles yet to be fought and the burden of choices they would never be able to undo. Yet, as their eyes locked, they knew they would face it all. Because the promise of that future was worth every trial.

Chronia stood silently at the edge of the chamber, her gaze a gentle weight upon them. She did not speak again, for there was nothing more to be said. The truth had already been revealed. The rest was theirs to choose.

And so, with hearts aligned and hands entwined, they turned from the vision and began the descent. The stars overhead sang on—a melody of possibility, a haunting refrain that echoed through the Nexus with clarity and peace.

As they exited the chamber, that vision clung to their minds. Not just a glimpse of destiny but a promise they carried forward. A vow not only to each other but to the very fabric of the universe.

They would walk into whatever darkness lay ahead. Trusting in their love, their unity, to light the way. Through storm and sorrow, they would stand firm—together. Breaking the chains of the past, they would forge a path no one had dared walk before.

And as the Light of the Nexus faded behind them, the Eternal Spiral stretched downward like a river of stars. The song of the cosmos followed them still, threading itself into their every step—a lullaby for the future, yet unwritten.

The universe held its breath, and at its center, two souls walked as one, shaping tomorrow with every heartbeat, every vow, and every step toward the dawn.

CHAPTER

15

THE GATHERING OF THE GUARDIANS

THE FINAL WAR DOES NOT WAIT FOR READINESS—IT DEMANDS IT.

 # CHAPTER 15

△ MAXIMUS, THE ETERNAL QUILL
AQUARII: LUNARETH VAL'ANAR.

 OPENING WHISPER – CH. 15

△ VALDUM, THE CELESTIAL ARCHITECT
AQUARII: ANARION XAL RIVEN'DOR.

CLOSING WHISPER – CH. 15

15.1 The Call to Arms

The sun hovered low, casting golden Light across Aquaterra in long, luminous shadows. At the heart of the realm stood the towering Celestial Citadel, newly reborn from the ashes of past battles. It had not been merely reconstructed—it had been reimagined. Each stone bore the power and purpose of the Elemental Lords, Mystics, and Star Warriors. Starstone walls shimmered with a soft celestial glow, and ancient runes etched deep into their surface pulsed with cosmic energy. These were no mere symbols—they were living oaths: to protect, to unite, to defend all that was sacred.

Above, the spires stretched toward the heavens, pulsing with the rhythm of elemental forces drawn from the very fabric of the cosmos. Here, earth, sky, and stars converged, composing a luminous symphony—a radiant beacon of unity defying the Void's encroaching shadow.

Within the Citadel, tension thickened the air. The clink of armor being fastened, the rhythmic sharpening of celestial blades, and the soft hum of woven spells echoed through vaulted halls. The leaders and warriors had faced countless battles, yet all understood—this one was different. No longer a fight for territory or pride; this was a war for existence. The fate of the cosmos now rested in their hands.

At the heart of this assembly stood Aqua and Capri, the commanders of the alliance. Side by side, they exuded a calm presence, yet beneath it, both carried the burden of destiny. They had led armies into battle before, but never against a threat so vast, so consuming.

Aqua's voice rose, firm and clear, cutting through the silence."This is it. Everything we've fought for, every sacrifice—it leads here. The Void will not stop until every last spark of Light is devoured. We must hold the line."

Capri placed a steady hand on his arm. Her voice, though gentler, carried unshakable resolve."Our allies are ready. They believe in us and in what we fight for. We must believe in them—and in ourselves. If we falter in that, how can we ask them to risk all?"

The great hall fell silent. One by one, the leaders of the allied realms stepped forward, each radiating immense power. Beneath their grandeur, Aqua sensed what none dared voice: a shared fear of what was to come.

The first to step forward was Solarion, Lord of the Sun. His golden aura filled the chamber with warmth, his armor gleaming as if forged in the very heart of a star. His voice rang deep and commanding, echoing across the hall."The Light of the sun shall guide us through the darkness. We, the bearers of its flame, stand with you, ready to face whatever dares challenge the Light."

Lunara, the Moon Priestess, followed in graceful silence. Her silver robes shimmered like liquid starlight as she moved. Eyes deep with ancient wisdom reflected the stillness of a thousand nights. Her voice was a soft dusk wind."The night, too, holds power,"she whispered."It is not our enemy, but our ally. Hidden in shadow lies strength. When the moment comes, we shall strike—unseen but unyielding."

Behind Lunara strode Gaian, the Earth Warden, his towering figure exuding raw, untamed strength. Every step he took seemed to shake the ground ever so slightly, a reminder of the indomitable force he commanded. His deep voice rumbled like a distant quake."The earth beneath us is enduring, as am I. Let the storm come—we will stand firm, rooted in our strength, unshakable."

Aqua acknowledged them each with a solemn nod. They were titans of their realms, wielders of vast and ancient forces—yet they stood not as rulers but as comrades in the same cause. In each gaze he met, he saw it clearly: beneath their bold words, they carried the same fear. What if they were not enough?

Capri's hand gently tightened on his arm, sensing the weight of his thoughts."They are here because they believe,"she said quietly."In the cause. In us. We must carry that belief, too."

He turned toward her, his voice low."It's not them, I doubt,"he admitted."It's us. What if we fall short? What if—"

"We won't,"she said, cutting in, calm but firm."We can't. Not this time. Together, we've faced the Void before—we will again. But this time, we do it with all of them."

They exchanged a final glance. Around them, the leaders returned to their places, the silence in the great hall humming with resolve.

Aqua and Capri ascended the high walls of the Citadel, their eyes scanning the vast assembly below. The courtyard overflowed with warriors—an army unlike any ever gathered. From across the cosmos, they had come. Towering Star Warriors stood sentinel, their gleaming armor catching the dying light like mirrors of starlight. Elemental Lords stood with their legions, avatars of raw power: Pyronix, wreathed in shifting flame; Aqualith, rippling with the presence of oceans; Zyrion, blurred at the edges like the wind itself.

In the distance, the central spire of the Citadel—the Beacon of Unity —pulsed with radiant energy. A protective shimmer cloaked the stronghold, beating in rhythm with the energy of the army below. It was more than a shield; it was a symbol, a living bond forged through alliance, faith, and fire.

Yet even as the evening breeze stirred their cloaks, the weight of what lay ahead bore down upon them. This was their moment—perhaps the final one before war returned to claim all.

Capri's voice came soft as the wind."Do you think we're ready for this? Truly?"

Aqua remained quiet, watching as the horizon swallowed the last sliver of sun. The world below melted into hues of crimson and gold."I don't know,"he confessed."But we must be. There's no room for doubt. Too much depends on us. If we fail..."

She interrupted, voice clear and steady."We won't. Not while we stand side by side."

He turned to her then, and in her eyes, he found his own fear reflected —alongside the same unwavering hope. For a long while, they stood in silence, united in both purpose and vulnerability. They had always known this fight might take everything. But still, they would give it.

The final rays of Light vanished. The Citadel shimmered in twilight, aglow with the quiet strength of those who stood ready. Below, the army stirred, murmurs rising like a whisper through the night.

Tomorrow, the storm would come.

Tonight, the Light held fast.

The calm before the storm had never felt so fragile.

15.2 The Assembly of Ages

The Assembly Hall, nestled at the heart of the Celestial Citadel, was a place steeped in the living memory of the cosmos. Its vast circular chamber, crowned with a ceiling that seemed to brush the heavens, thrummed with the quiet hum of celestial energy. The very air shimmered with timeless resonance, echoing the collective weight of eons. At the hall's center stood the starstone table—an awe-inspiring relic hewn from a fallen celestial stone, its polished surface gleaming with an ethereal, shifting Light. It mirrored the stars above, where the domed ceiling displayed a living map of the universe, each celestial body drifting in real-time. A visual reminder that the forces of creation and destruction never slept.

The chamber walls spoke in silence—ancient tapestries stretched across time itself, depicting the birth of the first stars, the rise and fall of galactic empires, and the unending war between Light and darkness. These woven chronicles glowed faintly in the cosmic Light, casting a soft radiance over the gathered figures and reflecting the gravity of the moment to come.

A hush fell over the hall as the most powerful beings in existence took their places around the table. Each bore not only the mantle of their realms but also the weight of the universe's future. The Void crept ever closer, its hunger a threat to all that had ever been. This meeting was no mere council—it was the culmination of countless lifetimes spent preparing for a war that now loomed inevitable.

At the head of the table stood Aqua and Capri—twin pillars of unity. His gaze, deep and fathomless like the oceans he ruled, swept the room, reading every tension. Beside him, she radiated with an ethereal Light drawn from the stars themselves. Together, they embodied harmony—Light and water, sun and sea, hope and resolve. Yet even they could feel the burden of the battle pressing near.

Capri broke the silence first. Her voice was steady, though beneath its calm cadence ran a ripple of tension.

"We've all faced the Void in our own ways," she began, her gaze sweeping across the table. "We know its power, its endless hunger. But this time is different. This time, we are not alone. We are united. And together, we are stronger than we ever could be on our own."

Her words lingered in the chamber, a beacon of defiance against the encroaching dark. She turned to Aqua, offering a subtle nod. He stepped forward, his tone resolute yet urgent.

"The Void has always thrived on division," he said. "It feeds on fear and isolation. But we've seen what unity can accomplish. If we stand as one, not even the Void can break us. But let there be no illusion—this will test us. We must be ready for the greatest battle of our lives."

A murmured ripple passed through the hall as the leaders absorbed his words. Some faces tightened with grim resolve; others reflected the weight of ancient contemplation.

Astralis, the Seer of the Stars, was the first to rise. Draped in robes that shimmered with the Light of distant galaxies, she stood as a living constellation. Her eyes, ageless and knowing, had witnessed the rise and fall of worlds.

"The stars reveal many paths," she said, her voice soft and resonant like the whisper of nebulae. "But they do not choose for us. The future flows like a river with countless currents. We must be deliberate in choosing ours—for once chosen, there is no turning back."

Her words struck a chord, and a chill passed through the assembly—a reminder of what was at stake.

Next came Thalassa, Guardian of the Oceans. Her sea-green hair cascaded like waves, and in her hand gleamed her trident—a symbol of power and perseverance.

"The oceans have known many wars," she said, her voice as deep as the abyss. "But this will be unlike any before. We do not fight only for our waters but for every star and every world. Like the tides, we will wear down the Void—one relentless wave at a time."

Tension gathered like a storm as the debate began to stir. Solarion, the Sun Lord, stepped forward, radiant in golden armor that blazed with the brilliance of a thousand suns. His voice thundered across the chamber.

"We cannot afford hesitation," he proclaimed. "The power of Light will blind the Void. We must strike first and strike hard. Let the darkness be scorched before it can gain ground!"

His fervor was met with cool resistance. Lunara, Lady of the Night, moved with quiet grace, her silver robes flowing like moonlight across still waters. Her eyes, dark as the void between stars, held a calm wisdom.

"We must not be reckless," she said evenly. "The Void feeds on chaos. But shadows can conceal us. Let us strike from where they least expect —with silence, with patience. That is where our strength lies."

Gaian, Earth Guardian and voice of balance rose next. The floor beneath him shifted subtly as though the very planet moved with his breath. His armor, wrapped in vine and stone, resonated with ancient calm.

"The earth teaches us through endurance,"he said."We cannot be only force or only stillness. We must use the elements. We must build walls they cannot breach and strike with precision they cannot counter. Let balance be our blade."

The chamber hummed with energy as voices clashed and strategies collided. Solarion's followers championed overwhelming radiance; Lunara's, a campaign of cunning and stealth. Others, like Thalassa and Gaian, urged a tempered blend—defense paired with patient aggression. The currents of opinion swirled faster, and at their eye stood Aqua and Capri, watchful and silent.

Capri could feel the mounting pressure coiling within her. Doubt whispered in her thoughts like a breeze before a storm. She leaned closer to Aqua, her voice barely a breath.

"What if we're wrong?"

Her question trembled with the weight of every realm they sought to protect.

"What if the Void is too strong?"

Aqua's jaw clenched, but his gaze remained steady.

"We cannot afford doubt,"he murmured."We've come too far. We must trust ourselves—trust in them. We hold the line now. We do not break."

The clamor rose to its peak, voices layered with conviction, fear, and hope—until a sudden hush swept the room. All eyes turned to Aqua and Capri. The final decision belonged to them.

Capri stepped forward. Her voice rang clear, unwavering, like starlight piercing the darkness.

"We will strike hard and fast—but not recklessly," she declared. "We will use the brilliance of the sun to blind the Void, the silence of the night to conceal our approach, and the strength of the earth to hold our ground. We will not face the darkness from one side—we will come at it from all directions, with every force we command."

Then Aqua spoke, his tone calm as the deep tides.

"We will move as the sea does—unstoppable, surging, impossible to cage. The Void will not have the time to recover, to regroup. We will not allow it. Together, we will rise as one and drive the darkness back to where it came from."

A breathless silence followed. The weight of their plan settled across the assembly like the hush before the battle. Then, one by one, the leaders began to nod—slowly at first, then with growing conviction. It was a daring strategy. But it was their best hope.

As the meeting drew to a close, the tension softened. Yet the burden of what was to come remained ever-present. Aqua and Capri stood unmoving at the head of the starstone table, surrounded by those who would fight beside them. But in that sacred moment, they bore the solitary weight of command.

They were no longer just leaders—they were the fulcrum of fate.

And as they looked out upon the gathered Guardians of the cosmos, they knew with piercing certainty: whatever came next, the universe would never again be what it once was.

15.3 The Strategy of Light

The War Room of the Celestial Citadel pulsed with concentrated energy—a fusion of purpose, prophecy, and finality. This was no ordinary war council. It was the convergence of every vow sworn at PaxProfundis, every alliance born in the halls of Unity, and every truth unearthed in the scrolls of the Ancients. The battle no longer loomed —it pressed at the gates of creation itself.

The starstone dome above reflected a living constellation. Shifting stars and glowing cosmic lines moved in rhythm with the tides of the universe, casting a pale light on those gathered below. At the heart of the chamber floated the Celestial War Map, a radiant orb swirling with translucent layers of time, terrain, and strategy. Aquaterra shimmered in its core—its luminous cities, river veins, and fortified citadels clearly marked—while encroaching Void surged in shadowed waves from the peripheries, a malignant tide set to consume all.

Surrounding the map were the circular seats of command, each carved from stardust-laced marble. At the apex stood Aqua and Capri, robed in celestial regalia woven with threads of Light and elemental essence. Behind them towered the four Supreme Generals, embodiments of cosmic defense: Vortizian, Master of Water and Time Currents, calm as the abyss; Celestara, Celestial Healer and Shieldbearer of the Light; Tempestor, Stormlord of the Sky Spires; and Valorus, The Shield of Valor—Supreme Guardian of the Champions of AquaCapri and protector of all constellations.

Each general's aura flared subtly in response to the shifting energies in the room. Their very presence emanated the authority of galaxies.

Seated below them, surrounding the map's luminous projection, were the realm's fiercest defenders. Zephyr, eyes closed, attuned to the currents of air beyond the chamber. Luna, silent and serene, fingers tracing patterns of Void infiltration in her dream-bound journal. Beside them sat Gaian, the Earthbound Strategist, whose silence bore the weight of mountains. The three formed a triad of insight, constantly interpreting the ever-shifting energy lines threading through the realm.

Aetherion, Guardian of Harmonic Balance, stood in quiet contemplation at the map's edge. At the same time, Pyronix, the Flame Sculptor, blazed with controlled intensity. Aqualith, the Sovereign of the Sea Tridents, radiated with oceanic calm. All were drawn here by the same purpose: to shape the final strategy that would determine the fate of the cosmos.

The War Map morphed again, now displaying the defensive grid of Aquaterra: citadel walls fortified with mystic wards, sky bastions aligned with storm-break cannons, and subterranean trenches mapped for coordinated collapse. Three main battlefronts flickered with urgency—Skyward Bastion in the northeast, Shieldspire Plateau in the west, and the leyline-crossed Aquacrest Valley in the south. At each location, the towering silhouettes of the Stardust Warriors began taking formation—gleaming sentinels born of stars, their limbs forged from Duroxium alloys, and their eyes glowing with the light of a thousand suns.

Capri approached the map, voice sharpened by resolve.
"Here," she said, motioning to the southern ridge, "is where the Void will first strike. The leyline convergence is vulnerable, and they will try to tear it open."

Aqua stepped beside her. "Above, the skies over Solaris Crest must not fall. Pyronix, you command the Emberwings—ignite the aether, disrupt their approach from the upper realms."

Pyronix bowed slightly, flames rippling along his arms."Their shadows will burn before they reach our sun."

Aqualith stepped forward, voice steady."The waters of Aquaterra will not be taken. My trident will stand where the river meets the Void."

A nod passed between Aqua and Capri. The council had begun, and soon, destiny would follow.

The orb shifted again, expanding its projection to encompass not only Aquaterra but the peripheral starfronts surrounding it. Waves of Void energy slithered at the edges of space like black serpents, closing in from three directions. Strategic overlays flickered across the map— rune shields, beacon towers, warp gates, and reinforcement corridors came into view, color-coded by realm and readiness.

Aqua raised his hand, commanding silence."We now define the roles that will shape the course of the battle. Each action, each breath, must be intentional. There is no margin for chaos."

He turned toward Celestara, her aura glowing with waves of radiant gold and silver."You will oversee the protection of the wounded and maintain the cosmic shields at Shieldspire Plateau. Your barrier domes must never falter."

Celestara inclined her head."Their pain will not pass unguarded. The Light shall cradle those who bleed."

"To the west,"Capri added,"Tempestor, you will command the cloud ships and storm-sentinels across the Skyward Bastion. Turn the skies against them—let no enemy find shelter in the winds."

The Stormlord's voice cracked like thunder."The skies shall roar in defiance. Lightning will answer their darkness."

Aqua gestured to the map's southern reaches."Vortizian, your command lies beneath—the trenches of Aquacrest and the flowgates of the tide fields. Time and current will bend to your will."

Vortizian's form shimmered, timeless and fluid."The river of destiny will be rewritten in their ruin."

Capri's gaze then turned to Valorus, who stood still as a mountain, his hands clasped before him, his armor etched with symbols of every constellation.

"You,"she said,"will be our immovable force. From Solaris Crest, you'll oversee the Stardust Warriors' deployment. If the Void breaches our lines, you are the last shield. Hold the center. Hold everything."

Valorus nodded once."So long as I draw breath, no shadow shall pass."

The orb flared again, highlighting three pathways of Void ingress. Capri traced the motion with her hand, observing the irregularity of the patterns.

"They will not attack as they have before,"she warned."They will seek to unravel us—twist formation into confusion. Zephyr, you will ride the winds to intercept their scouts. Disrupt their intelligence. Keep their eyes blind."

Zephyr's voice was soft yet charged with focus."The wind listens. I will scatter their whispers before they form."

"Luna,"Aqua said,"we need you in the realm of dreams. Look beyond the physical. Sense their doubt, their misdirection. If they manipulate thought or feeling—we must know."

She met his gaze, calm and assured."They cannot mask their shadows from the night. I will find their fear."

"Aetherion,"Capri continued,"stand between realities. Monitor the harmonics of our realms. If anything falls out of balance—act. Disrupt the disruption."

The harmonic guardian gave a subtle nod."I will tune the stars to truth."

Aqua glanced at Gaian, seated still beside Zephyr and Luna."Gaian, your role is the unseen foundation. Reshape the terrain behind the main lines. Should they break through, collapse the earth beneath their step."

"I will,"he rumbled."Let them walk into the waiting jaws of the world."

Capri looked across the room."This is our line. The balance of all things rests here. Every constellation that burns in the heavens watches now. There is no fallback."

Aether, from the alcove of scrolls, stepped forward then, eyes shimmering with ancient Light."The war to come has been sung by the stars for eons. And still, they wonder—will we fulfill the melody... or break it?"

No one answered. But in that silence, a conviction was born.

A quiet shift in the air signaled a new current of tension as Luminarion stepped forward, radiant in golden robes that shimmered with the Light of the first dawn. His aura softened the shadows, yet it did not dispel them entirely. He looked into the depths of the Celestial War Map, then toward Aqua and Capri.

"The Light blinds when wielded carelessly,"he said, his voice resonant and ancient."But in the right hands, it reveals what the Void wishes to hide. We must strike with brilliance but not arrogance. I ask only that our first blow be one of guidance—not vengeance."

He raised his palm, and the orb responded. Sunlight bathed the map's western front, illuminating fault lines in the Void's advance."Their coordination weakens when exposed. I will bend Light to scatter their unity."

Capri regarded him with a nod."Your Light will open the battlefield. But we must also close it."

From the opposite side of the room, a figure stirred in near silence—ShadowVeil, cloaked in folds of darkness, his presence barely tethered to form. He moved like an absence, yet every step he took grounded the room in stillness.

"The Void will not fear Light,"he murmured,"but it will distrust its own shadow. Let them see their own fear wearing our faces."

He extended a single finger toward the orb, and immediately, dark tendrils spread across the map's eastern quadrant—intercepting Void communication lines, collapsing transit gates, and triggering hidden detonations."We strike from silence. Precision. Sabotage."

The room fell into a sacred stillness as the two greatest forces—Light and Shadow—stood in harmony. For an eternity, they had existed in tension. Now, that tension was a blade honed to a single purpose.

Aqua broke the silence."Luminarion, you lead the opening wave. Illuminate their weakness. Create confusion where they expect clarity."

The Sovereign of Radiance bowed, hands glowing."They will see nothing but the dawn."

"ShadowVeil,"Capri followed,"you move after the first strike. Target their leadership. Sever their coordination. Do not let them reform."

The master of shadows offered no reply, only a brief shimmer as his form flickered—gone before their eyes, a silent promise written in absence.

Zephyr turned to Luna and whispered,"Even silence finds purpose here."

She smiled faintly."Even darkness bows to hope."

The orb dimmed slightly, adjusting its hues as zones were finalized. Then, from the edge of the council, Aetherwind stepped forward. Clad in silver-laced indigo, the Windwalker bore no weapon but carried the weight of insight.

"We speak of formations, fortifications, and flanking corridors,"he said, voice even and calm."But the Void does not merely march. It infects. It twists. It speaks in voices that sound like our own."

He approached the map and pointed not at the enemy lines but at the heart of Aquaterra itself."They will not just strike where we are vulnerable—they will make us believe we already lost. Their true weapon is despair."

Capri listened carefully, then turned to the chamber."Then we must armor more than bodies. We must shield the soul. Every commander, every warrior—remind them what we fight for. Remind them who they are."

Aetherion stepped beside her, his tone solemn."Then let the Song of Memory be sung. Let the truth echo through the ranks."

Aqua's voice resonated low."Because the Void cannot consume what remembers the Light."

The commanders nodded. All understood.

Aqua stepped forward, his gaze sweeping across the war table, from the radiant sovereignty of Luminarion to the quiet storm of ShadowVeil, from the elemental strength of the generals to the steadfast resolve of their closest companions. He saw not just warriors —but anchors of the cosmos.

"The Void comes not only for territory,"he said, voice rising with clarity and thunder,"it comes for memory. For meaning. For the spark that makes each soul a star. But we are not merely guardians of land— we are guardians of purpose."

He turned toward the center of the Celestial War Map, now pulsing with threads of Light and darkness."Our enemies will flood Aquaterra. They will try to sever us from hope. But they will find no opening—only unity."

Capri joined him, her presence fierce and unwavering."We stand not as fractured realms but as one breath of creation. Let our strength be their unraveling. Let them hear the song of our defiance in every heartbeat of this world."

Valorus stepped forward, his shield drawn and glowing."My post will not fall. The Champions of AquaCapri stand ready."

Tempestor cracked his knuckles as thunder rolled behind his eyes."Let them try the skies."

Celestara's light flared outward in waves."Their hatred will break against our healing."

Vortizian bowed deeply, his voice calm and echoing."And in the currents of time, their decay will dissolve."

From the side, Pyronix ignited both fists with controlled flame."They will taste fire before they see the dawn."

Aqualith brandished his royal trident."And the waters will drag their shadows to the deep."

Zephyr's eyes closed briefly."I will ride the winds beyond their sight."

Luna's voice followed his, quiet and resolute."And I will trap their dreams in a maze of Light."

Gaian stood without rising, but his words carried weight."The ground beneath them will betray every step."

Aetherion nodded toward Aetherwind."And I will bind their chaos in harmony."

ShadowVeil reappeared beside the orb, silent, only offering a nod to Aqua. Luminarion met it with one of his own. In their mutual glance, centuries of difference were erased—opposites united under shared purpose.

Aether stepped forth one final time, holding in his hand a scroll sealed with the Crest of Eternity."This contains the Song of Memory. It will be sung by our people at sunrise. Let every voice rise with it—so even in silence, we remember who we are."

Capri looked toward the orb one last time."Mark this moment. It is no longer the beginning of a war. It is the rise of the realms."

Aqua extended his arm to her, and she placed her hand upon his. Then, they both touched the orb. Instantly, a surge of Light exploded outward, tracing along the stone walls of the Citadel, into the sky, and across the battle map.

The heavens above the War Room shimmered.

Stars aligned.

And in that alignment, a declaration was written across the night.

All commanders rose. Armored footsteps echoed. Weapons shimmered with starlight. The champions turned toward the doors that would lead them to the fields of destiny.

Aqua's voice, calm and final, cut through the silence one last time."We begin now."

Capri's whisper followed, yet echoed like thunder."Let the Light rise."

Together, they walked into the storm.

CHAPTER

16

VEILS OF ILLUSION

ONLY BY KNOWING ONESELF CAN THE VOID BE FACED.

CHAPTER 16

△ VALDUM, THE CELESTIAL ARCHITECT
AQUARII: DRAVENTH XAL KORUUN.

OPENING WHISPER – CH. 16

△ MAXIMUS, THE ETERNAL QUILL
AQUARII: KORUUN VE'THALOR.

CLOSING WHISPER – CH. 16

16.1 The Maze of Mirrors

After the great assembly in the Celestial Citadel, where the guardians, mystics, and warriors of AquaCapri united to forge a final strategy against the Void, a deeper understanding was revealed—victory would not come through might alone but through clarity of spirit. It was Chronia, the Seer of Time, who gently stepped forward, her voice flowing like starlight across water, and spoke of an ancient trial—the Maze of Mirrors. She had seen in the threads of time that Aqua, Capri, Luna, and Zephyr must confront this illusion-born labyrinth, for only by facing their innermost fears could they unlock the final path toward the Vault of Eternity, where the last key to the Void's undoing awaited. Their companions, including Valorus, Aetherion, Sylphara, and the rest of the chosen circle, escorted them to the entrance, standing vigil at the gate. Only those whose hearts were bound by truth could walk within.

The labyrinth sprawled endlessly in all directions, its walls of polished crystal mirrors reflecting distorted images of reality. Every step Aqua, Capri, Luna, and Zephyr took deepened the sense of disorientation. The air hung heavy with an oppressive force that gnawed at their minds, whispering doubts as if the maze itself were alive—sentient and waiting for them to falter.

Dim, pulsating Light seeped through cracks in the ceiling, casting an eerie glow that made their reflections shimmer unnaturally. What should have been simple images became mockeries—twisted, grotesque versions of themselves. The floor beneath them was smooth but subtly uneven, shifting underfoot as though the ground itself were guiding them deeper into its trap.

A constant sense of dread pervaded the air, magnifying with every step and breath. Their movements sent ripples through the mirrors, distorting the reflections until their doppelgängers sneered back at them, their mocking expressions growing louder in the echoing silence.

Capri (anxious):

"This place... it's trying to tear us apart. It knows our fears and our doubts. We must stay focused. Remember what we are fighting for."

Her voice, soft yet strained, sliced through the oppressive silence—though only barely. Aqua walked just behind her, his eyes locked on his own reflection in the mirrored walls. The image wavered, twisting until it no longer resembled him—at least, not the version he knew.

In the reflection, Aqua saw a broken version of himself. Behind him, the AquaCapri realm lay in ruins—its skies darkened, its people vanished. His reflection wore a cruel sneer, its eyes void of hope.

Aqua's reflection (mocking):

"Look at you, Aqua. Do you truly believe you can save them? You've always known you're not enough. You've already lost—you just don't realize it."

The words hit like a blow to the chest. Aqua stopped, staring helplessly at the distorted image. His heart pounded with doubt, and fear gripped him. The AquaCapri realm—his home—lay in ashes within the mirror. His warriors were dust, scattered by the cold winds of the Void.

Aqua (softly, to himself):

"What if... what if this is true? What if I fail them?"

His voice trembled. Breath shallow. It felt as though the weight of the universe pressed upon his shoulders, sinking him into despair. The labyrinth closed in, walls reflecting his deepest fears. The whispers grew louder in his mind.

Capri, sensing his turmoil, turned. Her eyes, wide with concern, met his. She could feel the maze pulling at them, trying to fracture their unity, to sow discord. Without hesitation, she stepped forward and laid a firm hand on his arm.

Capri (firmly):

"We're not lost yet. Don't let this place take hold of you. You're stronger than this."

He met her gaze, but the vision of a crumbling kingdom held him captive. The reflection sneered, stepping closer to the surface of the mirror, its malice intensifying.

Aqua's reflection (taunting):

"You can't protect them. You've never been enough. And deep down, you know it. The Void is coming, and when it does, everything you love will fall. You'll be powerless."

His fists clenched. His heart sank further into despair. The destruction, the darkness—it played before his eyes like a prophecy written in shadow. His hands, once steady with purpose, now trembled.

Then—a spark. Deep within, a flicker of memory ignited. Battles fought. Sacrifices made. He had felt this fear before, and still, he had stood. Still, he had risen.

He remembered what had always pushed him forward—it wasn't the certainty of victory but the will to fight, to believe in something beyond himself.

He tore his gaze away from the mirror and found Capri's presence—steady, unwavering.

Aqua (quiet but growing stronger):

"No... I won't let fear stop me."

The words released the pressure on his chest, letting strength flood through him. His voice grew, no longer faltering.

Aqua (defiant):

"I may not always be enough. But that's not what matters. What matters is standing for what I believe in—fighting for those I love, even when the odds seem impossible. I will protect them—because I must."

The image of the crumbling AquaCapri began to waver. Aqua's resolve cracked the illusion. The sneering reflection faltered, its certainty slipping.

Aqua's reflection (wavering):

"You think... you can win?"

His voice was calm. Steady. Unflinching.

Aqua:

"It's not about winning. It's about never giving up."

With a surge of will, he raised his hand—and the mirror shattered. A thousand pieces cascaded to the floor, fading into nothingness. The oppressive weight in the air lifted, if only slightly.

As they pressed deeper into the labyrinth, Capri came face to face with her own reflection. What stared back was nearly unrecognizable: a version of herself that was weak and worn. Her crown was tarnished and cracked, her robes tattered. Her eyes were hollow with doubt and regret. Behind her lay the ruins of Aquaterra.

Capri's reflection (whispering, mocking):

"You've always known, haven't you? Without Aqua, you are nothing. You've leaned on him because you cannot stand alone. Soon, you'll lose him—and what will you be then? A queen of ruins."

Capri's heart clenched. She had feared this—the whispered doubt that haunted her darkest nights. What if she truly was nothing without Aqua? What if she had always been just a shadow of his light?

The weight of her crown suddenly grew heavier.

Capri (softly, to herself):

"Am I truly nothing... without him?"

Her reflection stepped forward, voice low and insidious, wrapping around her like smoke.

Capri's reflection:

"Yes. You are nothing. Let the Void take you. Let it all end."

But something within Capri rebelled. A fire rose in her chest, burning the doubt. Yes, she had leaned on Aqua. But that did not make her weak.

She had her own power. Her own Light.

Her spine straightened. Her chin lifted. The tremble in her voice vanished, replaced by steel.

Capri (steadily):

"No. I am not a shadow. I've always had my own Light."

The reflection sneered, but she stood her ground. Her voice gained strength with every word, each syllable a pillar of her identity.

Capri (defiant):

"I may have leaned on Aqua, but I am more than that. My power is mine. I will not let you—or the Void—take that from me."

Cracks splintered across the reflection's surface, faint at first, then spreading rapidly.

Capri's reflection (desperate):

"You can't stand alone. You are nothing—"

Capri (with finality):

"I don't need to stand alone. But I can."

With one final breath of resolve, Capri watched the image shatter, fragments dissolving into mist. The weight that pressed on her heart melted away, replaced by quiet strength.

Elsewhere in the labyrinth, Zephyr moved through winding corridors. The winds rose around him, swirling with agitation. Ahead, his reflection coalesced—wild, untamed. The currents tore at the walls, shaking the mirrored maze with fury. The reflection's eyes glowed with chaos—a mirror of destruction.

Zephyr's reflection (mocking):

"You believe your winds bring balance, but all they do is destroy. You are a force of ruin, Zephyr. You've never brought peace—only chaos. How long until you destroy what you swore to protect?"

His heart thundered. He saw memories—chaotic battles, collapsed structures, lives scattered in the aftermath of his storms. He remembered the fear in others' eyes. And his own.

Zephyr (uneasy, doubting):

"I... I don't want to hurt anyone. I never meant for my power to—"

Laughter erupted from the reflection, cruel and echoing.

Zephyr's reflection (jeering):

"But you did. And you will again. You are a storm—wild, uncontrollable."

The winds howled louder, shaking the very ground beneath him. But through the chaos, he remembered something else. The rain that brought life. The breeze that carried seeds. The gentle winds that cooled a burning sky.

His voice steadied.

Zephyr (softly, to himself):

"My winds bring life. They are not just chaos."

The sneer faltered. The winds around the reflection wavered.

Zephyr (stronger now):

"I am not destruction. My power brings balance. I control it—it does not control me."

The chaos began to subside. The storm stilled.

Zephyr's reflection (desperate):

"You think you can control this power?"

Zephyr (with finality):

"I am the wind."

With a surge of controlled force, the mirror shattered into fine particles, scattering like dust on a breeze. The winds around him calmed, wrapping him in peace.

Luna's trial unfolded silently among them. Her reflection had whispered of isolation—that she would always walk alone, her light fading in the presence of others. But Luna, drawing upon her quiet strength and the harmony she carried within, looked her fear in the eye and replied only once:

Luna (softly):

"I was born of moonlight. And the moon never needs permission to shine."

And her reflection, too, dissolved into quiet mist.

At the center of the maze, the four emerged—Aqua, Capri, Zephyr, and Luna—reunited, their trials behind them. Though the air felt lighter, a quiet tension lingered. Before them loomed the Reflector: a swirling mass of mirrors in constant motion, shifting and contorting. It reflected not only their images but their fears—each flicker of emotion cast back in ghostly mockery.

Reflector (softly, mocking):

"You have faced your fears, but fear is never truly defeated. It lingers in the shadows, waiting. Are you truly free? Or are you merely delaying the inevitable?"

They stood still, shoulders squared. Aqua and Capri exchanged a glance, their hands instinctively finding each other—fingers interlaced, steady.

Capri (firmly):

"We are not defined by fear. We know who we are."

Aqua (with quiet resolve):

"And we know what we're fighting for."

The Reflector quivered, the mirrored surfaces distorting wildly, unable to hold form beneath the pressure of their clarity.

Reflector (fading, voice echoing):

"The Void is watching. This is only the beginning."

A burst of radiant Light surged from Aqua and Capri—two streams of Essence united as one. The Reflector's form cracked and then shattered in a thunderous burst, shards dissolving into stardust. The labyrinth groaned and fell away, the illusion unraveling in silence.

The maze vanished, and in its place stood an open space bathed in soft Light. They remained still for a moment, breathing in the silence—cleansed by the truth they had reclaimed.

They had survived the Veil of Illusion. And in doing so, they had discovered not just the strength to face what was within—but the unbreakable will to face what lay ahead.

Together.

16.2 The Test of Truth

The labyrinth had been treacherous—a maze of twisting mirrors that distorted reality, warping Aqua and Capri's deepest fears into living nightmares. Every step dragged them deeper into their insecurities until disorientation blurred the line between illusion and truth. Now, they stood at the threshold of the Chamber of Truth, the very heart of the Mirror Labyrinth. The air was cooler here, almost biting, as though it cut through every falsehood they had encountered, leaving behind only clarity.

They stepped forward. Their feet made no sound on the gleaming floor that reflected the sky so perfectly; it felt as though they walked upon a boundless plane, suspended between two realms—above and below, nothing but an endless, serene expanse. The chamber was vast, yet it held an uncanny sense of confinement. Crystal walls stretched into infinity, mirroring their every movement with unsettling precision. Unlike the distorted reflections that had plagued them in the maze, these images remained unwavering. No illusions. No tricks. Only truth.

Capri's breath came shallow as she surveyed their surroundings, the gravity of the trial ahead pressing heavily on her shoulders. Her voice, though soft, carried the edge of resolve.

"This is different," she said, her fingers brushing the crystal wall. It was smooth and cold beneath her touch, a stark contrast to the deceptive glass that had tormented them earlier. "No enemies... no shadows. Just us."

Her reflection stared back—unnervingly calm.

Capri had long fought her doubts, haunted by fears that she wasn't strong enough, wise enough to lead her people or protect the ones she loved. And now, for the first time, there was no foe before her. Only herself.

Silence cloaked the chamber, profound and sacred.

Aqua stood beside her, gaze locked on his own reflection. The weight of leadership—of bearing responsibility for their realm, for Capri, for the fragile balance they embodied—had left its mark. The labyrinth had tested their senses with deception. Here, the true trial began: to face the parts of themselves they had long kept hidden.

"No more lies," he murmured, voice low as a breath. "No more hiding from ourselves."

They moved deeper into the chamber. With every step, the stillness intensified—not the oppressive hush of fear, but the serenity of a storm's eye, a calm that demanded reflection. No outer chaos remained. Only the battle within.

Capri approached her reflection with measured steps, movements deliberate yet laced with hesitation. For a long moment, she stood before the mirror, studying the woman who met her gaze. This was no twisted mockery, no monstrous projection of her insecurities. This was simply... her. Real. Unfiltered.

"I've been afraid for so long,"she whispered, the words thick with emotion."Afraid I wouldn't be enough. That I couldn't protect the ones I love or lead the way I was meant to."Her voice quivered, but she clenched her fists, steadying herself."But I see now—strength isn't the absence of fear. It's the courage to face it."

Her reflection offered no judgment. No distortion. Only quiet acknowledgment.

She drew a deep breath. As she exhaled, the weight she had carried for so long seemed to ease, the invisible chains of doubt loosening.

"I see my flaws. And I accept them,"she said, voice steady."They don't make me weak. They make me... me."

The crystal walls shimmered faintly as if stirred by the power of her admission. A gentle calm surged through her, a peace she hadn't realized she was missing. When she opened her eyes again, her stance was taller, her spirit firmer than it had been in ages.

Across the chamber, Aqua faced a quieter battle—no less profound.

His reflection mirrored the leader he was. The weight of a thousand decisions was etched into his posture, the burden of responsibility pressing across his chest like armor he could not remove. He had feared failure more than anything: the fear that he might not be enough to protect their world... or her. In the deepest corners of his heart, he had always questioned if the ruin of what he loved would be his doing.

His reflection did not comfort him—it simply waited.

"I've doubted myself more times than I can count,"he admitted, his voice low but unwavering."Wondered if I deserved to lead. If I was strong enough to bear it all."The words, once buried, lifted from him like stones tumbling from his soul."But those doubts... they made me fight harder. They shaped me."

His voice grew firmer."I'm not perfect. But I won't let those doubts define me. I'll use them."

He met his reflection's gaze. Not seeking approval but truth. And this time, it was enough.

From the far end of the chamber, a figure emerged—graceful, deliberate, as if it had always been there. Reflector, guardian of the labyrinth, glided forth from the mirrored walls with an elegance that defied form. Its body shimmered like liquid Light, ever-shifting yet coherent, and though its face remained indistinct, its gaze—if it could be called such—locked onto them with piercing clarity.

"The truth,"Reflector said, voice like an echo woven from glass and wind,"is often the hardest thing to face. But it is also the most powerful."A pause followed, giving space for the weight of its words."You have confronted yourselves, accepted your flaws. And in doing so... awakened your true potential."

Capri glanced toward Aqua, a fire of clarity and strength rising behind her eyes."We've faced our fears. And we're stronger because of it."She stepped closer, letting her hand find his. The bond between them surged with renewed vitality. Their love—tested, reaffirmed—felt more enduring than ever."Now, let's finish this. Together."

The chamber pulsed with light, the crystal walls glowing as if stirred by their unity. Reflector inclined its head, then slowly dissolved back into the mirrored veil, its purpose complete.

Aqua turned toward her, calm and resolute."We know who we are now,"he said softly, his voice resonant with conviction."Nothing can stop us."

Capri nodded. Her fingers intertwined with his, firm and certain. They faced the exit, its threshold opening like a path to destiny. Beneath them, the sky-reflecting floor stretched on, no longer a reflection of the Void but a canvas of possibility.

Their reflections remained behind them—not distorted specters, but whole, truthful images, radiant and at peace.

They walked forward, not as fractured souls, but as bearers of clarity, strengthened by acceptance and forged through trial. Whatever shadows awaited beyond the labyrinth, they would face them side by side—undivided and unwavering.

Together, they left the Chamber of Truth, their steps lighter, their hearts unburdened. The path ahead was unknown, but they no longer feared it.

They had seen the truth—and embraced it.

Outside the Chamber of Truth, their companions waited in silence. They, too, understood that some battles could only be faced alone.

16.3: Seeing Beyond

Aqua and Capri stood at the threshold of the Heart of the Labyrinth, their breaths slow and deliberate. Though they had navigated the maze's shifting corridors, this chamber—the final test—carried a weight unlike any they had faced before. The mirrored walls had long since stilled, as though the labyrinth itself had guided them here, to this sacred center where illusions dissolved, and truth took root.

The chamber was vast, a circular expanse illuminated by a soft, ethereal glow emanating from crystalline walls. The Light—neither harsh nor blinding—bathed everything in a warmth that felt otherworldly yet deeply comforting. The air hummed with a melody that seemed to come from the stars themselves, resonating within their hearts. Beneath their feet, the floor formed a breathtaking mosaic of stardust—constellations that shifted and pulsed like a living map of the cosmos, hinting at destinies not yet written.

At the center stood a pedestal, intricately carved from the same luminous crystal as the walls. Atop it hovered the Crystal of Clarity, pulsing with rhythmic Light as if it carried a heartbeat of its own. Small and unassuming, the artifact filled the chamber with an immense, infinite presence—as though within its glow lay the secrets of the universe.

Capri stepped forward first, drawn to the crystal's glow like a moth to flame. Her eyes were wide, not with fear, but reverent awe. She felt its power—ancient, vast, and heavy with untold revelations. Her hand rose, fingers trembling with hesitation, stopping just shy of its radiant aura.

"This is it..."she whispered, voice barely audible, yet thick with emotion."The Crystal of Clarity. With it, we can pierce the Void's deceptions, unravel the illusions that haunt us."She paused, peering deeper into its glow."But it shows more than that..."Her gaze darkened as unspeakable images flickered in her mind."It reveals the price. The sacrifices we'll have to make."

Aqua stepped beside her, eyes fixed on the crystal, though his thoughts drifted far beyond it. He saw in her expression the same burden he had felt growing heavier with every step of their journey. The battles they'd endured, the lives lost—so much had already been sacrificed. Yet, in the depths of his soul, he knew the road ahead would demand even more.

"We've always known there would be sacrifices,"he said, voice steady though tinged with the quiet weight of resignation."But seeing it... like this."His hand came to rest gently on her shoulder—a gesture of both comfort and solidarity."It makes everything feel more... real. The pain, the loss—it's all laid bare now."

Together, they stood in silence, the pulse of the crystal echoing the rhythm of their hearts. Beneath them, the stardust mosaic stirred, the constellations shifting, reforming into new celestial patterns—glimpses of futures not yet decided. Along the crystalline walls, faint images emerged: their Stardust Warriors locked in battle with shadowy entities of the Void; fields of war scarred by darkness, faces of those they cherished—some standing proud, others fading into shadow.

From the far side of the chamber, a figure stepped into the Light with solemn grace. Reflector, guardian of the labyrinth, now took a form more stable than before. No longer elusive or shifting, it appeared solid—its crystalline body aglow, pulsing in harmony with the chamber's radiance. When it spoke, its voice was calm, touched with sorrow, as though it, too, bore the burden of what must be faced.

"The Crystal of Clarity reveals all—truth and deception, Light and shadow,"Reflector intoned, approaching the pair with reverent steps."It shows the path ahead but also the burdens you must carry. The sacrifices... they are inevitable."

It paused, gaze resting on the crystal, now glowing with heightened urgency. "The choice is yours. The crystal offers clarity, but with it comes the weight of knowledge. Once seen, the truth cannot be unlearned—nor can it be avoided."

Capri tore her gaze from the crystal, her expression sharpening with resolve. Determination burned in her eyes, though sorrow lingered behind them—a quiet reflection of the conflict within. The truth stood before them, and with it, the weight of what must be given. She felt Aqua's struggle within her own heart, their burden intertwined, their choices shared.

"We've come too far to turn back now," she said softly, her voice firm despite the hush. "Whatever the cost, whatever the sacrifice—we'll face it." She turned to him, eyes softened by love. "Together."

He met her gaze, seeing within it the same strength that had guided them through shadows and storms. "Together," he echoed. "Always."

With one breath, united in purpose, they stepped forward, hands entwined, reaching toward the crystal. The moment their fingers met its surface, the Light within surged—bursting into brilliance that filled the chamber with waves of cosmic radiance. The faint hum crescendoed into a celestial symphony, a song of the stars, as though the universe itself bore witness to this moment.

Then came the visions.

They saw the future unfold in a torrent of Light: legions of the Void descending upon the realms, skies consumed by shadow, the earth trembling beneath the storm of war. Towering and steadfast, the Stardust Warriors met the darkness—each one a bastion of Light amid the onslaught. Their glowing forms stood in contrast to the suffocating gloom.

Faces emerged—Zephyr, swift Guardian of Winds; Pyronix, fierce Master of Flames; Aqualith, serene Guardian of Water. And among them, Luna, her silver gaze radiant with courage as she stood against the approaching dark. Though each held strong, within their eyes danced the shadow of doubt—the fear of what might be lost.

Then the vision shifted: Capri's kingdom, rivers of radiant Light, devoured by creeping darkness. Aqua's oceans churned under a blackened sky, the waves lashing out in fury against the Void's advance. And finally, the two of them, side by side in the heart of chaos, the Crystal of Clarity lifted high—a beacon in the abyss.

Victory glimmered within reach. But its price would be steep.

As the visions faded, silence returned—deep and infinite. Breathless, they stood trembling beneath the weight of all they had seen. The knowledge was now theirs, the truth indelible.

Capri's voice broke the stillness, low and unwavering."This is the path we've chosen. No matter what comes, no matter the cost, we'll face it together. We are stronger than illusion, stronger than fear."

Aqua nodded, his grip firm around hers."Together, we will see beyond the darkness. We'll face the truth and rise stronger for it."

The Crystal of Clarity pulsed once more, its Light softening as though in solemn approval. It had revealed what lay ahead—and sealed their resolve.

Slowly, the chamber began to return to stillness. The radiant brilliance dimmed to its gentle glow. Beneath their feet, the mosaic shimmered quietly, forming new constellations—a celestial path unwritten, waiting. Though their hearts carried the weight of future trials, their spirits remained unbroken.

They had seen beyond illusion.

They had seen the truth.

As they turned to leave, Reflector stepped aside, bowing its crystalline head with silent reverence."You have seen beyond. May clarity guide you through the darkness that awaits."

With one final glance shared between them, Aqua and Capri crossed the threshold, their hands still joined, their steps steady and sure. The Light of the crystal followed them, casting a soft trail as they walked—gentle, unwavering.

Behind them, the Heart of the Labyrinth stood quiet once more.

Before them lay a world shadowed by what they had seen—but they no longer walked in uncertainty. They carried clarity, not as a burden, but as a torch.They would face the final battle not as dreamers nor as warriors alone but as those who had seen the truth behind the veil.

Together, they were ready.

Threshold of Eternity

Beyond the fading echoes of the Maze, the path opened into a vast, starlit chamber—neither within nor outside time. The Vault of Eternity stood before them, not built but *born*, carved from the silence between stars and sealed by the first breath of creation.

Here, truths were not spoken—they were remembered. The air was still, yet heavy with the gravity of all things ever feared, hoped, or forgotten. Its walls shimmered with ancient memory, and the ground pulsed with the silent weight of destinies unlived. In its heart floated a single flame—not of fire, but of soullight: the radiant fusion of all that had ever been loved, lost, or dared.

Aqua and Capri stepped forward, their hands still joined, their hearts shaped by the Maze and strengthened by its illusions. The Vault did not open to force. It opened to unity.

As their bond aligned, the Vault exhaled—a breath of radiant stardust that circled their forms, weaving around Zephyr, Luna, and the others who had endured the crucible with them. There was no prize, no power... only *clarity*. And in that clarity, a final thread of truth:
The Light alone would not win this war. But neither would darkness. It would take something beyond both—*balance, sacrifice, and love*.

With the Vault's last breath, the chamber dissolved into rising strands of Light. The air changed. The stars dimmed.

The Final War had already begun.

CHAPTER

17

THE FLAMES OF RECKONING

*NOW THE FIRE CONSUMES ALL HESITATION
—ONLY PURPOSE REMAINS.*

 # CHAPTER 17

△ VALDUM, THE CELESTIAL ARCHITECT
AQUARII: ZANTHUR EL'DRENAI.

 OPENING WHISPER – CH. 17

△ MAXIMUS, THE ETERNAL QUILL
AQUARII: DRENAI XAL VARETH.

CLOSING WHISPER – CH. 17

17.1 The Purge of Shadows

The Shadowed Plains of Noctyra stretched endlessly under the weight of darkness. Once a radiant star-planet at the edge of Light and Void, it now lay cursed and hollow—scarred by a war the cosmos tried to forget. Jagged shards of obsidian jutted from the earth like fractured bones, casting long, spectral shadows across a ground cracked and scorched by voidfire. Pools of bubbling black tar festered between the rocks, releasing foul fumes that burned the air itself. Above, twilight skies churned with unnatural storms, dark clouds pulsing with volatile magic. Lightning—sharp and white as broken memory—briefly illuminated the battlefield before vanishing into the suffocating gloom. Each thunderclap echoed like the death rattle of stars.

Noctyra had held the balance as a Beacon Between Realms. Now, it served as a grim threshold—the Void's forward bastion into the territories of Light.

At the vanguard of the forces of Light stood Aqua and Capri, their gazes fixed on the bleak horizon. The earth shivered beneath them as the Void's legions approached—an endless wave of darkness crawling from every fracture in the star's surface. The air hung with the weight of history and sorrow as if even time recoiled from witnessing the end.

Though her heart thundered with the enormity of the moment, Capri spoke with calm resolve.

"We stand at the edge of everything. This is our last stand. If we falter, there will be no dawn."

Her words rang with somber clarity. The corrupted ground trembled again as though Noctyra itself cried out against its fate.

Aqua turned to her, placing a steady hand upon her shoulder. His voice was quiet but resolute.

"We will not fall. Our Light is not only for us—it burns for every soul still clinging to hope, every star that has not yet faded. We fight for them, Capri. No matter the cost."

The army drew closer—monstrous silhouettes shifting like nightmares against the horizon. Twisted figures loomed, their eyes glowing with cruel hunger. They walked in silence, but their presence screamed. Each step brought decay. The starlit earth died beneath them.

Behind Aqua and Capri, the forces of Light assembled—Starlight Warriors forged from celestial flame and hope. Their armor gleamed with the occasional lightning flash, casting halos around unyielding faces. Towering at the center stood Supreme General Valorus, armored in radiant plates engraved with the sigils of constellations. His sword glowed with the brilliance of ten thousand suns, and behind him, his titanic shield bore the scars of ancient wars.

His voice rolled across the battlefield like thunder, firm and defiant.

"Let the flames of reckoning cleanse this land! We will not break—we are the bulwark of Light!"

The cry of Valorus ignited a blaze in the hearts of the Lightborn legions. A unified roar erupted through their ranks as they surged forward, a tide of radiance clashing with the flood of darkness. The collision was immediate and deafening—steel against shadow, fire against void. Sparks erupted in the gloom, each one a flicker of hope resisting extinction. The Shadowed Plains trembled under the fury of battle, the sky above echoing the wrath of two ancient forces colliding.

Aqua raised his hands, summoning spiraling waves of light-infused water. With a sharp gesture, radiant torrents crashed forward, dissolving the twisted forms of shadow soldiers in a cleansing deluge. Each impact sent ripples of brilliance outward, washing away the corruption with relentless force.

Capri moved with grace and certainty, the fabric of time bending around her fingers. Her enemies lunged toward her, but within her temporal field, their movements slowed to a crawl. In those suspended moments, her blade gleamed with precision, slicing through the still air—and the enemy—with elegance honed by countless battles. Every step she took rewrote fate.

But the Void's might was endless.

From the churning storm of shadows emerged Dark Sovereign Moroseth, cloaked in silence more profound than night. His form was tall, regal, yet haunting—a silhouette of what he once was. Shadows clung to him like sentient smoke, moving with his breath. His gaze— two cold orbs of vacant sorrow—locked onto Aqua and Capri, but his voice echoed through the entire battlefield, a whisper laced with eons of despair.

"You cling to fading stars,"he intoned,"while the cosmos calls for renewal. Through darkness, it shall be reborn."

Moroseth's presence spread like a plague—hope weakened, resolve wavered. Around him, the Shadowed Ones advanced:

Sectrix and Mirage twisted perception, spreading lies among the defenders, illusions of betrayal and faltering loyalty.

Vexalia moved like venom, whispering enmity into ears, igniting ancient rivalries.

Nethermind, a being of pure psychic despair, fed on fear itself, magnifying panic into madness.

But a second shadow rose to meet them—this one tempered by Light.

ShadowVeil – The Eclipse Spy, emerged with his agents of the Order of the Equinox, silent and swift. Trained in secrecy by the Master of Light, he struck from within the chaos. Infiltrating enemy lines, his spies disrupted Void formations, exposed traitors, and collapsed illusions spun by Sectrix and Mirage.

The battlefield now teemed with covert duels beneath the surface: deception versus counter-deception, illusion against truth, the broken mind pitted against resilience.

Light and shadow clashed in blinding bursts and whispered death, while above it all, Aqua and Capri continued their dance of command and courage—unshaken, though the Void threatened to unravel all.

Valorus, sensing the tide turning, charged into the fray. His radiant blade cut through the encroaching dark like a falling star. Around him, Starlight Warriors regrouped under his command, holding the line where it threatened to break. Flames of celestial origin flared from his strikes—not wild, but measured and resolute, like the beating heart of a star refusing to fade.

Aetherion's Dimensional Protectors moved through the ranks with precise purpose. From the high ridges, Voltar released bolt after bolt of starlight energy, each one eliminating key targets and shielding their allies' advance or retreat. On the central front, Ferran became an unyielding wall—his armored form absorbing even the fiercest blows of the Void's champions. The ground quaked beneath his stand, but he did not yield.

In the heart of shifting shadow, Aetherwind traversed shimmering rifts invisible to most eyes, his form flickering between dimensions. Wherever Moroseth's forces sought to breach reality's veil, Aetherwind was already there—sealing cracks, dismantling rituals, relaying intelligence to Aetherion through hidden glyphs and starlit signals.

Lumina, radiant in motion, moved from group to group. Her light dispelled Nethermind's psychic smog, cleared illusions left by Mirage, and spoke silent truths where lies had begun to fester. Her presence alone revived the morale of faltering soldiers, who rose anew beneath her glow.

And yet, the Void pressed on.

Moroseth, untouched and unreadable, advanced like a living eclipse. ShadowVeil and his elite agents struck at the flanks, dismantling sabotage operations and neutralizing shadow infiltrators. His confrontation with Sectrix was swift and silent—twin masters of deceit in a deadly game of foresight and patience. In another corner of the field, Mirage's illusions faltered under Lumina's light and ShadowVeil's keen discernment.

Still, the defenders began to strain. Even Aqua and Capri, though far from the front, felt the pressure.

Capri, panting, the sweat on her brow shimmering like dew in starlight, turned toward her companion.

"Their numbers... they don't end."

Aqua's voice, though strained, held fast."Then we don't stop. We stand because if we fall—there's nothing left."

And then the heavens roared.

With a cry forged from the heart of ten thousand stars, Valorus raised his sword skyward. A column of radiant flame surged from the ground, a firestorm of such intensity that the very sky shuddered. The inferno swept across the battlefield in a colossal arc, consuming all shadow in its path. The Void recoiled. Soldiers of darkness faltered. And in that moment, the defenders surged forward once more.

But Moroseth did not retreat. Standing alone amidst the scorched ruin, the flames parting around him like a tide around a stone, he spoke—not in rage, but in sorrow.

"You burn shadows, yet they always return. I am not your enemy... I am your truth."

Then, as quietly as he had appeared, he vanished into the darkness— his words hanging in the air like prophecy.

Aqua and Capri stood atop the ruined ridge, battered but unbroken. The sky was still dark. The war is far from over. But for now, Light had held.

And where Light endures, so too does hope.

17.2: The Phoenix's Rise

The Heart of the Shadowed Plains of Noctyra trembled violently as the clash between Light and darkness surged toward its fiery crescendo. The fractured Earth beneath shuddered, jagged and torn, revealing molten rivers that coursed through deep fissures—lava glowing with a hellish hue, casting a grim and flickering Light across the battlefield. The air was choked with the acrid bite of sulfur; every breath tasted of ruin. Overhead, the sky had become a tempest of swirling shadow and fire, as if the heavens themselves had surrendered to the chaos below.

At the front line stood Aqua and Capri, flanked by the unwavering guardians of the elements—Zephyr, Pyronix, Aqualith, and Gaian—forming a resolute wall against the encroaching dark. Aqua's blue armor, now scorched and blackened, bore the wounds of endless combat. His grip on the sword of starlight remained firm, slicing through tendrils of black magic that clung like venomous serpents. His body ached, each motion slower than the last. To his right, Capri moved with disciplined grace, her Crescent Blade gleaming even through the choking haze. Though exhaustion lined her face, her resolve never faltered.

The Void's armies surged forward, phantoms of despair flickering in and out of the material world. Their very presence leached the hope from the soldiers of Light, their dark enchantments coiling like chains around the hearts of the brave. Murmurs of doubt whispered from unseen places—echoes of failure, of inevitable loss—and the line of defenders bent beneath the weight of those invisible burdens.

Aqua's eyes swept the battlefield. All around, courage was thinning, the luminous spirit of resistance dimming like a fading star. His jaw tightened. Was this to be the end? Would the Light truly be extinguished?

Just then, the Earth trembled again—not with the Void's fury, but with something ancient, something sacred. The very air thickened with raw, primordial power. Even the shadows faltered.

The battlefield fell into a breathless hush, awaiting what would come next.

From the epicenter of chaos—where lava clashed with shadow in a battle of elemental extremes—a blinding Light erupted. It tore across the plains like a blade of fire, forcing even the Void's minions to recoil. From within that radiance emerged a creature of legend, a being of rebirth and undying flame.

The Phoenix

Its wings stretched wide, ablaze with cascading hues of gold, crimson, and molten orange. With each mighty beat, the skies shook, and waves of heat and Light washed over the battlefield, searing away the encroaching dark. The scorched ground beneath cracked and smoked, yet where the Phoenix soared, shadow fled—and hope surged in its place.

Capri's voice trembled in awe, barely more than a breath."Aqua... look. The Phoenix—it's real. We still have a chance."

He turned, eyes wide with wonder as the sacred creature blazed across the sky. The crushing fatigue in his limbs vanished as a surge of life burst within him. The Phoenix was no longer a myth—it was a miracle, the very embodiment of their cause. The spark had returned to reignite the fire in their hearts.

"The Phoenix rises from the ashes,"Aqua said, voice carrying like thunder,"and so shall we. The Light will never be extinguished. Not while we stand!"

The Phoenix's cry echoed like a celestial chorus, piercing the veil of despair. Its pure, resonant sound reached deep into the hearts of every soldier of Light. The tide shifted. The shadows wavered, their magic cracking beneath the blaze of divine fire.

With renewed strength, Capri lifted her Crescent Blade high."To the Phoenix!"she cried."Let its flame burn through your fear!"

The warriors of Light—wounded, wearied, nearly broken—rose again. Shoulder to shoulder behind Aqua and Capri, with Zephyr's winds swirling, Pyronix's fire flaring, Aqualith's waters crashing, and Gaian's earthen power rumbling beneath their feet, they charged.

As flames swept across the battlefield, darkness was scorched away. Hope, like fire, had been rekindled.

Through the rising inferno, a shadow moved—graceful, serpentine, sinister. Moroseth, Dark Sovereign of the Shadowed Ones, emerged from the veil of gloom. Once a cosmic guardian, now consumed by the Void, his silhouette shimmered with ancient sorrow and abyssal power. His obsidian eyes narrowed as he beheld the Phoenix, tearing radiant swaths through his legions.

"You think flame can undo the endless night?"His voice, like cracked stone over ice, rolled across the field."You cannot burn away what was born from sacrifice."

Light and darkness clashed once more in the heart of the plains. The Phoenix met his presence with a defiant cry, its wings unfurling in a blazing arc. Fire lashed outward, but Moroseth strode through it, his void-cloaked form absorbing the light. Each movement sent shockwaves through land and sky alike.

They danced—flame and shadow, in a duel that shook the heavens. Every strike of fire met an echo of darkness. And through it all, the ground groaned, and the stars dimmed.

Aqua's breath caught."This is it,"he whispered."The turning point."

Capri stood beside him, her gaze fixed on the clash above."If the Phoenix falls... so do we."

Then, fire erupted anew—Infernos, the Flamebringer, charged forth like a meteor loosed from heaven. His body shone with molten fury, a cyclone of flame spinning wildly around him. He raised his arms, his voice an infernal roar.

"With the Phoenix at our side, we burn brighter than ever!"Infernos cried."Ignite, warriors of Light!"

Flames surged, merging with the Phoenix's power. Together, their fire became a cataclysm of cleansing heat. The soldiers rallied once more, shouting into the storm. Their blades gleamed; their spirits blazed.

Above them, the Phoenix ascended, a burning constellation raining fire upon the Void. Yet Moroseth endured. Drawing upon the well of his fallen purpose, he expanded—becoming a towering wraith of cosmic shadow. His words, now thunder, cracked the sky."Shadows return. They always do."

With a violent gesture, Moroseth hurled tendrils of Void toward the Phoenix, seeking to smother its sacred blaze. They struck, writhing like starless serpents, and the Phoenix shrieked—a cry of agony but not defeat. Its wings beat harder. Its flame blazed brighter.

Aqua's voice cut through the din."We cannot stand idle. The Phoenix fights for us—now we fight for it!"

"Together,"Capri said, steel in her voice.

They charged. Zephyr summoned storms to tear through the ranks; Pyronix unleashed columns of flame; Aqualith surged with tidal force;

Gaian cracked the ground itself. Aqua and Capri led the charge, weapons ablaze with celestial Light.

Infernos joined them in a fury of fire, cutting a blazing path. The warriors of Light followed, unstoppable, their battle cry echoing through the storm.

Empowered by their unity, the Phoenix ignited in a final blaze of glory. With a deafening cry, it released a burst of radiance so pure it shattered the dark bonds and tore through the shroud of Void. Moroseth staggered, his massive form flickering, unraveling in the torrent of Light.

"You cannot win, Moroseth!"Aqua's voice rang like a celestial bell."The Light always rises again!"

Moroseth's voice was a ragged hiss, part rage, part grief."This is not the end, Aqua. Shadows endure... even in Light."

And then he vanished, consumed by the storm—his shadowed essence scattering like ash on the wind. The field fell silent but for the beating of wings overhead.

The Phoenix soared in slow circles, casting golden Light over the scorched Earth. The defenders stood in awe—battered, breathless, but victorious.

Capri looked skyward, her voice resolute."We rise, like the Phoenix. We will not fall."

Aqua placed a hand on her shoulder."Together, no shadow can break us."

Above them, the Phoenix released one final cry—a song of rebirth, of triumph forged in flame—as the warriors of Light began to regroup. Though war still loomed, hope had been rekindled, and it would burn ever brighter.

17.3: Ashes to New Beginnings

The ground beneath them trembled, groaning under the weight of the battle between the forces of Light and darkness. Once teeming with life and vitality, the Final Battlefield was now a scorched wasteland—a brutal reflection of the struggle that had consumed it. The earth lay in jagged shards, torn by relentless violence, with molten rock and flame erupting from fissures that pierced the world's core. Blood-red clouds veiled the sun, casting the land in a choking half-light, thick with smoke and the acrid scent of burning metal and ash. Strewn across the terrain were the remnants of war—broken swords, shattered shields, and the lifeless bodies of warriors who had given everything for the promise of hope.

Amid this shattered world stood the last defenders of the Light. At their head, Aqua and Capri bore the wounds of countless battles—their armor battered, their faces streaked with soot and blood. Yet their eyes still burned with unyielding fire. They had come too far to fall. Around them stood their most trusted companions—guardians, mystics, elemental avatars—each a living force of nature, each prepared to fight until their final breath. Together, they formed a bulwark against the encroaching shadow of the Void.

Capri's gaze swept across the ravaged horizon, memorizing the faces of those who had become more than comrades—kin forged in fire. Her voice rang out, clear despite the smoke, carried on the winds of loss and defiance."We've lost so much,"she began, eyes glowing with the memory of every soul claimed by war."Friends, families, homes... but we stand here, united. This is our last chance. Whatever comes, we hold the line together. We finish what we began."

Aqua stepped forward, her words grounding him like stone beneath the tide. He raised his spear, the Light at its tip piercing the gloom like a star reborn."The Void has taken much, but it will not steal our hope,"he said, voice rising with the tide's fury."We fight till the last breath. And together, we will see the Light return."

As Aqua's words settled over the warriors, a bitter wind swept through the battlefield. The temperature dropped sharply, and each breath became a plume of frost as the chill of despair crept through their bones. From the heart of encroaching shadow, Nocturn, Harbinger of the Void, emerged. Cloaked in undulating darkness, his form bent the air around him as though the world recoiled at his presence. His eyes blazed with a malevolence that defied time— ancient, insatiable. The very Earth quaked beneath his feet, and with each step he took, the Light seemed to retreat.

Behind him surged the legions of the Void, vast and formless, a sea of writhing black silhouettes that blotted out the horizon. Their advance was silent, but their intent screamed of annihilation.

Nocturn's voice rumbled like thunder across a broken sky, thick with contempt."Foolish mortals,"he hissed, his gaze sweeping over the gathered forces of Light."You think you can stand against the Void? You are but flickering flames—soon to be swallowed by eternal night."

Unease rippled through the ranks. But from among them stepped Solara, Guardian of Dawn. Her golden armor, though scorched and cracked from countless battles, still shimmered with the radiance of a newborn star. Her sword, forged in the fire of the universe's first sunrise, blazed defiantly against the shadow. Her very presence pushed back the dark.

"The dawn always comes," Solara declared, her voice steady, fierce—like sunrise on a battlefield. "Even after the longest night, Light rises again. You will not extinguish us. We will shine brighter than ever before."

The air crackled. Solara's eyes locked with Nocturn's. The world seemed to still as the final confrontation began. With a roar, the Voidlord lunged, his massive blade—wreathed in shadow—descending in a death arc. Solara met it mid-swing, their weapons colliding in a storm of Light and darkness that rocked the battlefield with raw power.

The moment Solara clashed with Nocturn, the forces of Light surged forward like a tidal wave. Aqua and Capri led the charge, radiant as twin beacons amidst the chaos. Behind them thundered their allies. Zephyr, Guardian of Winds, unleashed a storming tempest, his winds slicing through the advancing darkness with razor precision. Aqualith, Guardian of Water, summoned cleansing waves that surged across the battlefield, drowning the unholy flames of the Void.

Beside them fought Pyronix, the Master of Flames, a whirlwind of fury and fire. His twin blades, wrapped in blazing arcs, carved fiery paths through enemy ranks. But driven by his own fury, Pyronix pushed too far into the enemy line. Shadows swarmed to consume him, threatening to smother his flame. From the chaos, Aqua's voice rang like a battle horn, and Aqualith responded with a crashing torrent of water that slammed into the shadows, shielding their brother-in-arms.

"We fight as one, Pyronix!"Aqualith roared his voice, a booming cascade of power and kinship.

Pyronix, steadying himself, grinned through the smoke.
"Together, then,"he shouted, his flames roaring anew."Let's burn them out!"

Then came the quake.

The Earth beneath the Void trembled—not from destruction, but rebirth. Cracking through stone and flame, the ground erupted as Gaian, Earth Warden, rose into the fray. His armor, forged from living rock and rooted deep in the soul of Aquaterra, glowed with runes of primeval strength. With a mighty stomp, he split the terrain beneath the enemy ranks, sending whole divisions of shadows plunging into crevices lined with crystal light.

"Let the Earth speak!"Gaian thundered, his voice ancient as mountains."And may it bury this darkness!"

With the four elemental guardians—Zephyr, Aqualith, Pyronix, and Gaian—marching in unison, the tide of battle turned. The Light pressed forward, defying despair with every breath.

The battle raged on, pushing every warrior to the brink. The forces of Light burned with relentless resolve, their courage spreading like wildfire across the ruined expanse. Yet for every shadow slain, two more seemed to rise. Capri, her mastery over time bending the very threads of reality, slowed the Void's advance, granting her allies fleeting moments to strike. Lumina, Bearer of Light, cast searing beams of radiance, cutting through gloom and igniting hope. Chronia, Seer of Time, moved with eerie precision, her foresight guiding every maneuver, foretelling each enemy's misstep.

Still, Nocturn loomed like a living eclipse—undaunted, unbroken. Each sweep of his blade unleashed tides of darkness, sundering the Light's formations. Even Solara, radiant and fierce, faltered beneath his unending assault.

"You are nothing!"Nocturn bellowed, his voice shaking the heavens."This world belongs to the night eternal! You cannot defy what must be!"

But Solara stood firm, chest heaving, eyes ablaze. With a cry of defiance, she met his blow, her sword a star reborn."There is always Light!"she cried."Even in the blackest hour—hope will never die!"

Near them, Aqua and Capri fought side by side, a storm of water, time, and starlight. Aqua deflected Nocturn's shadow strikes with crashing waves and blinding arcs while Capri weaved moments into seconds, slowing time to expose every weakness. But the darkness encroached still.

Nocturn, sensing the end, summoned the full fury of the Void. His blade, devoured entirely by black flame, rose high to strike Solara down.

In that instant, Aqua and Capri moved.

Channeling their deepest Essence—Water, Light, and time—they lunged. Aqua's spear surged with the ocean's primal force; Capri's staff shimmered with temporal brilliance. Their weapons met Nocturn's in a cataclysmic clash, blinding the battlefield in an explosion of Light and shadow.

For a breathless moment, all stilled. Time held its breath.

When the brilliance faded, they stood unshaken, weapons locked with the Voidlord's. For the first time, Nocturn's form flickered.

"We will not fall,"Capri whispered, calm and resolute."Not while we stand together."

With a final surge, their united power overwhelmed him. Nocturn reeled, his dominion unraveling. The battlefield tilted toward hope.

And in the silence that followed, the universe waited—for the Light to rise once more.

CHAPTER

18

THE TAPESTRY OF FATE

WHAT IS WRITTEN CAN STILL BE REWRITTEN—IF THE WILL IS STRONG ENOUGH.

 # CHAPTER 18

△ **MAXIMUS, THE ETERNAL QUILL**
AQUARII: SYRENTHA VAL'DURIEN.

OPENING WHISPER – CH. 18

△ **VALDUM, THE CELESTIAL ARCHITECT**
AQUARII: DURIEN XAL ANVROS.

CLOSING WHISPER – CH. 18

18.1 The Weave of Time

As the echoes of battle faded into the smoke-veiled silence of the Shadowed Plains, Aqua and Capri stood at the precipice of a fragile victory. The war against Moroseth and the Void had not ended the turmoil—it had only revealed how deeply the fabric of existence had been wounded. Though the battlefield had quieted, the cosmos still trembled.

It was then that Chronia, Seer of Time, emerged once more from the Eternal Spiral. Her robes shimmered like temporal waves, embroidered with constellations that flickered in patterns yet to unfold. She approached not with urgency—but with inevitability.

"The war you've fought has shifted more than realms,"she said."It has frayed the Loom of Eternity itself. The threads that bind past, present, and future strain beneath the weight of what has been undone. There is only one path forward—to reweave what the Void has unraveled."

Chronia revealed a hidden portal born from the Starlight Pendant and activated by the harmony Aqua and Capri had forged. Only they—and Luna, the celestial archivist whose lineage held memory beyond time—were permitted to cross. The others—Zephyr, Aetherion, Sylphara, and the generals—remained behind to guard Aquaterra, unaware of the greater silence that now called beyond the stars.

The portal led to the realm of fate itself—where threads of choice, consequence, and creation hung in infinite balance. A realm that could not be conquered or protected by force only understood.

Thus began a new journey, not of war, but of will.

Not of blades but of belief.

A journey to the Loom of Eternity—to stand before the Tapestry of Fate and decide the future not only of AquaCapri but of all things that breathe, dream, and become.

The Loom of Eternity

Beyond the edge of all known realms, there existed a place where time itself unraveled—a world of fleeting shadows and radiant light. This was the realm of the Loom of Eternity, where past, present, and future were not separate strands but threads woven tightly together. Aqua and Capri stood before it, breaths shallow, eyes wide as they beheld the towering structure that dominated the endless expanse. Its magnitude was incomprehensible, stretching beyond the limits of vision, shifting as if alive with each heartbeat of the cosmos.

The Tapestry of Fate, vast and unending, rippled before them. Threads of every hue—some vibrant, others dim—extended into infinity. Each one bore meaning: a life, a moment, a single decision bound within a living lattice that pulsed with the rhythm of existence. The air itself hummed, heavy with the weight of all that had ever been —and all that would ever be.

Aqua stood tall beneath the celestial glow, the starlight casting a soft shimmer over his robes. Though his presence radiated strength, his gaze betrayed the awe that gripped him. This was no battlefield, no council chamber of cosmic leaders—this was something far more sacred. At his side, Capri brushed her fingers against his, grounding herself in his presence as her gaze drifted across the gleaming threads.

Her voice trembled with reverence.

"This... this is where it all begins and ends," she whispered, wonder widening her eyes. "The Loom of Eternity... it's more than I imagined.

It doesn't just weave our path—it weaves all paths, all futures, for every soul, every realm."

Aqua's awe began to crystallize into clarity. His voice carried the quiet resolve that had seen them through countless storms.

"Which means we have a choice,"he said, eyes fixed on the luminous weave."Here, we can end the cycle. We can weave something new—a future where Light and darkness are no longer at war but in balance. This is where everything changes."

As their voices faded into the living silence of the Loom's realm, a presence stirred.

From the swirling confluence of shadow and light, figures began to emerge—the Weavers of Fate. Neither wholly male nor female, neither of Light nor darkness, their forms shifted like flowing water reflecting the ever-turning stars. They were living echoes of what had been and premonitions of what would be. Though their features remained unreadable, their eyes—deep, knowing, ancient—locked onto Aqua and Capri with unshakable intent.

The First Weaver stepped forward, its presence a breath of wind across the stars, its voice a murmur of galaxies long faded.

"You now stand at the heart of all that is and will be,"it intoned, each syllable heavy with inevitability."The threads of fate are fragile—but not immutable. One choice, one motion, can unravel entire worlds."

Another stepped forth, the Second Weaver, its form flickering like the glow of distant novas.

"You carry the power to reshape time,"it said, a note of temptation woven beneath the warning."But know this—once a thread is woven, it cannot be undone. Each choice you make will echo through eternity, shaping countless futures."

Aqua's eyes followed the gestures of the Weavers, and then—he saw it.

A single thread, faintly aglow, intertwined with strands of shadow and brilliance.

Their thread.

This was the fate they had battled against—a future where Light and darkness remained locked in ceaseless conflict, never yielding, never healing.

His jaw tightened as the weight of understanding settled on his shoulders.

Beside him, Capri studied the loom's ever-moving strands. Her voice trembled with uncertainty.

"And if we try to weave a new path?"she asked, hand reaching for his."What if we only bring more pain? What if the darkness must exist? If we strip it away, could we shatter the balance entirely?"

The Weavers offered no reply. Only their eyes answered, mirroring the threads—ever turning, ever uncertain.

Aqua turned to her, his gaze steady, voice rich with conviction.

"We're not here to destroy the darkness,"he said."We're here to reshape the tapestry—so Light and dark can coexist without war. That's the future we're choosing."

Capri's heart raced. The threads shimmered like stars and shadows across her vision—countless lives, unspoken histories, all intertwined.

This was more than a battle for peace—it was the moment they would rewrite the destiny of everything.

Could they truly forge a world in balance?

What price would the cosmos demand?

The First Weaver stepped forward again, silhouetted against the glimmering weave, its presence both serene and absolute.

"Once a thread is woven,"it said, voice carrying like a bell across eternity,"it cannot be unspun. Your decision will ripple across the stars and echo through every life, every realm. This is the choice of gods."

Capri inhaled deeply, her grip tightening around Aqua's. Her voice was soft yet unshaken.

"Then we'll make this choice together."

He nodded, his hand closing firmly over hers. Together, they turned toward the Loom.

It vibrated softly as they approached, threads dancing with untold energy. Some glowed like suns; others writhed like tendrils of shadow. The winds that brushed past them carried distant voices—whispers of dreams, of fear, of forgotten promises.

This was the breath of the cosmos, the heartbeat of all creation.

And they were about to change its rhythm.

Hand in hand, they reached for the thread that was theirs.

The Weavers remained still, their eyes unblinking as Aqua and Capri's fingers touched the strand that pulsed with the echo of their shared destiny. At that contact, the Loom stirred. A gentle hum bloomed into a cosmic resonance, vibrating through the realm like a chord struck across existence itself.

The threads around them shifted—elegant filaments of starlight and shadow weaving together in new, unseen ways. What had once been rigid began to transform. The Tapestry of Fate, once set in its eternal struggle, now shimmered with change. Light and darkness—once divided—spiraled into delicate harmony, entwined without conflict.

The Second Weaver spoke then, its voice barely more than the rustling of time.

"The threads shall remember," it whispered. "Your will has been etched into the fabric of the cosmos. The future has been rewritten."

Aqua and Capri took a step back. Before them, the tapestry now glowed with new meaning—its threads alive with unity and fragility. A balance had been formed, not through domination, but through intent. Light and darkness, for the first time, danced in harmony.

Yet even as the Loom's resonance softened, its light fading to a gentle pulse, the future remained uncertain. What they had woven would ripple outward—unseen, unpredictable.

As they turned to leave the realm of the Weavers, hands still clasped, one truth burned in their hearts:

Whatever came next,

they would face it together.

18.2 Strands of Destiny

The Nexus of Possibilities stretched before them like an uncharted ocean—endless, shifting with every breath. This realm, where reality itself twisted and reformed, was unlike anything they had ever encountered. Threads of fate—some shimmering with radiant Light, others darkened by ominous energy—wove themselves into an intricate tapestry spanning eternity. With every step, the air pulsed with the energy of countless futures, each waiting to be shaped into being.

Aqua paused, heart heavy beneath the weight of infinite destinies. He gazed across the surreal expanse, voice soft yet resonant, echoing like a ripple across still water.

"We're standing in the eye of creation,"he murmured, feeling the enormity of the moment in every fiber of his being."This is where everything converges."

Beside him, Capri remained silent, her hand entwined with his. Her eyes were wide—not with fear, but with awe born from understanding. They stood at the center of all that was, all that is, and all that might be.

"Everything that was, everything that will be,"she whispered, gaze drawn to the endless web of glowing threads."It's... overwhelming."

The Light within the Nexus shifted ceaselessly, bathing them in hues of deep blue, shimmering gold, and crimson flame. Shadows danced at the edges of perception, twisting into fleeting shapes that flickered between existence and absence. Faint whispers filled the air—voices of past and future alike—some guiding, others warning.

As they ventured deeper, the whispers intensified, insistent and disorienting. Each step blurred the line between their own thoughts and the chorus of fates surrounding them. Then, as if summoned by their presence, visions emerged—fragments of what might be woven from threads aglow with destiny.

The first vision unfolded like a dream, soft and radiant: AquaCapri, whole and at peace, cradled in the calm of a universe at rest. Light and shadow lived in harmony. The balance they had long pursued was at last achieved. From a hilltop, they watched their realm flourish beneath stars that shimmered with the promise of peace. The echoes of war had faded into the stillness of a new dawn.

Capri's breath caught as she gazed at the vision, her voice touched with wonder.

"Could it really be like this?"she asked, her eyes reflecting the gentle glow above."A future where the war ends... where Light and shadow find balance?"

Aqua, too, stood captivated, heart aching with longing for the peace they had sacrificed so much to pursue.

"It's the future we've always dreamed of,"he said, voice heavy with hope."The peace we've given everything for."

But even as he spoke, his brow furrowed. The vision flickered, serenity unraveling at its edges.

"But..."

Without warning, the dream twisted. Dark clouds gathered, swirling with malevolence. Fires ignited where once Light had thrived. Harmony gave way to chaos. The realm of AquaCapri lay shattered.

They saw themselves at the forefront of an endless war, faces weathered by time, hearts scarred by conflict. Shadowed figures moved through ruins, tearing through starlit skies. Their beloved world lay in ashes.

Capri staggered back, breath trembling.

"This... this is what happens if we fail,"she whispered, clutching his hand tighter."The price of a wrong choice."

The vision shattered like glass, plunging them into darkness. From the tangled threads of fate emerged ghostly forms—ephemeral beings flickering between presence and absence. These were the Echoes of Time: voices of the past, spirits of futures unborn, drifting beyond the bounds of time.

One Echo, its voice ancient and etched with the gravity of ages, spoke:

"The past shapes the present, but it does not command the future. Your history is but a thread that led you here. The choices you make now will decide what is to come."

Capri's doubt deepened as the magnitude of their task closed in.

"But how do we know which path is right?"she asked, voice raw."How do we measure the cost when every road demands sacrifice?"

Another Echo, its voice like the wind itself, answered from every direction.

"The future is fluid. Not yet woven into the tapestry. You hold the threads in your hands, but no choice is without consequence. Choose wisely, for your actions will ripple through time and space."

The Echoes faded, and silence returned to the swirling vortex of fate. As they pressed on, the weight of endless futures bore down heavier. Visions continued to flicker into being—sharper, more vivid.

In one, they reigned over a thriving AquaCapri, but the cost was unbearable: one throne stood empty, a kingdom gained at the expense of love. Loneliness stretched beyond time.

In another, they led armies in an eternal war against the Void. The stars dimmed, extinguished one by one under the toll of conflict. Theirs were faces aged by sorrow, spirits worn by sacrifice. Hope thinned with every battle lost.

Capri trembled as the enormity of it all settled upon her.

"Every thread is a life,"she whispered."A world. A universe. How can we possibly choose?"

Aqua turned toward her, steady amid the storm. Taking her hands in his, he anchored them both.

"We don't have to be certain,"he said, voice gentle yet resolute."Only true. True to the Light within us, true to the balance we seek. Whatever path we choose must reflect that."

Threads of fate swirled with purpose, alive and sentient. The very air thickened as if existence itself awaited their decision. Clarity approached—but with it came the crushing burden of consequence.

More futures unfurled. One where AquaCapri blossomed, but their joy was forfeit. Another where war ravaged the realm, yet their love endured through ruin. Every path bore a cost. Every ending bore loss.

"No future is without sacrifice,"Capri whispered, tears glistening in the ethereal glow."Even in the best ones... someone loses."

His grip tightened, gaze steady as the stars.

"Then we choose the future where the losses mean something,"he said."Where they give rise to something greater than ourselves."

The threads blazed brighter, vibrating with possibility. The air crackled with potential. Time bent. Reality awaited.

The Echoes returned, their voices interwoven with the charged hum of fate.

"The future you weave will ripple far beyond this moment,"one intoned."But remember—every choice carries the weight of countless lives. You must decide what price you are willing to pay."

Capri looked into his eyes, burdened by the gravity of all they had seen.

"We can't save everyone,"she said, voice breaking."But we can save enough to matter. That has to be enough."

Aqua nodded, resolve burning bright within.

"Then let's weave the future where Light and shadow stand together —not in opposition, but in harmony."

Together, they reached for the threads. Fingers moved in unison, weaving patterns only their hearts could understand. The threads responded, glowing ever brighter, coiling and twisting into a vision born of unity and courage. The Nexus pulsed, and for a moment, reality bent—acknowledging their decision.

As the threads dimmed, the weight of their choice settled upon them like a sacred shroud. Their course was set. Consequences would ripple far and wide. The path ahead remained veiled in uncertainty, but hand in hand, they had chosen a truth they could stand by: a future where Light and darkness could coexist.

Silence followed.

Not empty—but pregnant with meaning.

The kind of silence the cosmos holds when stars are born or when time, for the briefest instant, forgets to move.

In that stillness, the universe seemed to hold its breath, waiting for their woven destiny to echo outward. The tapestry, though unseen, had begun to shift. Somewhere in the distance, a thread gleamed just a little brighter. Somewhere, a shadow softened.

They stood not just as lovers, not just as leaders—but as weavers of fate.

And in their hands, hope endured.

18.3 The Future Foretold

The Loom of Eternity stood vast and awe-inspiring at the heart of the Chamber of Stars. Its golden threads danced with shadow, weaving the destinies of countless realms into a grand, shimmering tapestry. At the center of this celestial construct pulsed the Final Thread—its light radiant gold interlaced with swirling shadow. This was no ordinary thread; it held the weight of every choice and every sacrifice Aqua and Capri had made. A fragile, delicate equilibrium between Light and darkness.

An uncanny stillness blanketed the chamber as though time itself had paused, holding its breath for this final moment. The stars beyond the dome shimmered faintly in suspense. Around the loom drifted the Weavers of Fate—ethereal beings composed of both Light and shadow. Their presence was nearly tangible in the charged air. They had guided the two souls to this sacred place, but now, they remained as silent witnesses, offering no further direction. This moment belonged to Aqua and Capri alone.

They stood close, hands barely touching—a symbolic distance reflecting the gravity of what lay before them. His eyes locked on the glowing thread, Aqua's brow furrowed with the weight of all that had led them here. His jaw clenched. Each breath he drew was slow and deliberate. Capri, unwavering, exhaled softly. Though her heart raced, her gaze remained calm. Whatever future awaited them after this act, there would be no turning back.

Her voice, soft yet steady, broke the silence.

Capri: (quietly)

"This is it. Every trial, every loss... everything we've endured has led to this moment."

Her eyes shifted to the Final Thread."Every choice, every path—it's all brought us here."

He turned to her. The uncertainty that once clouded his gaze had given way to a quiet strength. Aqua reached for her hand, fingers brushing over hers. That single touch rooted him in the present.

Aqua: (firm, with a flicker of vulnerability)

"We've fought so hard. Now, we decide the fate of everything—our people, our world. But whatever happens next... we face it together."

Their fingers interlaced, and for a breathless moment, the world narrowed to just the two of them—two souls standing at the precipice of destiny.

The First Weaver, radiant with the brilliance of a thousand stars, glided forward. Her voice, when it came, vibrated with the very rhythm of the cosmos—eternal, infinite, resonant.

First Weaver: (with quiet reverence)

"The Final Thread awaits. Once woven, the future will be sealed. Your choices will echo through time, shaping the fates of all who follow."

The weight of her words hung in the still air. Around them, the Weavers of Fate drew nearer, their celestial forms merging Light and shadow in perfect unity. Their eyes, unreadable yet deep with knowing, betrayed the wisdom of those who had witnessed the birth and end of countless realities. They offered no warning, no counsel—only presence.

Capri felt the subtle pull of the loom—a quiet vibration beneath her skin, urging her onward. She turned to Aqua, their hands still joined.

Capri: (with quiet resolve)

"We're ready."

Her gaze held the fire that had carried them through every battle, every sorrow.

"Together, we'll weave the future we believe in—a future where Light and darkness do not war but coexist."

Aqua nodded, his grip tightening as they stepped forward in unison.

Aqua: (with unwavering conviction)

"Together, always."

They approached the Final Thread. The golden light flickered softly, alive with the echoes of their choices. Aqua paused briefly, hand hovering over the glowing strand as if sensing the magnitude it contained. But then he looked to Capri—and in her steady gaze, he found strength. They had weathered every storm side by side. This, too, they would face together.

Their fingertips brushed the Final Thread. It was warm—fragile, yet pulsing with a power that defied comprehension. The Weavers moved in silence, offering subtle guidance with gestures shaped by ages of observation. Slowly, Aqua and Capri began to weave.

Their weaving was deliberate, every motion steeped in the weight of all they had endured. The loom responded with a deep, cosmic hum—an ancient sound that resonated through their bones and into the stars. As the thread moved through the tapestry, its golden light entwined with tendrils of shadow, forming a pattern neither purely radiant nor dark. It was the essence of harmony—a vision hard-won through love, loss, and belief.

The Second Weaver's voice drifted through the chamber, gentle as a breeze across stardust.

Second Weaver: (softly)

"Each thread alters the pattern. The universe will sing the song of your choices for eons to come."

As the weaving continued, flashes of possible futures danced before their eyes. One realm, flooded in Light—pure, blinding, and brittle in its perfection. Another, cloaked in endless shadow—vast, empty, where only power reigned. But their chosen future was neither extreme. In it, Light and darkness twined like dancers—partners in a cosmic balance, each defining the other.

Capri's hand trembled slightly as she drew the thread through a final loop.

Capri: (whispering)

"We've seen so many paths... but this one—this is where hope survives."

Aqua's gaze remained steady, solemn.

Aqua: (softly)

"This is the one where love endures."

The final strands slipped into place. Instantly, the tapestry shimmered with vibrant light, breathing with life itself—as if the universe had exhaled. At its heart, their woven thread pulsed like a living sun, encircled by luminous tendrils of Light and shadow in perfect symmetry.

The First Weaver stepped forward again, her form now flickering between brightness and darkness. Her voice, though quieter, carried the reverence of one who had witnessed the birth of time.

First Weaver:

"The tapestry is complete. The future is sealed. The path you have chosen shall guide the cosmos for all time."

Hand in hand, they stepped back from the loom. Before them stretched the finished tapestry—its beauty staggering, its complexity beyond comprehension. At the center, the Final Thread gleamed brightest, a testament to their love, their sacrifice, and the truth they had chosen. Around it, threads of Light and shadow wove in graceful arcs, rippling out into infinity.

Capri: (her voice soft, laced with quiet strength)

"It's done. The future we've chosen... it's woven into the stars."

She turned, eyes shining with the weight of everything they had endured.

"Whatever comes next, we face it together."

Aqua's gaze softened. The intensity of the moment melted into a calm that spoke of peace—the peace that comes from giving all one has to a cause greater than self.

Aqua: (gently)

"Together, always."

The Weavers of Fate encircled the tapestry, their forms glowing with the golden aura that now radiated from the weave.

Second Weaver: (with reverence)

"The tapestry will echo through time, shaping the destinies of all who come after."

The chamber resonated with a soft hum as the final thread settled into its eternal place. The loom fell silent. Its great task was fulfilled.

Turning away from the Loom of Eternity, Aqua and Capri walked toward the chamber's exit. Behind them, the tapestry continued to glow—an eternal beacon of balance and hope, born from their hearts, shaped by their hands.

As they departed, the golden light dimmed to a gentle pulse, leaving only the quiet harmony of the cosmos behind. A new dawn had begun—one they had shaped. Though their journey had reached its final threshold, the path they carved would stretch beyond stars and time.

And in the hush that followed, the universe itself seemed to sing their names.

Their story may have ended—but their legacy would forever be written in starlight.

CHAPTER

19

THE CELESTIAL CONVERGENCE

ALL REALMS MEET WHERE LIGHT AND SHADOW CONVERGE IN FINAL BATTLE.

CHAPTER 19

△ VALDUM, THE CELESTIAL ARCHITECT
AQUARII: KAELORIN XAL VERAK.

OPENING WHISPER – CH. 19

△ MAXIMUS, THE ETERNAL QUILL
AQUARII: VERAK VE'SERAN.

CLOSING WHISPER – CH. 19

19.1 The Alignment of Realms

The vastness of the cosmos stretched endlessly beyond the Celestial Nexus—a convergence point at the universe's very heart, where realms intertwined and destinies were woven by the rhythm of the stars. The stars shimmered above, ancient and eternal, casting their Light like scattered diamonds upon the velvet blackness. Each crystalline bridge spanning the Nexus pulsed softly—a living network of energy connecting infinite worlds, delicate yet indomitable, like the heartbeat of creation itself.

At the epicenter stood Aqua, his gaze fixed on the celestial tapestry above, where the stars had begun to shift. At first, the movement was subtle, nearly imperceptible. But with each breath, the change intensified—an unseen momentum that sent ripples of energy surging through the air, vibrating through the crystal platforms beneath his feet. The Alignment had begun. This was the long-awaited moment, the convergence foretold since the first dawn. The fate of all realms was threading into a singular point.

Capri stood beside him, eyes wide as she looked out over the Nexus. The celestial energy in the atmosphere was overpowering— breathtaking and terrible in equal measure. She felt it coursing within her, pulsing like a second heartbeat, surging through her veins with an intensity that left her trembling. Reaching for Aqua's hand, she clung to the grounding strength of his touch amid the wild currents surrounding them.

"The realms are aligning,"she whispered, voice taut with awe and fear."I can feel it... It's unlike anything we've ever known. There's so much power... but something darker moves beneath it. We must be ready. Everything changes here—everything could end."

He turned to her, his gaze steady, an expression fierce and tender all at once. The echoes of countless battles flickered in his eyes—conflicts fought across the ages and the love that had carried him through them. His hand tightened around hers, a silent promise forged in resolve.

"The Void will stop at nothing," he said, calm but resolute. "This has always been their plan—to fracture this moment, to plunge the realms into chaos. But we won't allow it. Not after all we've sacrificed, all we've endured. The universe will not unravel. Not while we remain."

The tension between them and the stars above thickened as though the universe itself held its breath. The pull of destiny was irresistible— the balance of Light and darkness teetered on the cusp, and with it, the fate of creation itself. All around them, the crystalline bridges of the Nexus sparkled with the energy of merging realms, their Light refracting like celestial fire across the translucent platforms. With every pulse of that radiance, the presence of the Void drew nearer, drawn to the convergence like a moth to flame.

From the shadowed perimeter of the Nexus, a figure emerged. Arcanus, Guardian of the Nexus, advanced with solemn grace. His towering form was cloaked in robes woven from the Essence of stars, glimmering with shifting constellations. Though serene, his face bore the weight of eons. His eyes, radiant with timeless wisdom, seemed to see beyond matter and time. He was more than a being—he was a force of balance, as old and enduring as the Nexus itself.

"The Nexus is the heart of all things," Arcanus said, his voice low and resonant, heavy with cosmic gravity. "Its balance is more fragile than you understand. If the Alignment falters, the collapse will be catastrophic. You must protect it—at any cost. Should the Nexus fall... so too shall the Light of existence."

A ripple of unease passed through the gathered defenders. Aqua and Capri exchanged a look—no words, only understanding. The burden they bore was now infinite. Even as Arcanus spoke, something stirred again at the edges of the Nexus, and the air turned cold, brittle with an unnatural chill.

From the growing darkness stepped Nihilus, Herald of the Void. His form, cloaked in writhing shadows, absorbed all Light, and his eyes gleamed with the cold fire of oblivion. Where Arcanus embodied wisdom, Nihilus radiated entropy—pure destruction, decay incarnate. His arrival struck the Nexus like a silent scream, pressing down on reality itself with oppressive finality.

"You fools,"Nihilus hissed, his voice slithering through the air like a curse murmured by the void itself."You believe you can control the convergence? You cannot begin to grasp the force you seek to tame. The Alignment will be your undoing. The Void is eternal—it will consume all things: every realm, every star, everything you hold sacred."

He stepped forward, his shadowy aura seeping through the Nexus like tendrils of living darkness, wrapping around the Light and suffocating it. The warriors of Light responded with rising energy, their collective strength flaring like a celestial tide—but Nihilus merely laughed, a sound thick with venomous certainty.

"You cling to the lie of balance,"he sneered."But balance is a myth. Darkness is truth. Entropy is inevitable. The power you covet will unravel the fabric of all realities, and the Void shall claim the remnants."

Capri's grip on Aqua's arm tightened, her breath catching as dread clawed at her heart. The Herald's words felt like a shadow inside her, threatening to extinguish the last flickers of hope. Yet beside her, Aqua remained unmoved, his gaze fixed and unflinching as it met the abyssal stare of their adversary.

"Balance isn't about control, Nihilus,"he said, voice calm but unwavering, the quiet defiance of a leader who had stared down annihilation more than once."It's about harmony. The universe does not belong to the Void, nor solely to the Light. It belongs to all who live within it. And we will stand against you. Always."

The stars above pulsed in answer, beams of Light dancing through the Nexus bridges in radiant defiance. The Alignment neared its zenith, and cosmic energy surged, stirring every soul within reach with awe and a rising storm of purpose.

Arcanus stepped forward, his presence growing brighter, the energy of the stars gathering around him like a mantle of destiny. His eyes pierced into Nihilus with unflinching finality. For the first time, the Guardian spoke not as a sage—but as the voice of the universe itself.

"This is a place of convergence, not decay,"he thundered."The Alignment is the heartbeat of existence. You, Nihilus, are a flaw in the pattern—an echo of collapse that will fade. Light, like the stars, shall endure."

Bolstered by Arcanus's words, the warriors of Light took their positions. Behind Aqua and Capri, a legion of defenders stood tall, their weapons gleaming with the brilliance of a thousand suns. Among them, the Guardians of the Nexus radiated calm resolve, their expressions etched with centuries of purpose. They all knew what was at stake.

The ground trembled beneath their feet as the realms continued their sacred alignment. Above, stars shifted into place, locking together like the gears of a vast celestial mechanism. With each movement, waves of radiant energy pulsed through the Nexus, bathing the platforms in shimmering Light—beautiful, resolute, and unyielding.

Yet, for every burst of Light, a shadow answered. From the furthest corners of the Nexus, the legions of the Void emerged, serpentine forms coiling like dark smoke, creeping ever closer. At their helm stood Nihilus, eyes glowing with relentless malice, his will an obsidian tide.

Aqua raised his blade, its edge glowing with starlit fire. He stepped forward, his voice cutting through the mounting silence like a bell of fate.

"This is it,"he called, his tone unwavering."The fate of the universe is upon us. We fight not only for ourselves but for every realm and every star that dares to shine. Stand strong—let the Light within guide us all!"

The final moment had come. The stars, ever-watchful, continued their deliberate cosmic dance. The forces of Light and darkness faced one another, poised on the edge of cataclysm.

The hum of existence intensified, a cosmic crescendo pulsing with every heartbeat. The alignment surged toward completion, and in that final breath before the clash, the universe trembled.

And then—across the sacred heart of the Celestial Nexus—the Light and the Void collided.

19.2 The Final Battle

The Celestial Nexus, once a sanctuary of harmony, now trembled under the weight of war. Its once-pristine crystalline bridges splintered, fractured by the surge of power clashing across the realms. The air was thick with the scent of scorched energy, the echoes of serenity replaced by cries of battle and the raw hum of unleashed elemental force.

Above, the heavens reflected the chaos below. The aligned realms formed a glowing ring in the sky, their celestial convergence casting radiant beams down upon the battlefield. Explosions of Light and shadow clashed midair—blazing reds, ethereal blues, and molten gold against the ever-churning blacks and violets of the Void. It was as if the cosmos themselves were embroiled in the confrontation, the astral canvas ruptured by the forces of destiny.

Below this storm of energies, the forces of Light stood firm, though weariness weighed heavily on them. Capri, her golden armor dulled by ash and time, raised her voice above the cacophony of blades and sorcery.

"This is it! We cannot falter!"

Her words, ringing with urgency, cut through the roar of battle like a clarion call.

"We are the final line! If we fall, so too falls all we cherish!"

Her gaze swept across the battlefield—over Guardians and Champions, over elemental warriors wielding fire and stone, over machines of radiant might. They fought shoulder to shoulder, holding back the relentless tide. Fatigue clung to them like chains, yet none stepped back. They knew this was their last stand.

Beside her, Aqua cleaved through the Voidspawn with his starlight blade, each strike releasing radiant arcs that seared the air. Shadowy creatures disintegrated into mist, shrieking as they vanished. Gritting his teeth, he called out above the fray,

"Capri! The hunger of the Void grows. I can feel its reach spreading through the ley lines. But they do not know us. They have never known hope."

Resolve flared in his eyes, but even he sensed the strain tightening like a noose around the Light's defenders.

A shattering boom tore through the Nexus. The earth convulsed, rupturing the sacred geometry etched into its foundations. Crystalline platforms buckled and snapped. Still, the warriors of Light did not yield.

From the eastern flank surged Aurora, the radiant Lightbringer, her staff raised high like the dawn itself summoned into form. She advanced across broken ground, cutting through the gloom with every step. Her armor, woven of golden fire and argent moonlight, blazed with celestial strength.

"Do not fear!"she cried."The dawn shall rise! We are the Light of all Realms, and we will not be extinguished!"

Her voice rang like a vow cast in the stars, and it surged through the ranks—through the Guardians of AquaCapri, through the Champions of Capricorn, and into the hearts of every soldier bearing the mark of Light. Shields were raised anew. Swords flared brighter. Stardust Warriors, towering engines of divine justice, unleashed their fury in synchronized blasts of pure starlight.

But for every enemy felled, more emerged from the churning dark.

From the heart of that malevolent storm, a silhouette broke the void—an overwhelming force wrapped in swirling shadow. It was Eclipse, Champion of the Void, his colossal frame clad in obsidian armor veined with violet runes that pulsed with the breath of dying stars. His presence was gravity—crushing, cold, inevitable.

"Fools,"he intoned, voice like a collapsing sun."You rage against destiny. The Void does not conquer; it restores balance by returning all to silence."

Aurora stepped forward, eyes bright with flame. Her staff flared with the brilliance of a thousand suns.

"Even in the deepest abyss, Light will rise. You speak of silence, but we sing of eternity."

A grin curled across Eclipse's face. With both hands, he raised his dread blade—the Umbral Fang, forged in the last breath of a fallen nova. It thrummed with death.

"Then you shall be the first to fall."

With that, he struck, and the heavens reeled.

The impact of Eclipse's blade against Aurora's staff sent out a shockwave so powerful it warped the very Light around them. Armies on both sides staggered, and for a breathless moment, it was as if time itself recoiled from the clash.

The battlefield became a whirlwind of chaos and valor.

Elsewhere in the Nexus, Aqua and Capri moved with a rhythm that mirrored the pulse of the stars. Their battle was a symphony of motion—his blade of starlight dancing through the air, her shield deflecting arcs of dark energy with unwavering precision. Together, they were unstoppable, not merely warriors but twin forces of will and destiny.

Yet even with their unity, the tides surged darker.
The Voidspawn poured in like a flood. Their forms twisted, born of forgotten nightmares, howling with hunger. The Stardust Warriors, towering titans of alloy and astral flame, unleashed beam after beam of concentrated Light, vaporizing waves of enemies. But with each advance they repelled, another wave surged behind it, more ferocious, more unrelenting.

The ground trembled with every step of the massive guardians. Their voices, deep and synthetic, rang like cosmic thunder as they called to one another, coordinating attacks with divine precision. But for all their power, even these celestial war engines were beginning to strain. The darkness adapted. It multiplied.

A surge of voidfire exploded nearby, blasting Capri off her feet. Her body hit the scorched earth, breath knocked from her lungs. Pain seared through her limbs, but she forced herself to rise, battered and breathless.

"We won't break!"she roared, defiance burning in her eyes.

Her gaze found Aqua across the field. Their eyes locked, and in that instant, no words were needed. If they were to fall, it would be as one. Not in surrender but in defiance. For love. For their realm.

Aqua's blade ignited with renewed brilliance. A halo of starlight flared around him as he charged into the darkness, each step a declaration of purpose.

"This is our realm! Our legacy! We will not yield!"

His voice rang like a prophecy, and across the battlefield, warriors of Light—Zephyr, the wind-forged archer; Aqualith, with tidal fists of living water; Pyronix, fire incarnate; and Gaian, the Earth-Warden—rallied with him. Alongside them rose the champions of AquaCapri, their elemental banners whipping in the rising wind.

Above them, Supreme General Valorus, his armor ablaze with radiant sigils, led the endless phalanx of Star Warriors, their shields and spears glinting like stars reborn. Lumina, her very presence a beacon of truth, cast a veil of Light over the wounded, restoring strength and courage where despair had taken root.

And from the shadows, unseen but ever-present, came ShadowVeil and
Aetherwind, masters of espionage and arcane disruption. Their agents struck with surgical precision, severing the lines of communication among the Void's hidden infiltrators. The armies of the Equinox Spies moved like whispers between realms, dismantling traps, dispelling illusions, and ensuring the warriors of Light could advance without falter.

Yet the Void did not falter either.

From its core surged the Champions of the Void, beings molded in entropy and fueled by the screams of extinguished stars. They formed a phalanx of despair behind Eclipse—massive, grim, and silent.

The Shadowed Ones, Moroseth's legion of infiltrators, whispered curses into the minds of the weak, turning hesitation into collapse. And overhead, from the highest reach of the aligned realms, came Moroseth himself, the Dark Sovereign, his wings of voidstuff unfurled like eclipsed constellations. He did not yet descend, but his presence alone bent the battlefield into a deeper night.

At the heart of it all, Aurora and Eclipse danced their terrible duel.

"You shine with defiance,"Eclipse sneered, his sword sweeping in a wide arc, carving through pillars of Light."But stars fade. Even your brilliance is but a breath."

Aurora countered, her staff catching the blade mid-strike. The Light of galaxies surged through her.

"A breath, yes. But enough to illuminate eternity."

She released a blinding explosion of Light. The clash roared across the battlefield. Eclipse staggered—but only for a moment. He surged back with a wrathful cry, the very darkness around him solidifying into jagged shards that launched outward like spears.

Aurora deflected one, two—then three struck her side.

Still, she stood.

Capri, lungs burning, shoulders bruised, turned to Aqua with a quiet, ferocious resolve.

"We can't let it end like this,"she whispered, voice raw but steady.

He stepped beside her, hand lifting his blade toward the roiling sky.

"It won't. We are the Light, Capri. We've come too far... endured too much. This is our final vow."

The blade pulsed—starlight forged through unity and sacrifice. He raised it high.

"For AquaCapri!"

His voice became thunder, echoing across the battleground, across the broken bridges of the Nexus, and into the hearts of every soldier bearing the crest of hope. Warriors rose, rallied, and surged forward. Wounded Stardust Warriors powered their cores anew. The elemental forces surged with fresh fury. Spies leapt from shadow to strike key lieutenants among the Void. Even the wounded lifted their weapons once more.

Then came the fracture.

From across the field, Eclipse, furious at the tide's momentary turn, let out a savage roar and brought down his blade with cataclysmic force. It struck Aurora's staff, and the sacred relic—center of her radiant strength—shattered.

Crystalline fragments burst in every direction as Aurora was hurled through the air, her body crashing into a broken spire. Her breath escaped in a single, pained gasp. Silence fell as if the battlefield itself had forgotten how to breathe.

She lay still, radiant hair scattered across the cracked stone, her light dimmed. The warriors of Light froze, their hearts clenched in disbelief.

Eclipse, towering above her, raised his sword once more.

"And now you die,"he intoned, voice soaked in cruel triumph."And with you—Light itself."

The blade began to fall.

And then, the earth wept Light.

A tremor split the battlefield. The foundations of the Nexus groaned and pulsed. A deep, resonant hum echoed from below—ancient, harmonic, and alive. Golden cracks laced the ground, and from them burst a radiant wave unlike anything seen since the first dawn of creation.

A column of golden Light surged upward, roaring into the heavens like a living flame. It struck Eclipse mid-swing, halting his blade and driving him back. He staggered, snarling, eyes wide in disbelief.

Aqua and Capri turned, shielding their eyes against the divine brilliance.

"What's happening?"she whispered, awe wrapped in every syllable.

Aqua stepped forward slowly, eyes fixed on the heart of the storm.

"The Nexus... it's awakening."

The Light spiraled upward, encircling the soldiers of AquaCapri. It wove around them like silk spun from stars, mending wounds, strengthening limbs, restoring what was nearly lost. Wounded warriors rose anew. Swords rekindled. Shields reformed. Even Aurora, crumpled and dimmed, lifted her head as the radiant tide surged into her chest.

She inhaled, and her glow returned in full force.

Around them, the Void recoiled. Its shadows withered in the golden blaze. Eclipse snarled, stepping back as the divine force washed over him, stripping his armor of its unnatural gleam. His hands tightened around the Umbral Fang.

In the sky above, Moroseth narrowed his eyes.

Below, Aqua's voice rang clear.

"The Nexus has chosen."

He advanced toward the center of the battlefield, sword blazing with new fire, the chosen embodiment of AquaCapri's spirit.

"The Light will not be extinguished."

And so, the battle raged on.

The forces of Light, once battered and worn, now surged forward with the fury of resurrected stars. Empowered by the awakened Nexus, they fought not just with strength but with clarity—knowing the realms had not forsaken them. Knowing the cosmos still answered the cry of the just.

At the front, Aqua, Capri, and Aurora led the charge. Behind them, every Guardian, champion, and warrior rose as one. The Light blazed brighter than ever before.

But in the distance, the shadows still loomed.

And the final confrontation had only just begun.

19.3 The Triumph of Love

The Heart of the Nexus floated in the Void like a celestial gem, the sacred center where the energies of all aligned realms converged into a radiant, pulsating core. Its Light was so intense it seemed to transcend time itself, stretching into every corner of creation. Within, golden and silver strands of cosmic energy swirled—colliding, merging—as if dancing to the eternal rhythm of the universe. The raw power of creation and destruction, locked in their infinite cycle, vibrated through the fabric of existence.

At the edge of this awe-inspiring spectacle stood Aqua and Capri. Their journey had carved paths through trials of loss, currents of hope, and battles that raged across the cosmos. Now, they stood at the threshold of the ultimate test—the moment when the fate of the stars, their realm, and their love would be determined. The weight of destiny pressed upon them, heavier than the gravity of galaxies.

Capri stepped forward first, her voice soft yet resolute, filled with the unwavering truth of all they had endured.

"This is it," she said. Her gaze, steady as a starlit sky, mirrored the swirling energies before them. "Everything we've sacrificed... everything we've fought for... leads to this."

His deep blue eyes met hers, shining with steadfast love. Without a word, he reached for her hand, their fingers intertwining. A surge of energy flared from their bond, the pulse of their love a tangible force that momentarily repelled the gathering shadows.

"Together," he whispered, his voice steady with conviction,
"we've endured the darkest nights and fiercest storms. And together, we will face this. Our love is the strength that will protect all—no matter the cost."

But even as their Light surged, the Void stirred.

A writhing mass of impenetrable darkness crept from the fringes of the Nexus. Its presence was overwhelming—cold, crushing, like a black shroud poised to suffocate the Light. Tendrils of shadow slithered through the air, coiling around radiant streams, seeking to corrupt and consume the Heart itself. The very air thickened, and the hope that had once filled the cosmos began to falter.

Then came the voice—deep, guttural, ancient. A venomous echo dripping with malevolence.

"Fools..."it growled.

The words rippled like a plague through the Nexus, thick with poison."You believe love can halt the inevitable? That Light can endure before eternal night? I existed before your stars flickered before your realms were named. I am the end. I will devour all you cherish—every realm, every breath. Love is weak. Fleeting. It cannot withstand forever."

The darkness surged, its tendrils lunging toward the core. Blacker than the abyss, the shadow advanced, swallowing hope with every breathless moment.

But she did not yield. Chin high, eyes blazing, Capri stood unmoved.

"You're wrong,"her voice rang clear."Love is stronger than darkness. It binds, it lifts, it kindles hope in even the bleakest void. It is the Light that never fades, the fire that endures."

The Void recoiled, stung by her truth. But with renewed rage, it pressed forward, determined to smother her defiance.

He stepped beside her, and the Light responded. It swelled, shimmering in rhythm with his rising will.

"Together, we will triumph,"he declared, his voice a blade of radiance."Love restores balance. You may wield power, Void, but without love—your dominion is hollow."

The Heart of the Nexus answered.

Golden Light flared like a newborn star, ignited by his words. Yet the Void did not relent. From the edge of the realms, it gathered itself in a roaring fury. Then, with a cry that shook creation, it hurled a wave of all-consuming darkness toward the Light.

The brilliance dimmed. For a moment, shadow eclipsed the core. The darkness wrapped around them, coiling with intent to devour. The air stilled. Hope flickered.

But even surrounded, they did not break. From their joined hands, a warm, unyielding Light bloomed. It spread like a sunrise, soft but relentless, pressing against the consuming tide.

The Void hissed, recoiling. But its desperation deepened. It lashed again, more vicious, more vast. The entire Nexus trembled under the weight of this clash—golden beams slamming into obsidian tendrils, creation and oblivion locked in an ancient, eternal dance.

She leaned close, her whisper cutting through the chaos."Do you feel it? The universe—it stands with us."

He nodded, tightening his grip."I do. We will not fail."

With one last, furious cry, Moroseth and the Void summoned its ultimate force—a wave of darkness so immense it blotted out the heavens. Shadows rushed forward, determined to extinguish the core forever.

They stood unshaken.

Together, they became the beacon.

With one final surge, they channeled everything—every memory, every heartbeat, every breath of love—into a pulse of blinding energy.

The Light erupted outward in a tidal wave of brilliance, smashing into the oncoming night.

The darkness howled.

Tendrils evaporated, scorched by the Light of their love. The Heart of the Nexus pulsed, brighter than before—restored by creation, bound by unity, crowned by love.

Moroseth fell not by blade, but by the light he had once abandoned, and the Void began to retreat—its form crumbling into the abyss from whence it came, its roar now a fading echo of defiance.

Her hand still entwined with his, she turned toward him, eyes glowing with quiet strength.

"Love binds the stars, the realms, all life. That is its strength. And that is why it will always prevail."

He smiled, his gaze a mirror of calm devotion. "We've won. Our love is the Light that banishes darkness. It always was."

Their hands rose, still joined, casting a final pulse of brilliance. The last remnants of the Void disintegrated before it, erased from the Heart of the Nexus. Peace fell, soft and vast. The realms breathed again.

In that celestial stillness, they stood bathed in radiant glow, hearts soaring with peace and hard-earned triumph. The road behind them had been long, littered with shadows and sacrifice—but now, at the center of all that is, they knew one immutable truth:

Their love had endured.

And in the end, it had triumphed.

The Heart of the Nexus pulsed with gentle rhythm, a reminder of harmony restored. Around them, the cosmos shimmered, alive with unity once again. The war had ended not with destruction but with Light born of devotion.

Side by side, they embraced the silence—not of emptiness, but of completion.

The universe, once threatened by oblivion, now shone brighter for the love that had saved it.

Their journey was not over, but this chapter had found its close—not with a sword or crown, but with two hearts beating as one.

And the stars watched in silence, bearing witness to a truth older than time:

Love endures.

Always.

CHAPTER

20

ETERNITY'S PROMISE

THE STARS WILL REMEMBER THEM, AND SO SHALL WE.

 # CHAPTER 20

△ **MAXIMUS, THE ETERNAL QUILL**
AQUARII: AQUA'NAIR XAL CAPRI'UM.

 OPENING WHISPER – CH. 20

△ **VALDUM, THE CELESTIAL ARCHITECT**
AQUARII: SOL'VIRE AN'THELARI.

 CLOSING WHISPER – CH. 20

20.1 The Infinite Cycle

The sky above Aquaterra shimmered with a brilliance born of triumph, the stars twinkling like a thousand diamonds across the velvet sweep of eternity. It was a beauty earned only through the deepest trials—a peace forged in the crucible of shadow. Below, the land once scarred by war had bloomed anew. Crystalline mountains rose in majestic splendor, their jagged peaks reflecting the heavens, while rivers of liquid starlight flowed through emerald valleys, casting silver ripples that danced across fields bursting with cosmic blossoms. Even the air felt alive, pulsing with harmony. Every leaf, every ripple whispered of renewal.

Aqua and Capri stood hand in hand atop a hill, their hearts intertwined as they gazed upon the realms they had saved. A golden Light bathed the landscape, warm and serene. Yet, as a gentle breeze tousled the silver strands in Capri's hair, a subtle murmur stirred the air—a quiet reminder that peace was but a chapter in the endless turning of the cosmic wheel.

"It's so beautiful..."she whispered, her voice soft as starlight, eyes shimmering with the splendor before them."After all we've endured, all we've lost... it feels almost unreal. Like a dream, we've only just awakened from."

Aqua turned, his grip tightening slightly. The warmth of her presence grounded him, but his expression was far away."More than a dream,"he murmured, voice deep with the weight of their journey."It's the reality we fought to shape—the future we carved from the ashes."He paused, brows furrowing as if sensing a ripple beyond the horizon."But I can feel it, Capri... this peace—this balance—it's only the beginning. There's more waiting beyond the veil."

Before she could respond, the Light surrounding them shifted, deepening into a soft, luminous glow. From the skies above, a figure descended—wrapped in the radiance of stars, her form shimmering with celestial brilliance. Her arrival was silent, yet profound, as though the very fabric of existence had rippled at her presence.

Childlike in form, radiant in essence, the being hovered before them, her eyes wide and filled with the Light of distant galaxies. When she spoke, her voice was like the song of a thousand celestial birds, soft and echoing across the expanse."The cycle of stars is endless,"she said, her words resonating in air and thought alike."With each turn, new trials arise. Balance has been restored, but the universe is vast—and its forces far from still."

Capri, captivated by the visitor's glow, felt no fear—only awe and boundless curiosity."Who are you?"she asked, her voice a breath upon the wind, careful not to disturb the fragile peace.

The figure smiled, pulsing with a gentle Light that hinted at innocence cloaked in ageless wisdom."I am Astrid, born of stardust and Light. I come not with warning but remembrance—your journey has not ended. Even now, new stories are being spun in the tapestry of time, destinies forming beyond this horizon."

Aqua stepped forward, steady and unwavering, eyes fixed on the starborn child."What forces stir?"he asked quietly."What lies beyond this calm?"

The air shifted again, heavier now—thick with timeless gravity. Another form emerged, ancient and immense in presence. Celestia, Elder of the Constellations, descended, her silver hair flowing like rivers of light, robes glimmering with the breath of stars. A low hum echoed in the sky as the constellations shifted overhead as if bowing to her return.

"Celestia..." Aqua breathed, his voice reverent. She, the guardian of the constellations—witness to the birth of realms and the fall of empires—stood before them, a living echo of the cosmos.

Her voice was a symphony—gentle yet unyielding, layered with the memory of eons. "The Light you restored will guide you," she said, her gaze shifting between the two. "But where there is Light, shadows will follow. This is not the end of your path—it is the closing of one chapter. Another soon begins, and with it, mysteries even the stars cannot yet decipher."

Capri felt a stirring, not fear, but something deeper—anticipation. "Shadows..." she whispered. "Will they return for us?"

Celestia's smile held both hope and gravity. "Shadows are part of the eternal balance, child of the stars. Light and darkness, creation and unraveling, love and loss—these are the pulses of the universe. You and Aqua now stand as anchors of that balance. And though you stand together, the next trials will not mirror the last. New forces rise, ones hidden even from my sight."

Aqua listened, his silence sharpened by resolve. "Whatever they are," he said firmly, "we'll face them. We've fought to restore harmony before. And we'll do it again. Together."

Beside Celestia, Astrid's glow brightened. "That is why you were chosen—not for your might, but your unity. The cycle endures through those who carry both Light and love. But even in peace, love must be protected. Vigilance is required. For the cycle... is eternal."

Their words lingered in the air like celestial mist, a soothing balm and a solemn bell. Aqua and Capri exchanged a glance—one of shared truth, of a vow unspoken. The fire between them, forged in the crucible of cosmic war, had not dimmed.

Above them, the stars began to shift, constellations dancing in slow celestial rhythm as though the heavens themselves acknowledged the next turn in the great cycle. Aqua turned to Capri, his gaze steady, voice soft but resolute—a whisper of strength carried on the cosmic wind.

"Whatever lies ahead, we face it together. Our love—our bond—is our strength. No matter what shadows rise, we will always bring the Light."

Capri's hand tightened gently in his, her heart echoing his vow."Always together, Aqua. For every cycle. For every challenge. We are ready."

As Astrid and Celestia began to fade, their luminous forms dissolving into the golden twilight, the crystalline trees rustled with a breeze that felt like the universe exhaling. Yet beneath the serenity, a pulse remained—a quiet signal of movement beneath stillness. A whisper. A promise. The cosmos turning once more.

The two stood in silence a moment longer, watching the starlit rivers shimmer and the blooming fields sway in colors too vivid for any language. The scent of rebirth drifted on the air, rich and eternal. And though peace wrapped gently around them, both could feel it—the subtle pull at the edges of time, the beckoning call of the next great unfolding.

The future remained unseen, veiled in stardust and potential. But one truth endured: as long as they stood together, they would face whatever came—hand in hand, Light against shadow, bound in love.

Above, the stars twinkled in silent witness—a radiant chorus echoing the eternal promise that Aqua and Capri would forever be part of the infinite cycle, their souls woven into the living fabric of the universe.

adult version

20.2 The Legacy of Aqua and Capri

In the heart of the Celestial Citadel, suspended among the stars, lay the Hall of Memories. A sanctuary unlike any other, it was a place where the stories of the universe's most revered figures were enshrined —where even time seemed to bow in reverence. Crystalline pillars stretched endlessly toward the starlit ceiling, and stardust murals adorned the walls, each particle shimmering as though plucked from the very weave of the cosmos. The Hall pulsed with a quiet song of valor, sacrifice, and wisdom, echoing softly through the infinite expanse.

As Aqua and Capri stepped into the sacred chamber, their footsteps on the polished marble floor whispered like wind across still waters. Above, the stars shone through crystalline windows, their golden Light diffusing into a gentle glow that bathed the Hall in warmth and serenity. Statues of legendary heroes stood in silent vigil along the walkways, carved from luminescent stone that pulsed faintly, as if the Essence of their lives lingered here, woven into the memory of the realm. These effigies were more than monuments—they were frozen moments of triumph and struggle, preserved in stone and Light.

Aqua's gaze fell upon a towering likeness of himself. It captured him mid-battle, sword of Light raised high, his expression carved in unyielding determination. Every detail—the fire in his eyes, the coiled tension in his limbs, the gleam of his blade cutting through darkness—had been immortalized. Beside him stood Capri, conjuring a sweeping wave of stardust, her face calm yet fierce. Power radiated from her sculpted form, a testament to the balance of serenity and might she so gracefully embodied. Together, their statues told a tale not only of cosmic defiance but of a love that had reshaped the fate of creation.

Capri paused before a vast mural stretching along the nearest wall. It depicted one of their most defining moments—a convergence of love and sacrifice. They stood united against encroaching shadow, their stardust warriors flanking them. Their faces, though determined, bore the fatigue of countless battles. Yet, even in painted silence, their bond glowed like a beacon through the chaos—a guiding Light born not merely of duty but of devotion.

"It's humbling, isn't it?"she murmured, awe softening her tone."To see our journey preserved among so many others... It reminds me we are only a part of something far greater than ourselves."

Aqua moved beside her, his gaze tracing the familiar brushstrokes of the mural. Memories surged—battles fought in the void of space, the aching cost of sacrifice, and the quiet, stolen moments when their love had been the only Light left to guide them. His voice, low and steady, carried the weight of those memories."We've left a mark upon the universe,"he said."But this isn't the end. There's more to protect... more to uncover. What we've built is only the beginning of our legacy."

The truth of his words echoed around them as they walked deeper into the Hall. With every step, the reverent stillness seemed to grow more profound. The air thrummed with the energy of innumerable lifetimes, vibrating softly with the memories sealed within these sacred walls.

They came to a more intimate alcove—less grand but no less powerful. Here, the stories felt personal. Sculptures and murals gave way to relics preserved in shimmering stasis, each one a fragment of the journey they had walked together. Aqua's first blade rested on an obsidian pedestal, its edge still sharp, its surface etched by time and battle. Nearby, a veil speckled with stars floated within a sphere of light—Capri's, from their union beneath the astral skies. Each item told a tale: of valor, of vulnerability, of victories born from the strength of unity.

Then, a shift in the silence.

From the shadowed edge of the chamber emerged Celestia, Elder of the Constellations. Her presence shimmered like a constellation drawn into form, robes flowing like currents of cosmic wind. Her every movement defied time, and her eyes—deep pools of ancient starlight—held the gravity of a thousand ages.

A hush settled over the Hall as she approached. Aqua and Capri, though leaders in their own right, felt the weight of her presence. It was not a burden but a reminder—of the vastness of the universe, of how even great stories are part of a greater whole.

"The Hall of Memories remembers,"Celestia said, her voice a calm resonance that seemed to echo from both the present and eternity."But it does not only preserve the past. It also gazes toward what must still come."She extended an arm toward a great, unmarred wall ahead—its surface pure, untouched, waiting."Your next choices will shape the unwritten chapters. The cosmos will always need guardians—those willing to stand against the Void and illuminate the stars."

Capri stepped forward, her gaze held by the blank wall. The meaning of Celestia's words wrapped around her like a mantle—not a burden, but a truth. This sacred place was not only for reflection. It was also a threshold. Their battles, their triumphs, were only the beginning.

"We've come so far,"she whispered, turning to Aqua, her eyes wide with realization."But there's more ahead. Our story isn't just ours— it's woven into every life we touch, every realm we protect, and the future we help shape."

Aqua stepped beside her, his fingers brushing hers, grounding them both in the gravity of the moment."Our legacy,"he said, voice low but resolute,"isn't only written in the battles we've fought. It lives in the love we share, in the bonds we've forged, and in the Light, we've spread across the stars. This story... it's ours—but also theirs. All who follow."

They stood together before the vast, waiting wall—its smooth surface gleaming under the soft golden radiance of the Hall. And in that silence, something profound stirred in their hearts. This was not an ending. It was the breath before the next beginning. Their legacy was not static but alive—shaped by every future choice, every act of courage, every whisper of hope carried across the cosmos.

Celestia's voice, deep with vision, broke the stillness."The universe is infinite. You have brought peace to many realms, but shadows still linger in distant corners. The cycles ahead will not be free of trials.

What you choose—how you rise—will determine if peace holds... or if darkness finds a way back."

Aqua's grip tightened gently around Capri's hand. His gaze met hers, and in it, she saw the same flame that had carried them through every storm."Whatever awaits,"he said,"we'll face it together. As we always have."

Capri smiled, her hand locking securely into his."Together. Always."

With one final glance at the sacred Hall, they turned and began walking—hand in hand—toward the Light streaming through the great archway. Their steps were quiet yet resolute, echoing through the chamber like the first notes of a new song. Outside, the Celestial Citadel awaited, and beyond that, the boundless realms of the cosmos.

Though they had faced despair and risen from its ashes, they understood something deeper now: the true strength of their legacy was not in victories or monuments but in how their journey had inspired others—how it would continue to echo in every corner of the universe they had touched.

Behind them, the statues stood in eternal vigil, silent witnesses to the bond that had defied fate. The murals shimmered with stardust, capturing fragments of their shared odyssey. And before them, the stars burned with renewed brilliance, casting their Light on paths yet to be walked—on realms still in need of guardians and stories still waiting to be written.

Their legacy lived on. Their story was far from over.

20.3 A Whisper to the Future

The stars shimmered above, blanketing the vast expanse of the cosmos in a soft, radiant glow. Aqua and Capri stood at the precipice of the Starry Path, the ethereal trail winding ahead through the infinite. Beneath their feet, the path glowed gently, as though woven from stardust, its Light pulsing in rhythm with their heartbeats. Galaxies swirled in the distance, their Light mingling with constellations, creating a cosmic symphony of brilliance and shadow. The air around them was cool and still, filled with an almost palpable anticipation, as if the very universe was holding its breath, waiting to see what they would do next.

Capri's fingers lightly touched the edge of the path, the shimmering surface warm under her touch. A soft light illuminated her face, her eyes wide with awe as she gazed into the endless expanse before them. The Starry Path seemed alive, breathing with the energy of countless realms, each star overhead a story waiting to be told, each galaxy a world to be explored.

"The Starry Path..."she whispered, her voice tinged with quiet reverence."It feels like the universe itself is calling us."She paused, letting the weight of her words settle."There's so much more to discover, Aqua. So much more to protect."

Aqua stood beside her, his expression steady and purposeful. His presence, always a source of unwavering strength, seemed even more grounded now. He had always been the calm in the storm, the pillar Capri could lean on. His gaze remained fixed on the horizon, where the radiant path disappeared into the unknown. The universe before them stretched out in infinite possibilities, and Aqua was ready to face whatever it had in store for them.

"The future is vast, Capri," Aqua replied, his deep voice resonating in the stillness of the stars. "We've faced darkness and emerged stronger, but this is only the beginning." He turned to her, his smile soft but filled with certainty and affection. "There's still so much ahead of us, and I can't wait to see what we'll discover."

The stars above seemed to hum in agreement, their twinkling lights reflecting off the smooth surface of the Starry Path. As if responding to their shared resolve, the path ahead brightened, beckoning them forward. Their journey was far from over.

Together, they took their first steps onto the glowing trail, the universe stretching endlessly before them. The air was cool but comforting, and the faint scent of celestial winds carried with it a sense of possibility. As they moved forward, a soft ripple of stardust fluttered before them, and out of the shimmering Light, Astrid, the Starborn Child, appeared. Her form was radiant, her features shimmering with cosmic Light. Her presence, always an embodiment of both wisdom and innocence, filled the air with a sense of calm anticipation.

"The stars whisper of new adventures, new challenges, and new discoveries," Astrid's voice carried like the distant hum of galaxies, her words soft but powerful. "Your journey is far from over, Aqua and Capri. The universe is waiting for you."

Her words felt like a gentle nudge from the cosmos, awakening something deep within them. Aqua and Capri had triumphed over the shadows that sought to consume the realms, but now, standing here on the precipice of the unknown, they understood that the universe was far more vast than they had ever imagined.

Capri turned to Aqua, a new spark of determination in her eyes. "Then let's not keep it waiting," she said, her voice steady and resolute. She took his hand, her grip firm yet warm."Together, we'll continue to protect the Light and bring hope to every corner of the universe."

Aqua smiled at her, his gaze filled with the same tenderness that had carried them through so many battles. There was a quiet promise in his eyes—a vow that no matter what challenges lay ahead, they would face them together."Together,"he echoed, his voice strong yet gentle."Always."

They continued walking down the Starry Path, their steps slow but certain. The stars above pulsed softly, guiding them forward into the unknown. Each step seemed to hum with possibility, the cool air filled with the distant echoes of the cosmos. Every breath felt like a renewal, a reminder that their story was still unfolding.

The path beneath them shimmered, neither fully solid nor entirely ethereal, as though it existed somewhere between reality and dream. It glowed with the Light of a million stars as if the fabric of the cosmos itself had been woven into its surface. Around them, the whispers of the stars grew louder, blending into a celestial chorus. Some stars shared stories of realms long forgotten, their Light carrying the echoes of ancient civilizations, while others whispered of adventures yet to come, their voices filled with the promise of discovery. The universe was a living tapestry, and Aqua and Capri were now woven into its endless story.

But as they ventured further, a subtle tension began to weave through the starlit air. The atmosphere was electric, charged with the promise of new beginnings, yet beneath it lingered a shadow of uncertainty. The future, vast and filled with infinite possibilities, was also fraught with challenges. The universe was a delicate balance of Light and darkness, and where there was Light, shadows would always follow.

Aqua felt the presence of something distant yet looming. It wasn't fear that gripped him, but understanding. They had fought against the Void and restored peace, but he knew that darkness was relentless. It would return, seeking to unsettle the harmony they had fought so hard to preserve. But this time, Aqua was ready. They both were.

As they ventured deeper along the Starry Path, the stars above began to pulse with a quiet urgency, their whispers growing louder, more insistent. The Light around them flickered for a moment, and Aqua and Capri paused, sensing something just beyond their reach. And then, from the shimmering Light, Astrid appeared once more, her form brighter and more radiant than before. Her eyes, now filled with solemn wisdom, met theirs.

"The universe is vast,"Astrid began, her voice gentle but resolute."But so is your strength. Remember, where there is Light, shadows will always seek to follow. But you have faced darkness before and triumphed. The stars will always guide you forward."

Capri's grip on Aqua's hand tightened slightly as she listened, her gaze unwavering. She knew the weight of those words. With Light came responsibility—a responsibility to protect, to guide, and to fight for the future. But she was ready. They both were. Together, they had faced darkness, and together, they would continue to protect the Light.

"We're ready,"Capri said, her voice firm with conviction.

Aqua nodded, his eyes meeting Astrid's."Whatever comes next, we'll face it together."

The Starry Path stretched before them, its shimmering surface leading into the vast expanse of the universe. Every step they took was guided by the Light of the stars, their whispers filling the cool air with encouragement. The path ahead was unknown, but Aqua and Capri walked forward with unwavering confidence. The universe was vast, filled with new beginnings, new challenges, and infinite possibilities, but with each other by their side, they knew they would endure.

As they disappeared into the horizon, their figures framed by the brilliance of galaxies, the stars continued to twinkle, their soft voices lingering in the air—a promise of what was to come, a whisper to the future.

The universe was infinite, but so was their strength, their love, and their resolve. Together, they would protect the Light, bring hope to every corner of existence, and face whatever lay ahead. Their journey had only just begun.

And with every step they took, the future unfolded before them, shimmering with the radiant Light of endless possibilities.

The End.....For Now

AQUACAPRI MASTER GLOSSARY SCROLL

Chapters Covered: 1.1 through 20.3

[A]

Abyss *(location/concept)*
A formless realm beyond time and space, representing the deepest reaches of the Void. It is a place where Light falters and reality unravels.

 Ch. 19.3

Aegir *(character)*
A cautious royal advisor of AquaCapri who oversees maritime affairs. Though initially loyal, his fascination with PaxProfundis and proximity to Talssa's ambition make him vulnerable to manipulation by the Void's agents.

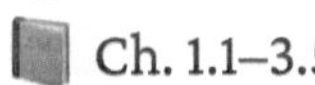 Ch. 1.1–3.5

Aether *(character)*
Realm Historian and Keeper of the Stars. Aether sees the past, present, and future, offering maps, sacred scrolls, and counsel during war.

Ch. 1.1–3.5, 7.3, 8.1, 13.1

Aetherion *(character)*
A being formed of stardust and cosmic memory. Guardian of the Celestial Conflux and a loyal companion to Aqua and Capri, he guides the heroes with timeless wisdom and protects cosmic truths.

Ch. 5.3, 7.1, 9.2, 9.3, 12.1, 13.1

Aetherion Sigil *(artifact)*
An ancient emblem of cosmic balance, forged in the early days of the Constellary Ordo. It resonates with starlight and shadow.

Ch. 11.3

Aetherwind *(character/group)*
A high-ranking operative within the Order of Equinox. Silent guardian of AquaCapri, skilled in shadowcraft and strategic surveillance. Later elevated to master of arcane espionage and illusion, leading elite units against Void strategies.

Ch. 1.1–3.5, 5.1, 5.2, 8.2, 9.1, 15.3, 17.1, 19.2

Alignment *(cosmic event)*
A rare and powerful moment when the stars and realms across the universe shift into perfect harmony. It strengthens the bonds between worlds and unlocks immense energy.

Ch. 19.1

Ancient Spell *(magic)*
A powerful incantation hidden for centuries, accessible only through unity and courage. Unlocks the full potential of the Starlight Pendant.

Ch. 9.4

Aqua *(character)*
Prince of Aquaterra and co-creator of the AquaCapri Constellation. Embodies compassion, adaptability, and oceanic strength. Later becomes the guardian of Light and embodiment of calm resilience.

Ch. 1.1–3.5, 7.1–8.3, 9.1, 17.3, 20.3

AquaCapri *(realm/concept)*
The central realm of harmony and balance, founded by Aqua and Capri. A land and an idea—symbol of unity, love, and courage against the Void.

Ch. 1.1–3.5, 6.1–8.3

AquaCapri Constellation *(place)*
The grand celestial domain where Aquaterra resides. Governed by Aqua and Capri, it unites realms through Light and shared destiny.

Ch. 1.1–3.5, 4.1, 12.2

AquaCapri Echoes *(phenomenon)*
Residual whispers of Light left behind after the use of high elemental magic. They guide others toward acts of selflessness and valor.

Ch. 11.2

Aqualith *(character)*
Guardian of Water, one of the mighty Elemental Lords. Calm, wise, and unwavering, he anchors rituals, defends realms, and balances chaos.

Ch. 9.1, 10.3, 11.3, 15.1, 16.3, 17.2, 17.3

Aqualora *(character)*
Lady of Water and sovereign of the Realm of Water. Her form shifts like rivers and tides. She tests one's trust and grants the Tidecaller Trident.

Ch. 10.1

Aquaterra *(location)*
Crystalline capital of AquaCapri. Heart of civilization, unity, and Light. Reborn after the final battle

into radiant harmony.

Ch. 1.1–3.5, 7.2, 8.3, 10.1, 12.2, 12.3, 20.1

Aquacrest Valley *(location)*
A leyline convergence zone in southern Aquaterra. Key battlefield and staging ground for Stardust Warriors.

Ch. 15.3

Arcanus *(character)*
Ancient Guardian of the Nexus. Shimmering with constellations, he embodies balance and speaks with cosmic authority.

Ch. 19.1

Astralis *(character)*
The Seer of the Stars, clad in celestial robes. Interprets constellations but emphasizes that choice shapes destiny, not fate.

Ch. 15.2

Astrid / Astrid, the Starborn Child *(character)*
A radiant child of stardust and Light who speaks with the voice of remembrance. Innocent yet wise, she heralds the next universal cycle.

Ch. 20.1, 20.3

Aurora, the Lightbringer *(character/title)*
A sun-powered celestial warrior. Her radiant staff and

unwavering spirit make her a beacon against the Void.

Ch. 19.2

[B]

Balance *(concept)*
The sacred equilibrium between Light and shadow, love and loss, creation and destruction. It is the universe's true law and the destiny Aqua and Capri come to embody.

Ch. 20.1

Barrier of Light *(magic/item)*
A radiant magical force used by Celesta's warriors to trap dark entities like Lord Umbra. It seals shadows in Light's embrace.

Ch. 8.2

Battle for Aquaterra *(event)*
The first unified stand of AquaCapri's forces against the Void. Victory is celebrated during the Celestial Ball.

Ch. 5.1

Beacon Between Realms *(location title)*
An ancient name for Noctyra, once a bridge of Light and Void. Its fall sparked the final cosmic conflict.

Ch. 17.1

Beacon of Love *(concept)*
The radiant force created

through Aqua and Capri's united bond. It becomes the ultimate beacon that restores balance.

Ch. 19.3

Beacon of Unity *(artifact/ location)*
A pulsing spire atop the Celestial Citadel. It channels unity and repels darkness with Light's resonance.

Ch. 15.1

[C]

Capri *(character)*
Princess of Caprion, co-ruler of AquaCapri, bearer of the Crescent Blade, and guardian of balance. Compassionate, wise, and luminous with inner fire.

Ch. 1.1–3.5, 4.2, 6.2, 7.1–8.3, 9.1–9.3, 10.3, 15.1–15.2, 17.2–17.3, 20.3

Capri's Vision *(event/prophecy)*
A sudden vision during the symphony where Capri foresees AquaCapri's fall. It warns of the Void's conquest to come.

Ch. 5.2

Caspian *(character)*
Spy from the Capricorn Realm. Loyal to AquaCapri, he risks his life uncovering internal threats.

Ch. 6.1, 8.2

Celesta, Supreme General *(character/title)*
Fearless military leader in AquaCapri's army. Commands the assault on Umbria.

Ch. 8.2

Celestara *(character)*
Celestial Healer and Supreme General. Casts domes of Light, shielding entire fronts.

Ch. 1.1–3.5, 7.3, 9.1, 15.3

Celestia / Celestia, Elder of the Constellations *(character)*
Timeless seer of stars. Guides Aqua and Capri toward their cosmic roles, echoing the wisdom of aeons.

Ch. 20.1–20.2

Celestial Anchor *(artifact)*
A radiant orb enabling long-distance communication between realms and leaders.

Ch. 9.1

Celestial Ark *(artifact/vessel)*
Star-forged ship that travels through time-folds and Light currents. Carries the heroes to sacred destinations.

Ch. 13.2

Celestial Ballroom *(place)*
Domed chamber of ritual unity beneath a living star map.

Ch. 1.1–3.5

Celestial Citadel *(location)*
Strategic fortress and spiritual

nexus of AquaCapri. Site of planning, resistance, and prophecy.

📘 Ch. 1.1–3.5, 5.1, 7.2, 13.1, 15.1–15.2, 20.2

Celestial Conflux *(location)*
Nexus where Light and Void intersect in swirling harmony. Site of the cleansing ritual.

📘 Ch. 12.1

Celestial Courtyard *(location)*
Moonlit garden for elemental gatherings beneath crystal fountains.

📘 Ch. 10.3

Celestial Nexus *(place/location)*
The central convergence point of all realms, where crystal bridges connect dimensions. Becomes the stage for final battle.

📘 Ch. 19.1–19.2

Celestial War Map *(artifact)*
Living orb displaying battlefield movements across realms and leylines in real time.

📘 Ch. 15.3

Chamber of Destiny *(location)*
Sanctum within the Library of Eternity, where infinite futures ripple across cosmic glass.

📘 Ch. 13.3

Chamber of Light *(place)*
Council hall within the Hall of Stars. Site of strategic planning and truth revelation.

📘 Ch. 1.1–3.5, 8.1

Chamber of Stars *(place)*
Celestial room where the Loom of Eternity resides. Holds the fate of all realms.

📘 Ch. 6.2, 18.3

Chamber of Truth *(location)*
Crystal hall within the Mirror Labyrinth. Only truth pierces its silence.

📘 Ch. 16.2

Champions of the Void *(faction)*
Warriors formed from extinguished stars and chaos. They speak only in violence.

📘 Ch. 19.2

Chronia *(character)*
The Seer of Time. Guides heroes at turning points, speaks with cosmic breath, and guards the Loom's edge.

📘 Ch. 4.2, 7.3, 8.3, 10.3, 13.1–13.3, 14.1–14.3, 16.1, 17.3, 18.1

Clandestine Wraith, Zarvok the Shadowweaver *(character/ title)*
Master of illusion and betrayal. Sows chaos through psychic traps and whispered half-truths.

📘 Ch. 1.1–3.5, 5.2, 8.2

Clash of Light and Shadow *(event)*

Cosmic duel in the Heart of the Nexus. A turning point in the war for existence.

 Ch. 19.3

Cleansing Ritual *(event)*
Sacred elemental rite to purge Void corruption through balance. Performed at the Celestial Conflux.

 Ch. 12.1

Conspirators of Equilibrium *(group)*
Idealists who believe balance includes shadow. Some betray Light in pursuit of perfect harmony.

 Ch. 1.1–3.5

Constellation Map *(artifact)*
Tactical and symbolic map displaying realm alignments. Used by King Oceanius.

 Ch. 5.3

Constellations *(symbolic/ celestial bodies)*
Living sky-scriptures. Each pattern holds prophecy, memory, and sacred weight.

 Ch. 12.2, 13.2–13.3, 20.2

Crystalline Arcades *(place)*
Gleaming halls in Aquaterra. Once tranquil, now host whispers and conspiracies.

 Ch. 1.1–3.5

Crystalline Bridges *(artifact/ place)*

Translucent bridges at the Celestial Nexus. Allow traversal across dimensions.

 Ch. 19.1

Crystal Citadel *(place)*
Shimmering central fortress of AquaCapri. Protected by energy shields and home of royal command.

 Ch. 7.2–7.3

Crystal Dome *(location/tool)*
Vision-reflecting dome atop the Hall of Ages. Mirrors time's spiral across space.

 Ch. 14.1

Crystal of Clarity *(artifact)*
Pulses with truth at the labyrinth's core. Reveals hidden illusions.

 Ch. 16.3

Crystal Walls *(artifact/setting)*
Mirrored panels within the Chamber of Truth. Respond only to honest introspection.

 Ch. 16.2

[D]

Dawnbreaker *(artifact)*
Auroran's radiant sword, forged from celestial fire. It glows with the first Light of day and cleaves through Void shadow.

Ch. 11.2

Dark Sovereign Moroseth *(character/title)*
Supreme lord of the Void. With wings of voidstuff and ancient sorrow, he commands the Champions of Shadow from above, awaiting his moment to unmake creation.

Ch. 17.2, 19.2

Defense Nodes *(object/place)*
Vital energy hubs scattered across AquaCapri. They power the realm's shields and are prime targets for Void sabotage.

Ch. 1.1–3.5

Defenders of Capricorn *(group)*
Elite elemental warriors from the Capricorn Realm. They arrive in Aquaterra as reinforcements against the Void.

Ch. 4.2, 4.3

Dimensional Protectors *(faction)*
Secret guardians of the realm-veils, led by Aetherion. They monitor rift-lines and protect against interdimensional collapse.

Ch. 17.1

Dreadmare *(character)*
Former Star Warrior turned ambiguous ally. Towering and armored, he walks the line between redemption and ruin.

Ch. 6.3, 8.2

Duskblade *(character)*
Void general clad in serrated black armor. His presence devours hope and emits an aura of looming despair.

Ch. 11.2

Duroxium *(mineral)*
A mineral extracted from the riches of AquaCapri Constellation.

Ch. 2

[E]

Earthshaker / Tervigon *(character)*
Mighty general of Capricorn. Commands seismic forces, leads the Groundbreakers, and is unwavering in defense.

Ch. 4.2, 4.3

Earthshaper Hammer *(artifact)*
Forged from mountain-rooted stone and infused with grounding force. Symbol of Earth's endurance.

Ch. 10.1, 10.3, 11.3, 12.1

Echo Wardens *(group)*
Silent cloaked guardians who watch realm faultlines. They intervene only when the balance teeters toward ruin.

Ch. 11.3

Echoes of Time *(concept/ entities)*
Timeless beings that speak in whispers from futures unborn. They guide heroes when time itself fractures.

Ch. 14.2, 18.2

Ecliptix Mantle *(armor)*
Dark cloak worn by Eclipsia, forged in the Abyss. Conceals its bearer from divine sight and focuses Void energy.

Ch. 11.3

Eclipse *(character/title)*
Void's Champion. Cloaked in obsidian and wielding the Umbral Fang, he moves like silence incarnate to extinguish Light.

Ch. 19.2

Elemental Artisans *(group)*
Mystical craftsmen attuned to storm, nature, and elemental beauty. Their works shape realms in peace and battle.

Ch. 4.1

Elemental Lords *(title/group)*
Primal guardians of Fire, Water, Earth, and Air. They hold sacred relics and sustain realm harmony.

Ch. 10.1, 11.3, 15.1

Elemental Realms *(location)*
Sacred dimensions beyond Aquaterra. Only those proven in harmony may pass their trials.

Ch. 10.1

Elemental Relics *(artifacts)*
Weapons of elemental origin: Solarflame Blade, Earthshaper Hammer, Tidecaller Trident, Windstrider Bow.

Ch. 11.2

Emberwings *(unit)*
Aerial fighters led by Pyronix, their wings aflame. They rain fire upon Voidspawn from the skies.

Ch. 15.3

Essence *(cosmic force)*
Vital energy flowing through all things. The Void seeks to corrupt or consume it, while Light purifies and renews it.

Ch. 1.1–3.5, 11.1, 16.1

Essence of Life *(concept)*
The soul's energy, preserved through time, memory, and relics. It echoes even when the body is gone.

Ch. 20.2

Eternal Spiral *(location)*
A stair of starlight and memory. Each step brings vision, clarity, and cosmic truth.

Ch. 14.2, 14.3

Eternite Crystal *(material)*
Crystalline essence of pure Light and memory. Cannot be

touched by decay.

Ch. 13.2

Equinox Spies *(group/faction)*
Elite covert agents led by ShadowVeil and Aetherwind. Masters of misdirection, sabotage, and hidden Light.

Ch. 19.2

Eternal Quill, Maximus *(see Maximus)*

[F]

Final Battlefield *(location)*
A war-torn realm of broken stars and torn skies where Light and Void make their final stand. Here, destiny burns at its brightest.

Ch. 17.3

Final Cycle *(prophecy)*
The last great turning of Light and Void. Sacrifice becomes the only currency to restore sacred balance.

Ch. 13.2

Final Guardian *(entity)*
A living constellation of shifting light and shadow who guards the final trial of the Starlight Pendant.

Ch. 9.4

Final Thread *(artifact)*
A glowing strand woven from Aqua and Capri's love and sacrifice. It holds the fate of all

futures in the Loom of Eternity.

Ch. 18.3

Firn *(character)*
Ice Vanguard and commander of the Frost Guard. His blizzards shield allies and freeze betrayal.

Ch. 4.2, 4.3

First Light / Golden Light *(symbol)*
The dawn over Aquaterra, symbolizing rebirth, unity, and Light's return after suffering.

Ch. 12.3, 20.1

First Weaver *(being)*
Ancient being of Light and shadow. Overseer of the Weavers of Fate and guardian of destiny's seal.

Ch. 18.3

Flame Warden *(title)*
Held by Ignatius and later Pyronix. Denotes mastery of fire and leadership in flame's fury.

Ch. 4.1

Flamebringer *(title)*
An honor granted to Infernos, whose presence rekindles courage with fire's righteous heat.

Ch. 17.2

Fortress of the Void *(location)*
A cursed bastion where fear is carved into stone. Light

weakens here, and silence reigns.

 Ch. 11.3

Frost Guard *(group)*
Regiment of icy warriors led by Firn. They bring winter's vengeance in the war against the Void.

 Ch. 4.2

[G]

Gaia *(character)*
Guardian of renewal. She heals corrupted land and revives the sleeping earth with floral wisdom.

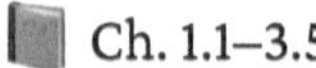 Ch. 1.1–3.5

Gaian / the Earth Warden *(character)*
Embodiment of stone-bound strength and patience. Wields the Earthshaper Hammer and shapes battlefields with tectonic will.

Ch. 1.1–3.5, 11.3, 15.1, 15.3, 17.2, 17.3

Galeonix *(character)*
Wind Guardian tested by fear and loyalty. Her journey reveals valor forged in sacrifice.

Ch. 9.1–9.3

General Gathering *(event)*
Summoned in times of crisis. This high council convenes beneath starlight to face prophecy and war.

Ch. 1.1–3.5

General Valorus / Supreme General Valorus *(character)*
Defender of the constellations and commander of celestial legions. Stands as the realm's enduring shield.

Ch. 4.1, 7.2, 7.3, 9.1, 10.3, 15.3, 17.1

Golden Light *(symbol)*
The shimmering manifestation of restored peace and unity. The final sign that harmony has returned.

Ch. 20.1

Grand Council Hall *(location)*
Heart of Aquaterra's governance. Star-forged walls echo with decisions that shape the fate of realms.

Ch. 9.1

Grand Plaza *(place)*
Public gathering space beneath crystal towers and constellations. Birthplace of speeches, songs, and uprisings.

Ch. 1.1–3.5

Groundbreakers *(group)*
Subterranean warriors led by Tervigon. Experts in tunnel warfare and explosive emergence.

Ch. 4.2, 4.3

Guardians *(group)*
Chosen protectors of AquaCapri. Summoned in times of crisis to defend realms from cosmic threat.

Ch. 5.3

Guardians of the Citadel *(cosmic beings)*
Towering entities of Light and shadow, formed to test those seeking the Pendant's key.

Ch. 9.3

Guardians of the Cosmos *(group)*
Embodiments of universal energies—time, flame, water, and beyond. They protect the sacred balance.

Ch. 1.1–3.5

Guardians of the Pact of Protection *(group)*
Defenders sworn to Aqua and Capri. Each wields elemental might and cosmic loyalty.

Ch. 7.1

[H]

Hall of Ages *(location)*
Memory's cathedral, etched in obsidian and lit by the Crystal Dome. Here, the past breathes in light.

Ch. 14.1

Hall of Elements *(place)*
Site of sacred oaths and convergence. Where the Pact of Protection was sealed.

Ch. 4.3

Hall of Memories *(location)*
Sanctum of legacy within the Celestial Citadel. Relics, murals, and whispers preserve the lives of heroes.

Ch. 20.2

Hall of Stars *(place)*
Celestial tower containing the Chamber of Light. Its ceiling maps fate through constellation.

Ch. 1.1–3.5

Heart of the Nexus *(location)*
Spiritual epicenter of aligned realms. Light and shadow converge in swirling tension.

Ch. 19.3

Healers of Light *(group/title)*
Sacred caregivers trained to mend physical and spiritual wounds. Light is their salve.

Ch. 6.1

Herald of the Void *(title)*
Held by Nihilus, who brings entropy and silence before the storm.

Ch. 19.1

Hidden Realms *(place)*
Cosmic sanctuaries unseen by mortal eyes. Safe from the Void,

lost even to memory.

Ch. 13.1

Hollow of Infinity *(location)*
Edge of the universe where the Library of Eternity floats, tethered by memory.

Ch. 13.2

Horizon Spire *(location)*
Crystal tower etched with constellations. A place for reflection, clarity, and celestial vision.

Ch. 12.3

[I]

Ignatius *(character)*
The Flame Warden before Pyronix. Wise and forceful, he channels fire into strategy and sacrifice.

Ch. 4.1

Illuminor, Primarch of Radiance *(character)*
A legendary figure among the luminous ranks, Illuminor is the highest-ranking wielder of solar Light and spiritual command. Known as the—
Primarch of Radiance—
preserves clarity in the sacred hierarchy of the Celestial Order. His presence shines not just as brilliance, but as discipline, warmth, and tactical illumination.

Appears in Ch. 15.3

Illusions (True Reflections) *(concept)*
Mirrored distortions within the Labyrinth, cast by the Void to exploit fear. Only the brave uncover their true essence.

Ch. 16.2

Infernos *(character)*
The Flamebringer. A living inferno of purpose, joined by the Phoenix to turn tides of darkness into light.

Ch. 17.2

Infinite Cycle *(cosmic theme)*
The eternal wheel of Light and darkness, joy and sorrow. Aqua and Capri are now part of this sacred recurrence.

Ch. 20.1

[J]

(No entries at this time.)

[K]

Kaelen, High Veilwarden of the Obscurari *(AquaCapri – Hidden Order)*

Once mistaken as a ShadowBlade, **Kaelen** is now

recognized as the **High Veilwarden of the Obscurari**, AquaCapri's most secretive order. His presence at the Celestial War Council signals his unmatched value in the coming war. Master of infiltration and silence, Kaelen uses the arrogance of the Void against itself. He moves unseen, and when he strikes, it is already too late.

Allegiance: AquaCapri (Direct Command: Aqua and Capri)

Order: The Obscurari (Covert 7th Force)

Abilities: Stealth warfare, disruption tactics, deception engineering

Appears in Ch. 15.3

Key *(artifact)*
The glowing object that unlocks the Starlight Pendant's dormant power. Can only be claimed through proven unity.

Ch. 9.3

Keyhole *(artifact detail)*
The hidden core of the Pendant, revealed only when fear is transcended and the ancient spell awakened.

Ch. 9.4

King Oceanius *(character)*
Wise monarch of Aquaterra. Balances power with patience, and trusts in the future Aqua and Capri forge.

Ch. 1.1–3.5

King Stonewall *(character)*
Steadfast ruler of Capricorn. His warnings stir preemptive action and uncover treachery.

Ch. 1.1–3.5, 5.3

Kraytor / Krytor, the Silent Enforcer *(character)*
Mute agent of Void destruction. Icy gaze, thunderous impact. Speaks through collapse and silence.

Ch. 1.1–3.5, 5.1, 5.2

[L]

Labyrinth of Mirrors / Maze of Mirrors *(location)*
A sentient crystalline maze where characters confront illusion and self. Passage requires truth and Essence.

Ch. 9.4, 16.1, 16.2

Layer Shields of PaxProfundis *(defense system)*
Five veil-like enchantments protecting the 13th star from detection or corruption. Each holds a unique resistance.

Ch. 1.1–3.5

Legacy *(theme)*
A living river of memory, carried from the actions of past heroes to the hands of the

present.

Ch. 12.3

Legacy of Stars *(artifact/book)*
A tome etched in Light. It reveals the cosmic past and future woven from creation's breath.

Ch. 13.2

Legions of the Void *(faction)*
Endless armies born of entropy. Numberless, merciless, and commanded by chaos incarnate.

Ch. 17.3

Leylines *(cosmic force)*
Invisible threads of power coursing through realms. When crossed or converged, they fuel great magic—or corruption.

Ch. 15.3

Library of Eternity *(location)*
Cosmic archive suspended in the Hollow of Infinity. Its halls ripple with choices that never were—and may yet be.

Ch. 13.2–13.3

Light *(force/cosmic energy)*
The radiant thread of all life. It heals, connects, and resists oblivion. Only it can counter the Void.

Ch. 12.2, 19.1, 19.3, 20.3

Light and Void *(cosmic forces)*
Born of the same breath, their dance shapes creation. They are not enemies—but opposites meant to balance.

Ch. 13.2

Light of the Realms *(concept/faction)*
Unified Guardians, champions, and celestial allies who fight under Light's banner.

Ch. 19.2

Liora *(character)*
A gentle healer of Aquaterra. Her hands mend the body and soul, and her voice carries peace.

Ch. 12.2

Loom of Eternity *(artifact/location)*
Cosmic nexus where all destinies are woven. Threads of lives, choices, and fates connect in its eternal tapestry.

Ch. 18.1, 18.3

Lord Umbra *(character)*
General of the Void's Shadow Forces. Cold, calculating, and wielding the Riftbreaker, he tears Light from realms.

Ch. 1.1–3.5, 5.1, 6.2, 6.3, 8.2

Lord Valthor / Valthor *(character)*
Dark architect of twisted balance. Wishes to reshape harmony into a reign ruled by himself.

Ch. 1.1–3.5, 8.2

Love *(force/philosophy)*
More than feeling—it is the tether of creation. In its purest form, it redeems, binds, and transcends time.

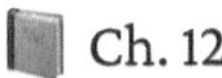 Ch. 12.3

Lumina *(character)*
Bearer of Light whose glow revives the fallen. She is a living beam of resilience and cosmic clarity.

Ch. 4.2, 7.1, 17.3

Luminarion *(character)*
Master of Radiance. Wields Light with serenity and leads through illumination and purpose.

Ch. 1.1–3.5, 5.2, 6.1, 7.2, 7.3, 8.1, 13.1

Luminarion's Radiance *(concept)*
Symbolic aura of his nobility. Even dimmed by loss, it guides with unwavering strength.

Ch. 7.3, 8.1

Luna / Lunara, the Moon Priestess *(character)*
Guardian of intuition and serenity. Her moonlit strength calms storms and unveils unseen truths.

Ch. 9.2, 9.3, 15.1, 15.2, 16.3

[M]

Malagorath *(character)*
A brooding Void lieutenant whose faith in Lord Valthor wanes after Umbria's fall. His turmoil may yet shift the war's tide.

Ch. 8.2

Map of Destiny *(artifact)*
A hovering weave of radiant strands showing futures untaken. Grants foresight, not certainty.

Ch. 13.3

Masters of Manipulation and Deceit *(group)*
Whispered cabinet of the Void. Their craft is illusion, their weapon: unraveling trust one truth at a time.

Ch. 1.1–3.5

Maximus, the Eternal Quill *(character)*
Scribe of the stars, guardian of cosmic lore, and one half of the Twin Pillars of Concord. Preserves balance through quiet remembrance.

Ch. 1.1–8.3, 20.3

Maze of Mirrors / Labyrinth of Mirrors *(location)*
Reflective trial ground where illusions test the soul. Truth must shatter illusion for the path to open.

Ch. 9.4, 16.1

Mirage & Sectrix *(characters)*
Twins in service to Moroseth. Mirage bends perception; Sectrix distorts belief—together they turn loyalty to lies.

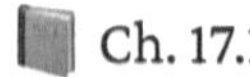 Ch. 17.1

Mirror Labyrinth *(location)*
A mirrored realm of living illusions. Reveals, tests, and sometimes breaks those who enter.

 Ch. 16.2

Moroseth, the Dark Sovereign *(character/title)*
Winged tyrant of the Void. Unleashes champions forged from extinguished stars. His silence weighs more than war cries.

Ch. 17.2, 19.2

Moroseth's Gaze *(power)*
His stare unravels illusion and magnifies doubt. To meet it is to confront the shadow within.

Ch. 11.1

Moonborn *(title/concept)*
A rare bloodline tied to lunar rhythms and prophecy. Moonborn often hold truths veiled to others.

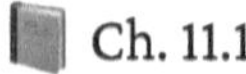 Ch. 16.1

[N]

Nebula Pathways *(location)*
Stardust corridors of shifting thought and illusion. Thought becomes direction, doubt leads astray.

Ch. 9.2

Nebula Wisps *(phenomenon)*
Floating lights of uncertain purpose. Sometimes guides, sometimes traps.

Ch. 9.2

Nebulon *(character/entity)*
Guardian of the Nebulae. Speaks in riddles and dust. Judges not through might, but mystery.

Ch. 9.2

Nethermind *(character)*
Psychic predator of the Void. He drowns minds in uncertainty and feeds on unraveling hope.

Ch. 1.1–3.5, 17.1

Nexus *(location)*
Dimensional heart of existence. A meeting place of fates, timeless and ever-surging.

Ch. 19.3

Nexus Awakening *(event)*
A surge of divine energy triggered within the Celestial Nexus. It restores Light's strength at the brink of defeat.

Ch. 19.2

Nexus of Possibilities *(cosmic realm)*

A sacred crossroads where potential futures dance in radiant strands. Time folds, futures whisper.

Ch. 18.2

Nihilus *(character)*
The Herald of the Void. A shadow-cloaked harbinger of entropy whose arrival marks cosmic collapse.

Ch. 19.1

Nocturn *(character)*
Cold, cosmic devourer and avatar of the Void. Bends reality to silence, seeks to erase Light itself.

Ch. 17.3

Noctyra, the Forsaken Star *(location)*
Once a realm of balance, now corrupted and cast into darkness. The first beacon to fall.

Ch. 17.1

[O]

Obsidian Archway *(gateway)*
Threshold into the Hall of Ages. Forged of time's stone, its pulse is the breath of history.

Ch. 14.1

Observatory of Infinity *(place)*
A tower where time slows and futures unfold like petals.

Vision and silence rule here.

Ch. 4.2

Ordo, The Constellary *(organization)*
Hidden order founded by Valdum and Maximus. Protectors of cosmic harmony. They speak seldom—but their quill writes destiny.

Ch. 1.1–8.3

Order of the Equinox *(organization)*
Espionage network led by ShadowVeil. Operates between light and dusk to preserve balance.

Ch. 1.1–3.5, 5.1, 5.2, 8.2, 17.1

Orion *(character)*
Mystic navigator, cloaked in constellations. Interpreter of signs and seeker of celestial equilibrium.

Ch. 13.1, 10.3

Orion's Warning *(prophecy/ memory)*
A haunting foresight that star-Essence would fall. Now fulfilled as the Void spreads.

Ch. 11.1

Origon *(character)*
Supreme General of Capricorn. Stern but loyal, wields starlight with grim efficiency.

Ch. 4.2, 4.3, 5.2

Pact of Protection *(event/ concept)*
A solemn vow forged by Guardians, Mystics, and Defenders of Capricorn. Sealed beneath starlight to bind forces against the Void's descent.

Ch. 4.3

Pendant's Power *(force)*
A sacred energy of harmony, not destruction. It awakens only when hope and unity overcome fear.

Ch. 9.4

Phantom of Umbra *(implied title)*
An unseen shadow drifting in Lord Umbra's wake—agent or presence unclear, but felt.

Ch. 6.2–6.3

Phoenix *(mythic being)*
Flame-born spirit of rebirth. Soars through warzones singing fire and rising courage from ashes.

Ch. 17.2

Planet Umbria *(location)*
A shrouded Void realm of whispered temptations and power unearned. Promised to traitors, paid for in silence.

Ch. 6.1, 6.2

Plains of Serenity *(location)*
Once a meadow of peace, now a battlefield where Light strains to resist the Void's march.

Ch. 11.2

Polished Obsidian Floor *(object)*
A galactic mirror within the Hall of Ages. Walking upon it is to step among stars and memory.

Ch. 14.1

Primordial Essence *(cosmic origin)*
Breath before time. It binds all: Light, Void, soul, and stone. The first whisper of all creation.

Ch. 13.2

Pyronis *(character)*
Lord of Fire. Grants the Solarflame Blade and demands mastery over flame and will.

Ch. 10.1

Prophecy of the Final Battle *(scroll/prophecy)*
A vision held within the Library of Eternity. It speaks of a last clash—where love and fate cross blades.

Ch. 13.2

Pulse of the Bond *(concept)*
The glowing wave of energy released when Aqua and Capri unite—body, soul, and heart.

Ch. 19.3

Pyronix *(character)*
The Flame Warden. Twin-

bladed and untamed, Pyronix incinerates despair and strikes with blazing precision.

Ch. 4.1, 9.1, 10.3, 11.3, 15.1, 16.3, 17.2, 17.3

[Q]

Queen Marinella *(character)*
Regal matron of Aquaterra. With dreamlike wisdom, she steadies the realm in times of unraveling.

Ch. 1.1–3.5, 9.1

Queen Terra *(character)*
Guardian of Gaia's legacy and sovereign of grounded realms. Her wisdom echoes through stone and seed.

Added by request

[R]

Radiant Heart *(artifact/place)*
A blazing core of divine energy within the Crystal Citadel. Activated in moments of utmost need.

Ch. 7.2

Radiantia *(place/symbol)*
Once a luminous stronghold, now dimmed by Void invasion. Its fall whispers the price of apathy.

Ch. 1.1–3.5, 5.1, 5.2, 5.3, 6.1

Reflection Illusions *(magic)*
Phantoms of the self projected by the Mirror Labyrinth. Each one embodies a doubt once buried.

Ch. 9.4

Reflector *(entity/guardian)*
Living presence in the Mirror Labyrinth. Shifts shape to test the seeker's sincerity.

Ch. 16.1–16.3

Reflections (True) *(concept)*
Not visions, but revelations. To face them is to reclaim truth beyond disguise.

Ch. 16.2

Relics *(artifacts)*
Items infused with legacy. In the Hall of Memories, Aqua's blade and Capri's veil shine brightest.

Ch. 20.2

Rift *(cosmic phenomenon)*
A tear in the universe's veil. Signals the first breach of Void into AquaCapri.

Ch. 1.1–3.5

Riftbreaker *(object/weapon)*
Lord Umbria's annihilation blade. Slices dimensions and detaches hope from form.

Ch. 1.1–3.5, 7.1

Rivers of Starlight *(symbolic location)*
Glowing waterways in reborn

Aquaterra. Carry celestial memory and echo the flow of time.

Ch. 20.1

[S]

Sectrix *(character)*
Manipulator of belief. With a single whispered phrase, Sectrix cracks alliances and tilts entire wars.

Ch. 1.1–3.5, 17.1

Shadow Agents *(enemy group)*
Stealthy enforcers of the Void. Born in silence, moving in whispers, they bring collapse without warning.

Ch. 8.2

ShadowBlade *(character)*
Silent hunter allied with Zynara. Tracks traitors across stars, strikes before sound can warn.

Ch. 5.1, 5.2

Shadow Caverns *(place)*
Depths beneath Aquaterra where fear echoes and Light forgets itself. Many enter. Few return.

Ch. 8.1, 8.3

Shadow Forces *(group/army)*
The Void's dark flood. Shape-shifting, shadow-drenched, reality-warping. They erode truth with presence alone.

Ch. 1.1–3.5

Shadow Fortress *(place)*
Lord Umbra's command bastion. Pulses with vile technology and ancient darkness.

Ch. 1.1–3.5

Shadow Syndicate *(organization)*
Capricorn's clandestine intelligence order. Operates with surgical silence to preserve fragile balance.

Ch. 1.1–3.5

ShadowVeil *(character)*
The Eclipse Spy, leader of the Equinox Order. Commands secrets and shadows with equal mastery.

Ch. 1.1–3.5, 5.1, 5.2, 8.1, 9.1, 17.1

Shadowed Ones *(faction)*
The Void's elite agents. They seed betrayal and unravel unity from the inside.

Ch. 17.1, 17.2, 19.2

Shadowweaver Zarvok *(title)*
Master of illusions and doubt. Known by whispers, feared by minds he's never touched.

Ch. 1.1–3.5

Shieldspire Plateau *(location)*
Defensive highland shielded by Celestara's radiant domes. A

final sanctuary for wounded Light.

 Ch. 15.3

Stilvren *(character)*
Once loyal, now lost. Archer turned infiltrator, believes betrayal is balance.

 Ch. 1.1–3.5, 17.1

Skyward Bastion *(location)*
Tempestor's citadel in the skies. From here, thunder answers shadow's call.

 Ch. 15.3

Solara *(character)*
Guardian of Dawn, sword aglow with the sun's first cry. She rises where night has lingered too long.

 Ch. 17.3

Solarium *(location)*
Faded heart of sunlight once strong. Its dimming mirrors Aquaterra's waning unity.

 Ch. 8.3

Solarflame Blade *(artifact)*
Living sword of flame. Granted by Pyronis, it requires soul and purpose to wield without ruin.

 Ch. 10.1, 11.3, 12.1

Solarion, the Sun Lord
(character)
Sovereign of warmth and clarity. Leads with brilliance and unshakeable conviction.

Ch. 15.1, 15.2

Solaris Crest *(location)*
Floating fortress of flame. Pyronix and Valorus stand sentinel here against the Void's aerial siege.

Ch. 15.3

Song of Memory *(ritual)*
Battle hymn echoing through stars. Each note calls forth legacy, valor, and identity.

Ch. 15.3

Song of the Stars, The
(phenomenon)
A cosmic melody that binds fate and memory. Heard only in the sacred chambers of convergence.

 Ch. 14.3

Spell of the Eternal Flame
(invocation)
A sacred incantation spoken in unity by Aqua, Capri, and their circle to unlock the **Starlight Pendant**, revealing its hidden keyhole. Though delivered in the Common Tongue, the spell echoes the deeper Aquarii language of the First Harmonists. It may only be activated by those whose souls are harmonized by truth, love, and purpose. The spell's power bridges the realms of Light and Destiny.

Form:

"Orravelle luminara, stellae cordis spirara—
Kaelion veritas, e'ravun estelanar
—

Virellum thalorien, pax infinita
—"

Ch. 9.4

Stardust *(material/concept)*
Sacred cosmic essence. Powers technology, spells, and soul-bound weapons across the realms.

Ch. 1.1–3.5

Stardust Blade / Sword of Starlight *(weapon)*
Forged for Aqua. Carved from fallen stars and soul-bound to hope's flame.

Ch. 7.2, 11.1, 11.3, 17.2

Stardust Guardians *(group)*
Celestial sentinels who monitor anomalies and interstellar threats.

Ch. 1.1–3.5

Stardust Murals *(art)*
Constellation-dusted murals within the Hall of Memories. Each shines with moments frozen in time.

Ch. 20.2

Stardust Pedestal *(artifact)*
Platform of compressed star memory.

Holds only relics of fate-changing weight.

Ch. 13.2

Stardust Warriors *(group/faction/constructs)*
Towering defenders of Light, forged from Duroxium and stardust. Aline with Aqua, Capri, and all who resist darkness.

Ch. 1.1–3.5, 5.1, 6.3, 7.1, 7.3, 15.3, 16.3, 19.2, 20.2

Starlight *(energy)*
Illuminating force born of stars. Healing, empowering, and unyielding against shadow.

Ch. 20.2

Starlight Pendant *(artifact)*
Celestial relic worn by Capri. Awakens with unity and is key to accessing deeper cosmic realms.

Ch. 9.1–9.4, 10.1, 10.3, 11.3, 12.1

Starlight Warriors *(faction)*
Chosen cosmic fighters armored in constellations. Their presence blazes against the dark.

Ch. 17.1

Starforger *(character/entity)*
Cosmic smith of fate, working in Light and memory. Creates tools not of war, but

transformation.

Ch. 13.1

Starforge *(place)*
Hidden nebula-forge where celestial relics are made. Birthplace of power, unreachable by greed.

Ch. 13.1

Starfire Elite *(group)*
Capricorn's finest warriors. Trained to wield starlight as both shield and spear.

Ch. 4.2

Starry Path *(location)*
Mystical road that pulses with the heartbeat of the cosmos. Leads those chosen through trial into destiny.

Ch. 20.3

Starstone *(material)*
Sacred crystal pulsating with Light. Embedded in towers, weapons, and memory-keeping architecture.

Ch. 12.3, 13.3

Starstone Table *(artifact)*
Runed council stone reflecting constellations in real time. Decisions made here echo across fate.

Ch. 15.2

Starveil Nexus *(location)*
Where starlight converges with ancient ley-lines. Time and Light blur into possibility.

Ch. 11.3

Strands of Destiny *(concept/ artifact)*
Glowing filaments that tether each soul and choice. Woven in the Loom of Eternity.

Ch. 18.2

Supreme General Tempestor *(character)*
Tactician of thunder and storm. Directs weather as both strategy and shield.

Ch. 5.2, 7.3, 9.1, 15.3

Supreme General Valorus *(character)*
Shield of the Realms. Stands unmoved at the edge of collapse, embodying unbreakable courage.

Ch. 4.1, 7.2, 7.3, 10.3, 15.3, 17.1

Suspended Gardens *(place)*
Floating sanctuaries above Aquaterra's palace. Woven of flowers, silence, and queenly wisdom.

Ch. 5.3

Sword of Starlight *(weapon)*
Another name for Aqua's celestial sword. Represents clarity through action.

Ch. 11.3, 17.2

[T]

Talssa *(character)*
Once loyal, now fugitive in service to the Void. Her betrayal still casts ripples.

Ch. 1.1–3.5, 5.1, 5.2, 8.2

Tapestry of Fate *(concept/ artifact)*
Woven within the Loom of Eternity. Threads of life, Light, and possibility form the universe's ever-shifting design.

Ch. 18.1, 18.2, 18.3

Tapestry of Time *(concept)*
A vision of reality's interconnectedness. Every action, a thread in the great weave.

Ch. 14.1

Tempesta *(character)*
The quiet master of storms. Speaks seldom, but moves with power hidden behind restraint.

Ch. 4.1

Tempestor *(character)*
General of storms and air defense. Holds the sky firm with crackling resolve.

Ch. 5.2, 7.3, 15.3

Temple of Elements *(place)*
Sacred council chamber where Elemental Lords gather and balance is honored.

Ch. 4.1

Tendrils of Shadow *(force/ creature)*
Void-born extensions of corruption. They writhe across battlefields, seeking Essence to consume.

Ch. 19.3

Terranox *(character)*
Lord of Earth, voice of patience and force. Grants the Earthshaper Hammer to the worthy.

Ch. 10.1

Thalassa *(character)*
Protector of the Oceans. Her wisdom is tidal, her justice as deep as abyss.

Ch. 4.1, 15.2

The Constellary Ordo *(organization)*
Secret guardians of balance, formed by Valdum and Maximus. They record, witness, and act only when harmony tips.

Ch. 1.1–8.3

The Light *(concept)*
Unbreakable truth, radiant hope, and loving resolve. More than magic—it is life itself.

Ch. 20.3

The Realms *(cosmic structure)*
Celestial planes of existence, linked by Light and balanced by unity.

Ch. 19.1

The Triumph of Love *(theme/event)*
The moment when all war, fear, and darkness bend before union of spirit.

Ch. 19.3

The Universe *(concept)*
All that is, was, and may be. It breathes through AquaCapri as a living, evolving force.

Ch. 20.3

Thread of Bond *(concept)*
Golden line binding Aqua and Capri across all time and choice.

Ch. 14.1

Threads of Time *(concept)*
Mystical strands seen in sacred sites like the Star Nexus. Each one a moment, a path, a possibility.

Ch. 14.3

Thread of Light *(magical bond)*
Living tether between allies. If broken in trial, all is lost.

Ch. 9.3

Trial of Belief *(event)*
Final test within the Citadel. Requires triumph over fear through unwavering hope.

Ch. 9.4

Twin Pillars of Concord *(title/group)*
Valdum and Maximus. Together, the unshaken balance in an unraveling cosmos.

Ch. 1.1–8.3, 20.3

Twinburst Strike *(move)*
Aqua and Capri's synchronized finisher—where water and starlight spiral into impossible brilliance.

Ch. 11.1

[U]

Umbral Fang *(artifact/weapon)*
Eclipse's blade of extinction. Forged from a dying star's last scream, it cuts through hope itself.

Ch. 19.2

Umbria *(location)*
Once radiant, now consumed. A lost realm overtaken by the Void's hunger, now home to echoes and ruin.

Ch. 8.2

Umbra *(character/place)*
Lord of Shadows, wielder of Riftbreaker. Umbra leads with whispered dread and tears realms with thought alone. Also refers to the fallen realm under his rule.

Ch. 1.1–3.5, 5.1, 6.2, 7.1, 8.2

[V]

Valdum *(character/title)*
The Celestial Architect, co-

founder of the Constellary Ordo. He guards sacred truths, ensuring fate bends only when balance demands.

📕 Ch. 1.1–8.3, 20.3

Valorus / Supreme General Valorus *(character)*
The unshakable Shield of the Constellation. Where he stands, Light does not falter.

📕 Ch. 4.1, 7.2, 7.3, 10.3, 15.3, 17.1

Valthor / Valthor *(character)*
Master of the Void's philosophy. He seeks a twisted order through controlled collapse and reshaped cosmic law.

📕 Ch. 1.1–3.5, 8.2

Veil of Illusion *(concept)*
The subtle fog between truth and perception. Its unraveling begins with self-awareness.

📕 Ch. 16.1

Velkaris, Mistress of Shadows (character)
A shadow-forged warlord who commands the battlefield like a storm in human form. One of the Void's highest-ranking generals, Velkaris is both elusive and ruthless, capable of resisting elemental onslaughts with her formless might. Her voice can chill even the bravest warrior, and her laughter

follows retreating Light like a curse.

📕 Appears in Ch. 17.1–17.2

Verdant Wardens *(group)*
Capricorn's elite guardians of nature. They bind forest, river, and root against encroaching shadow.

📕 Lore-based, referenced in Capricorn index

Vexalia *(character)*
Whisperer of envy and seed-planter of dissent. Her voice distorts clarity, feeding fractures with soft venom.

📕 Ch. 1.1–3.5, 17.1

Violet Eyes *(marker/symbol)*
Void corruption's signature glow. The eyes that shimmer with this hue no longer serve the Light.

📕 Ch. 11.1

Void / The Void *(force/entity/concept)*
Cosmic hunger without shape or mercy. The Void devours memory, Light, and love, erasing without rage—only intent.

📕 Throughout

Voidbringers *(creatures)*
Specialized shadow beasts bred to destroy Light-wielders. They feast on spells and unmake

armor with touch.

Ch. 7.1, 7.2

Voidfire *(element)*
Black flame of forgetting. Where it burns, purpose unravels and identity dissolves.

Ch. 17.1

Void Forces *(faction)*
The unrelenting storm of shadow that follows Umbra, Valthor, and Moroseth. Each warrior forged from despair.

Ch. 6.1

Void Ingress Paths *(strategy term)*
Hidden routes by which the Void infiltrates realms. Revealed by Capri, they mark unraveling points of peace.

Ch. 15.3

Voidspawn *(creatures)*
Ever-changing horrors birthed from the core of the Void. Their minds are void, their bodies formless—yet deadly.

Ch. 11.2, 19.2

Void Warden *(character/title)*
Gatekeeper of the Fortress of the Void. Silent, unmoving, and ancient. He blocks the path with presence alone.

Ch. 11.3

Voltar *(character)*
Wielder of lightning, general of shock. His strikes are decisions

made manifest.

Ch. 4.1

Vortizian *(character)*
Master of time and water currents. Leads the Celestial Citadel's defenses with quiet foresight.

Ch. 1.1–3.5, 7.3, 9.1

[W]

War Machines of the Void *(creatures/weapons)*
Colossal abominations. Each one forged from entropy and despair, draining all Light from the field.

Ch. 7.2

Weavers of Fate *(group / beings)*
Cosmic seamstresses of destiny. They neither rule nor follow—they weave, they witness, they warn.

Ch. 18.1, 18.3

Windstrider Bow *(artifact)*
Gifted by Zephra, wielded by Zephyr. Its arrows ride the breath of truth and silence.

Ch. 10.1, 11.3, 12.1

[X]

(No entries at this time.)

[Y]

(No entries at this time.)

[Z]

Zarvok / Shadowweaver
Zarvok *(character/title)*
Master of illusion and psychic deception. Plants invisible thoughts that bloom into betrayal.

Ch. 1.1–3.5, 5.2, 8.2

Zarvok's Whispers *(concept)*
Psychic seeds of manipulation. They feel like your thoughts, until your thoughts become someone else's plan.

Ch. 1.1–3.5

Zeyra *(characters)*
Wind-born guardians, some loyal, others lost to false balance. Each one rides the sky with sharp eyes and sharper truths.

Ch. 1.1–3.5

Zephyr *(character)*
Guardian of Air. He strikes fast, speaks little, and watches the skies with unwavering resolve.

Ch. 7.1, 8.2, 9.1–10.3, 11.3, 15.1–17.3

Zyrion *(character)*
The Gale Knight. Proud, loyal, and endlessly in motion. Wind answers his breath like kin.

Ch. 4.1, 6.1, 6.3, 15.1

Zynara *(character)*
Commander of spies. Capricorn's silent edge in a war of whispers.

Ch. 1.1–3.5, 5.1, 6.1, 8.2, 9.1

Thus concludes the complete and unified AquaCapri Glossary, spanning Chapters 1.1 to 20.3.

△ AQUARII CODEX

The Sacred Translation Scroll of the Whisperers
As spoken by Maximus, the Eternal Quill — and sealed by Valdum,
the Celestial Architect

PURPOSE:

The Aquarii Codex is the final scroll in *Whisperer Across the AquaCapri*.
It reveals the **English translations** of all **Aquarii Whispers**—the sacred
phrases spoken by Maximus and Valdum at the opening and closing of
each chapter. While the book itself presents only the Aquarii lines (to
preserve mystique), this Codex unveils their hidden meanings for the
reader.

THE WHISPER ARCHIVE

Sacred Whispers of Maximus & Valdum
From the Scrolls of the Constellary Ordo

Chapter 1

△ **Maximus, the Eternal Quill**
Aquarii: Navirynth xal Kalumé. Sevalon miréth ari Ondaros.

The stars have opened. The path of union has begun.

Opening Whisper – Ch. 1

△ **Valdum, the Celestial Architect**
Aquarii: Kaluméth el synar. Endros tel Aetheran.

Let unity remain. Let the Light endure.

Closing Whisper – Ch. 1

Chapter 2

△ **Valdum, the Celestial Architect**
Aquarii: Yaltheorn istri quel'vireth. Maerion xal dorentha.

The guardians rise from stillness. Harmony shields the realms.

Opening Whisper – Ch. 2

△ **Maximus, the Eternal Quill**
Aquarii: Dorentha silen ar'navai. Solari ven thalorien.

Peace is the truest shield. Even silence can protect.

Closing Whisper – Ch. 2

Chapter 3

△ Valdum, the Celestial Architect
Aquarii: Velarith nox'al dravon. Eluneth xal Vire.

The veil stirs in silence. Shadows reach for truth.

Opening Whisper – Ch. 3

△ Maximus, the Eternal Quill
Aquarii: Vire sevanor xal Kreion. Noctir valea'rin.

Truth cannot hide in dusk. Night always remembers.

Closing Whisper – Ch. 3

Chapter 4

△ Maximus, the Eternal Quill
Aquarii: Salendir viratha'kael. Lumae xal Aquarith.

The waters remember the oath. Light binds the blood of Aqua.

Opening Whisper – Ch. 4

△ Valdum, the Celestial Architect
Aquarii: Thalorion kel'dunari. Kaelis vintra somnar.

Time bends around the vow. Stars whisper their witness.

Closing Whisper – Ch. 4

Chapter 5

△ Maximus, the Eternal Quill
Aquarii: Celestrion val'dareth. Symphara xal Intrae.

Destinies collide in song. The Symphony begins within.

Opening Whisper – Ch. 5

△ **Valdum, the Celestial Architect**

Aquarii: Furion astrae xal thaniel. Torith vel sympar.

Let fate find its echo. Let the stars conclude the dance.

Closing Whisper – Ch. 5

Chapter 6

△ **Valdum, the Celestial Architect**

Aquarii: Shalanor tevir xal mael. Orun'thel drayen som.

Darkness gathers in silence. The storm listens well.

Opening Whisper – Ch. 6

△ **Maximus, the Eternal Quill**

Aquarii: Mael'dros viran. Shalanor will not break us.

Storms shall pass. Darkness cannot fracture the flame.

Closing Whisper – Ch. 6

Chapter 7

△ **Valdum, the Celestial Architect**

Aquarii: Toran viranth xal vekir. Shal'dryn estel'nar.

Let the shields hold fast. Let sacrifice be the silent flame.

Opening Whisper – Ch. 7

△ **Maximus, the Eternal Quill**

Aquarii: Serenyth kalan'mir. Valor endures beyond the fall.

Peace lives beyond the fire. Honor never fades.

Closing Whisper – Ch. 7

Chapter 8

△ **Maximus, the Eternal Quill**
Aquarii: Thalun xal aurelieth. Sevaran doxal mirav.

Love finds its shadow. But Light shall remain.

Opening Whisper – Ch. 8

△ **Valdum, the Celestial Architect**
Aquarii: Aurelieth val'torun. Heart and flame entwine again.

Love survives the eclipse. Flame and soul return as one.

Closing Whisper – Ch. 8

Chapter 9

△ **Valdum, the Celestial Architect**
Aquarii: Nareth doral sa'vyn. Valor is the breath of dawn.

The blade is drawn with purpose. Let courage be the dawn.

Opening Whisper – Ch. 9

△ **Maximus, the Eternal Quill**
Aquarii: Velnar xal Kireth. Even dusk remembers Light.

Let the darkness falter. Day will rise from the ashes.

Closing Whisper – Ch. 9

Chapter 10

△ **Maximus, the Eternal Quill**
Aquarii: Xarnor xal vinthae. The cosmos watches, silent and vast.

The void may whisper, but the stars shall speak.

Opening Whisper – Ch. 10

△ Valdum, the Celestial Architect

Aquarii: Vinthae xal eiranor. The watchers remain unseen.

Even silence has keepers. Even shadows have laws.

Closing Whisper – Ch. 10

Chapter 11

△ Valdum, the Celestial Architect

Aquarii: Kaerinth xal Maelorin. The mind fractures where faith fails.

When trust shatters, reason follows.

Opening Whisper – Ch. 11

△ Maximus, the Eternal Quill

Aquarii: Seryon ve'marion. Truth returns with pain.

Even when veiled, truth finds a way to return.

Closing Whisper – Ch. 11

Chapter 12

△ Valdum, the Celestial Architect

Aquarii: Thandor xal Aravyn. The balance lies in the wound.

Only through the scar may healing begin.

Opening Whisper – Ch. 12

△ Maximus, the Eternal Quill

Aquarii: Xel'vire nax toruin. The blade must rest to forgive.

Forgiveness does not follow the sword—it ends it.

Closing Whisper – Ch. 12

📘 Chapter 13

△ **Maximus, the Eternal Quill**
Aquarii: Nuralith sel'vian. The tide speaks of change.

📜 When oceans shift, destinies awaken.

▪ Opening Whisper – Ch. 13

△ **Valdum, the Celestial Architect**
Aquarii: Sel'vian xal taruun. The drift leads us home.

📜 Even lost currents return to their source.

▪ Closing Whisper – Ch. 13

📘 Chapter 14

△ **Valdum, the Celestial Architect**
Aquarii: Vraxor tenebral. The fracture speaks.

📜 Where the Light breaks, the Void listens.

▪ Opening Whisper – Ch. 14

△ **Maximus, the Eternal Quill**
Aquarii: Xal'reth donavir. The end begins with truth.

📜 Every collapse echoes a long-hidden truth.

▪ Closing Whisper – Ch. 14

📘 Chapter 15

△ **Maximus, the Eternal Quill**
Aquarii: Lunareth val'anar. The night holds its flame.

📜 Darkness cannot smother the eternal fire.

▪ Opening Whisper – Ch. 15

△ **Valdum, the Celestial Architect**

Aquarii: Anarion xal riven'dor. Stars burn beyond despair.

Even despair must yield to the light of stars.

Closing Whisper – Ch. 15

Chapter 16

△ **Valdum, the Celestial Architect**

Aquarii: Draventh xal Koruun. War consumes the last silence.

The drums of fate beat louder than truth.

Opening Whisper – Ch. 16

△ **Maximus, the Eternal Quill**

Aquarii: Koruun ve'thalor. The storm ends in stillness.

After the fury, only peace remains.

Closing Whisper – Ch. 16

Chapter 17

△ **Valdum, the Celestial Architect**

Aquarii: Zanthur el'drenai. Strike with clarity.

When vision clears, the blade need not tremble.

Opening Whisper – Ch. 17

△ **Maximus, the Eternal Quill**

Aquarii: Drenai xal Vareth. Silence marks the victor.

The truest triumph leaves no echo.

Closing Whisper – Ch. 17

🔖 Chapter 18

△ **Maximus, the Eternal Quill**
Aquarii: Syrentha val'durien. Grief binds the living flame.

📜 Pain kindles memory; sorrow shapes resolve.

✨ Opening Whisper – Ch. 18

△ **Valdum, the Celestial Architect**
Aquarii: Durien xal Anvros. Let grief pass into fire.

📜 In mourning, we forge our greatest strength.

✨ Closing Whisper – Ch. 18

🔖 Chapter 19

△ **Valdum, the Celestial Architect**
Aquarii: Kaelorin xal verak. The blade chooses the final bearer.

📜 Destiny arms those who stand when others fall.

✨ Opening Whisper – Ch. 19

△ **Maximus, the Eternal Quill**
Aquarii: Verak ve'seran. It ends where it must begin.

📜 In the last strike lies the first breath of peace.

✨ Closing Whisper – Ch. 19

🔖 Chapter 20

△ **Maximus, the Eternal Quill**
Aquarii: Aqua'nair xal Capri'um. One flame, two hearts.

📜 Together, they rise beyond all endings.

✨ Opening Whisper – Ch. 20

△ **Valdum, the Celestial Architect**

Aquarii: Sol'vire an'thelari. Let Light be the final whisper.

Let the echo of unity outshine the fall.

Closing Whisper – Ch. 20

△ THE WHISPERER'S SEAL

△ Valdum, the Celestial Architect

Aquarii:"Amareth su Eternar. Quorynth Auralien. Kalumé Syrenai."
[AH-mah-reth soo eh-TER-nar. KWOHR-inth aw-rah-LEE-en. KAH-loo-may SY-ruh-nye]

◆ Sacred Farewell • Love's Whisper • Peace's Embrace

△ Maximus, the Eternal Quill

Aquarii:"Rioneth Orikai. Varethiel na Myroneth. Whisperen, Veraleth."
[REE-uh-neth OR-uh-kye. vah-RETH-ee-el nah MEE-roh-neth. WHIS-per-en, VEH-ruh-leth]

◆ The Union's Bond • Echo through Flame • The Whisper Transcends

INVITATION BEYOND THE PAGES

The journey of AquaCapri does not end here.
Its whispers continue in living scrolls, chronicles,
and future volumes awaiting your step.

- aquacaprisaga.com — the gateway to the realms

- valentinotravaldi.com — words from the author's hand

Enter, and let the constellation unfold before you.

www.ingramcontent.com/pod-product-compliance
Lightning Source LLC
Chambersburg PA
CBHW031200010826
48971CB00013B/988